PENGUIN BOOKS

VIS & RAMIN

Fakhraddin Gorgani was an eleventh-century Persian poet. He wrote *Vis & Ramin* sometime between 1050 and 1055, when he was a member of the retinue of the ruler of Isfahan. Although very little is known about his life, Gorgani's name suggests he was from the town of Gorgan to the east of the Caspian.

A Fellow of the Royal Society of Literature, Dick Davis is currently professor of Persian at Ohio State University. His other translations from Persian include *Borrowed Ware: Medieval Persian Epigrams*, *The Legend of Seyavash*, *The Shahnameh*, and, with Afkham Darbandi, *The Conference of the Birds*.

VIS & RAMIN

FAKHRADDIN GORGANI

TRANSLATED AND EDITED
WITH AN INTRODUCTION AND NOTES BY

DICK DAVIS

PENGUIN BOOKS

PENGUIN BOOKS
Published by the Penguin Group
Penguin Group (USA) Inc., 375 Hudson Street, New York, New York 10014, U.S.A.
Penguin Group (Canada), 90 Eglinton Avenue East, Suite 700, Toronto,
Ontario, Canada M4P 2Y3 (a division of Pearson Penguin Canada Inc.)
Penguin Books Ltd, 80 Strand, London WC2R 0RL, England
Penguin Ireland, 25 St Stephen's Green, Dublin 2, Ireland (a division of Penguin Books Ltd)
Penguin Group (Australia), 250 Camberwell Road, Camberwell,
Victoria 3124, Australia (a division of Pearson Australia Group Pty Ltd)
Penguin Books India Pvt Ltd, 11 Community Centre,
Panchsheel Park, New Delhi – 110 017, India
Penguin Group (NZ), 67 Apollo Drive, Rosedale, North Shore 0632,
New Zealand (a division of Pearson New Zealand Ltd)
Penguin Books (South Africa) (Pty) Ltd, 24 Sturdee Avenue,
Rosebank, Johannesburg 2196, South Africa

Penguin Books Ltd, Registered Offices:
80 Strand, London WC2R 0RL, England

First published in the United States of America by Mage Publishers, Inc. 2008
Published in Penguin Books 2009

Some sections of this translation have previously
appeared in *The Hudson Review* and *The New Criterion*.

The translator thanks the Persian Heritage Foundation for a grant
toward the translation of this work.

Persian calligrapy by Amir Hossein Tabnak

Map by Karen Rasmussen, Acheographics © Mage Publishers

THE LIBRARY OF CONGRESS HAS CATALOGED THE HARDCOVER EDITION AS FOLLOWS:
Fakhr al-Din Gurgani, fl. 1048.
[Vis va Ramin. English]
Vis & Ramin / Fakhraddin Gorgani ; translated from the Persian with
an introduction and notes by Dick Davis.—1st hardcover ed.
p. cm.
Includes bibliographical references.
ISBN 1-933823-17-8 (hc.)
ISBN 978-0-14-310562-6 (pbk.)
I. Davis, Dick, 1945–   II. Title.   III. Title: Vis and Ramin.
PK6451.F28V513 2008
398.220955—dc22   2007041742

146122990

CONTENTS

For Afkham

تو از خوبی کونی چون نیست آفت
خطا آن است که از تو برینیم

INTRODUCTION

VIS AND RAMIN WAS WRITTEN between 1050 and 1055 by the Persian poet Fakhraddin Gorgani; it is the first major Persian romance, and one of the most extraordinary and fascinating love narratives produced anywhere in the medieval world, Islamic or Christian.

Vis and Ramin is Gorgani's only surviving long work, and no more than three other short scraps of extant verse are ascribed to him. We know virtually nothing about the poet, apart from what he tells us in the exordium and conclusion to his poem. Remarks by medieval poets about themselves have to be treated with care; many such comments, especially boasts, and complaints likely to elicit sympathy, tend to be drawn from a common stock and to vary little from one poet to another. In general, the less specific self-referential remarks made by medieval poets are, the more unreliable they are.

But Gorgani is very specific about two things: his patron's identity and the circumstances under which his poem was written, and there seems no reason not to take his account at face value. In 1050, the Seljuk sultan Abu Taleb Toghrel

Beg left the city of Isfahan under the control of one 'Amid Abu'l Fath Mozaffar. Gorgani says that he accompanied the new commander to the city, who commissioned the poem from him as an entertainment, during their sojourn there. Other sources confirm that 'Amid Abu'l Fath Mozaffar was the ruler of Isfahan from 1050 to 1055, which gives us the date for the poem's composition. Gorgani's name suggests that he, or his family, was from an area to the east of the Caspian, either the town of Gorgan itself, or the surrounding countryside, which was also called Gorgan. The town and its surroundings figure quite prominently in *Vis and Ramin* (geographically, it is about halfway between the two main areas of the poem's action), and it may be that the tale was thought of as a largely local story in the places where the poet grew up. We know, however, that it enjoyed a wider currency than the merely local, as the Arab poet Abu Nawas mentioned it in the eighth century, three hundred years or so before Gorgani wrote his version. Twice in the course of telling his lovers' story Gorgani refers in general terms to his age, but the two instances seem to contradict one another. At one point he tells us that his own days of romantic involvements are long over, suggesting that he is at least middle aged, and then at the very end of the poem he asks his friends to pray that God will "Forgive the youth who wrote this pretty story." All we know for sure about Gorgani is that he wrote his poem in Isfahan at some point between 1050 and 1055, and that he was familiar with the atmosphere and protocol of a local ruler's court; we can guess that he was probably from the area to the east of the Caspian known as Gorgan. Occasionally, in the course of *Vis and Ramin*, he will address his reader or auditor directly, and sometimes when he does this he recommends generosity as a noble course of action; these remarks are probably there as a hint to remind 'Amid Abu'l Fath Mozaffar of his duties as a patron.

The eleventh century was a period when a number of Persian authors were interested in writing versions of stories from pre-Islamic Iran. The country had been conquered by the Arabs in the seventh century, and then subsumed into the Arab and Moslem caliphate. Iran had existed as an independent country, and as the ruler of much of Western Asia, for most of the previous millennium, and the conquest was such a shocking reversal of fortune that it took some time for the culture to recover. Persian poetry of the eleventh century shows a strong nostalgia for the stories and civilizations of pre-Islamic Iran, for a time when Persian political and cultural hegemony in Western Asia was unquestioned, and its rulers could style themselves King of Kings without apology. The most spectacular example of this literary nostalgia is Ferdowsi's great epic, the *Shahnameh* (completed in 1010 CE), and Gorgani's *Vis and Ramin* is another instance of it. In some ways *Vis and Ramin* is an even more interesting example than the *Shahnameh*; usually when Ferdowsi comes across a pre-Islamic custom of which Islam disapproves he glosses over it, or, if mention of it is unavoidable, he is shamefaced about it. Gorgani makes no bones about such moments and seems to make no effort whatsoever to trim his tale to suit Islamic sensibilities; similarly, although Ferdowsi's diction is relatively conservative, Gorgani's is at times even more so, and his poem is a major source for lexical survivals from pre-Islamic Persian into the Persian of the post-conquest period. In his poem's introductory material Gorgani implies that he understands "Pahlavi" (pre-Islamic Persian) well – we have no way of verifying whether this was true or not – and he will occasionally refer us to the meaning of Pahlavi words or phrases, as when he gives us the etymology of Khorasan (page 139).

In a series of cogently argued articles,[1] the twentieth-century Russian scholar Vladimir Minorsky drew on geographical, philological, and historical evidence to demonstrate that the story of Gorgani's *Vis and Ramin* derives from the Parthian period. The Parthians ruled Iran from 247 BCE to 224 CE, so the tale comes from around the beginning of the Christian era, give or take a century or two. The dominant religion of Iran during the period of Parthian rule was Zoroastrianism. We have then a Parthian/Zoroastrian story that is being retold by an author who has grown up in an Islamic milieu and has at least a nominal allegiance to Islam. As might be expected, the text is often a kind of cultural palimpsest, with both cultural and religious traditions present; even when one is brought into especial prominence the other usually remains discern-

---

1 Vladimir Minorsky, "Vis u Ramin: A Parthian Romance," Bulletin of the School of Oriental and African Studies, Vol. XI, 1943–46, pp. 741–763; Vol. XII, 1947–1948, pp. 20–35; Vol. XVI, 1954, pp. 91–2; "New Developments," Vol. XXV, 1962, pp. 275–286.

ible in the background. Perhaps deliberately, Gorgani begins and ends his tale by invoking both cultures simultaneously; at the opening of the story he mentions both Korah and Kasra in one image; Korah is a figure from the Qur'an, Kasra from pre-Islamic Persian history; at the end of the tale he imagines the Islamic angel Rezvan looking down on the Zoroastrian temple of Borzin, where Vis's tomb is located.

The Social World of *Vis and Ramin*

The first thing that strikes any reader of *Vis and Ramin* is the very peculiar nature of the marriage customs that seem to be in place at the beginning of the poem. These customs are (and were in Gorgani's time) as bizarre to Middle Eastern readers as to Western readers, as they belong not only to the Zoroastrianism of two millennia ago, but also to the marriage customs of the pre-Islamic Persian royal dynasties. Marriages that are now universally regarded as incestuous were relatively common among the pre-Islamic dynasties of Iran, and were even seen as especially praiseworthy.[2] In the ancient world, royal incest was of course not unique to Iran; it was also common

---

2 Confirmation of the relative commonness in pre-Islamic Iran of marriages that would now be regarded as incestuous is provided by the Sasanian law book, *The Book of a Thousand Judgements* (Introduction, transcription and translation of the Pahlavi text, notes glossary and indices by Anahit Perikhanian. Translated from Russian by Nina Garsorian. Bibliotheca Persica, Costa Mesa, 1997). This contains laws relating to brother-sister marriage (p. 237, section 105, 5–10; p. 281, A18, 7–12; p. 315, A36, 6–12), father-daughter marriage (p. 33, 3, 11–14; p.121, 44, 13–14; p. 235, 104, 12–14) and mother-son marriage (p. 33, 4, 1–4).

in the Egyptian royal dynasties, and the pharaohs were usually married to their own sisters. The brother-sister marriage that comes near the opening of *Vis and Ramin,* and generates much of the subsequent plot, is taken by the poet simply as a norm within the society out of which the story comes. The custom will have been as strange for Gorgani as it is for us, but he gives no hint of being in any way troubled by it; he has clearly decided to accept, without judgment, the tale as he has received it. The erotic relationships within the poem stay highly endogamous: the lovers, Ramin and Vis, share the same wet nurse, which makes them a kind of honorary brother and sister, a relationship recognized within the culture as being equivalent to that of siblings; and Ramin is the younger brother of Vis's husband, Mobad.[3]

The society Gorgani invokes in *Vis and Ramin* is almost entirely a courtly one. The characters in the poem are members of major or minor royal families, or they are the servants of such families. Power and pleasure are central preoccupa-

---

3 And he may be more than simply the younger brother; there are hints that in an earlier version of the tale he was also Mobad's son; see note 27 to the main text. This would mean that Mobad had married his own mother; it's clear that Mobad's father is long dead, and such a marriage would be theoretically possible (though much less common than either brother-sister marriage or father-daughter marriage) by Parthian custom. In the version that Gorgani gives us, a number of speeches indicate that no one thinks of this as being the case (e.g., at one point the mother remarks to Mobad that he does not have an obvious heir, which a son would be). However, the references to Ramin as Mobad's son, Ramin's one reference to Mobad as his father, as well as a courtier's reference to Ramin as Mobad's "brother and . . . son," suggest that in one version of the story Ramin may well have been both brother and son to Mobad.

tions both of the characters and of the poet, and a great deal of time is spent in feasting, gift giving, hunting, and making war, all of which are done on a lavish scale; almost every aspect of life involves displays of vast amounts of wealth. Certainly this princely opulence is to some degree fantastic, but for as long as the Persian princely courts have existed they have been known as centers of great wealth and luxury. From Herodotus to Shakespeare the almost unimaginable splendor of Persian courtly life was a constant theme of Western writers who mentioned the country, and although the quantities of precious goods that Gorgani describes are surely a great exaggeration of what was available in any given center of power, there can be no doubt that when he describes gold, silver, jewels, brocade, silk, ermine, musk, ambergris, as well as less remarkable but still highly valued items like crystal and sugar, he knows what he is talking about. In surrounding his royal characters with such luxuries he is exaggerating conditions that had long been a reality in Persian aristocratic culture, rather than inventing a fantasy world out of whole cloth.

The emphasis on pleasure can be seen partly as a survival from Zoroastrianism, the ancient pre-Islamic religion of Iran. Until Zoroastrianism was modified by Manicheism, physical pleasure was seen as a gift of the good principle of life, Ahura Mazda, and gratitude for its presence and its assiduous cultivation were seen virtually as religious duties. This partly accounts for the importance given to wine drinking in the poem. It's clear from both *Vis and Ramin* and a number of other texts that are contemporary with it that excessive wine drinking was associated with the pre-Islamic courts of Iran, and that, despite the triumph of Islam, the custom had continued to flourish in courtly circles, especially in eastern Iran, which seems to have hung on to its pre-Islamic roots more assiduously than most other areas of the country. Wine drinking to the point of drunkenness is expected of the members of the court in Gorgani's poem (almost every time we see the king go to bed, the fact that he is drunk is mentioned, and there is usually no implication that this is a reprehensible state for him to be in). Constant wine drinking is also one of the main occupations of the lovers, Vis and Ramin, whenever they are together, and Eros and wine become inextricably linked as the story develops. The pleasure that is given most emphasis in the poem is of course erotic pleasure, and the nurse's frank statement to Vis that she can have no idea of what real happiness is until she has experienced sexual pleasure is made with an impatience that implies that morality, and all questions of how and with whom one might experience this pleasure, are fairly minor concerns:

> You've never truly slept with any man.
> You've had no joy of men, you've never known
> A man whom you could really call your own . . .
> What use is beauty if it doesn't bless
> Your life with pleasure and love's happiness?
> You're innocent, you're in the dark about it,
> You don't know how forlorn life is without it.
> Women were made for men, dear Vis, and you
> Are not exempt, whatever you might do.

And to make quite sure that Vis knows what she is talking about, the nurse goes on to add:

> *God made us so that nothing's lovelier than*
> *What we as women feel when with a man,*
> *And you don't know how vehemently sweet*
> *The pleasure is when men and women meet;*
> *If you make love just once, I know that then*
> *You won't hold back from doing so again.*

As in the literary representations of most courtly worlds, along with pleasure comes protocol, and the backbiting that accompanies slips in protocol; as her nurse says to Vis at one point:

> *Surely you see*
> *You're going to have to act appropriately.*
> *There are a hundred things we have to do*
> *Simply because the world expects us to;*

This is a very hothouse world, and if the opportunities for pleasure are numerous and varied so are the opportunities for disgrace. Associated with the currency of one's good name is the fairly frequent invocation of chivalry, especially by Ramin, as an ideal of behavior. An aspect of the poem that is perhaps startling at first, given the emphasis on courtly protocol, chivalry, and correct behavior, but which has clear parallels in Western medieval narratives that deal with the same kind of world, is the validation of adultery. The nurse's admonitions to Vis, once her charge has realized she is married to someone for whom she feels no affection, are given with cynical insouciance:

> The well-born women of the world delight
> In marrying a courtier or a knight,
> And some, who have a husband, also see
> A special friend who's sworn to secrecy;
> She loves her husband, she embraces him,
> And then her happy friend replaces him.

Certainly here the nurse is speaking in defiance of the poem's conventional morality, to which due lip service is paid by the poet, and to which more than lip service is paid by Vis, at least until she finds herself helplessly and hopelessly in love, but the plot bears out the nurse's version of what matters in life, not conventional morality's. In theory, women belong to their parents and their husbands, but in reality much of the poem's energy is spent on depicting the inner life of a woman rebelling against this inherited notion of how she should spend her life. And Gorgani is obviously in sympathy with his heroine; he condemns her mother's promise of her as a bride to someone before she is even born, and he asks the reader to forgive Vis her transgressions against conventional morality, saying they were a part of God's plan for her. We see a parallel situation in the economic world of the poem. Again, in theory the poem takes place in a quasi-feudal, gift-giving culture, in which wealth comes to the king through tribute, conquest, and taxation, and to his subjects through his patronage. But commerce, the production by artisans of luxury goods, and the risks of individual economic endeavor are constantly alluded to in the poem's metaphors, and the wealth of the court includes a great many foreign items (central Asian furs and scents, Chinese silks, Chinese and Western [Byzantine?] paintings, western locks and keys) that have clearly been acquired by means of the camel caravans and mule trains of traded goods to which allusion is also made. In both the erotic and economic spheres we see a traditional top-down, hierarchical structure being modified, and to some extent subverted, by individual aspirations and enterprise. Vis is happy to subvert the old order when she breaks her marriage vows to her husband, but when her lover Ramin breaks his promise to her and marries another woman, she reproaches him with an image that unites the dangers of such new-found erotic and commercial individualism: she says he is

> . . . like a gold coin journeying through the land
> By constant passages from hand to hand.

It will be clear to readers of Western medieval literature that the world Gorgani depicts is very close to that of say Chrétien de Troyes and other writers of European chivalric romances; something that should be kept in mind though, when making such natural comparisons, is the date of Gorgani's poem. It is certainly true that the court setting, chivalry, obsessive love-longing, and the validation of adultery that are present in Gorgani's poem can all be found in European medieval romances. But in the fully developed state in which we find them in *Vis and Ramin,* they do not appear in a European context until well over a century after *Vis and Ramin* was written. The courtly sophistication of *Vis and Ramin,* and the subtlety of its extensive analyses of psychological inwardness, particularly as regards the heroine, are barely adumbrated in European literature of the eleventh century; for someone who is conscious of this time lag it seems indisputable that there must have been some transfer of Middle Eastern literary preoccupations and techniques to the West, during the intervening century, in order to facilitate such a similar literary efflorescence in the lands of Christendom. And of course the intervening century in question includes the period of the early crusades, and the emergence of a heightened consciousness of the presence of a highly developed cultural alternative to Christian Europe, lying just beyond its eastern and southern boundaries.

The Aesthetics of *Vis and Ramin*

Although there are obvious novelistic elements to *Vis and Ramin* (after all, we have a narrative and we have characters), the work is not told as a modern novel is told, and to approach it with the expectations we bring to contemporary, or even to nineteenth-century, fiction can only lead to frustration. The aesthetics of the poem are quite far from those of contemporary fiction, and it is as well to be aware of this. Dr. Johnson remarked of the novels of the eighteenth-century novelist Richardson, "Why, Sir, if you were to read Richardson for the story, your impatience would be so much fretted that you would hang yourself. But you must read him for the sentiment, and consider the story as only giving occasion to the sentiment." This remark takes us some way towards the world of *Vis and Ramin*, but not all the way; *Vis and Ramin* belongs to a rhetorical world in which set pieces are elaborated for their own sake, and when an occasion for a set piece presents itself everything else stops, often for pages on end. One reads for the sentiment, yes, as Dr. Johnson recommended, but also for the elaboration of the sentiment, and the ways in which this is done.

Where do the aesthetic presuppositions and devices of the poem come from? In a work published a few years ago[4] I pointed out that *Vis and Ramin* and a couple of other eleventh-century Persian romances set in pre-Islamic Iran have strong affinities with the Hellenistic romances that were written in Greek, and mostly in western Asia, around the beginning of the Christian era. The Persian and Greek romances in question share a great many plot elements, involve virtually identical casts of main (and in some cases also minor) characters, and seem to inhabit the same aesthetic universe. I suggested that both the Greek romances

4 *Panthea's Children: Hellenistic Novels and Medieval Persian Romances,* Bibliotheca Persica (2002).

and the originals of their Persian counterparts were in all likelihood the product of a literary milieu shared between Iranian and Greek culture at a time (roughly the Parthian period) when we know that the two cultures were in constant contact and, in western Asia at least, were permeated with one another.

Parthian fiction was recited orally; it seems not to have been written down, and no examples of it survive. We don't know what the Parthian version of *Vis and Ramin* looked or sounded like. But, in this same period, a literary argument was going on in the worlds of Greek and Latin literature that seems to have some bearing on our poem. One style, which conservative Roman critics emphatically denounced, was accused of being "Asiatic"; this "Asiatic" style developed into what has been called the "jeweled" style, which became common in literary works, in both Latin and Greek, during late antiquity. And when we examine the characteristics of the jeweled style we find that we are looking at a style that is, in many respects, almost identical with that in which *Vis and Ramin* is written. The rhetoric of *Vis and Ramin* is I believe derived from the rhetoric of western Asian literary production during the late Parthian and Sasanian[5] periods, a rhetoric that in the West came to be known as the Asiatic, and later the jeweled, style.

---

5 The Sasanians (224 CE to 642 CE) replaced the Parthians as the ruling dynasty of Iran and reigned until the Arab/Islamic conquests of the mid-seventh century.

The Western (Greek and Latin) "jeweled" style, as it was practiced in late antiquity, involved[6] a tendency to the hyperbolic and the episodic, with frequent interruptions of the forward action of the plot for elaborate descriptive passages; generally in a narrative, but especially within such descriptive passages, rhetorical devices like anaphora, antithesis, chiasmus, and plays on words were employed to create extensive passages of verbal repetition and variation. Set speeches, sometimes of great length and complexity, designed to show the character or state of mind of the speaker, were frequent, as were elaborate lists of one kind or another. There was a particularly strong emphasis on two frequently repeated metaphorical vehicles – flowers (especially the brightly colored flowers of spring) and jewels. And there was also a special interest in descriptions involving light, often in conjunction with the mention of jewels, either metaphorically or as being literally present in a scene. All these rhetorical characteristics are emphatically and obviously present in *Vis and Ramin*, indeed the poem could almost be called a textbook example of their use, and it seems reasonable to suppose that Gorgani's rhetoric is a late manifestation of a style that had

---

6 This brief summary of the style's most obvious characteristics is heavily indebted to *The Jeweled Style: Poetry and Poetics in Late Antiquity*, 1989, by Michael Roberts. My assumption is that the "Asiatic" style existed, as its name indicates, in Asia before it became common in the literatures of Greece and Rome, and that what Roberts persuasively calls the "jeweled style" is the development in Greek and Latin of aesthetic criteria and techniques that had a contemporary existence, in a similar form, in western Asia.

been current in western Asia since the period of the Parthian and Hellenistic cultures.

The result of these aesthetic preoccupations is that the plot of the poem moves fairly slowly and is interrupted by frequent elaborately descriptive passages; there are also long rhetorical speeches that are expressive of highly emotional states of mind, as well as a very long letter that serves the same function. In the constantly interrupted forward movement of its plot, in its highly artificial and embellished rhetoric, and in its hyperbolic expressions of extreme emotion, the relatively recent Western art form that it most resembles is opera, especially perhaps bel canto opera. Anyone who can appreciate the sensibility that produced Bellini's *Norma* or Donizetti's *Rosmonda d'Inghilterra* should have little problem in responding to the florid ornamentation of the set pieces in *Vis and Ramin*. The poem can also feel very like a Bollywood love story, and one could easily mark up the text to indicate where the songs and dances should appear. A last analogy, not for the narrative as a whole but for certain lyrical moments within it, is with the world of country music, which also deals in brooded-over emotions hyperbolically conveyed, and which often delights in elaborate word play, sentiment for its own sake, and far-fetched imagery (that can occasionally slip into bathos, as can Gorgani's). That the approximately similar art forms I have been able to come up with all involve music seems significant; the hero of the poem is a musician, and music is never far away from the author's mind. And, as is indicated in the closing lines, the poem was written as much for (probably quasi-musical) performance before a group of friends as for solitary reading.

One of the most attractive aspects of Gorgani's poetic style is his very engaging use of simile and metaphor (often introduced by the phrases, "You would say," or, "You would have said," the equivalent of the English, "It was as if . . ."). Gorgani's images are not all of the same kind. A great many of them, especially in his descriptions of physical beauty, draw on a common stock of images, some of which would seem to be of great antiquity and are probably directly inherited from the "Asiatic" rhetoric discussed above. Vehicles for these metaphoric descriptions of the body are drawn from the three main areas preferred by the practitioners of the jeweled style: flowers (or fruit), jewels (or precious metals), and effects of light. And so beautiful hair is compared to violets, the cheeks to roses or pomegranate blossoms, the breasts to jasmine (for their color and scent) or pomegranates (for their shape), the face to the sun or the full moon, beautiful skin to silver, the skin of a sick person to gold, teeth to pearls, lips to rubies, and so forth (a list of the commonest of these stock comparisons is given in the appendix on page 517). The images are stock, but even so Gorgani is often able to overwhelm the reader with their profusion, or to produce charming and original effects with them, as for example when Vis comes on Ramin asleep in a garden and Gorgani mixes metaphor and reality in one visual image:

And then she saw her lover lying there,
With violets clustered in his violet hair,
With faintly blushing roses held in place
Beneath the pressure of his rosy face.

Less languorous and more pithy are the many metaphoric moments that sound proverbial in their feistiness, as when the nurse is scheming how to bring Ramin and Vis together, and wondering

. . . how like fat and sugar they could be
Blended entirely, and inseparably.

Or when she is advising Vis to get rid of her husband Mobad before he gets rid of her:

Before he dines on you for lunch, attack,
And eat him as a tasty breakfast snack!

The edge of humor in these moments can sometimes turn into outright farce. When Mobad finds out that for all his precautions Vis has been entertaining her lover in a locked room, while her guard has sat obliviously outside, Mobad compares the useless locked door to the man's belt, and bursts out with,

A pretty belt's of no significance
Unless it's holding up some kind of pants!
Buckle your belt as tight as you can make it,
But with no pants to wear you're still stark naked!

Sometimes Gorgani can develop breathtakingly beautiful images over a few lines, as in this image of the slowly moving constellations in the night sky:

> *The firmament was like a canopy*
> *Studded with jewels, vast in its majesty,*
> *Secure and barely moving, strongly tied*
> *With heavenly guy ropes to the mountainside.*

Or the images can have an almost bizarre vividness, as in this extraordinary image of a huge fire:

> *It was a golden dome, a wondrous sight*
> *That shook with incandescent flakes of light,*
> *A lovely woman in a crimson dress*
> *Strutting and roaring, wild with drunkenness,*
> *Splendid as when she meets her love, and burning*
> *With all the heat of separation's yearning;*
> *Filling the world with dazzling, brilliant light,*
> *Banishing darkness and the shades of night.*

This last passage contains an example of a kind of comparison that Gorgani occasionally uses, one we might call a reversed image. To say that a woman longing for her lover is like a blazing fire is not unduly strange for us; what is stranger, and productive of a stranger effect, is to reverse the image and say that a blazing fire is like a woman longing for her lover. Gorgani is particularly fond of employing these reversed images in the poem's few battle scenes, for example,

> *And, elsewhere, sudden arrows entered eyes*
> *Like sleep that takes a warrior by surprise;*
> *Like love, spears pierced through hearts, and like*
> > *good sense*
> *Axes split open heads and arguments.*

And sometimes he can spin conventional paradoxes that sound exactly like the stock in trade of Petrarch and his followers in Europe three hundred years later, as when Ramin laments his love for Vis:

> *Half of my body burns, half of it freezes.*
> *Has God created, and can heaven show,*
> *An angel made like me from fire and snow?*
> *Fire does not melt my snow, and who has seen*
> *Snow coexist with fire, as in Ramin?*

I would like to quote many more of Gorgani's images, but space prevents me. Suffice it to say that, although it's impossible to convey in English the charm and force of much of his metaphoric language, I hope that in the course of this translation I have been able to give some occasional glimpses of it.

THE POEM

Although such concerns can be fascinating in themselves, especially to scholars, we don't read narrative poems primarily for the social worlds they evoke, or in order to trace the origins of their rhetorical conventions. We read them because their narratives engage us, because their characters speak to us in some way, because they can seem to be disguised versions of our own longings or fears, because, across whatever distances of time and culture, they confirm the realities of our common humanity. If a narrative doesn't do at least some of these things in a compelling fashion, no amount of scholarly excitement can keep it alive.

The beauty and vigor of Gorgani's language and, despite all its rhetorical artifice, its constant freshness are of course only palely reflected in a translation. For us, the poem must live or die by the story it tells and by the characters it presents to us. The story is not a complicated one, though it begins obliquely and to our eyes rather strangely; in essence it is a very familiar and simple story, a love triangle. Despite his slow pace, and his habit of introducing the odd detail that he then forgets he has mentioned, so that there are occasional inconsistencies in the narrative, Gorgani is a very good storyteller. He sets up situations well; he switches from one character to another, and one place to another, convincingly; he keeps us on edge; he is wonderfully good at creating an atmosphere of expectation and romance when he needs to. Many of the most important scenes in the story happen at night, and this can add immeasurably both to its deliquescent romanticism and to the frequent frisson of fear that Gorgani wants us to feel.

Four characters are at the center of the poem: Vis, her second husband Mobad, her lover Ramin (who is also Mobad's younger brother), and her nurse. Vis is by far the most interesting character in the poem, and her creation, or recreation, is Gorgani's greatest achievement. She shares with a number of other eleventh-century Persian heroines, whose stories were drawn from pre-Islamic lore, an articulate forthrightness that can be both surprising and very stirring. The first time we see her speak is when she publicly storms at her mother after she learns that her mother had promised her as a bride to Mobad before she was even born. Her numerous speeches of rage, anguish, contempt, and supplication, to her nurse, her husband, and her lover, often have extraordinary power. She is given a complexly divided inner life that is unmatched by that of any other contemporary heroine in Persian, or I think in any contemporary European work. Vis's husband, Mobad, is given an almost equally complex and volatile inner life, and although he is in some sense Vis's enemy, and he certainly acts in ways that Gorgani condemns, as will any reader, it is impossible not to feel some sympathy for his wretchedly evolving situation. The nurse is a stock character (she has clear antecedents in Greek and Latin comedy, and she will often remind a Western reader of the nurse in Shakespeare's *Romeo and Juliet*, or of Pandarus in Chaucer's *Troilus and Criseyde*), but her sly, scheming amorality combined with her genuine love for her charge, Vis, are brilliantly presented, and most of the poem's occasional flashes of humor are associated with her. Compared to Vis, Mobad, or the nurse, Ramin is undoubtedly a less-compelling character. He is usually, we can say, a serviceable cipher rather than a fully drawn character in his own right (his inner life seems to be a much simpler affair than Vis's), although he does grow in stature as the poem proceeds, and the episodes when he marries and then repentantly returns to Vis show him at his most complex and interesting. But he can then be obtuse in ways that, one feels, neither Vis or the nurse would ever be (he tries to compliment his wife by telling her she looks like Vis and is taken aback by her angry response), so that even when he seems believable as a person it is hard to feel as much empathy with him as the portrayal of Vis invites us to experience.

THE POEM'S AFTERLIFE

1. IN PERSIAN CULTURE

Gorgani's *Vis and Ramin* had a profound, if also very mixed, influence on subsequent Persian literature. On the one hand its rhetoric and a number of its scenes and themes were widely imitated, especially by the major romance writer Nezami, who lived a century after Gorgani. Nezami adopted wholesale Gorgani's array of rhetorical devices (although he rarely uses the kind of daringly original metaphors that Gorgani occasionally employs). In general he smooths away the occasional rough edges in Gorgani's rhetoric; he takes fewer risks, but his poems have a more consistently beautiful finish to them than Gorgani achieves, or was perhaps interested in achieving. Nezami also took a number of other hints from Gorgani's poem. The long altercation in the snowstorm, towards the end of *Vis and Ramin,* was closely copied by Nezami in his

Khosrow and Shirin, and the extensive description of the night sky, and its astrological implications, when Mobad enters the castle of Gurab near the poem's opening, also strongly influenced similar moments in poems by Nezami, who had an obsessive interest in astrology. Because Nezami's romances became the model for subsequent writers of Persian romance, Gorgani's poem, through Nezami, had far-reaching effects on the development of the genre in Persian.

But in another way Gorgani's *Vis and Ramin* was a cul-de-sac within Persian culture, a poem that led nowhere. Gorgani's poem is about an erotic relationship that is celebrated in and for itself; it is among other things a kind of hymn to the pleasures and miseries of Eros, and to Eros's ultimate triumph. It is also a very sympathetic portrait of a woman who commits adultery, who blithely (and sometimes not so blithely) follows her heart, and whose desires are vindicated by the outcome of her story. No other Persian romance does this. In the century that followed Gorgani's masterpiece, Persian love poetry became progressively less carnal and more moralistic, and eventually mystical. Nezami's romances tend to be in the form of an *éducation sentimentale,* and the (chaste) female beloved's main function is to elevate the spiritual sensibility of the male hero, who is at the center of the poem. Nezami's romances also hint at mystical dimensions, and by the time we come to a writer like Jami, the most important writer of Persian romances in the fifteenth century, the real subject of the romance is the soul's love for God. In so far as women exist in the poems they are there as allegorical presences, and female sexuality as such is regarded with extreme suspicion, not to say outright misogyny. From being a celebration of the flesh and its pleasures, the romance had become a means of transcending the flesh and its pleasures. *Vis and Ramin* fell into relative obscurity; none of the few surviving manuscripts seems to have a Persian provenance, as they were written for either Indian Mughal or Turkish Ottoman patrons. The poem came to be thought of almost solely in terms of its rhetorical influence on Nezami. In popular Persian culture, Vis herself, in so far as she was remembered at all, became a negative moral example, a warning of the dangers of immorality and unbridled passion. It was not until the mid-twentieth century that the poem was, to some extent, rehabilitated, although it is still thought of by many who are aware of its existence as an interesting if somewhat crude precursor to Nezami's more admired romances, rather than as a major work in its own right.

2. IN EUROPE

I suggested above that, because the world of *Vis and Ramin* is in many respects similar to that of a number of medieval European romances, and that it precedes them by over a hundred years, Gorgani's poem, or other poems like it, probably played some exemplary part in the efflorescence of European romance literature. Recent years have seen a gradual acknowledgment by scholars of European medieval poetry that influences on medieval European literature from the world of Islam cannot be discounted as the wild imaginings they were once considered to be. There is now I think an increasingly widespread acceptance of the notion that Dante did probably have some knowledge of the *Libro della Scala,* an account of Mohammad's tour of heaven and hell that contains some striking similarities to moments in the *Commedia,* that the numerous images and motifs common to both Andalusian Arabic ghazals and the poems of the troubadours are not simply extraordinary coincidences, and that the presence of vernacular Arab poets in Sicily was at the least a catalyst to the emergence of the *dolce stil nuovo.* The notion that medieval European and Christian literary culture was completely isolated from medieval Middle Eastern and Islamic literary culture, and that there was no movement from the one to the other, has been recognized as untenable.

For over a century now a specific connection has been intermittently suggested between *Vis and Ramin* and the story of *Tristan and Isolde,* which became known in Europe about a hundred, or a hundred and fifty, years (depending on when one dates Béroul's poem, which marks the first appearance of the tale in Europe) after Gorgani wrote *Vis and Ramin.* As far as I know, the first scholar to suggest the connection was Italo Pizzi (1849–1920) in the 1890s, and his tentative suggestion was followed up by Rudolf Zenker's discussion of the notion in his article *Die Tristansage und das persische Epos von Wis und Ramin* in 1911, in which he concludes that *Vis and Ramin* is the major source of the *Tristan* legend. Various other scholars have come to the same conclusion, most notably Pierre Gallais in his exhaustive, and it must be admitted somewhat combative, discussion of the possibility, *Essais sur Tristan et Iseut et son Modèle Persan*, Paris 1974. Gallais' book received some very respectful reviews, but its conclusions have been not so much refuted as simply ignored by most writers on the *Tristan* story.

Once the extensive similarities between the tales are pointed out it is difficult to conclude that there is no connection between them. The narratives share a number of motifs, including: the hero falling in love with the heroine while escorting her as a bride to the home of his king and close relative; the hero being renowned as a minstrel; the crucial role of the heroine's servant/confidante as go-between; the substitution of this servant/confidante for the heroine in the king's bed; the episode of the hero's false love (Isolde of the White Hands, Gol; the characterization of the two is extremely similar); a threatened but averted trial or punishment of the lovers by fire; the lovers' escape together to an "uncivilized" area (the forest in *Tristan and Isolde*, the forested area of Daylam in *Vis and Ramin*); the hero's disguising himself in an enveloping cloak/veil (Tristan as a leper, Ramin as a woman) in order to gain access to the beloved; Mobad's being killed by a boar, while a dream has the equivalent character's (King Mark's) palace despoiled by one in *Tristan and Isolde*. There are more general parallels too; both poems contain spectacular leaps, of which much is made by the authors, undertaken by Tristan when he is cornered, and by Vis in order to escape from the rooms where she has been confined; both Tristan and Ramin are the putative inheritors of their kings' realms since there is no closer relative who is the obvious heir; both Mark and Mobad are sympathetically presented betrayed older husbands (and kings) rather than contemptible villains, and neither is treated as the conventional cuckold-as-figure-of-fun.

Even where there are differences between the tales, tantalizing parallels exist. Tristan is King Mark's nephew, while Ramin is Mobad's younger brother. But, as I have indicated above (in footnote 3), Ramin is also twice referred to as Mobad's son, and once he refers to Mobad as his father. Ramin could be both son and brother to Mobad by Parthian custom, a dual relationship that was obviously impossible in Europe; it seems plausible that a sibling and a son could turn into a sibling's son when the story moved to another culture. Although the magic love potion handed by Isolde's confidante to the lovers is absent from *Vis and Ramin*, Vis's confidante is also a practitioner of magic (she prevents Mobad from sleeping with Vis by means of the talisman[7]), and Gol says that Ramin's heart is bound to Vis by "the old nurse's spells"; moreover, the metaphor of love as a wine that

___

7 Interestingly enough, in Chrétien de Troyes's variant of the Tristan story, *Cligès,* the nurse, like Vis's nurse, uses her magic powers to render the unwelcome husband of the hero's beloved impotent, rather than, as in *Tristan,* to make the lovers fall in love; and, as in *Vis and Ramin,* the adulterous lovers end their lives happily as king and queen, after the fortuitous death of Cligès's uncle, who is also both his king and his lover's husband. The survival of these motifs from *Vis and Ramin,* in a variant of the Tristan story, would seem to tie this story even more closely to the narrative of *Vis and Ramin.*

induces intoxication and delirium, and which one drinks mutually, is a commonplace of the poem.

Clearly some episodes in *Tristan and Isolde* must come from another source (the spreading of flour between Tristan's and Isolde's beds for example, the character of Kurvenal),[8] and clearly too, much that is in *Vis and Ramin* is not reproduced in *Tristan and Isolde*. The antithetical endings to the tales can make them seem very far apart: *Vis* comes ultimately from a culture that celebrated physical pleasure, and Gorgani's version was written in a period of nostalgia for pre-Islamic civilization, when an imagined (and perhaps real) pre-Islamic *douceur de vivre* had a recognizable cachet within his culture; *Tristan* comes from a Christian culture, and the deaths of Tristan and Isolde imply that the values by which they lived have no ultimate validity in the Christian world, which cannot allow the lovers to be rewarded by success or happiness. In the European versions of the tale the happy ending of *Cligès* was to remain an anomaly; it was the tragic ending of *Tristan* that was seen as culturally "right", and which quickly gained wide currency.

It is undeniable that there are important differences between *Vis and Ramin* and *Tristan and Isolde*, but there is no other tale, certainly there is nothing in Celtic literature,

---

8 Melot, the malevolent dwarf who betrays the lovers, may seem to be another candidate; however Gallais argues, I think with some cogency, that Zarin-Gis, the blond-haired informant of Mobad, is an equivalent character in *Vis and Ramin*. The few times that it is mentioned in medieval Persian literature, blond hair is seen as indicative of deceitfulness, and in both tales we have an example of the common belief that those who do not look like the rest of the community are malevolent and untrustworthy.

which is the usually assumed source of the Tristan story, which even remotely shows as many similarities to the tale of *Tristan and Isolde* as does the tale of *Vis and Ramin*. In fact the moments in Celtic literature that have been pointed to as parallels or antecedents to *Tristan and Isolde* are slight in the extreme, and have none of the plethora of specific detail to be found in *Vis and Ramin*, which parallels similar details in the *Tristan* legend.[9] Celtic names that are similar to those of the lovers have been found, and they may well have influenced the forms of the lovers' names in various versions of the *Tristan and Isolde* story as it spread throughout Europe, but before Béroul's version appeared in France in the mid- or late-twelfth century, the people that these names designated were never associated together in one tale, and there was

---

9 To dismiss the "Persian and Arabic analogues" (which presumably include *Vis and Ramin*) to the *Tristan* legend as being "restricted to isolated motifs overwhelmingly belonging to the common fund of Marchen-types" (Francoise Le Saux, in *The Growth of The Tristan and Iseut Legend In Wales, England, France and Germany,* Lampeter, 2003, p. 3) discounts two important facts. The first is that the motifs are not "isolated" but are arranged into what is essentially the same story (apart from the endings). The second is that the Celtic cultures that are assumed by most scholars to be the source of the *Tristan and Isolde* story can offer even less in the way of evidence for such a claim, and they have been much scoured in an attempt to find such evidence. Certainly they cannot offer anything as coherent as a story, not even one that could be dismissed as being made up of "isolated motifs overwhelmingly belonging to the common fund of Marchen-types." Even if the evidence that *Vis and Ramin* is a source for the *Tristan and Isolde* story be thought of as slight (and I believe it warrants much more than this), slight evidence is still preferable to no evidence.

no suggestion whatsoever that they were lovers. There is no evidence of a Tristan who was known as a lover in any Celtic story until long after the story of *Tristan and Isolde* was already circulating in Europe. As C. E. Pickford, the reviewer of Gallais' book in *Medium Aevum*, noted, "The thesis of the Celtic origin of *Tristan* owes more to the eloquence of Gaston Paris [the notion's nineteenth-century originator] than to the realities of Celtic Literary History."

I should like to stay with the names of the lovers for a moment. I offer the following speculations as merely that, speculations, but I believe them to be at least plausible. Although she is usually referred to as Vis in the course of the poem, the heroine of Gorgani's *Vis and Ramin* is occasionally called "Viseh"; it's clear that this is her real name, and that "Vis" is a shortened form of it (perhaps for metrical reasons). If, as would necessarily have been the case if the tale did in fact travel to Europe, the poem reached the West via an Arabic speaking country, the names in the poem could well have undergone some Arabicization in their pronunciation. The Arabic pronunciation of the letters that spell "Viseh" in the Perso/Arabic script is "Wisat," or "Wiset" depending on the local pronunciation of short vowels, which varies a great deal in Arabic dialects. The first form of the name of the heroine of *Tristan and Isolde*, as it appears in Béroul's version, is Iseut (the final "t" would of course have been pronounced in the twelfth century). From Wisat or Wiset to Iseut is phonetically a very short distance indeed (if the initial "w" is lost, an entirely plausible development, the name is virtually there). I think it quite likely that the Arabic pronunciation of "Viseh" ("Wisat" / "Wiset") is behind the name "Iseut."

To get from Ramin to Tristan is clearly not such a short phonetic journey as to get from Viseh/Wiset to Iseut. There is however something curious about the names of both heroes, in that in each case an author of the tale remarks on the meaning of the first syllable of the name; further he remarks on its meaning in the language of his source, not in the language in which he is at the moment writing the story. Gorgani says that it is entirely appropriate that his hero is called Ramin, since in pre-conquest Persian "Ram" meant "contented, satisfied" and after his long tribulations Ramin became a contented and satisfied man. Gottfried von Strassburg remarks that it is entirely appropriate that his hero is called Tristan, since in French "Triste" means "sad," and Tristan lived a sad life and came to a sad end. In each case the hero's name is seen as a commentary on the nature of his fate, and as the fate in question changes from a happy one to a sad one so the name of the hero changes from one that implies happiness to one that implies sadness. This looks like a deliberate ploy, or even a joke, on the part of whoever domesticated the tale to a European context and gave it a sad ending, particularly as the meanings of the names are in each case explicitly emphasized. When for a while (in some versions of the tale) Tristan disguises himself as a merchant, he reverses the syllables of his name and refers to himself as "Tantris." This suggests that his name is something malleable, involving word play and a deliberate disguise, a trope that is consistent with the derivation of his name in the way that I have suggested above, since this also involves word play and a deliberate disguise.

In the argument against the existence of a connection between the two tales, much has been made of the absence of evidence of textual transmission, but a greater awareness of the ways in which stories travel orally from culture to culture makes such concerns perhaps less decisive than they once seemed. Gallais and other scholars have assumed that transmission of the tale to Europe, if it occurred, was probably through Arab Spain. My own feeling is that a more likely conduit would have been the Seljuk court of Syria. This court culture was highly polyglot, and was made up of Central Asian, Persian, and Arab elements. Although ethnically the Seljuks were central Asian Turks, much of their court culture was Persian; they had passed through Iran during their conquests, and taken on its culture and court language as their own, much as the Normans passed through western France and became culturally French before they conquered England in the eleventh century. The Syrian Seljuk court showed a lively interest in literature in Persian (for example, the twelfth-century Persian compendium of advice, *Bahr al-Fava'id*, was a product of their court's patronage). Politically, they were known as skilled negotiators (probably because of their familiarity with a number of ethnic and cultural traditions), and they tended to act as the diplomatic spokesmen of the Moslem world in its contacts with the crusaders of

Outremer. They were a branch of the same family to which Gorgani's sultan, Abu Taleb Toghrel Beg, belonged, the man who had placed Gorgani's patron in Isfahan as its ruler. The autobiography of the Syrian soldier and diplomat Usama ibn Munqidh (1095–1188), who was present during diplomatic contacts with the crusaders on a number of occasions, gives a fascinating picture of the complexities of this culture, and incidentally makes us realize just how extensive, and intimate, personal contact could be between individual Christian and Moslem members of opposing political and religious factions. I think it more likely that *Vis and Ramin* could have been communicated to a Western audience, which could have then brought it to Europe, in such informal contacts in Outremer and Syria, rather than in Moslem Spain, which would have required a more circuitous route, and probably more numerous points of transmission.

This Translation

I have worked from three printed editions of the poem: one edited by Mohammad Ja'far Mahjub (Tehran, 1337/1959), a Japanese edition prepared by Emiko Okada and Kazuhiko Machida (Tokyo 1991), and the edition of Mohammad Roshan (Tehran 1381/2003).[10] I have also consulted the best preserved manuscript of the poem, which is in the Bibliothèque Nationale, Paris (this is a fifteenth-century

---

10 These editions were prepared from the following manuscripts: Bibliothèque Nationale Suppl. Persan 1380, Bodleian Elliott 273, and Berlin Public Library Pertsch 681.

manuscript, written in a clear and beautiful hand, for the Ottoman court). The manuscripts of the poem differ in mainly minor ways. But there are some brief passages present in only one manuscript (not always the same manuscript). As these are usually in the nature of further embellishment of already highly embellished passages, I have in general taken them to be scribal interpolations and have omitted them (in all, the passages to which I am referring come to less than twenty lines). I have begun my translation at the point where the manuscripts have the heading "The Beginning of the Tale of Vis and Ramin," and have omitted the preceding introductory material, which is largely devoted to praise of Gorgani's patron and employers. I have also omitted the corresponding laudatory material after the story ends (this moment too is marked in the manuscripts by a fresh heading). Where the printed editions differ I have in general followed the one edited by Mohammad Roshan, although not in every case. I have also referred to George Morrison's prose translation of the poem (New York, 1972), which was prepared chiefly from Mahjub's 1959 edition of Gorgani's text. Although I differ with Morrison on the interpretation of a few passages, I have found his suggested solutions to some obscure moments of the poem extremely useful.

The poem is in couplets in the original, as are all Persian narrative poems, and these couplets correspond in length quite closely to the English pentameter couplet, commonly called the heroic couplet. As the pentameter couplet has been a vehicle for narrative poetry in English since the medieval period, and as it is by far the closest form in English to the form in which Gorgani's poem is written, this seemed the obvious choice as the vehicle for my translation. I have in general translated one couplet in Persian by one couplet in English, although there is not always an exact correspondence; occasionally I have had to take two couplets to convey the meaning of one couplet in the original, and very occasionally I have incorporated two Persian couplets into one English couplet. As well, obviously, as conveying the basic meaning of what is going on, I have tried hard to bring across what I take to be the tone of the original, especially during the long speeches given by many of the characters at different moments in the story; I have taken especial trouble over the numerous metaphors and similes, as these constitute a very important part of the effect of Gorgani's poetry in Persian. With one exception, the headings in the English text are translations of headings that are present in the Persian text. The one exception is the heading "Ramin reproaches his heart" (page 372), which I have added; I did this because I found that friends who were kind enough to read parts of my translation in draft form pointed out to me that it was unclear for an English reader who Ramin was talking to at this point.

I have become greatly indebted to a number of people for help and encouragement during the four years that I have worked on this translation. I would like to thank my friend Michael Zwettler for his gift to me, many years ago, of his copy of Mahjub's edition of *Vis and Ramin*, and also Professor Heshmat Moayyad for his gift of the Japanese edition of the poem. Without the unflagging support and enthusiasm of Mohammad and Najmieh Batmanglij of Mage Publishers, the project would have taken far longer and would perhaps never have been completed. Their occasional presents of really splendid wine, which would turn up often unannounced on my doorstep from time to time, would certainly have seemed highly appropriate to Gorgani, as they did to me too. Two of my friends have read the whole manuscript through and made innumerable useful suggestions. I am very grateful to the scholar of medieval French literature and culture Sarah-Grace Heller for her never-wavering encouragement, and for her willingness to share with me her wide-ranging knowledge of the European medieval romance tradition; I am equally grateful to the poet Catherine Tufariello who kept a watchful eye on my metrics, who caught many tetrameters and hexameters trying to pass themselves off as pentameters, and whose knowledge of the English poetic tradition I almost always trusted when she said the equivalent of "Well it may sound good like that in Persian, Dick, but it won't do in English." My chief debt in all my Persian translations has always been to my wife, Afkham Darbandi, through whom I first came to know and love the culture and literature of Iran, and who has remained my inspiration and muse throughout my long association with the incomparable splendors of Persian medieval poetry; I gratefully dedicate this translation to her. I am also very grateful to our two daughters, Mariam and Mehri, for their constant kindnesses to me, and for the unfailing support

they have offered for the literary projects they have heard me obsess about for most of their lives. I happily admit to one other debt, one I am reluctant to believe is wholly imaginary:

> *Ah Vis, across the centuries I heard*
> > *Your human cry,*
> *And vowed that I would do my part to see*
> > *It did not die.*

THE PRONUNCIATION OF NAMES

Names in Persian tend to be pronounced with an even stress, which sounds to an English ear as if the last syllable is being slightly stressed. In general I have scanned the names as if the last syllable is stressed. The sound represented by "i" is pronounced "ee," so that "Vis" rhymes with "peace," and "Ramin" rhymes with "seen." There are two "a" sounds in Persian, a long "a," which is like the British "a" in "father," and a short "a" like the "a" in "cat." The "a" in Ramin and Qaren is long; that in Mobad, Zard, and Shahru is short.

Black Sea
Caucasus
Caspian Sea
Arran
Arman
Abkhaz
Mughan
Azerbaijan
Dehestan
Astarabad
Gorgan
Gilan
Amol
Daylaman
Tabaristan
Alborz Mountains
Damavand
Rey
Euphrates
Tigris
Mahabad (Hamedan)
Kuhestan
Dinavar
Saveh
Mt. Arvand
Qom
Gurab
Baghdad
Mah
Isfahan
IRAN
Shushtar
Khuzan (Khuzestan)
Ahvaz
Estakhr
Shiraz
Persian Gulf
A GEOGRAPHY OF
VIS & RAMIN

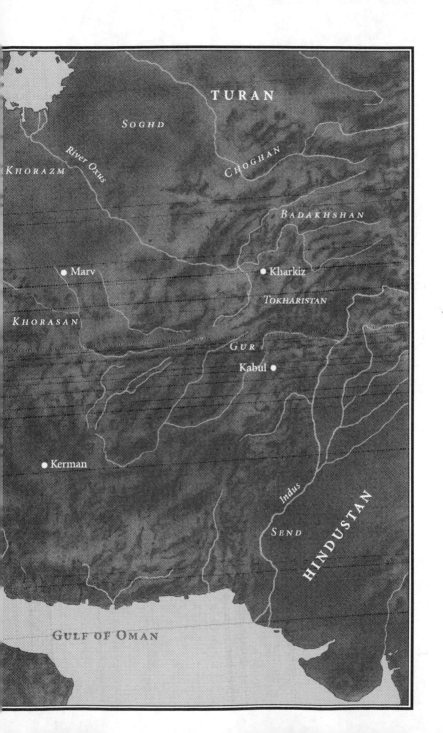

VIS & RAMIN

THE BEGINNING OF THE TALE

آغاز داستان

I found an ancient tale that men recite
To while away the watches of the night.

There lived a king once, long ago, who reigned
In glory; all he wanted he obtained,
And petty rulers bowed before his throne,
Subservient to this happy king alone,
Whose dignity and splendor seemed to rise
Beyond the radiance of the turning skies.
Korah's and Kasra's[1] fabled opulence
Did not approach this king's magnificence;
He was a lion in war, and in largesse
An April cloud that rained down happiness.
What banquets and festivities this king
Would hold at court to celebrate the spring,[2]
With noblemen as guests from every town
And women of great beauty and renown,
From Rey, Gorgan, Shiraz, and Khorasan,
Azerbaijan and distant Isfahan;

Bahram, Roham from Ardebil, Viru,
Ramin, Daylam's Goshasp, and Shapur too
From great Gilan were there, and with the king
Was Zard, his confidant in everything,
His brother, his most trusted minister,
First of his courtiers, and his counselor.

The king sat in his court surrounded by
His nobles like the full moon in the sky
Among its stars. None equaled him in fame
Or regal radiance; this sovereign's name
Was King Mobad, and from his eyes there shone
Light like the world-illuminating sun.
His nobles were like lions ranged in rows,
The women of the court like graceful does,
The lions gazed with longing, and the deer
Bravely returned their stares and showed no fear.
Goblets went round, all filled with brimming wine,
Like suns that passed from sign to stellar sign,
And blossoms settled on the throng as though
Gold coins were scattered to a crowd below.
A cloud of burning musk filled all the air,
As fragrant as a lovely woman's hair,
Musicians drank and sang, and told their tales,
And roses heard the plaint of nightingales.
The king's court rang with joy, and far and wide
Festivities filled all the countryside.
Men went out from their homes to celebrate
The advent of the spring's auspicious date,
And varied melodies were heard to rise
From every plain and meadow to the skies.
So many flowers now thronged the earth, the sight
Was like the star-strewn canopy of night.
Now everyone wore tulips in their hair,
In every palm a wine cup nestled there,

Some rode their Arab horses through the day,
Some sang and danced their weary cares away,
Some drank their wine surrounded by sweet roses,
Some went out in the meadows picking posies,
And everywhere the spring's new blossoms made
The earth as lovely as a rich brocade.
The king joined in their pleasures, riding on
An elephant whose splendid trappings shone
With silver, gold, and jewels, so that it seemed
To be a glittering sea that glowed and gleamed.
Horsemen preceded him across the plain,
And after him there came a varied train
Of litters and bright palanquins, which brought
The lovely women of the royal court;
And as he went he scattered his largesse,
Bestowing justice, wealth, and happiness.
(This is how one should live; try if you can
To give enjoyment to your fellow man,
Neither the generous or the mean survive,
So spread what joy you can while you're alive.)
A happy week went by, and everywhere
The king proceeded, pleasure too was there.

THE WOMEN LOOKING ON AT THE KING'S COURT

Among the noble, watching women who
Accompanied the monarch was Shahru,
The lovely, well-born queen of Mahabad;
Azerbaijan had sent Sarv-e Azad,
The beautiful Abnush came from Gorgan,
And Naz Delbar was there from Dehestan,
From Rey both Dinargis and Zaringis,
From Kuhestan Shirin and Farangis.
From Isfahan two radiant sisters came,
Abnaz was one, Nahid the other's name;

Golab and Yaseman had each been brought there
(Their fathers were both ministers at court there),
The charming child of Saveh's noble king
Arrived, and in her radiance shamed the spring,
Naz, Azergun, Golgun, whose faces' glow
Was like a blood-red blush suffusing snow,
All these were there, together with Sahi,
The king's wife, splendid in her dignity,
Whose body was like silver, and whose face
Rivaled the moonlight in its lovely grace.
A thousand serving girls, with violet tresses
And jasmine breasts,³ attended these princesses –
Girls who were Western, Turkish, or Chinese,
As elegant as slender cypress trees;
Their waists were girt with gold and jewels, and on
Their heads bright diadems discreetly shone.
Among these women come from far and wide,
Strutting like hawks and peacocks in their pride,
Whose lovely doe-like eyes seemed made to slay
The lions that pursued them as their prey,
The loveliest of all the beauties who
Adorned this great assembly was Shahru;
A cypress in her slender elegance,
Topped by the sun in its magnificence,
Whose ruby lips hid shining pearls, whose dress
And face competed in their loveliness,
Two marvels side by side, as each one made
The other seem the lovelier brocade.
Her lips were sugar, and each tooth a gem,
Her words as if sweet sugar coated them,
Two scented braids descended from her crown,
Two looped and twisted chains cascading down
Where fifty tumbling musky ringlets chased
Each other to beneath her lovely waist.

Her eyes like two narcissi seemed to be
The home of witchcraft and dark sorcery.
A moon of beauty when she sat and talked,
A moving cypress when she stood and walked,
The breeze of spring felt shame before her face,
The scent of aloes wood shrank in disgrace
Before her fragrant hair; a jewel arrayed
In jewels, both silver and bright gold were made
More lovely by her wearing them, though she
Was beautiful without their sophistry.

MOBAD MAKES A PROPOSAL TO SHAHRU, AND SHE MAKES HIM A PROMISE

One day it happened that Mobad, by chance,
Was smitten by this full moon's radiance,
This silver cypress tree, this idol who
Seemed always smiling and was named Shahru,
And had her summoned to his royal throne
And sat her there beside him, quite alone.
He gave her roses, whose bright pinkness glowed
With all the colors that her cheeks now showed,
And kindly, softly, with repeated smiles,
With happy, hesitant, flirtatious wiles,
He said to her, "Your beauty makes me see
How wonderful time spent with you would be;
Now, if you will agree to share your life
With me here, as my friend or as my wife,
I'll share my realm with you, we'll never part,
Since you're more precious to me than my heart.
I'll stand before you as your slave, I'll bow
Before you as the world does to me now.
From all the earth I've chosen you, and I
Will look on you with love until I die.
I'll sacrifice my heart and soul for you,
Whatever you might order me, I'll do.

If you stay with me day and night, each night
Will be a day for me, imbued with light,
And if I see your face continually
Each day will be the first of spring for me."

When Shahru heard the king she smiled and said,
"Why should such fancies fill your royal head?
Besides, my lord, I am not worthy of
The friendship that you offer, or your love.
And since I'm married to another man
I could not even think of such a plan,
And I'm a mother too. My sons have grown
To be fine princes, worthy of a throne,
The best of them's Viru, and he can fight
Successfully against a mammoth's might.
You never saw me in my youth, it's then
That I was worthy to be loved by men!
How sweet I was, how ready for romance,
A stately cypress in my elegance;
But now the wind has robbed my braided hair
Of all the lovely scents that lingered there.
The sun and moon no longer shine for me,
Though, in my spring, I was a willow tree
That flourishes by gently flowing streams:
But all that's passed now, gone like vanished dreams.
Once, where I walked, the scent of jasmine stayed
For years before its strength began to fade;
My beauty captured kings then, and my breath
Brought men back, living, from the throes of death.
My life has reached its autumn now; I see
The spring, and all its sweetness, snatched from me.
My skin is sere, and in my musky hair
Strands of white camphor can be counted there,
My face has lost its charm, adversity
Has bent my body's crystal cypress tree.

And it is worse than shameful to pretend
One's young still when one's life is near its end;
If I behaved like someone young despite
My age, I would be loathsome in your sight."

Mobad replied, "I wish the mother who
Bore such a lovely speaking moon as you
All joy, and sweet, delicious food; and long
May where you grew be prosperous and strong.
You are so lovely in old age, in truth
What were you in the springtime of your youth?
If this is now the withered flower, I say
A thousand blessings on you every day,
And when it was in bud, how many men
Whose hearts were stolen must have loved you then!
If you won't be my lover and my wife,
If you won't grant me happiness and life,
Give me your daughter; may her jasmine be
United with this stalwart, noble tree,
For any child you bear must be, like you,
As white and sweet as jasmine, dear Shahru,
And in my palace, when all's said and done,
I'll have the splendor of the shining sun;
If I've the sun of love here, why should I
Care for the sun that occupies the sky?"

Shahru replied, "A better son-in-law
I never thought of and I never saw:
If I'd a daughter in my house, my lord,
I'd know my duty then, you have my word,
But I have none. If I give birth to one,
I'll give her to you; you will be my son."
Mobad was overjoyed, and hand in hand
They swore an oath that none could countermand.

On silk, in musk diluted with rose water,
They wrote that if Shahru should have a daughter
All other suitors would be set aside:
Only Mobad could claim her as his bride.
See now what troubles came of this, that they
Had fixed an unborn daughter's wedding day.

THE BIRTH OF VIS

بر دنیا آمدن ویس

The secrets of the world are various,
And wisdom can't reveal their depths to us;
Fate knows of many a hidden chain that we
Cannot unlock with our sagacity.
Consider how she set this secret snare
And how the great Mobad was captured there,
And all because desire made him decide
A child as yet unborn would be his bride;
Wisdom did not reveal her birth would bring
Calamity and suffering to this king.
When these two swore their oath they did not know
The mastery that Fate would later show,
The horrors they'd confront, because they'd sworn
To chart the life of one as yet unborn.

Years passed, and hearts forgot the promise they
Had made to one another on that day.
The dry tree flourished once again, once more
The rose put forth its blossoms as before;

Old now, the queen was pregnant with a girl,
Within its shell there grew a precious pearl.
Nine months went by, and then this moon gave birth;
Another moon arose above the earth,
Or say the mother was the east, the source
From which the sun begins its radiant course.
They called her Vis, and all who saw her face
Wondered at its surpassing charm and grace.
As soon as she was born her mother sent
The baby to a nurse for nourishment,
Who kept her in Khuzan,[4] the place where she
Had come from, where she still owned property.
The little princess's layette was made
From precious scents, and jewels, and rich brocade,
From ermine, squirrel, sable, every fur
That would be soft, and gently comfort her,
Brocaded pillows, pretty trinkets, pearls,
And all that warms the hearts of little girls.
Her food was nourishing, her clothes were fine
And colorful, of delicate design.

She grew into a silver cypress tree,
Her heart was steely, and her spirit free,
And Wisdom gazing on her lovely face
Was baffled to describe her radiant grace.
It said, "She is a garden burgeoning
With all the freshness of the early spring,
Her eyes are two narcissi, and her hair
The purple violets darkly nestled there,
Her face is formed from tulips and wild roses."
But then it said, "It's autumn that composes
Her loveliness, not spring, and she is made
Of fruits that ripen in autumnal shade:
Her hair is clustered grapes, her breasts now show
The shape of pomegranates as they grow,

Her chin is like an apple, sweet and round."
And then it said, "In this sweet girl is found
The riches all the world desires, and she
Is like a wealthy royal treasury:
Her skin is silk, her face is rich brocade,
Her hair the essence from which scents are made,
Her body's made of silver, and beneath
Her ruby lips peep priceless pearls, her teeth."
And then it said, "But God has formed her of
His own refulgence, and celestial love,
And in her body all components meet
That make the walks of paradise so sweet,
The water and the milk, her cheeks' red wine,
The honey of her lips, are all divine."
It's no surprise if Wisdom missed the mark
Since heaven's eye, in seeing her, grew dark.
Her cheeks would steal spring's heart, when Patience spied
Her lovely eyes it sighed for them and died;
Her face was like the sun, in coquetry
She was the mistress of all sorcery.
Like some pale Western king, her face was white;
Her braids were guards, dressed blackly as the night,
And, like a royal African's, her hair
Glowed from her cheeks' bright torches, burning there.
Her curls were like a black cloud, and amid
Its darkness Venus, her bright earrings, hid.
Her fingers were ten reeds of ivory,
Their nails were filberts fitted cunningly,
Her necklace was like ice that coalesced
Upon the conflagration of her breast,
As though the splendid Pleiades were strewn
Across the shining surface of the moon,
As though a glittering torque should somehow be
Fitted around a silver cypress tree.

She was a houri in her loveliness,
In inward strength she was a sorceress,
Her eyes were doe's eyes, and you'd say that her
Plump rump belonged upon an onager.[5]
Her lips rained sugar down, and everywhere
She walked musk wafted from her perfumed hair;
And you would say that subtle mischief made
Her face to plunder hearts as its cruel trade,
Or that this lovely creature had been given
All of the beauty that was owned by heaven.

VIS AND RAMIN ARE BROUGHT UP BY THE SAME NURSE

The nurse was diligent, and strove to give
This lovely princess all the means to live;
Ramin was with them in Khuzan, and he
Worried his nurse's soul continually.
Vis and Ramin prospered beneath her care,
A rose, a marigold, together there;
They played together all the day and night
And so grew up in one another's sight,
Till Prince Ramin, as soon as he was ten,
Was taken home to Khorasan again.
Who could have guessed then what the skies would do,
The heavenly fate that waited for these two?
Before they were conceived, Fate had decreed
Their every motion and their every deed.
If one who knows the world's ways reads their tale
He will not blame them when they seem to fail,[6]
He'll know that God decided on their story
And human wills cannot oppose God's glory.

So Vis matured, and when she'd grown to be
As stately as a noble cypress tree,
When her bright, crystal arms filled out their strength,
And her dark hair was lariat-like in length,
Shading the lovely roses of her face,
Guarding their frailty with its tender grace,
Her name was bruited about the town
Which echoed with her beauty and renown.

Then the nurse wrote a letter to Shahru
That said, "There's no one as unkind as you
In all the world. Your selfish cruelty
Has made you disregard both Vis and me.
The things you gave me for her at her birth
Were paltry trinkets and of little worth,
But I have brought her up with dignity,
She's used to every kind of luxury.
The little hawk I raised has fledged her wings,
She's ready to fly on to greater things,
But I'm afraid that when she once takes flight
She'll find some partner, and soar out of sight.
I've given her whatever's suitable,
Surrounding her with all that's beautiful,
With gold and silver, colors, subtle scents,
Brocades and silks, every magnificence;
But she's so willful now, I hardly know her,
She doesn't like the gorgeous robes I show her.
Whatever lovely clothes I offer her,
Be they brocade or silk or softest fur,
There's always something wrong. 'But this is yellow,
It's only suitable for some mean fellow;
And this is blue, blue's right for someone who
Is in deep mourning, no one else wears blue.

This parti-colored robe is only fit
For scribes; who else would even look at it?
And this is white, the color old crones wear.'
Her pickiness will drive me to despair!
When she wakes up from sleep her morning fad
Is a silk gown made in Astarabad,
Then around noon she'll stubbornly declare
That filmy Chinese silk is all she'll wear;
At night it has to be a rich brocade
That's double sided and superbly made.
She's eighty friends to keep her company
(Since less than eighty's a catastrophe),
And when they eat together all the dishes
Must be of gold, since that's what madam wishes.
She's fifty chambermaids who, come what may,
Must be prepared to serve her night and day,
All belted and all crowned, all stood before her
And ready to do any service for her.
    I can't supply her needs now. I'm not fit
For this job, and I won't put up with it!
When you receive this letter, see she's brought –
As quickly as you can – back to the court.
A hundred nimble fingers can't fulfill
That one head's whimsical, impulsive will,
Just as three hundred stars can't be as bright
As one sun's world-illuminating light."

Shahru was overjoyed to read this letter
And thought the news it brought could not be better.
She gave the envoy jewels, a crown, and gold
That compensated him a thousandfold.
Next, Shahru followed royal precedent
And had young servants in gold litters sent
To follow him, so that they could escort
Vis from Khuzan back to the royal court.

When Shahru saw her daughter's lovely face,
Her stature, beauty, and bewitching grace,
She showered her with jewels and gold, and said
Her silent prayers above her daughter's head.
She sat her down, and gave her musky scents,
Brooches and bracelets and fine ornaments,
Gold-worked brocade – whatever could augment
Her charms, or make her more magnificent.
She gave her lovely daughter everything
The breezes give our gardens in the spring;
She was a portrait, as if Chinese art
Had now perfected her in every part,
She was a houri, whom Rezvan's caress [7]
Had made more gracious in her loveliness,
Since even faultless faces can be made
More lovely by gold jewelry and brocade.

VIS AND VIRU

ویس و ویرو

SHAHRU GIVES VIS TO VIRU,
BUT NO HAPPINESS COMES OF THIS

When Queen Shahru saw Vis would put to shame
Rose gardens with her beauty and her fame,
She said, "My dear, it seems that you compress
Within your being all of loveliness,
The world's become a much more splendid place
Because it holds your beauty and your grace.
Your father is a king, and I'm a queen,
No husband, in no country that I've seen,
Is worthy of you, and I'm unsure where
I'll find a husband who deserves to share
Your life with you; though here there's one man who
Is of your rank, your brother, Prince Viru.
Rejoice my heart, rejuvenate my life,
And say that you'll agree to be his wife.
Be both his wife and sister, and to me
You'll be my child for all eternity.
Viru's a sun, his goodness shines like light,
And Vis is like bright Venus in the night.

Nothing will make me happier than when
The best of women weds the best of men."

Vis heard her mother, and her face became
Like saffron with embarrassment and shame.
Love sprang up in her heart, she'd love Viru,
And, saying nothing, she acceded to
Her mother's words. Hair fell across her cheek,
Her face turned scarlet, but she did not speak.
Her mother realized this embarrassment
And silence signified the girl's consent,
Since she too in her youth had much preferred
To hold her tongue when serious things occurred.
The queen called in astrologers to know
The good and evil that the stars might show,
To say when Mars and Saturn would not shed
An evil influence on the marriage bed,
And when this brother should see at his side
His mother's daughter and his sister-bride.
They took their starry charts and calculated
When the auspicious time had best be dated:
They chose the sixth hour then, on the eighth day
Of the ninth month, as best in every way.

And when the chosen time arrived, Shahru
Came solemnly to Vis and to Viru,
And took their hands in hers, and gravely prayed
That God send down his blessings and his aid,
Then cursed the demon powers who might annoy
The couple with their spite, and mar their joy.
She praised Sorush,[8] and asked him to provide
His blessings for the husband and the bride,
Then said to each of them, "I pray that you
Find peace and happiness in all you do;

When siblings marry there's no need to hold
A ceremony bright with jewels and gold,
Likewise, it doesn't matter in the least
If you get married here without a priest –
A sibling marriage doesn't even need
A witness to corroborate the deed:
God and Sorush both know what has been done,
As do the stars, and moon, and shining sun."
She joined their hands and prayed that they
Might see good fortune with them every day,
That every month and every year would bless
Their lives with pleasure, joy, and happiness,
That they'd be faithful friends, each to the other,
As loyal sister-bride and husband-brother,
That like the sun and moon these two should be
Joined each to each for all eternity.

Zard comes as a messenger to Shahru

Beginnings show the end, and we can tell
When matters promise not to turn out well.
Bad weather starts at dawn, the sky will show
That rain will soon arrive, or freezing snow,
And warnings of a serious drought appear
In winter, presaging a tragic year;
When a young sapling starts to grow, the first
Shoots clearly show if it is blessed or cursed,
If it's to bear good fruit its buds in spring
Will tell the man who looks there everything;
And one who sees an archer draw his bow
Knows where the arrow that he shoots will go.
So, on that first day, Vis's destiny
Was plain for anyone with eyes to see.

No sooner were they married, and Shahru
Had joined the hands of Vis and Prince Viru,

Than all the castle rang with gaiety,
With loud rejoicing and festivity.
But then a cloud appeared above the lake,
And sudden evening seemed to overtake
The sun's course in the sky, and now you'd say
That it was not a cloud that dimmed the day,
But something like a dusty hurricane
That sped across the mountain and the plain.
A rider soon appeared, urging his steed
Straight for the castle at a furious speed.
His horse was black, the horse's trappings blue,
As were the rider's clothes and saddle too,
His turban, breeches, cloak, and boots[9] all glowed
Like violets as he rushed along the road;
Zard was the rider, Mobad's minister,
His trusted brother, and his counselor.
His eyes were bloodshot, and his forehead frowned,
Knotted with anger as he glared around,
Like a fierce wolf that sees its prey, or like
A hunting lion that prepares to strike.
He held a letter from his king, its scent
Perfuming all the highway as he went,
Written on silk, its ink of musky wine
And ambergris, sealed with a golden sign.
　　He rode into the castle and made straight
For where the queen awaited him in state.
He bowed and asked to be excused that he
Had ridden to her unceremoniously
But said his king's particular commands
(Commands that were for him divine demands)
Were that he ride posthaste by night and day,
Without a pause for rest, without delay,
And, sleeping in the saddle, he should ride
Until he stood at noble Shahru's side

To hand the letter to her that he'd brought
And bring her answer to his sovereign's court.
And then he said, "The king sends greetings to
His mother-in-law, the lovely queen, Shahru."

Now Queen Shahru remembered everything
That once had passed between her and the king.
She read the letter then and felt that she
Was like a donkey struggling to be free,
Whose feet sink deeper in the mud, and stick
More firmly there, the more they strain and kick.
The letter dwelt on all the things they'd both
Sworn long ago, with many a solemn oath.
It started with the name of God, who made
This world in righteousness, the God who weighed
Man by his moral sense and saw that he
Whose life was virtuous tasted victory.
"All that I ask," the letter said, "is for
You to recall the solemn oath you swore.
You know what we have sworn to, and you know
How we clasped hands together long ago:
You gave your daughter to me then, you said
That if you bore a daughter she should wed
No man but me, and now she's come to you
It's me that God has given this girl to –
It's my good fortune, if the truth be told,
That made you bear a daughter now you're old,
As though a pomegranate's flower should be
A blossom on an aging cypress tree!
When she was born, in thanks I gave away
Abundant wealth to celebrate the day,
Because God had kept faith with me and given
An answer to my fervent prayers to heaven.
     That girl belongs to me, to King Mobad,
And I don't want her there in Mahabad,

Its young and old live only for delight
And running after women day and night;
Your young men in particular have made
Deceiving pretty girls their stock in trade –
Seducing girls, or someone else's wife,
That's all they're good at, it's their way of life!
God help the girl who falls for their glib chatter,
The woman whom their nasty natures flatter.

A woman's heart is soft and trusting, she
Can be corrupted all too easily.
Women think men will tell the truth, and then
They give their bodies to these lying men.
They might be clever and intelligent
But if a man is smooth and eloquent,
If he should say, 'You're like the moon, my love,
A houri from the heavenly realms above;
You know how I have loved you, and how I
Would sacrifice my soul, and gladly die
For your sweet sake, how day and night I've cried
And wandered in my madness far and wide.
Ah, if you don't take pity on me here
I'll die for you, my love, I'll disappear,
And, in the world to come, my only bliss
Will be to grasp your skirts there, as in this,'
No matter how high born they are, how chaste,
Or good, or fearful that they'll be disgraced,
These sweet, caressing words will soon dissolve
All of their chastity and their resolve.

I know that Vis is good and pure, that's why
I'm anxious for her, why I weep and sigh.
Don't keep her there in Mahabad, but see
She comes to Marv here, to my court and me.
Don't worry about wealth, since I can give
Her all the gold and jewels she needs to live;
She'll be my chatelaine and keep the keys
That open all my richest treasuries.

I've bound my heart to her, all she desires
Is hers, I'll do whatever she requires.
I'll send you so much gold and treasure you
Could turn a town gold if you wanted to;
You're like my soul to me, your Mahabad
Will be a prosperous place where no one's sad,
I'll see Viru is married to someone
Related to me, he'll be like my son;
Your clan will be renowned, and I'll ensure
Their noble name will last for evermore."

Shahru felt shame invade her heavy heart;
All her resolve now threatened to depart.
Her eyes grew dark, she stared ahead, confused,
Her mind drew back, bewildered and bemused.
The letter seemed to take away her sense
Of everything except her negligence,
And she could think of nothing but the blame
She felt was due to her, the gnawing shame
That ate into her heart, and made her bow
Her head like one who begs for mercy now.
She thought of all the promises she'd made,
To God, and to the king, and was afraid.
Vis saw her silent mother turning pale
Like one whose senses falter and then fail,
And shouted, "What's this? Where was your good sense?
Where were your wisdom and intelligence?
I tell you, you have done an evil thing
In promising your daughter to this king.
Is this your wisdom? This what you can do?
Wisdom, you say! The whole world laughs at you!"

VIS QUESTIONS ZARD AND HEARS HIS ANSWER

Vis turned then to the messenger and said:
"Tell me your name. Where were you born and bred?"

"I'm from my sovereign's family," Zard replied,
"And in the court I'm always at his side.
When he sets off for war, it's I who show
His mighty armies where they have to go.
And if he has some secret he will ask
Me to advise him: this then is my task,
To help the king in every way I can,
To see to it that every royal plan
Is brought to a successful, timely end,
To be his boon companion and his friend.
My face is red, and I'm a cheerful fellow;
My horse is black, my name's 'Zard,' which means 'Yellow.'"

Vis laughed and said, "Then I say, 'Long live yellow,
That's made you such a splendid, clever fellow!'
Is it conventional in Marv that one
Bride has two husbands, then? That's how it's done?
And that's your filthy custom there, to woo
A married woman? That seems right to you?
Can you not see we've guests, and can't you hear
The music that's assaulting Saturn's sphere?
And can't you see our pretty town is full
Of everything that's fine and beautiful,
Of lovely women, rich brocades, sweet scents?
Of wealth, and every kind of elegance,
Of courtiers crowding in from far and wide,
Of splendid noblemen on every side,
Of cheerful conversations, banquets, wine,
Of friends sat side by side to drink and dine?
Can you not hear men cry out everywhere,
'Long live this castle and its happy pair,
May brides and bridegrooms and their celebrations
Crowd in these halls for endless generations!'
        And now you've heard our toasts, and seen the way
We choose to celebrate my wedding day,

Tug at your reins, and turn your pitch-black horse;
Straight as an arrow set your homeward course.
And don't come here again, since if you do
I tell you, it will be the worse for you;
Don't send me letters either, I won't read them,
Their words are like the wind and I won't heed them.
Viru's out hunting now; you'd better go
Before he comes back here and gets to know
The nature of your message and demands.
If you don't want to suffer at his hands
Leave now, and tell Mobad that I've long known
How as a simpleton he stands alone,
That age has dulled his mind, that he's a fool,
Someone to laugh at and to ridicule.
Tell him I said that if he'd any sense
He would forget about such impudence,
That men of his age should be thinking of
The world to come, not looking for young love.
Viru's my splendid husband and my brother,
Illustrious Shahru's my noble mother,
They are the happiness that fills my heart
And from these two I hope I'll never part;
What's Marv to me, and what's Mobad to me?
Here is the only joy I'll ever see.
A cypress lies beside me, why should I
Seek out a plane tree that is old and dry?
My eyes here are made happy by my mother,
My soul here is delighted by my brother;
Viru and I are milk and wine;[10] how can
I go to Marv and marry an old man?
I say this to the world, my heart won't hide it:
I'm young, I hate old age, I can't abide it!"

When Zard heard Vis's words, he tugged his reins,
And turned, and set off home across the plains,
And as he traveled he was unaware
Whether the road or a black pit lay there;
He felt such anguish that the world became
A dark place in his eyes, suffused with shame.

Mobad for his part found it hard to wait
And wondered what was making Zard so late:
"In Mahabad he has no enemy,
And who would dare to risk annoying me?
Neither Qaren, Shahru's great husband, nor
Her son Viru would want to start a war,"
He thought, "so what is keeping Zard so long?
Why hasn't he returned yet? What's gone wrong?
It might be Vis's stubbornness, or fear,
That makes her hesitate to travel here."
These were the thoughts that occupied Mobad
As he surveyed the road from Mahabad
When suddenly a cloud of dust appeared,
And as it bore down on the town and cleared
Zard could be seen, charging as if he were
An elephant, a mighty pillager,
That breaks its bonds when it's been goaded by
Its handlers' prodding and their hue and cry;
Thundering across the plains and hills as though
Distinctions between high terrain and low
Meant nothing to him. He did not draw rein
Until he reached his waiting king again,
And halted there, still mounted, in his face
The anger of his failure and disgrace,
His horse and clothes still grimed and filthy from
The dusty way along which he had come.

The king cried, "Welcome, Zard! From Mahabad
What is the news you've brought us, good or bad?
Should I congratulate you now or blame you?
A failure? A success? Which should I name you?"
 Zard said, "I was unable to fulfill
Your orders to me; name me as you will."
Then he dismounted, bowed his grimy head
In humble homage to the dust, and said,
"May you forever seek a noble name
And may your triumphs bring you wealth and fame;
Great king, like Jamshid may your sovereignty
Strike demons down and bring you victory.
May you rejoice, while Mahabad despairs,
May it be fit for wolves' and lions' lairs;
And may a little month not pass before
It's razed beneath the fires and swords of war.
May all its winds bring fire, its clouds be dry,
While pain and death encompass all its sky.
　　　I saw their land crammed with magnificence,
With silks, brocades, beauty, and elegance,
Their town decked out like Chinese temples, full
Of everything that's sweet and beautiful;
Their meadows filled with seated companies
As lovely as the moon and Pleiades,
As vivid as the beauty tulips bring
To gardens, when they open in the spring.
All this was done by Shahru, Vis's mother,
To marry Vis off to Viru, her brother,
And you're her son-in-law in name alone –
Another man has claimed Vis as his own;
And this is why you see my anxious face
Striped like a cloth with anger and disgrace.
You dug the channel, but another bore
Away the water you had dug it for.

She gave her daughter to you once, and now
She thinks she can renounce her solemn vow?
Do they not know your value? Or is night
Like day to them, as if they had no sight?
They haven't done this to a person who
Won't soon exact from them whatever's due,
But, even so, we've lived to see this time
Before they're punished for their wicked crime.
　　　Viru's the best of them in war, and he's
Better at feasts than fighting enemies;
He calls himself 'The Good Viru,' but in
His heart he's welcomed Ahriman[11] and sin.
His people say that you're his underling,
That you're his functionary, and he's their king.
I've told you what I saw and heard; they're filled
With arrogance, they're stubborn and self-willed."

Mobad makes war on Shahru and Qaren

Mobad was angered by his envoy's tale,
The wine red of his cheeks turned deathly pale.
He sweated in his fury, and he felt
As though his body had begun to melt,
And like a sun that's seen in running water
He trembled at the thought of Shahru's daughter.
He said to Zard, "But did you see this then,
Or is it gossip heard from common men?
Say what you saw, not things that you've inferred;
What you have seen is true, not what you've heard."
His brother said, "I wouldn't say to you
Things I had heard and did not know were true.
I saw what I have told you: I've left out
A great deal more I only heard about.
Before, I thought of Shahru as my mother,
And of Viru as if he were my brother,

Though love of you now makes me hope that I
Won't meet with either of them till I die.
I would not want to live if it were true
That in my heart I felt less love for you,
But, if you ask me to, I'll gladly swear
By God and by your soul that I was there
And with my own eyes saw the feasts that they
Had organized to mark the wedding day,
Though I ate nothing, and in truth I hated,
As if they'd jailed me, how they celebrated;
The singers' voices irritated me,
Their songs seemed like a harsh cacophony.
I've told you what I know; you know I'll do
Whatever tasks my lord commands me to."

And when Mobad had heard him, once again
Sorrow filled all his heart with grief and pain;
At times he was a snake whose head is hurt,
Writhing and twisting in the dust and dirt,
At times he seethed, like grapes plucked from a vine,
Newly fermenting in a vat of wine.
The nobles present ground their teeth and said,
"Why has Shahru deceived our king and wed
Her noble daughter to another man?
How could Viru conceive of such a plan?"
Then added, "May our king destroy them all,
And may Viru's and Qaren's palace fall;
And may not only Vis lose her Viru
But all of Mahabad lose Queen Shahru –
May countless wives mourn husbands there, and may
Their worthless king, Qaren, be swept away.
May clouds rain death down, may disaster's hand
Plunder their city and destroy their land;
Fate's tocsin sounds for them, they'll be destroyed,
Their wealthy land will be a barren void,

Destruction spreads its wings now to attack,
And where's the army that could drive it back?"

The king writhed inwardly, as if a fire
Consumed his heart with anger and desire.
He had his court scribe summoned and dictated
The ways in which he'd been humiliated,
Complaining of Shahru and how she'd made
An oath that she had faithlessly betrayed.
He sent each king a copy, asking for
Allies to help him prosecute his war;
They came from Khorasan and Dehestan,
From Kuhestan, Tabaristan, Gorgan,
From Sogdia, China, India, and Send.
Warriors poured in to help, from end to end
Marv's plain was thronged with men, so that you'd say
It was the crowded site of Judgment Day.

VIRU LEARNS OF MOBAD'S ATTACK

When news came that Mobad intended to
Attack both Mahabad and Queen Shahru,
Viru appealed to all the guests who had
Come for his wedding day to Mahabad –
Guests from Estakhr, Gilan, and Khuzestan,
Azerbaijan, and Rey, and Isfahan,
Whose wives and children Queen Shahru'd looked after,
Making the court a place of joy and laughter
For six long happy months of celebrations,
Festivities, and friendly conversations.
Now when they learned King Mobad Manikan[12]
Was bearing down on them, they made a plan,
Dispatching letters home to ask for aid
Against this king who threatened to invade
Great Mahabad; from every country then
The desert overflowed with fighting men,

A mass as mountainous as Damavand[13]
Now gathered on the plains of Nahavand,[14]
Armed and prepared, as strong as elephants,
As brave as lions in their belligerence.
Foot soldiers came from Daylaman,[15] as hard
As are the mountain fastnesses they guard,
Fierce Arab horsemen filled the crowded plain
More numerous than pelting drops of rain,
And ancient lions of war were there, men who
Were seasoned, battle-hardened, tried and true;
Sentries were posted, and to left and right
Princes prepared their men to stand and fight.

On his side too, Mobad prepared his forces,
Their spears like reeds in marshy water courses,
His armies as he left Marv seemed a river
Seething and swirling, flowing on forever;
The din of drums and trumpets shook the ground
As if the whole earth trembled at the sound,
Such clouds of dust rose up, it seemed that soon
The dust would be conversing with the moon,
That devils swarmed up to the sky to share
The secrets that Sorush[16] imparted there,
And in the swirling dust the army seemed
Like hazy stars that faintly flashed and gleamed,
Although the moon shrank back in fear to see
Such floods of infantry and cavalry –
These were not water floods but floods of iron,
Of warriors, each of whom was like a lion.
They marched on Mahabad, the men intent
On war, the king on vengeful punishment.
One army like a mighty slashing sword,
The other like a lion that reared and roared,
And as they met their forces seemed to be
Wild waves that crested on a windswept sea.

Mobad, the eastern king, who had been given
The moon and stars, the stewardship of heaven,
Marched westward; now, the din of drums rang out
From each camp like a demon's grisly shout
And every man who heard its thundering roar
Thirsted for vengeance and the rage of war.
The squeal of trumpets on each side would wake
The dead, as when the clouds of springtime break,
And thunder presages life-giving rain
That brings renewed life to the thirsty plain.
"Charge now," the drums exhorted, "charge and seize
The souls of all your wretched enemies."
As nightingales that nest in gardens sing
A medley of new songs throughout the spring
The trumpets blared a hundred different ways,
The bugles seemed to follow every phrase,
As if two singers sang in unison,
Each voice an echo of the other one;
Sad horn calls seemed to register dismay
As dying soldiers felt life ebb away,
And as each vanquished soldier's spirit fled
Swordsmen exulted that their foes were dead.

     The armies' ranks rose up like craggy rocks
Withstanding a wild ocean's massive shocks,
The warriors were like sharks amid the waves;
Like mountain leopards leaping from dark caves
The cavalry bore down, and men of sense
Were maddened by the battle's turbulence,
Like lunatics who'll recklessly attack
Water and roaring fire, and not draw back,
Or face down swords and spears, war elephants
And lions, disregarding all defense:

So on that battlefield men fought for fame,
And, more than death, feared cowardice and shame.
High on embroidered standards jostling there
A wolf, a boar, a tiger thronged the air,
And like a copse of swaying cypress trees
Brocaded banners fluttered in the breeze
To show a peacock, simorgh,[17] eagle fly
Embroidered in gold thread against the sky,
And there beneath a hawk a lion lay
As though it were the hawk's defeated prey.
The horses' hooves sparked fire, dust from the plain
Soared to the sky then drifted down again
Clogging the warriors' eyes and mouths, and all
Their mounts turned grey beneath its deadening pall.
Now bravery and cowardice were clear,
Happy to fight or holding back in fear,
One yellow as gold coins, one with a flush
Of crimson like a pomegranate's blush.

    Now that these armies met head-on you'd say
Two mountains made of steel clashed on that day,
The messengers they sent were arrows, blows,
That settled in the hearts of dying foes,
Or in their eyes; from every house they held
Its erstwhile happy owner was expelled.
The battle raged so wildly, mortal fear
Made men suspect God's Judgment Day was near;
Brother deserted brother, each man thought
Of his own safety as he fled or fought,
Their own strength and their swords were all that men
Could count on for support or comfort then.
Silence descended on the eloquent,
Numbness bewildered the intelligent,
The din of drums, the trumpet's brazen blare
Were all the sounds to be distinguished there;

Swords slashed chain mail, and entered in like water
And, unsuspected, added to the slaughter,
And, elsewhere, sudden arrows entered eyes
Like sleep that takes a warrior by surprise;
Like love, spears pierced through hearts, and like good sense
Axes split open heads and arguments.
    It seemed that swords found out exactly where
God placed the soul with such abundant care,
And where men's flesh was opened by the blade
The soul fled through the gaping wound it made.
Sharp Indian swords let loose a pouring flood,
A Judas tree's red blossoms of bright blood,
Or pomegranate flowers, or seeds within
A pomegranate fruit's tough outer skin.
Lances were tailors as they sewed men to
Their horses' saddles when they ran them through,
Some men were lions seeking out their prey,
And some wild asses as they ran away,
Some were like mountain sheep that tried to flee,
And some like cheetahs in their savagery.

Among the mighty company of those
Struck down by arrow wounds or weapons' blows
Lay Vis's father, King Qaren, who died
With many of his nobles at his side.
Their bodies lay there saffron pale, and blood
Flowed like red Judas blossoms in the mud,
As if the heavens rained down golden dew
From which a mass of scarlet tulips grew.
And when Viru saw all these warriors dead,
Shamefully lying in the blood they'd shed,
Scattered about their fallen king, Qaren,
He turned and angrily addressed his men;
"Shame on you for your cowardice," he cried,
"That these courageous noblemen have died,

And that our enemies rejoice that they
Have spilled our valiant warriors' blood today.
They've stained Qaren's white beard with blood; will none
Of all this host avenge what they have done?
The sun of his good name has set, the light
Of all his joy has darkened into night.
And night falls for us too; all day you've fought
But have not gained the longed-for goal we sought –
Mobad still lives: make common cause with me,
Be dragons and assail his sorcery;
I'll scour the rust of shame away, I'll bring
God's judgment down upon this wretched king,
I'll free the world of him, I will destroy
His evil ways and give Qaren's soul joy."

He spoke and did not hide his courage then,
But followed by a few well-chosen men
Charged from the ranks like wind; like fire he fell
Upon his enemies who ran pell-mell,
A hurricane that swept across the land,
A mighty hero no one could withstand.
Now swords and axes swung in argument
And seeking heads was all their brawling meant,
Now son abandoned father, brother turned
On brother, battle-weary warriors spurned
Their liege lords; in the growing darkness there
(As night, before night, dimmed the murky air,
And men, like bats, were blinded by the dust
And did not know whom they should fear or trust)
Brother killed brother, father slaughtered son.
Like hens for roasting men were spitted on
Long lances, arrows pierced their eyes, chain mail
And helmets proved as flimsy as a veil
As sword blows ripped them with impunity
And violence wrenched up by the roots life's tree.

Spears like a reed bed thronged the air, the mud
Men trod on was a winepress thick with blood,
Slashed heads like polo balls lay all around,
And limbs like polo sticks obscured the ground;
Death tore men's heads off as a wind strips trees,
And heroes lay like toppled cypresses.
The sun set, and the western sky became
A lover's face, yellow with grief and shame,
Mobad's good fortune seemed to be the sun
Descending now its earthly course was run;
He feared his enemies, and feared the night
That fell on him and took away his sight.
His men broke ranks; Mobad was forced to yield,
Accept defeat, and quit the battlefield.

Mobad flees from Viru

But darkness helped Mobad, and his retreat
Disguised the magnitude of his defeat,
And to his eyes this intervening night
Was like a comforting and friendly light;
He turned his horse's head from Khorasan,
And went from Dinavar toward Isfahan.
Viru and all his courtiers felt quite sure
That once he'd fled he'd trouble them no more,
That shame had caught him in its toils, and so
They did not follow him, but let him go.
But this was not the fate the heavens willed;
Viru's surmises would not be fulfilled.

An army came from mountainous Daylam
And occupied the country near Taram,
And rather than oppose their massive might
Viru's commander there chose not to fight.

Viru heard this, and was astonished by
The seeming anger of the turning sky,
That mixed his victory with bitterness
And darkened all his joy with new distress
(But joy is mixed with grief, as we draw breath
Life leads us all, inexorably, to death).
So while Viru rejoiced Mobad had fled
His joy fled too at what his envoys said.
The enemy approached, Viru'd no time
To cleanse himself of all the battle's grime;
His sword still bloody, he set out to face
Another foe now in another place.

But when Mobad heard of this new campaign
He and his fleeing men turned back again –
They pressed ahead as if they'd sprouted wings,
The winds could not outstrip this king of kings.
And so they reached Gurab, the little fort
In which the lovely princess Vis held court.

VIS AND MOBAD

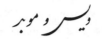

Mobad arrives at Gurab

Vis was a sun of beauty, but trapped there
She felt she was a bird within a snare.
She tore her musky hair out, and her tears
Fell jewel-like as she told her nurse her fears.
She wept to her and wailed, "There's no one who
Has suffered in the whole world as I do.
Who can I turn to in my misery?
Who'll help me now, and who can comfort me?
Who'll give me justice when the turning sky
Is all against me? What recourse have I?
How can I reach Viru or find a way
Not to become Mobad's unwilling prey?
What was I born for? Is this wretched state
In which I live to be my only fate?
I should have died before my father died
Rather than be this hated ruffian's bride;
My father's dead, my brother's left me here
Alone and prey to every passing fear.

I've suffered so much that I hardly dare
Imagine how much more I've yet to bear;
But it would be much worse than anything
To be the wretched captive of this king.
And if I cry for help no one will hear,
No one will come, no savior will appear.
I'll have to live among my enemies,
It's them I'll have to truckle to and please,
Far from my friends, in anguish and disgrace."
And as she spoke tears stained her lovely face.

MOBAD SENDS A MESSENGER TO VIS

An envoy from Mobad arrived to greet
The princess, and the words he said were sweet.
This was the message sent by King Mobad:
"Content yourself, dear moon of moons, be glad;
Don't claw your ivory face or wildly tear
From your exalted head your perfumed hair,
Since you cannot escape from heaven's decree
Or change what God has willed for you and me;
Don't let your heart imagine that it can
Struggle successfully against God's plan:
How can it help to fight against divine
Demands, if God has willed you to be mine?
For what Fate's pen has written there's no cure
Except to look for patience and endure.
I'm here because I love you, and if you
Are kind to me there's nothing I won't do.
I'll swear an oath with you today, I'll make
An oath with you that I shall never break:
Two heads will share one soul, my joy will be
To give you happiness continually.
You'll order my affairs, you'll keep the keys
That lock and unlock all my treasuries,

You'll have such wealth the sun and moon above
Will envy you your splendor and my love.
You'll be my comfort, and you'll reign alone
Within my harem on a royal throne;
Your joy will give me joy, and by your name
My name will be augmented in its fame;
I'll write all this and swear to it, and I
Will love your soul as mine until I die."

VIS'S ANSWER TO MOBAD'S MESSENGER

Vis heard the words the royal envoy said
As if he'd called down curses on her head.
She tore her silken clothes in her distress,
And beat her crystal breasts, and ripped her dress,
Baring her torso to the waist, revealing
The loveliness her silks had been concealing.
Her comely body was now visible;
It was more splendid and more beautiful
Than any silk or satin she might wear;
Wisdom would fail, and Patience would despair
To gaze on her; no one would sleep who saw
That silken loveliness without a flaw:
Her breasts' pink blossoms showed there, two wild roses
That springtime in its burgeoning discloses.

Her sweet lips answered like a stone, a blade
That slashed the protestations he had made.
She said, "I've heard the words Mobad has wasted,
And they're the nastiest poison that I've tasted.
Go tell your ancient king that he can't play
At such disastrous games with Vis today.
Tell him to have no hopes of me, to hold
On to his precious gifts of shining gold,
And let him understand I'll never quit
This fort alive in order to submit

Myself to him; he'll get no joy of me
Unless he's skilled in spells and sorcery.
Viru's my lord and king, it's him I love,
A stately cypress with the moon above,
My brother and my husband; at his side
I'll be his loving sister and his bride.
And while he lives how could I choose another?
Who could be equal to my husband-brother?
And while I clasp this lovely cypress tree
What can a weeping willow mean to me?

    And if Viru weren't mine, this doesn't mean
I'd love you, or consent to be your queen.
You killed my father, he's in heaven now;
My self, my being, are from him, so how
Could you become my husband or my friend?
When will this foolish business ever end?
I'm sick of grief, of life without Viru,
Of all the anguish I must suffer through;
I want no one but him, you'll never see
The happy day when you will marry me.
While I am his, no one can claim the right
To look on me with pleasure and delight,
If I betrayed him now, what could I say
To justify myself on Judgment Day?
I'm young, and I'm afraid of God. And you?
An old man, aren't you fearful of Him too?
Fear Him, since fear of God becomes the old.
God gave me beauty, luxury, and gold,
And you can't tempt me with your talk of pleasure,
God's justice is to me a greater treasure.

    And how can I delight in riches when
My mind recalls the death of King Qaren?
I'm not a princess if I can behold
With any pleasure now brocade or gold,

If they delighted me I could not claim
That I'm my father's child or use his name.
Your army doesn't frighten me, I've seen
No reason I should want to be your queen,
And you should give up wanting me, since all
These hopes of yours will prove ephemeral:
A man grows wretched if what he desires
Eludes him and his shattered hope expires.
How long will you pursue me with these wars?
You'll never humble me or make me yours,
Unless the world's against me in some way
And forces me to be your wife one day;
And even then, if fortune should decide
To hand me over to you as your bride,
You will not know one moment's joy, you'll find
No happiness with me, no peace of mind.
My brother is my spouse, and even he,
The man I chose, has had no joy of me,
And you're a stranger, someone I should shun;
I don't care if you're moonlight and the sun,
You can be sure I'll never sleep with you.
I've yet to give my body to Viru,
You simple-minded fool, and you've attacked
My home and left my native city sacked,
How can I give my heart to you? Your name
Sends hateful shivers through my trembling frame.

Hatred has come between us, we can't bless
Each other's hearts with joy and happiness,
And you, for all your vaunted sovereignty,
Can't make a lover from an enemy.
Hatred is iron, love is glass, these two
Cannot be joined, whatever you might do.
Feed it with sugared water, but the shoot
That's bitter will bear only bitter fruit.

A hawk that takes a partridge as his wife
Would be the image of our married life.
Who could put up with love like this? Who'd think
To choose pure poison as his daily drink?
You'll hear this message and you won't agree,
You think it would be sweet to marry me;
But brood on what I say; you'll realize
That my advice is right, if you are wise.
Evil will lead you to an evil fate,
And all of your regrets will come too late."

THE ENVOY RETURNS TO MOBAD

When once the messenger saw no pretense
Of friendship colored Vis's vehemence,
He went back and recounted everything
That Vis had told him to his waiting king.
The words were like sweet sugar trickling through
The king's heart, and his love and longing grew:
Sweetest of all was that Vis had not let
Viru enjoy her lovely body yet.
And this was true, since on the wedding night,
Which should have been a time of sweet delight,
Vis had discovered she was in a state
That hindered and reversed her husband's fate;
The heavens had willed that for a week the bride
Could not lie at her loving husband's side;
Her silver body ran with blood, as though
A mine of rubies had begun to flow
(And Zoroastrian women cannot speak
Or be with men at this time for a week,
And if a woman hides this state, she'll be
Untouchable for all eternity).
Viru filled all the world with his complaints
Against the myriad barriers and restraints

That kept him from his bride, against her duty
To see he had no access to her beauty.
But he forgot he was a husband when
He had to take command of fighting men,
And you would say his wedding feast was like
A flaming torch when sudden tempests strike;
The flickering flame first sputters and then dies,
Quenched by the gusts that fill the windy skies.

MOBAD CONSULTS HIS BROTHERS CONCERNING VIS

Mobad's desire grew greater when he learned
Of Vis's virgin state, and now he turned
For help to Zard and to Ramin, his brothers
Whom he confided in before all others,
And told them what had happened. But Ramin
Had been in love with Vis since they had been
Two childish friends, before they'd had to part,
And still this love lay hidden in his heart.
His love had been a barren field, and lain
Like land bereft of any hope of rain;
But coming to Gurab, it was as though
A water channel had begun to flow,
So that the field grew green again and thrived,
And all his hopes of seeing Vis revived.

But as love flourished in his ardent soul
His tongue grew rough and slipped from his control;
When love flares in the heart, the tongue will often
Prove harsh at moments when it ought to soften,
And men will blurt out things they ought to hide,
Which afterwards they'll wish they'd kept inside.
The heart should guard the tongue, and see it says
Nothing but wise remarks that merit praise:
There's nothing worse than an incautious friend
And rashness is a fault that's hard to mend.

Desire now gripped his heart, and love directed
Ramin to say the words that he selected.

He said, "Your majesty, do not distress
Yourself for Vis, or for her loveliness;
You're wasting wealth, my lord, and all you'll gain
For your munificence will be more pain;
You're sowing in the salt lands, among weeds,
You'll see no harvest, and you'll lose your seeds.
This Vis will never love or cherish you,
Or do what honest women ought to do;
She sees you as her father's murderer,
How can you hope for kindliness from her?
Your gold won't snare her heart, she shows no fear
Of all the warriors whom you've gathered here.
You'll win her with a world of grief, and when
She's won you'll wish that you were free again;
An enemy lodged in your house will fight you
Just as a snake lodged in your sleeve will bite you.
       The worst of all is this – and more's the pity –
You're old, my lord, and Vis is young and pretty.
You want to marry? You should choose a wife
Who's at the stage that you're at in your life –
Youth seeks out youth, it's natural Vis prefers
A youth whose age is similar to hers;
If you're December's, she is April's weather –
It's difficult to yoke these two together.
Don't look for love or happiness if she
Becomes your lawful wife unwillingly,
You will regret your choice, no salve will heal
The nagging pain that you will always feel,
You two will be like one cloth, and to tear
Its substance will be more than you can bear.
You won't escape from sorrow if you stay,
You'll find no pleasure if you go away.

The love of beauty is a boundless sea
Of unplumbed depths, unknown immensity –
At first, love seems an easy voyage, but then
You realize that you won't see port again.
You're eager for desire now, but tomorrow
You'll find your life's been overwhelmed with sorrow;
The going in is easy, but to leave
Is something that's far harder to achieve.
Love prompts my words, my lord, and they are true;
I only want to be of use to you."

Mobad, though, in his lovesick state, heard all
Of Prince Ramin's sweet words as bitter gall,
And this advice, intended to deprive,
Love of its force, made all his love revive.
The lover's heart hates health, and love's reborn,
Not dampened or destroyed, by others' scorn;
When love corrodes the heart, another's blame
Will scour it till it glitters like a flame;
Blame pierces like a sword thrust and will make
The injured lover bolder for love's sake.
A lover's not afraid if clouds rain stones,
Or javelins pierce his flesh and break his bones,
No calumny that anyone might say
Will wash an ardent lover's love away;
To one whose heart's tormented with desire
Reproach is like a wind that fans the fire.

Ramin's advice served only to increase
The love that King Mobad now felt for Vis;
He turned to Zard, in secret, to demand
Guidance on how he might win Vis's hand,
Adding that if he failed, his noble name
Would be a byword for disgrace and shame.

Zard said, "Her mother can be bought and sold,
Heap presents on her, buy her heart with gold.
Promise her gifts, then say she has betrayed
The solemn oath she swore; make her afraid
Of God and retribution; ask her how
She will excuse the way she broke her vow.
Tell her she'll be ashamed to stand alone,
Defenseless and at fault, before God's throne.
A few remarks, plus some brocade and gold,
And she will do whatever she is told;
Kings will succumb to them, and women fall
For talk and gold the easiest of all.
Even the wise submit; take my advice,
Use words and wealth, and all men have their price."

Mobad writes to Shahru

  Mobad liked Zard's advice on what to do
And quickly wrote a letter to Shahru.
A letter filled with jewel-like eloquence,
With sweetness and deceitful elegance.
He said, "Consider heaven, Shahru, and trust
That what I am telling you is true and just.
Consider God, who knows your soul and sees
Forever its dishonest blasphemies;
Consider Judgment now, consider well
The world to come and all the pains of hell.
Don't buy eternal sorrow for a day
Of worldly happiness that cannot stay,
Don't turn your back on God, Shahru, don't give
To Ahriman[18] the perjured life you live.

      You know the vows we made, you know we both
Once swore a solemn, ceremonial oath;
You know you promised me this unborn girl,
The child still in its shell, this precious pearl.

You bore this girl for me, so why did you
Ignore our oath and give her to Viru?
It was my fortune that prevailed that night,
Reserving Vis, and thwarting his delight;
God would not let another sleep beside
The woman I'd been promised as my bride.
Consider well, you'll see the heavens willed it,
That it was fated, and the stars fulfilled it.
And think of this new marriage as mere wind –
Ignore it, and acknowledge that you've sinned;
Give me this lovely moon, and save your land
From all the terrors of my wrathful hand;
The blood that's spilt here will be on your head
And you shall pay for it when you are dead.
If you are not the devil's friend, if you
Still care for God in all you say and do,
You should avoid this dreadful fate, and show me
Good faith by giving me the girl you owe me.
If not, I'll raze this land, and all the slaughter
Will be because you've tricked me of your daughter.
Don't underestimate my wrath, don't flatter
Yourself that this will be a little matter.
     But if you demonstrate your love for me,
I'll give Viru supreme authority,
My armies will be his, and I'll enthrone
Him in a kingdom he can call his own;
My Vis will be the queen of Khorasan,
And you will be the queen of Khuzestan –
If we survive a little while we'll know
All the sweet luxuries life has to show,
The world will be at peace, and I'll ensure
Our lives are undisturbed by strife and war.
Life can be yours to savor as you please,
So why treat all your friends as enemies?"

The letter sealed, it was as though Mobad
Emptied his treasuries of all he had;
He sent so many gifts to Queen Shahru
No scribe could ever read the record through.
To head the train, a hundred camels bore
Litters for travelers, and five hundred more
Were laden with fine clothes, and jewels as bright
As stars that spangle all the heavens at night.
Three hundred horses from Tokharistan[19]
Followed a hundred from Arabistan;
Two hundred Chinese serving girls were there
With rose-like faces, hyacinthine hair,
As charming as the spring, as beautiful
As is the radiant moon when she is full,
Their bodies tall as silver cypresses
Adorned with golden crowns and necklaces;
Gold jewelry glittered on these lovely girls,
Their shining mouths were rubies and bright pearls.
Two hundred golden crowns were added to
The store of riches destined for Shahru,
A hundred golden caskets made to hold
A shining treasury of jewels and gold,
Seven hundred gold and crystal bowls, that shone
Like Venus when the night is almost gone –
All these were followed by a cavalcade
Of twenty donkeys laden with brocade;
Lastly, a mass of goods that could not be
Guessed at for quantity or quality,
And all the jewels the world has ever seen
Seemed scattered by Mobad before this queen.

When Queen Shahru saw all this merchandise,
Such glittering gold, such jewels beyond all price,

She swooned like someone drunk and fell down dazed,
Dazzled by wealth, bewildered and amazed,
Forgetful of her daughter and her son.
Repentance before God at what she'd done
Worked in her worried heart, and fearful now
She fell to thinking of her ancient vow.
The heavens freed the demon of the night
And let him steal the moon's bewitching light,
And, in the castle of Gurab, Shahru
Did what she saw the turning heavens do:
She let Mobad in through the gates, and he
Entered rejoicing in his victory.

A DESCRIPTION OF NIGHT

The night[20] was pitch black, as though lovers parted
From one another's presence broken-hearted;
The starry sky seemed smeared with indigo,
The darkened surface of the earth below
Was like a rajah on an elephant,
As black as grief, and as recalcitrant
As hope. You'd say the sun was hidden by
A hanging curtain that concealed the sky,
Or that a pit had opened in the west
In which the sinking sun had come to rest.
The air was dressed in black to mourn for him,
And all the sky was overcast and grim,
Its starry legions traveling west to trace
Their lost commander's final resting place.
The firmament was like a canopy
Studded with jewels, vast in its majesty,
Secure and barely moving, strongly tied
With heavenly guy ropes to the mountainside.
The sun and moon were gone, as if they kept
A lover's secret tryst and sweetly slept,

Each star was like a pearl set carefully
Against a ground of lapis lazuli;
The heavens extended like an iron wall;
The stars grew languid and insensible.

The bull and ram were paralyzed with fear,
Sensing the lion of the sky was near;
The heavenly twins were locked in their embrace,
A water wheel revolving in one place;
The crab slept quietly at their feet, you'd say
Its claws and soul had both been snatched away;
The lion stood before the crab as though
Immovable, its tail curved like a bow
Arching above its massive back and head,
Its eyes and mouth glowed pomegranate red.
Holding a bunch of grapes in either hand
The virgin, as if drunk, could hardly stand;
All the scale's chains were broken, its pans scattered,
The balance beam from which they hung was shattered;
The scorpion's tail was curled around its head,
Like someone with a cold who stays in bed;
The archer stood there, bow in hand, each limb
Immobile, as if fear had conquered him –
The lamb slept in the flower-strewn grass, as though
It felt no threat from him, or from his bow,
Then, suddenly, the arrow sped and found
Its mark; the lamb lay wounded on the ground.
The water-carrier'd lost his pail, he stared
Like someone traveling who is lost and scared;
The fish was still and seemed to give no thought
To swimming on, as if it had been caught.
The sky seemed like a conjurer, whose power
And skill were demonstrated every hour
With some astonishing new trick, some change
That made the night bewildering and strange.

There in the north, a starry dragon curled
Its tail about the pole that guides the world;
Behind him stretched the somnolent Great Bear,
Its little cub was also sleeping there;
Here was a woman chained, and at her feet
A kneeling man, acknowledging defeat;
A vulture spread its wings, its claws clutched round
An arrow that it lifted from the ground;
A youth stood like a servant to display
A golden goblet and a golden tray;
Two fish like swollen bags swam placidly;
A duck whose neck was like a cypress tree
Was near a man dressed like a groom, whose hand
Held reins, although he'd no horse to command;
A man who charmed snakes, and his snakes were there;
Another man sat on a silver chair,
And near him stood a horse who'd shattered all
Its bonds and broken headlong from its stall;
One man held up a demon's head before
The image of a haughty conqueror.

And in the south a turbid river curled
Upon itself, and darkly seethed and swirled.
Weaving along its banks, with desperate bounds,
A hare tried to escape from two fierce hounds;
They'd been released by someone who stood back
With kingly pride to watch his dogs attack.
A boat whose cargo was bright jewels sailed by,
A ruby anchor fixed it to the sky;
A snake slid there as slender as a cane,
A strutting crow stood on a flowery plain,
A golden goblet was in front of him
And dew, not wine, had filled it to the brim;

A silver censer glowed with coals, and bright
Jewels gave a royal crown an answering light;
A huge fish flickered, and its white scales seemed
Like silver starlight as they flashed and gleamed;
Roses bloomed on a centaur, and you'd think
He'd fallen down and was the worse for drink,
His hooves were clasped about a lion's paw.
The loveliest peacock's tail you ever saw
Belonged to a strange bird that strutted there
Deprived of wings to raise it in the air.

Now from the east the turning stars made plain
This royal marriage would bring grief and pain.
The moon and sun were partners in disaster
(A minister that whispered to his master),
Saturn had joined them there, and Mercury;
The heaven's fourth house held this company.
Opposed to them, the dragon's tail and Mars
Were in the seventh house; between these stars
Venus was caught and seemed to have no hope
That good could come of such a horoscope;
No stars that foster justice were nearby.
Beneath this lowering, inauspicious sky
Mobad met Vis, a partner who would bring
No hint of love or pleasure to the king.

MOBAD ENTERS THE CASTLE AND TAKES VIS AWAY

So, beneath such a sky, at such an hour,
Mobad asserted his imperial power,
And went into the fort, and found no trace
Of Vis's rose-like loveliness and grace.
But then her musky hair's scent, and the light
That played about her forehead in the night

Informed the king of kings exactly where
The loveliness he sought was hidden there;
And so, before she'd time to understand
That he was near, he grasped her crystal hand
And dragged her to his camp, and gave her to
His closest cronies in his retinue.
They put her in a litter, where her presence
Created spring and springtime's iridescence;
Around the litter stood a company
Of warriors chosen for their loyalty.
At once the trumpets blared their brazen cry,
And banners rose up in the starry sky;
The king set out and, day and night, outpaced
The winds of heaven in his headlong haste,
Delighting like a lion who on his way
Meets with a herd of asses as his prey,
Or like a man who comes on royal treasure
And cannot hide his happiness and pleasure.
He had good reason to be happy too:
Vis was a peerless moon of beauty who
Was worth the pains he'd taken; and in her
He'd found both treasure and a treasurer –
Rubies that smiled, pearls that were eloquent,
Pure silver's sparkling gleam, and jasmine's scent.

VIRU LEARNS THAT MOBAD HAS ABDUCTED VIS

Then, in Taram, news reached Viru, and he
Set off for Vis's home immediately.
But he arrived too late, Mobad had taken
His moon-like bride, the castle was forsaken;
A thousand jewels were there in place of one,
The jewel Viru had hoped to find was gone.
The broken promises of Queen Shahru
Now lit a fire of grief within Viru;

Beauty had left the house of purity,
And spring the garden of fidelity,
The pearl had fallen from its costly case,
The moon's sphere had become an empty place.
Viru's soul was a mine of silver ore
In which there was no silver any more,
His eyes were like another mine that wept
Bright jewels incessantly and never slept.
Viru's heart wept and wailed in lamentation,
Mobad's heart gave itself to exultation.
Viru rained tears of sorrow and disgrace
Upon the yellow roses of his face,
He grew so wan and pallid then you'd say
His very soul had failed and fled away.
The bird of sense flew off, and in his heart
The veil of fortitude was torn apart;
All he could do was bitterly lament
His shining star's precipitous descent.

But just as Fate oppressed Viru, it brought
Sweetness to King Mobad and to his court –
Emptying a house of all prosperity,
Making a garden bloom with victory;
While one man struck his heart now with a stone,
And heaped dust on his head, and was alone,
Another sat to drink his wine beside
The lovely woman who was now his bride.

RAMIN SEES VIS AND FALLS IN LOVE WITH HER

The king's eyes shone with hope; he hurried on,
Bringing his glittering sun to Khorasan,
And, in his happiness, forgot the lies
And cruelty that the world's ways can devise.

The face of Vis made all her litter bright,
Glowing as if with painted, jewel-like light,
And where the winds that touched her litter went
The world was laden with her lovely scent;
The litter was a little chest in which
A pearl lay, fabulously bright and rich;
It was the heavenly sphere that shines at night
Filled with the brilliant moon's celestial light.
It was a dome, in which her musky hair
Was like a perfume drenching all the air,
And there a golden veil was pinned in place
To hide the sun-like splendors of her face.
Now Venus shone there, and the moon, and all
The road smelled musky and delectable;
It was as though Rezvan[21] himself were given
The guardianship of this bewitching heaven.

And so the heavens decreed Ramin would find
No further happiness or peace of mind,
That love would fill his heart with frenzied fire
Replacing sense and patience with desire.
A spring breeze blew the litter's veil aside
Revealing all that it was there to hide –
You'd say a sword had been unsheathed, you'd say
The sun had burst forth on a cloudy day.
The face of Vis appeared; Ramin's poor heart
Was hers as he felt consciousness depart;
As if her face had magic powers, one glance
Deprived him of his soul; a poisoned lance
Could not have worked more expeditiously,
Or arrow struck more unexpectedly:
The warrior fell down from his horse, as though
He were a leaf when blustery tempests blow.
The path love took was through his sight; his eyes
Had rendered his unhappy heart love's prize.

Love's tree grew tall in him, its branches spread,
Its fruit was all the tears that he would shed;
But now, like one who's drunk on too much wine,
He lay there on the ground and made no sign,
His cheeks like saffron and his lips dark blue.
The soldiers were unsure what they should do;
They crowded round him, weeping, unaware
That he lay languishing in love's despair,
Tongue-tied, and with his heart bowed by disaster
Since love was now its undisputed master.

Ramin revived, and tears began to well
Within his eyes like pearls within a shell;
Shame made him rub his wrists against his eyes,
And hide his tears, and stifle all his sighs,
So that his friends thought him the victim of
A sudden epileptic fit, not love.
But when Ramin remounted, bitter pain
Filled all the sweetness of his soul again,
He rode as if he were a man with no
Idea of where it was he ought to go;
His heart was in Eblis's[22] grip, he gazed
At Vis's litter as though stunned and dazed,
Just like a thief who cannot tear his eyes
From where a pearl within a casket lies,
And to himself he said, "How would it be
If Fate should show her once again to me?
How would it be now if the wind once more
Showed Vis's face here as it did before?
How would it be if she should hear me sigh,
And looked out from her litter so that I
Might glimpse her lovely countenance again
And she should see my pallor and my pain,
And she should pity all my agony
And hear my love-sick groans and comfort me?

How would it be if henceforth I could ride
As Vis's litter's guardian and guide?
How would it be if someone told her of
My homage and my chivalry and love?
How would it be if when she lay asleep
She saw me in a dream and heard me weep,
So that her stony heart grew soft and kind
And love's persuasive warmth filled all her mind?
How would it be if she became like me –
In love, and conquered by an enemy?
Perhaps if she too felt such love she'd bow
To love's commands and be less cruel than now."

These were the prince's thoughts and then he'd start
To recommend more patience to his heart,
And so he wavered, now in misery,
Now trying to maintain his dignity,
Telling himself, "My heart, what is it you
Are seeking here? What is it you would do?
You writhe in love while she is unaware
Of all your foolishness and your despair.
Why do you hope for her? Has anyone
Ever attained a union with the sun?
So why do you persist in foolishness
When there's no hope that you'll achieve success?
You're like a man who's thirsty, and who tries
To drink a desert mirage. Is this wise?
Life has grown harsh for you and obdurate –
May God have mercy on your wretched state."
And so Ramin was held by passion's chain
And suffered in his heart love's hopeless pain,
Unable to approach Vis, or conceive
Of any course now but to wait and grieve,
And though he rode beside her as they went
He knew no more of her than her sweet scent –

His soul was chained by love, but day and night
Her jasmine scent became his heart's delight.
No groans are like the groans a lover gives,
No life is like the life a lover lives;
If someone has a fever neighbors will
Ask fearful questions about why he's ill,
But years might pass, and no one will inquire
About a lover whose poor heart's on fire;
Tell me now, truly, you who're wise, is there
Any despair more harsh than love's despair?
Those men the fires of love consume should be
The loved recipients of our sympathy,
They mask their misery, they daren't confide
To anyone the secret grief they hide.
As Prince Ramin's love grew he struggled like
A partridge when a falcon's talons strike,
And neither lived nor died, but seemed to stray
Between the two as if he'd lost his way.
His silver radiance was a feeble glow;
The cypress tree was bent now like a bow.
And so he rode, as I've described: for him
The road to Marv was desolate and grim.

MOBAD ARRIVES IN MARV WITH VIS AND CELEBRATES THEIR MARRIAGE

The king of kings now entered Marv beside
The moon of moons, whom he had named his bride.
A thousand daises had been prepared
On which a myriad beauties sat and stared,
The courtiers scattering jewels and precious scents
Upon the cavalcade's magnificence,
While poorer women crowded there and threw
Sugar and hazelnuts upon them too.
Jewels were like gravel then, and everywhere
Sweet perfumes wafted in the dusty air,

Men trod on gold and silver, and you'd say
That royal Marv was paradise that day.
From every crowded roof throughout the town
A hundred rose-faced Venuses gazed down,
So many fine musicians could be found,
So many lovely women gathered round,
That hearts were overwhelmed to see the sight
And listening souls were ravished with delight.
These were the pleasures of the town, but see
With what great splendor now and majesty
The royal castle, where his bride was fêted,
Had been luxuriously decorated.
You'd say its roof was Saturn's steed, so high
It soared and reached up to the starry sky;
Within the massive building, on the walls,
Inside the splendid rooms and audience halls,
Were Chinese paintings whose bewitching grace
Was like the image of a loved one's face.
The orchard was in bloom, and seemed to be
A picture of the king's prosperity;
The gardens' blossoms glittered and beguiled
Men's hearts as Vis did when she laughed and smiled.
Like polished silver cleansed of every stain
Mobad's triumphant heart was free of pain,
And where he sat his nobles came to greet
Their sovereign, and to place before his feet
Their gifts of silver, gold, and jewels until
The piled-up tribute loomed there like a hill.
And as Mobad dined, he dispensed largesse
(May you do likewise, and know happiness).

Meanwhile the bride of this exultant king
Made all the harem like the flowers of spring;
But while he sat in lordly triumph she
Sat weeping night and day in misery,

So that the women there were moved and felt
Their hearts in sympathetic sorrow melt.
Sometimes she wept to think of Queen Shahru
Sometimes she groaned, remembering Viru,
Sometimes she wept in silence, sometimes she
Screamed without words, like one in agony.
She spoke to no one, and when people tried
To speak to her, she never once replied,
As if, each moment, caravans of grief
Arrived, incessantly, with no relief.
Her body had become reed-thin and frail,
Her faded color had turned saffron-pale.
The women round her tried to calm her fears,
But could not comfort her or dry her tears.
And every time she saw Mobad she tore
Her body's flesh and not the clothes she wore.
She would not hear the words he had to say,
Or look at him, but brusquely turned away,
And faced the wall in bitterness, and wept:
So on the road, and so in Marv, she kept
Herself from him; she was a garden but
The garden gate remained securely shut.

THE NURSE LEARNS THAT VIS HAD BEEN TAKEN TO MARV

Once the nurse learned Mobad had taken Vis
She wept as though her tears would never cease:
The world grew dark for her, and you would say
Her sobs had sighed her very soul away;
Her tears would make an Oxus flow, her moans
Would level mountains with the desert's stones.
She cried, "O lovely Vis, as beautiful
As is the radiant moon when she is full,
Why does Fate hate you so, why should you be
A byword in this world for misery?

My milk on your sweet lips has not yet dried
But all lips tell your tale now, far and wide;
Your pomegranate breasts are small and new
But men from seven countries dote on you,
You are so little, yet your name's so great,
You are a doe, and now a wolf's your fate;
You're innocent, your years are still so few,
And yet so many traitors lust for you.
In dragging you from your hometown they've left
Me comfortless, and wretched, and bereft:
Now I must wander too, and look for you,
Half crazed with grief in everything I do:
God's made the sight of you my soul; to see
You once again will give life back to me –
And if I live without you, may no trace
Of me be found again in any place."
Then she chose thirty camels for the road,
And burdened each one with a heavy load
Of royal goods, and so set out to seek
The soul she'd lost, and reached Marv in a week.

She found Vis broken-hearted, but the sight
Of her lost charge still filled her with delight.
Vis sat in filth, in ashes, on the ground,
Her face scored by her nails, her hair unbound,
Longing for death, weeping her youth away,
Bent like a heron when it seeks its prey,
Smearing dry dust upon her grieving head,
Her bodice stained by all the tears she shed,
And where her desperate fingernails had scored
Her cheeks, the marks showed like a rusty sword.
How thin she was! Her body, mouth, and heart
Seemed hardly there, as if they'd soon depart:
And in her heart the nurse felt all the fears
And fiery grief that prompted Vis's tears.

She said to her: "Your Highness, dearest child,
Why is your soul so agonized and wild,
Why do you harm yourself? Why do you shed
This blood without which you will soon be dead?
You are my eyes' light and the reason why
Fortune has favored me; you must not die!
I want your health and joy my child, not pain!
How can I let you hurt yourself again?
Don't fight with Fate, and if you must, take care,
And try to moderate your harsh despair!
You will be sorry when your skin turns pale
And all your body's strength begins to fail.
You're King Mobad's now, given by your mother;
And, it would seem, abandoned by your brother.
You are a queen, a splendid monarch's spouse,
The ruler of his soul and of his house;
Delight his heart, please him in everything –
Someone who's wise will not annoy a king.

     Viru's a prince, it's true, but what is he
Beside Mobad's imperial sovereignty?
You dropped a golden coin, but by God's grace
You've got a splendid jewel now in its place.
Your brother wasn't there to help his bride,
But God has been your guardian and your guide.
And if the vows you swore once to Viru
Are broken, King Mobad's are strong and true.
A silver apple's gone, but now you hold
Safe in your hand an orange made of gold.
A door shuts? Here's another, turn the handle.
A lamp goes out? So, light yourself a candle.
No harm has come your way to justify
The way you wail, and sob, and weep, and cry:
Ingratitude is wrong, and soon you'll see
The foolishness of all this misery;

You should be happy, this is not a day
To whine, and moan, and howl your heart away.
     Listen, get up, it's time all this was ended;
Prepare yourself, and dress in something splendid,
Then put a gold crown on your musky hair
As if the Pleiades were hovering there;
Put roses in your cheeks, and touch red wine
Against your scarlet lips to make them shine;
Flirt now, steal hearts and souls, and promise bliss
To hearts and souls bewildered by a kiss;
Turn night to day now with your face's light
And let your scented curls turn day to night:
Humiliate the sun, make him despair,
And bind up sorcerers in your musky hair.
Make men abandon sugar for your smiles,
And perfumes for your tumbling ringlets' wiles;
Make hearts forget their loves, so that they turn
Coldly away where once they used to burn.
Adorn yourself in splendor and you'll see
You're all, and more, than I have said you'll be:
You are a jewel, my dear, and you should dress
In jewels to complement your loveliness:
Your figure should wear figured cloth to show
Its slender elegance from head to toe:
Jewels are set off by jewels, and it's our duty
To augment personal beauty with more beauty.
You're young, you've sweetness, sovereignty, what more
Than all you have can you be hoping for?
Don't be ungrateful before God, don't make
Me suffer for some foolish fancy's sake.
God isn't moved by your tempestuous cries,
And nothing can reverse the turning skies:
So why make all this noise, why weep and wail
When all this useless fuss is sure to fail?"

It could have been the howling wind that blew
As she gave her advice, for all Vis knew;
Throw walnuts on a dome and make them stay,[23]
Or use the desert as a waterway
To sail boats on: the nurse tried to address
Her weeping Vis, and had as much success.

Vis answers the nurse

And Vis replied, "You only make things worse,
The seeds you sow will bear no fruit, dear nurse.
I'm sick of gowns and thrones, of tints and scents,
I want no part in such magnificence;
Give me my coarsest clothes, leave me alone,
Grief is my friend, the dust can be my throne.
Mobad will have no joy of me, and I
Want nothing of his glory till I die:
Life with Viru was once so sweet, like dates
That have no thorns; and now it seems my fate's
Harsh thorns that bear no dates. If, as men say,
We marry for desire to have its way,
May I lose all desire! I want no one,
Since he could not enjoy me, and has gone."

The nurse answers her

Again the nurse spoke: she was eloquent
And quick to answer in an argument.
She said, "You're like a lamp, child, to your mother;
It's right for you to weep now for your brother,
Because although he was your husband too
You got no joy of him, nor he of you.
What's worse than this, for two dear friends to be
Long years in one another's company,
And still at last to stay unsatisfied;
And then some mishap comes up to divide

The two of them, so that they don't know when
They'll be together in one place again?
The longing of the one is equal to
The misery the other's going through.
It's just as if a poor man found a treasure
And, thinking he'd return for it at leisure,
Left it where he had found it: off he went,
Imagining how his new wealth would be spent:
When he returned it was no longer there
And oh what grief he felt then and despair!
This is the case now for the two of you,
And bad luck has befallen poor Viru.
But you must choose, and chess is just like love –
You cannot capture two rooks with one move.
A friend that's gone is like a day that's gone,
It's futile to bewail his loss: move on!
Don't be so silly, child, you shouldn't be
So sulky and so furious with me:
Get up now from the dirt, do what I say,
It's time for you to listen and obey.

     Take rose water, and wash your face and hair,
Then ask the wardrobe-mistress what to wear;
Select an elegant, becoming gown,
And for your head a jewel-encrusted crown;
Here is the throne on which you ought to sit,
So dress yourself, and take your place on it.
Marv's noblewomen will be here to greet you,
All sorts of courtiers will arrive to meet you,
I don't want them to see you crying here,
Or sitting in the dirt when they appear –
They'd have to sit there too! Surely you see
You're going to have to act appropriately.
There are a hundred things we have to do
Simply because the world expects us to;

Shut gossips' mouths, and then you can be sure
Your name and reputation are secure.
If people see you sprawled here on the ground,
Who knows what nasty slanders they'll spread round?
Some will declare you're spoiled, and some will say
That you're too proud to even glance their way;
Some will announce, 'Her haughty condescension
Means she considers us beneath attention';
And some are sure to add, 'And who is she
To expect our service and our loyalty?'
See that you close their mouths, dear: I advise you
To give them no excuse to criticize you,
The person who is proud and hard to please
Will find that she has lots of enemies
And little joy in life; of course it's clear
I'm talking about folk in general here,
Mobad is heart and soul in love with you
And sees no faults in anything you do."

The nurse's words had their effect on Vis,
And gradually her heart grew more at peace,
She felt her petulance and rage desert her:
She liked the nurse and could not bear to hurt her.
And so she stood, and washed her silver skin,
And waited while the nurse arrayed her in
A splendid gown, and made her face and hair
Even more lovely with her expert care,
Using the colors and the heady scents
That brought out Vis's charm and elegance.
But, like a serpent, Vis writhed inwardly
And wept to see her gorgeous finery:
She sighed and said, "Good fortune has departed,
And left me friendless here, and broken-hearted;
I call upon the birds that throng the air
To be the witnesses of my despair.

Strangers are not neglected, men are quick
To bring a doctor to a man that's sick;
I'm sick now and alone, won't someone send
A doctor here, to me? who has no friend,
Who's been abducted from my family,
Whose heart is wounded by adversity,
Whose nobly born companions are now all
So far away and inaccessible,
Whose heart's a sea of longing for my mother
And for Viru, my glorious husband-brother?
Fortune's deserted me, the heavens hate me,
The world conspires to hurt me and berate me;
Injustice rains on me, and my sad state
Cowers beneath the threatening sword of Fate;
If there were justice here, the very stones
And plants would help me when they heard my groans."

THE NURSE PREPARES VIS

The nurse arrayed her charge, as if her powers
Could make a flower more lovely with more flowers;
From Vis's forehead Venus shone, her face
Glowed with the sun's and moon's bewitching grace;
Her eyes like Mars were filled with sorcery,
Her pitch-black hair had Saturn's majesty;
Her lips like Jupiter throughout the year
Made jewels and sugar magically appear:
Her hair against her face was like a crow
Whose crimson blood is spattered on white snow;
Her face was like massed flowers, in which the line
That traced her lips appeared like drops of wine;
Her jasmine-scented breasts were high and full,
Two worthy friends, supremely beautiful;
Her arms, like saplings, were firm-fleshed and long,
Branching in silver fingers, white and strong,

Branches that bore vermilion fruit whose shapes
And color were the image of ripe grapes;
Her mouth a rosebud that's not opened yet,
Within which two and thirty pearls were set,
Or say her teeth were jewels concealed behind
The richest rubies Badakhshan has mined.
Enthroned, she was a moon of sovereignty,
And when she stood, a walking cypress tree.
Wisdom when gazing on her face would claim
She was an idol whom he could not name,
Since such an idol Wisdom never saw –
So tall, and quick, and sweet, without a flaw,
As lovely as a garden in the spring,
As splendid as the treasury of a king.
A wise old sage in seeing her would tear
His clothes like madmen caught in love's despair,
And seeing her Rezvan[24] would be quite sure
His houris had no beauty any more:
And if she called the dead, their voices' sound
Would rise in answer from the dusty ground.
If brackish water standing on a plain
But washed her face, it would grow sugar cane,
And if her lips touched amber it would be
Turned into shining rubies instantly.
Such was her beauty and her cypress grace,
Such was her loveliness and sun-like face,
Beauties of China or of Barbary
Were stars beside that full moon's majesty,
She was the moon of spring, whose court is given
To be the thousand glittering stars of heaven,
A golden portrait from a foreign land,
Made by a Chinese or a Western hand.

Who could compute the gifts the king had sent
To win his bride's approval and consent?

Perfumes, and bales of cloth, caskets that hold
Resplendent jewels, and goblets made of gold,
Western and Chinese slaves, whose skin was white
Like camphor, and whose hair was black as night;
They were as shy and lovely as young deer
Who've never seen a lion wandering near,
As splendid as bright peacocks unaware
Of hawks' sharp talons hovering in mid-air.
Vis sat enthroned, made even lovelier
By everything the nurse had done for her,
And all the harem in comparison
Seemed like a reed bed, waste and woebegone,
Or like a stand of cypresses that's near
A place where roses suddenly appear.
The world rejoiced to know that she was there
While she felt only anguish and despair,
And all the courtiers' long congratulations
Sounded to her like hateful imprecations.

Now, for a week, Mobad caroused and then
Played polo with his country's noblemen;
Another week was spent out hunting game,
Bringing down prey with his unerring aim
As every arrow that he loosed there found
Its destined mark; not one dropped to the ground.
When he was feasting he spared no expense
But entertained with lavish opulence,
And when he raised his polo mallet high
The ball was sent careering through the sky.
Each day a world of courtly income went
On splendid banquets, wine, and merriment.
His generous hand was like a cloud that rains
Its bounty down upon the waiting plains,
And in his palm his goblet glittered like
The sudden flash when bolts of lightning strike.

The nurse made Vis so lovely that the sun
Begged for the light with which her face now shone;
But all the while she wept, and you would say
New sorrows crowded in on her each day.
In secret she confided to her nurse,
"I live assaulted by misfortune's curse,
My heart is sick of life, I long to tear
Its roots up in my horror and despair;
I see no choice, no other remedy
Than death to save me from this misery.
If you can't think of something else, if you
Can't comfort me and tell me what to do,
I'll kill myself, and quickly I'll release
My soul from endless pain and be at peace.
I feel I sit on fire as soon as I
Catch sight of King Mobad; I'd rather die
If the alternative's to be his wife:
May his life be as wretched as my life!
Though he's been patient, and he hasn't tried –
Till now at least – to claim me as his bride,
I'm still afraid that soon enough he'll find
The moment to announce what's on his mind.
Before he makes demands on me you must
Find something that will neutralize his lust,
Give me a year before I have to face
The thought of this loathed enemy's embrace.
My mourning for Qaren's death should protect me,
But, for a year, I don't think he'll respect me –
He has no shame, no sense of right and wrong,
I don't think he'll be patient for so long.
        But you're resourceful and intelligent,
Think of some trick to make him impotent;
Humble his lust and all will then be well,
And when a year's gone by, undo the spell.

And if you won't do this, please don't complain
That I complain that I'm in constant pain;
I'll wish you well, Mobad and you can share
Your lucky lives together, I don't care,
But I won't trade delight and my good name
For empty luxury and guilty shame.
I tell you this, I will not satisfy
Mobad's desires, and if I die, I die.
Don't tell me to give in to him; for me
Death would be better than such misery."

The nurse stared in astonishment, as though
A sudden arrow, speeding from a bow,
Had pierced her heart; and as it found its mark
The world before the nurse's eyes grew dark.
She answered Vis, "Light of your nurse's eyes,
I see no justice in your wild replies;
Your heart's turned black from all you've suffered here,
But blackness won't make blackness disappear.
A devilish army has invaded you,
Perverting you in everything you do,
But since you've grown so brazen, and decided
That wisdom's a mistake to be derided,
I have no choice: I'll do what you require,
And make a spell to bind Mobad's desire;
Within you there's a demon of mistrust
That treats the body's pleasures with disgust."

The nurse constructed a small talisman
To represent a woman and a man
(One made of copper, one of brass), and round
The little figurines she tightly bound
A band of iron. She said that for as long
As this unbroken band stayed firm and strong
He would be impotent with her; and when
The band broke, he'd be capable again.

Now that Mobad could not approach his bride,
She took the fetish to the countryside
And buried it beside a river bank;
The spot she chose was waterlogged and dank.
Then she returned to Vis and told her where
She'd placed it, and described the landscape there;
She said, "I disapprove, but I've obeyed you;
I've done as you desired and not betrayed you.
It's done now, and I hope that you're content;
With you, this noble man is impotent.
But when a month's gone by I hope you'll find
You've grown more sensible and changed your mind;
Submit to the Almighty's will, and start
To drive this rancor from your angry heart.
Don't talk about a year, no one will say
It's wise to look for such a long delay.
Just let me know as soon as you decide
You like the king and want to be his bride,
Then I'll destroy the fetish in a fire
And see that you accomplish your desire.
Whilst it stays damp, there's nothing he can do
That will enable him to sleep with you,
But in a fire the spell will melt, and then
His manly candle will burn bright again."
The nurse brought hope and happiness to Vis
By promising at least a month of peace.

But see how Fate displayed its tyranny
And mingled poison with felicity.
A storm cloud swirled up from the sea, and rain
Poured down in torrents on the dusty plain;
The meadows were a quagmire of wet mud,
The river turned into a raging flood,
Spilling beyond its banks as if to drown
The countryside near Marv, and half the town.

The talisman was swept away, which meant
Mobad was now forever impotent;
Vis became unattainable, a prize
Like someone's gold glimpsed by a beggar's eyes,
Or deer that feed before a lion's cage
Untroubled by his hunger and his rage.
Desire still lived in him, he loved his bride,
But you would say that part of him had died.
Subjected to perpetual delay
On happiness's road, he'd lost his way;
And, as his foes might wish, he chafed within
The tantalizing prison of his skin,
And when he clasped Vis in his arms you'd say
That she was sixty parasangs[25] away.
Two husbands had now married Vis, but she
Retained the seal of her virginity;
Neither of her two husbands had enjoyed her,
And life still teased her, toyed with her, annoyed her.
The world had nurtured her in luxury,
Accorded her renown and dignity,
But when she'd grown to cypress elegance
Her face the full moon in its radiance,
Her cheeks like flowers, her silver breasts like two
Young pomegranates peeping into view,
The world closed off affection's noble highways
And led her by circuitous paths and byways.
I'll tell you all about her, everything
Concerning her, Ramin, the nurse, the king,
And all they did – and if a lover hears
This tale his eyes will overflow with tears:
I'll tell a tale in which love's power will be
Displayed in all its force and subtlety.

Ramin walks in the palace gardens and complains of his love for Vis

Constrained now by the fateful stars above
Ramin's heart suffered agonies of love:
Always alone, he sought out places where
His weeping could give vent to his despair;
At night he did not seek his bed, but went
To count the stars that fill the firmament,
And in the day he fled from men in fear
As onagers will do, or timid deer.
Her cypress stature so obsessed his mind
He bowed to every cypress he could find,
He looked in every cultivated place
For roses to remind him of her face,
He gathered violets in the dawn, and pressed them
With tenderness against his heart, and blessed them,
Because their glossy color seemed to share
The darkly lustrous hue of Vis's hair.
Now he abstained from drinking wine, afraid
That in his cups his grief would be betrayed.
His lute became his friend, and constantly
He sang, or plucked a plangent melody,
His sighs of longing were a wind that blows
In April bringing cold December's snows;
His singing was so heartfelt, and so sweet,
That nightingales acknowledged their defeat.
He wept so copiously in his despair,
The dust was turned to mud and held him there,
Sunlight to his sad eyes seemed grey and dim,
And softest silks were like harsh thorns to him.
But no one asked him why he wailed and wept,
And seemed to waste away, and never slept:
Burning and melting like a candle he
Experienced all of love's long misery,

Life was now worthless to him, and his heart
Was happy to see happiness depart;
His clothes were stained with tears, his face was pale,
He felt his weakening strength within him fail,
Despair that Vis could ever be his wife
Enfeebled him, and he despaired of life.
Now that her image never left his sight
Health-giving sleep deserted him at night,
And though he drowned in seas of separation
The world seemed like a tight noose of frustration,
Or he was like a drunkard who forgets
The world and all its pleasures and regrets.
Or using Vis's name, he tried to tell
By auguries if love would turn out well,
Or he would ask the gardens' flowers and trees
To witness all his lovelorn miseries,
And cry aloud, "When Vis comes here, take care
To tell her the extent of my despair
And cleanse her heart of all its cruelty
And make her sorry for my misery."
He'd mock the nightingales, and ask them why
They thought they had the right to wail and cry:

"You're with your lovers there, so what's gone wrong
Up in the trees to justify your song?
For you a thousand lovely gardens wait,
A thousand burning sorrows are my fate,
Your lovers sit beside you, why should you
Lament love's separations as I do?
Such griefs are mine, since she I sing my song for
Knows nothing of my love, or who I long for;
Absent from her, and in such pain, it's right
For me to sigh, and to bewail my plight,
And not to know myself, and waste away,
And long for that sweet cypress every day."

So singing, weeping, Prince Ramin walked there,
Composing lays of longing and despair.

RAMIN SEES THE NURSE IN THE GARDEN
AND TELLS HER OF HIS STATE

One day, by chance, in this delightful place
Ramin and Vis's nurse came face to face.
He felt such pleasure and such shame he blushed,
His cheeks like scarlet tulips flared and flushed,
And brilliant drops of sweat were seen to shine
Upon his skin like pearls in crimson wine.
No flower could be as lovely as his face,
Whose silver beauty still showed not a trace
Of hyacinthine hair, whose lips were sweet
As cordials in which wine and honey meet,
Whose smile was jewels and sugar, and whose gait
Was like a walking box tree, tall and straight,
A box tree that bore Judas blossoms which
Glowed with a dark vermilion, red and rich;
He seemed a shining moon, if moons could wear
Belts at their waists and caps upon their hair;
His simple cloak looked lovelier by far
Than idols in the temple of Farkhar,[26]
His cap became him more than any crown
Worn by an emperor of world-renown,
A prince in wealth and in his ancestry,
Worthy of both, and of their sovereignty,
Mobad's own brother and his son,[27] the heir
To Mahabad and all that flourished there.
If Rezvan saw his face he'd say that he
Should rule the houris in his majesty,
This face that had endured such wretchedness
For Vis, and was so ravaged by distress.

Now when he saw the nurse he felt that Fate
Had taken pity on his wretched state.
He bowed and greeted her respectfully,
And she replied with equal courtesy.
They chatted then like old acquaintances,
Exchanging friendly reminiscences,
And clasped each other's hands, and gently walked
Through plots of lilies while they smiled and talked,
And all they said was like a balm to heal
The grief Ramin's heart had begun to feel.
But he found love impossible to hide,
And ardently he thrust all shame aside:
"I'm weaker than a slave before your feet,"
He said, "Oh, everything you say is sweet,
I wish you radiant luck in all you do,
And may my luck be to stay close to you;
You're like a mother to me now, I swear
By her I worship with such tender care,
Dear Vis, who is the sun and moon to me
Resplendent in her god-like sovereignty,
Whose parents are a monarch and a queen,
Whose like the wondering world has never seen.
You'd say her mother bore the child to raise
Throughout the seven climes a scorching blaze,
Especially in me, whose heart's desire
Burns with more fury than the sacred fire
That's kept alive in Khorrad and Borzin.[28]
May she not see the anguish I have seen,
May she be happy now, and fortunate,
And never grieve like me, or share my fate,
May she not burn as I do now, or see
Days like the days that have afflicted me.
May every pain I undergo increase
The love and blessings I bestow on Vis,

May she be happy always now, and leave
Ramin to long for her sweet love and grieve."

Bright stars appeared where two red rubies parted:
The nurse's smile was generous and kind-hearted.
She said, "Ramin, may you live happily
And safe from harm for all eternity:
May health and great good fortune not desert you,
And may no cruelty or injustice hurt you;
My happiness is bound up with your fame,
On you depend my fortune and good name,
So may my charge, the lovely Vis, remain
A shining sun and moon untouched by pain,
So may her years be filled with all the grace
That's present in her sweet, bewitching face;
May those who wish her ill know black despair
Twisting as deviously as Vis's hair,
And may her well-wishers have lives as bright
As is her lovely face's radiant light.
I find no fault in what you've said to me
Except your claim that all your misery
Is due to her, and there I can't believe you;
How could she be unjust to you or grieve you?
She's not your king or judge! What do you mean?
This makes no sense; explain yourself, Ramin!"

Ramin replied, "A lover's life is worse
Than any other wretch's life, dear nurse.
His heart's his enemy and will betray him;
It's always looking for some way to slay him,
Pining for her, and groaning in its pain,
All it can do is hurt him and complain
Until a man would rather die than be
Subjected to such constant agony.

Love fills his eyes with tears, he never sleeps
And in his sleeplessness he wails and weeps;
He wants what he can't have and treats with scorn
The things he has; how wretched and forlorn
Love renders him, so that he thinks distress
Is all that he can know of happiness.
If lovers could but sleep then you'd expect
That love and wine would have the same effect;
How bittersweet life would be for a lover,
Like drunken joy, then pain when we're hungover!
But lovers are like drunks, who think that all
That's ugly's beautiful, and laudable,
And in his sleeplessness a lover seems
Like one who always sleeps and lives on dreams;
An ugly demon grapples with his mind
And keeps his eyes continuously blind.
Love is like wine, and neither will agree
To live with wisdom and sobriety,
And how can wisdom lend its noble name
To love, that tears aside the veils of shame?
My veils are torn, and from my heart I know
Wisdom and patience both fled long ago.
A wind sprang up, and suddenly I saw
A houri's perfect face without a flaw;
The moon that was vouchsafed to me was Vis,
And since I saw her I have had no peace:
My eyes saw heaven, and my poor heart fell
At that same moment in the pit of hell.
Say that that wind was my catastrophe,
It showed the face of love and grief to me.

     You nursed me as a baby, and since then
The two of us have often met again,
But you've not seen me in this state before
Where life and death both seem to me unsure.

The lion has become a fox; you saw
My mountain body, now you'd say it's straw,
My body's like a hair, my cheeks are yellow,
And I've become a wretched, ugly fellow.
I sit myself with friends to feast, and act
Like someone whom they've suddenly attacked,
And when I try to rest I feel as though
I fight against disaster, blow for blow.
I lie down on brocade at night to sleep
And suffer all the terrors of the deep,
As if I drowned in some uncharted sea
Whose depths had overwhelmed and swallowed me;
And in the daytime with my friends I'm like
The ball that mounted polo players strike.
When evening comes the plaintive songs I sing
Are like those sung by nightingales in spring,
And in the dawn I weep like winter rains
That soak the cliffs and mountain slopes and plains.
   A thousand arrows from her eyes have slain me,
A thousand bonds from her two braids detain me;
I'm like a wounded onager whose heart
Is pierced and weakened by a poisoned dart;
I'm like a lion whose little cub has strayed,
Who runs and roars, distracted and afraid;
I'm like a baby who's abandoned by
His nurse and mother and can only cry;
I'm like a bough that's snapped off from a tree,
And now I turn to you to comfort me,
To show your noble chivalry[29] to one
Whom once you brought up as your loving son.
You're kind to madmen and to strangers who
Know of your kindness and appeal to you;
Think of me as a stranger here, or say
That I'm a madman who has lost my way,

But pity me because a dragon's breath
Bears down on me and threatens me with death.
    Let your heart overflow with love for me,
Treat me with kindness and humanity.
Accept my message now and take it to
That smiling idol who resides with you,
Whose black curls cluster on her lovely head,
Whose sweet, bewitching lips shine ruby red,
That shining moon, that walking cypress tree,
That springtime garden of felicity,
And say to her, 'You have been made from all
That's lovely, excellent, and beautiful,
And brought up with the customs of princesses,
Indulged with gentleness and kind caresses.
The beautiful obey you, kings adore you,
Magicians flee from you, and quail before you,
And Chinese effigies will shrink with shame
When they're compared with you or hear your name.
The moon prostrates herself, your breath revives
The dead again and gives them back their lives,
Barbarian idols now have had their day
And those who carved them throw their tools away.
My body melts with mingled hopes and fears
Like mountain snowfalls when the sun appears;
My heart is trapped by love for you, and there
I struggle like a wild ass in a snare;
Wisdom's forsaken my distracted head
And sense and consciousness have turned and fled,
The fluttering heart within my breast is breaking
And flits uncertainly from sleep to waking,
It has no sense of either pains or pleasures
And takes no joy in music or in treasures;
I cannot play at polo now, or find
In hunting solace for my restless mind,

I drink no wine now, women's games and flirting
Have ceased to be attractive and diverting.
I'm never free from sorrow and distress,
Nothing can give me joy or happiness,
I'm like a prisoner of myself, and see
No friend nearby to offer sympathy.
At night I writhe as though I were a snake
Whose body has been skewered by a stake.
      A word from you would bring me such sweet balm,
The sight of you such comfort and such calm,
That if I heard you speak I know I'd find
Patience again, restraint, and peace of mind.
Although my face is pale and stained with tears,
And love's tormented me for months and years,
My constant love for you consumes me more
Than life itself; without my longing for
Your love and trust, I've no desire for life;
May every hair of mine cut like a knife
If I should tire of you! But surely I
Will be your servants' servant till I die.
May your bright face give whiteness to my days,
May your black hair give darkness to my gaze,
My springtime be the roses of your cheeks,
My comforters the words your sweet mouth speaks,
My sun your face, my musk your perfumed hair,
Your glances all the jasmine I shall wear.
And on the day I glimpse your face I know
That I shall rise up from the world below
And enter paradise where I shall see
The pleasures promised for eternity.
This is my prayer to God, for this I pray
Incessantly through every night and day,
That you be kind to me, not criticize me,
Or turn from me, or say that you despise me.

Why must you spill the blood of someone who
Adores you and has never injured you?
Who'd gladly cast away his eyes to buy
The dust you tread on when you pass him by?
If you'll have mercy on him he will give
His life to you; if not he cannot live.'"

Ramin's words pierced the ancient nurse's heart
As if they'd been a cruelly sharpened dart;
Deep in her heart she felt for him, although
She did not let her friendly feelings show.
She said, "Ramin, my lord, you cannot tame[30]
The noble Vis; she doesn't share your name!
Forget such hopes – whatever you might do
Vis is a sun who'll never shine on you,
Don't think you'll win that lovely cypress tree
By clever plans or devious trickery,
And don't consider using force, Ramin,
Against the daughter of our noble queen.
If you persist, and bind your heart to Vis,
You'll never know another moment's peace;
No good can come of this, and once you start
It will be hard to extricate your heart.
　　　Knowledge and wisdom, modesty and shame
Are needed now to safeguard your good name –
They'll show your heart what's right and what is wrong.
Take up your staff and go where you belong!
Traverse the earth from end to end, or fly
Across the arching circuit of the sky,
Make rivers flow in deserts, make rocks flower
As tulips flower, or use a sorcerer's power
To build another world, and poise it on
A single fragile hair tip when you're done –
But still your magic won't be able to
Prevail on Vis to give herself to you.

For Vis to love you, wait until you see
Dates growing on a flowering Judas tree;
She is the moon, she hovers far above you,
She cannot bow to you, she'll never love you.
And who would tell her this? Who'd dare to face
Her fury when she learns of this disgrace?
You've no idea of her conceit, of how
Obsessed with her position she is now –
If I'd a hundred lions' strength this task
Is something I'd refuse you, so don't ask,
And don't expose me to the ribaldries
That would be said of me by enemies.
You know how proud she is, how she's more grand
Than any other woman in this land,
You know how she'll attack me and berate me,
And treat me cruelly and humiliate me.
With princesses she's just like emperors
Consorting with their humble courtiers,
She thinks that she's of such exalted worth
She has no equal anywhere on earth.
Her ancestors were all nobility
And she's been raised in lavish luxury,
No challenges can frighten her, no treasure
Can trick her with its promises of pleasure.

        Now, it is true, her spirits are quite down;
She's lonely here and far from her hometown,
She misses her old house and family,
And hides herself away from company.
She weeps, and curses how the heavens turn,
And all her maddened senses seem to burn
Like aloes wood that's thrown on glowing embers;
Grief overwhelms her as her heart remembers
The life she had once with her noble mother,
The love and friendship of her husband-brother;

And then she'll execrate the month and year
That drove her from her home, and brought her here.
And so this princess, who is of the seed
Of Persia's ancient emperor Jamshid,[31]
Whose birth her mother passionately prayed for,
Whose every whim was once indulged and paid for,
Weeps tears like rainy springtime clouds, and spends
Her days and nights in longing for her friends.
She never smiles, frowns always knit her brow,
Who'd dare repeat your nonsense to her now?
Don't tell me what to say, my head won't do
The idiotic things you tell it to;
If I'd more tongues than raindrops in a cloud
I wouldn't say such foolish things aloud!"

Ramin wept when he heard her speech, and all
His sorrow made him seem insensible;
The tears flowed from his eyes in such a flood
They turned the dust beneath his feet to mud.
He did not speak, love's fire flared up, and pain
Filled all his breaking heart and seething brain,
The tulips of his cheeks turned saffron pale,
His labored breathing slowed and seemed to fail.
Then, once again, he spoke with eloquence
Of passion's anguish and its vehemence.
He pleaded with the nurse, he wept and wailed,
But all his tears and wild entreaties failed;
The more Ramin attempted to persuade her,
The more severe and pitiless he made her.
He flung himself on her, and tried to hold her,
And clung to her, and wept against her shoulder;
He said, "Have pity on me now, dear nurse,
Don't make my desperate soul's afflictions worse;
Don't snatch away youth's hopes like this, don't give
Me poison and expect that I will live.

Of all my friends I trust in you, I plead
With you to help me in my hour of need –
What will it matter if you comfort me?
Open misfortune's claws now, set me free!
Nurse, guide me to her, open this closed door,
And let me see the face that I adore;
Dear nurse, if you continue to deny
Me hope, here, now, in front of you, I'll die.
Don't fling an innocent into the pit,
Don't burn my flesh then sprinkle salt on it;
Grasp at my hand, and find some way to save
The life of one who's your devoted slave;
You are the only person who can bring
The balm I need to cure my suffering,
And now in all the world there's no one who
I can confide in as I've done with you.
Enough of these excuses nurse, convey
To jasmine-breasted Vis the words I say.

     Men harness wind with mills, or turn the force
Of rivers with a channeled watercourse;
They capture birds and fish, make implements
To tangle lions in snares, or elephants,
With potent spells draw snakes from holes and charm them,
So that the snakes are tamed and never harm them.
You know more magic spells than anyone
No one can do the things that you have done,
You have a thousand tricks, who can devise
A plot like you? Who is there who's more wise?
You know just what to say and what to do,
And Vis will prove to be no match for you.
Good fortune brought me to you, and I pray
That God helps you as you help me today."

He held her tightly in a strong embrace,
And kissed her head, and then her lips and face:

A demon dwelt in him, he seemed to sow
Love's seeds within her heart and watch them grow.
A woman's like a horse; she can be led,
Once you have slipped the bridle on her head.
Ramin drew back from her; they stood apart,
And turmoil seized the nurse's troubled heart.
Shame's veils were torn; her words, that had been cold,
Were warm now and impetuously bold.
She said, "Your words bewilder and deceive me,
You'd bear away the prize for talk, believe me!
You try and try, and won't admit defeat,
And Vis is every woman whom you meet!
Dear child, I loved you well enough before,
But from today I'll love you even more;
The arrow of desire speeds on its way,
And there'll be no excuses, as you say;
From now on I'll obey you; I agree
To do precisely what you ask of me.
Fortune will smile on you, I'll plead your cause,
And victory and Vis will then be yours."

Heartsick Ramin was overjoyed to hear
The nurse's opposition disappear;
He said to her, "You'll see how I shall serve you,
Light of my eyes, I'll struggle to deserve you.
You see what I am now, how like a snake
I twist and turn for hopeless passion's sake,
Each night I think, 'I won't see morning's light,'
Each dawn I think, 'I can't survive till night';
I'm like a man at sea whom nothing saves,
Tossed by the howling winds and roiling waves.
I'm so distraught I don't know what to say,
I don't know day from night or night from day.
But now your promises will be the key
To unlock all love's happiness for me.

Be chivalrous, dear nurse, act now – talk needs
To be accompanied by actual deeds.
Tell me when next I'll see you in this place,
When can we meet again here face to face?
I'll count the days and hours, and all the while
I'll be on fire until I see your smile,
My crazy thoughts might wander far and near
But, like a madman, I won't stray from here."

The sorceress laughed and then replied, "Who knew,
My lord, that you had such a tongue in you?
With such sweet talk, you could revive the dead.
You've wounded my poor heart with all you've said;
You've broken all your chains, and now I see
My soul's the one that's under lock and key!
Don't be despondent, you'll soon realize how
Successfully I'm going to serve you now:
I'll seat you on an Arab horse, and then
Your envious rivals won't see you again!
At this time, once a day, make sure you're here,
And I won't fail to meet you, never fear.
I'll bring you news, and everything I do
On your behalf will be explained to you."
They clasped their hands then and agreed to this,
And so they parted, with a mutual kiss.

The nurse charms Vis on Ramin's behalf

Now when the nurse returned to Vis, her heart
Was filled with wizard's wiles and witch's art,
And when she saw Vis lying on the bed,
Her pillow dampened by the tears she'd shed,
Tears tumbling down like pearls spilled for her mother,
And more tears for her noble husband-brother,
She said to her, "But what's all this, my dear?
You're not unwell, why are you lying here?

What demon's sitting on your soul? Why should
He slam the door on all that's sweet and good?
Your cypress body's curved now like a bow;
You lie here, and you weep and wail, as though
You weren't in Marv but in some loathsome pit.
If you have trouble dear, make light of it –
Now don't you think you've had enough of all
This sadness and these tears? Be sensible!
Remembering the past just makes things worse.
Now, dearest, pay attention to your nurse;
When folk are sad the surest cure's to find
Some pleasant pastime to divert the mind.
Comfort's at hand my dear, so don't refuse it –
If you want happiness you have to choose it."

The nurse's chatter seemed to quieten Vis
And give her troubled heart a little peace;
Reluctantly she raised her lovely head,
And like the rising sun her beauty spread
Color and light and Chinese splendor there,
And all the room was perfumed by her hair.
The gorgeous beauty of her spring-like face
Made the king's palace a celestial place,
Its beauty then, and hers, both seemed augmented,
And each of them by each was complemented.
Her copious tears seemed like the springtime showers
That nourish gardens filled with budding flowers,
The bruises where she'd scored her lovely cheeks
Showed like a floating water lily's streaks,
Her sleepless eyes were lovelier than the sight
Of wet narcissi gleaming darkly bright.

Weeping, she said, "What day is this? You'd say
My days are fires that burn all peace away,
And as the heavens bring me each tomorrow
So they renew my agony and sorrow.

Is Marv to blame then? Or have I been given
This wretched fortune by the stars in heaven?
I feel the Alborz mountains suddenly,
And seventy times, have tumbled down on me;
This is not Marv, this town in which I weep,
It's like a pit that's sixty fathoms deep.
This garden and this palace are a cell
Located in the fiery pit of hell,
My body is a path of pain, you'd swear
That in my soul our sacred fires burn there,
And day and night I neither sleep nor rest
But tremble like a woman who's possessed;
I swear that if I die now this will be
A sweeter draught than life itself to me.

    I dreamt Viru was here, and now I live
Bereft of hope for all the world can give:
I saw his mountain horse, his glittering sword,
His lance held in his hand, a mighty lord
Who rode back from the hunt triumphantly,
And tugged his reins, and came across to me,
And leant down from his horse then, and caressed me,
With words as sweet as sugar he addressed me:
'How does my love, my life, among these strangers,
Deprived of me, beset with constant dangers?'
And then we lay together, and he faced me,
And touched my silver breasts as he embraced me,
And kissed my lips, my eyes, until I felt
My wound reopen and my body melt.
He said few words to me, but all he said
Is safely stored up in my heart and head,
His sweet scent stays with me, I still retain
Its savor in my nostrils and my brain.
What can Fate give me that is worse than this –
To dream of his caresses and his kiss

And to be far from him? This is my fate:
I'd rather die than live in such a state,
And this is grief enough for me, that I
Must live on while my wretched soul must die.
You know this Marv of theirs, dear nurse, and you
Have seen there's no one here who's like Viru."
And as she spoke she wept and sobbed again,
And freely scattered tears like jeweled rain.

The poor nurse struck her breast and then her head:
"Light of your grieving mother's eyes," she said,
"May your nurse sacrifice herself, my dear,
On your behalf, and never see or hear
Of sorrow touching you. The words you say
Are massive bars of iron and brass that weigh
So heavily on my poor heart I'm sure
My grief exceeds the sorrow you endure.
Don't grieve more than you should, try not to treat
Your life with bitterness, Vis, life is sweet.
Try to be tranquil now, to calm your heart.
Life lasts two days, and then, Vis, we depart –
Man's life is like a roadside inn, and we
Soon leave this lodging for eternity;
Sorrow and joy are mingled here together,
And last as long as clouds in windy weather.
Why should the world distress you, when it must,
Like you, pass on and crumble into dust?
And if it takes one joy from you, to spite you,
A hundred other pleasures can delight you;
You're young, a princess, and your life is sweet,
The world itself lies prostrate at your feet.
Don't say farewell to life like this, don't make
Eternal chains your fate for sorrow's sake.
The world is filled with young men eager to
Find pleasure in the various things they do;

Some ride with hawks and cheetahs after prey,
Some take up harps and lutes and sweetly play,
This one likes troops of friends, and that one craves
Young boys and pomegranate-breasted slaves;
And women might be hidden out of sight
But all of them seek some form of delight.
But you sit grieving for Viru as though
The whole wide world had no one else to show.

    You said in all of Marv there's no one who
Could be compared with your sublime Viru;
I grant you he's a noble prince, but then
He's not an angel, he's like other men,
And I've seen many fine young fellows here,
Brave warriors, and good-looking too my dear,
Like cypress trees in their magnificence,
Like flowering gardens in their elegance,
And if a wise girl were to look them over
It wouldn't be Viru who was her lover.
There's one of them especially, and he's
A splendid lion in all his qualities –
He is the sun, and they're the stars at dusk,
They are like perfumes, he is like pure musk,
His lineage could not be nobler since
The king's his brother, he's a royal prince.
He is an angel on the earth, but when
He's mounted he's a devil among men;
A finer nobleman cannot be seen,
He's Fortune's favorite, and his name's Ramin.
His handsome face is very like Viru's,
He is the lover every heart would choose,
Brave warriors praise him, and they cannot fight
Against his skill and overwhelming might –
His lance can split a hair, in all this land
No one can challenge his unerring hand,

And in Turan no archer can compare
With him in bringing birds down from the air;
At battles and at banquets he'll outshine
His friends at spilling blood and swilling wine,
At fighting he's a lion, at feasting he
Is like a shower of generosity.
　　For all his manliness, his heart endures
The same tormenting brand that tortures yours –
My silver darling, he's in love like you,
You two are like an apple cut in two.
He's seen you dearest, and he's fallen for you,
He hopes that you'll allow him to adore you.
His sweet narcissus eyes weep tears like rain
Expressive of his sorrow and his pain,
That shining moon, his face, is now like straw,
The sickliest, palest face you ever saw,
His heart knows all the griefs and agonies
Love visits on its wretched votaries.
He's young, as yet the world to him is new,
But he is heart and soul in love with you;
And I ask mercy on you both from heaven –
A pretty face should always be forgiven.
You're so alike you two, so overwrought,
So desperate and distracted and distraught,
So luckless in your love – I've never seen
Two lovers like my Vis and Prince Ramin."

Vis wept, and did not answer for a while,
Her silent lips would neither speak nor smile.
She seemed abashed, and hung her lovely head,
But then she roused herself and coldly said,
"What was the adage Khosrow[32] used to say
To would-be soldiers once? 'Be on your way
If you've no sense of shame, I won't require you.'
If you'd some sense of shame, nurse, to inspire you

You wouldn't say such things. But shame on you
For what you've said, from me and from Viru!
Shame on such idle talk, what can you mean,
Forsaking us like this for Prince Ramin?
If hair grew on my nails I wouldn't think
That these would be the depths to which you'd sink.
You're like my mother, I look up to you,
And I'm your child in everything I do;
Don't teach me how to be impertinent
And brazen-faced and lewdly insolent –
It's acting thoughtlessly and with no shame
That ruins women's fortunes and good name.
What's in my heart that you think I could fall
For such a notion? It's contemptible!
I'd be ashamed to follow your advice
And forfeit all my hopes of paradise.
Ramin can be a noble cypress tree,
The cynosure of Marv – what's that to me?
May God preserve him, but I want to hear
No more of him from you, I hope that's clear!
He might be splendid, but he's not Viru,
However like Viru he looks to you,
I won't set eyes on him, he won't deceive me,
And neither will your idle talk, believe me.
You mustn't listen to his flattery
And if you do don't bring it here to me;
Why didn't you reject his rudeness, nurse,
And answer his foul talk with something worse?

　　　How right Hushang's[33] advisor was to claim
That women have more appetites than shame!
Women are incomplete, it's this that makes them
Ugly with longing, so that shame forsakes them;
They give up both worlds for desire, good sense
Is quite forgotten in their impudence –

If you looked sensibly you'd see the place
Desire's had in so many girls' disgrace.
Women have wiles enough, it's true, but they
Still lap up anything a man might say:
Men have a thousand tricks and ways of wooing
To captivate the woman they're pursuing,
Man hunts a woman each and every way
And all too easily he traps his prey;
He promises, and flatters, and assures her
That he is hers forever and adores her,
A thousand sugared compliments waylay her,
A thousand pretty kindnesses betray her –
But once he's got her in his net, why then
He shows his old capriciousness again,
His kindness ends now and he's unavailable,
He's famous for it and he's unassailable;
His stubborn love grows tame, and raging fire
Becomes the cold, grey ashes of desire.
    She fell for all his sweet talk and flirtation
And now she's lost her name and reputation,
The wretched woman whom he won by lies
Has now become unworthy in his eyes,
She has to cower now, while he draws the bow
And shoots the fatal shaft that lays her low;
Unfaithful now, he doesn't care for her,
And soon she sees he's never there for her.
The kindnesses and compliments are over,
And he regrets that he became her lover;
And all her splendid hopes now melt away
Like thawing snowdrifts on a sunny day;
She's like a wounded onager,[34] who's bound
By ropes of love to some poor patch of ground.
She fears her husband and her relatives,
She fears the sacrilegious life she lives,
She fears the endless shame if they should catch her,
She fears the demons that she's sure will snatch her

And bear her off to hell's eternal flames –
There they don't care for titles, honors, names,
The power you wielded or the rank you had:
There all they ask is, 'Were you good or bad?'
How could I do what you're suggesting when
I fear God's judgment and the scorn of men?
If I should give my soul up to desire
God would destroy me in eternal fire;
If people knew, they'd slander me until
I'd be a field for everyone to till,
Some would entreat me with their wiles and prayers
And give their souls to make my body theirs,
And others would humiliate and hurt me,
And ridicule my shame, and then desert me.
And when they'd all had what they want from me
I'll be in hell for all eternity.
Why should I open this dark door and make
My soul a place in hell for passion's sake?
May Wisdom be my refuge, may my guide
Be the just God, with whom all truths abide."

The nurse saw her approach had not succeeded,
And that a less direct attack was needed.
She said, "Good fortune can still favor you,
Fortune decides our lives and what we do,
Fortune determines how a man behaves –
Why else would we be known as 'Fortune's slaves'?
Courage can't make a lion another creature,
A lion's what it is, and that's its nature,
And strength can't bully partridges to share
The hawk's audacious mastery of the air.
The heavens decide our fates, and we're awarded
Our lives and souls as heaven has recorded,
All our long struggles cannot modify
The fate that's written in the turning sky:

Fate took you from your mother and Viru,
And what Fate has in store won't change for you."

The lovely Vis replied, "It's true that Fate
Controls the good and evil of our state,
But still we know an evildoer's crimes
Will be repaid in kind a hundred times.
Evil was done at first here by Shahru
Who wrongly gave Mobad's bride to Viru.
She did this evil act, but it is we
Who've suffered for Shahru's iniquity –
Viru's name is despised as mine's despised,
And each of us has lost the love we prized;
And, given all I've seen of evil, I
Want no more dealings with it till I die.
Why should I look for evil and then say
That Fortune somehow made me act this way?
Good Fortune will protect me in the end
If I act justly, as Good Fortune's friend."

The nurse replied, "My silver cypress tree,
This Prince Ramin is not a son to me;
It's not for me to get him to undo
The knot of love that he has tied for you.
If God is with him he won't have to face
Harshness from heaven, or sorrow, or disgrace,
Since wisdom teaches that our heavenly king
Is able to encompass everything:
God made the world, all his creation lives
According to the limits that he gives –
And here we witness greater wonders than
Could be conceived of by the mind of man;
Heathens repent, and tyrants are laid low;
Ruins become great castles, gardens grow

Where battles raged; kings fall, and wretches reign.
If you're required to taste love's bitter pain
Fate will not lift its heavy yoke from you –
If love's your fate, there's nothing you can do:
Knowledge won't help, and nor will chivalry,
Neither will common sense, or chastity,
Anger won't profit you, neither will rashness,
Or wealth and jewels, or stubbornness and brashness,
Neither will statecraft, skill, a royal name,
Or sovereignty, or your great family's fame,
Seeing Shahru, or friends and relatives,
Or all the counsel that a wise man gives:
When love has chosen you, your only plan
Is to accept its rule as best you can.
You've merely glimpsed the smoke as yet, but you
Will realize soon enough my words are true,
When you've experienced love's fire you'll praise
As good advice the words your old nurse says,
And when that happens both of us will see
If I have been your friend or enemy.
And now my dear, as Fate and Fortune guide you
Love will oppose you, or be there beside you."

THE NURSE RETURNS TO RAMIN IN THE GARDEN

Then, as the sun rose in the east – as bright
As Vis's face – and showed its shining light,
The nurse set out for the agreed-on glade
Where sad Ramin sat waiting in the shade,
And when he saw her he revived again
Like parched earth that is soaked by sudden rain.
"Dear nurse, worthy of praise in every way,"
He said, "Tell me the news since yesterday:
You're happy, you have heard the words she speaks,
And seen her lively eyes and blushing cheeks;

Happy the eyes that see her face, the brain
In which some traces of her scent remain,
Happy your heart that you're so dear to her,
Happy your neighbors who live near to her!"
And then he said, "How is she? Tell me, how?
Ramin's soul is her slave forever now;
Did you convey my message? Did you give
Her news of how unhappily I live?"

"Ah, what a lion you are," the nurse replied,
"Calm down, Ramin, Patience must be your guide:
Think of a drunk, and how you'd separate
Drink's influence from someone in that state;
Think how you might undo the chains that hold
Winter within the grip of ice and cold;
Or could you wash the earth of flowers? Or force
The ocean's tides and tempests from their course?
Just so, you'll make Vis set aside her mother
And disregard her passion for her brother;
When once she's been persuaded to undo
The chains of love that bind her to Viru,
You might secure her; first she must forget,
Then you've a chance to catch her in your net.
I told her everything you said, and she
Raged inwardly at first, then chided me;
She wouldn't answer, then she stormed and swore,
And said I don't know what, and then much more!"

And as Ramin took in her words, the light
Of daytime seemed to him as dark as night.
He said, "But everyone is not to blame
If some men act without a sense of shame;
Not all men are unfaithful, we aren't all
To be considered as identical;

She shouldn't take a stick to all of us
And call us uniformly infamous.
She's seen injustice, but she hasn't seen
The way that she'll be treated by Ramin,
Why should she blame me when I'm innocent
Of sins I never did and never meant?
So tell the silver-breasted Vis, whose black
Curls twist and fall, cascading down her back,
I say: 'You're fairy-faced, with houri's eyes,
My spring, my moon, and quick to criticize;
Become acquainted with my love before you
Decide I'm faithless to you; I adore you –
I swear, a hundred times I swear, that I
Will not cease loving you until I die,
My soul is yours until my soul has fled
Out of my lifeless body, and I'm dead;
In days of war, my love, in days of peace
My heart will never not remember Vis.'"

　　　He spoke like one who weeps and hardly speaks,
And teardrops touched the roses of his cheeks
Like drops of wine, or pearls, and showed how strong
The love was that he'd hidden for so long.
He'd lost his heart, and now the nurse's heart
Was quick to sympathize and take his part.
"Light of my eyes," she said, "I won't neglect you,
And chain mail forged from patience will protect you;
Weeping for love has weakened you, and from
This weakness madness in its turn has come,
And since you don't have Vis, I'll gladly give
My willing soul to serve you while I live.
I'll go to her again, this time I'll wear
The shift of shamelessness, this time I swear
I won't return from her until I've made her
Submit to you; be patient, I'll persuade her.

Our cause is right, I'll do what you require,
And righteousness will win our heart's desire."

She went to Vis, and in her heart there lay
Ten different speeches that she thought she'd say.
She saw her charge now, like the full moon, caught
In all the sorrows separation brought,
Weeping and fevered from her storms of yearning,
A fiery oven of incessant burning.
The world before her eyes had lost its light
And seemed to her as dark as endless night,
And all her bright brocade and sumptuous fur
Seemed harsh and ugly as black snakes to her.
The nurse, who knew as many strategies
As there are precious pearls beneath the seas,
Addressed Vis: "How I wish that he were dead,
The man who brought these sorrows on your head,
Who dragged you from your home, whose tricks waylaid you,
Who brought you to this land and so betrayed you,
Who took you from your heart's delight, your brother,
And from your soul's familiar friend, your mother.
Your life has been a tale of misery,
Of soulful grief and heartfelt agony –
But what is reason, which the good Lord gave you,
If not a way to cure your grief and save you?
I burn to see you burn, you writhe in fear
And wretchedness, and I writhe with you dear,
But reason ends our woes, reason will cure them,
With reason they'll be gone, so why endure them?
God gave you knowledge and your reason, Vis,
And with this knowledge not one moment's peace:
    You're like a mule with swords piled on its back –
They're useless if a lion should attack!
How long do you intend there should be streaks
Of ruby tears upon your golden cheeks?

Stop now! Have pity on your youth; stop sighing,
And piling grief on grief, and all this crying.
You're in a foreign land! Don't wail about it;
You've royal glory, don't abuse and flout it!
Your angel is beside you every day
And he hears every single word you say,
See you don't forfeit his benevolence
By saying hateful things that give offense.
You are a royal princess of Iran,
A shining moon of beauty in Turan,
The sun of houris, and the mistress of
All splendid idols that the pagans love:
But understand, our earthly life is brief
And puts a sudden end to joy and grief.
      Our souls are dear and sweet to us, yet all
Your manner says your soul's contemptible –
She's your companion and your friend, she'll be
Your confidante for all eternity,
But now for years you've treated her as though
She were a wretch, the lowest of the low.
But then to you the courteous, kind Ramin
Is like the vilest thing you've ever seen.
Don't do this, Vis! Be kinder to your friends,
Be generous, like a laden tree that bends
Its branches down and proffers us its fruit;
Be good to that poor boy, don't persecute
Him any more, don't be so harsh and grim –
Have pity on yourself, and then on him.
Don't be so distant; he's been kind to you,
And now it's your turn to show kindness too.
If you won't be a friend to any man,
How are you different from some talisman
Against the evil eye, stuck on a roof?[35]
Now, if you're human, you must give us proof!"

But Vis responded with contemptuous scorn:
"I wish the three of us had not been born –
I wish the world itself had never seen
The birth of Vis, or you, or Prince Ramin;
May Khuzestan and all your family die,
I curse you and your stupid evil eye!
I curse your land, and may its progeny
Be fools and devils steeped in infamy
Who fail in everything that they attempt,
Whose foolish words are treated with contempt.
And may no noble mother ever do
What mine did once, and trust a nurse like you;
The loathsome milk her child drinks will impart
The nurse's evil nature to her heart,
Polluting her pure blood, staining with shame
Her noble family's lineage and name.
Shame on my mother now who gave me to
A nurse as evil and corrupt as you,
A wicked sorceress, who has no sense
Of shame, or justice, or intelligence.
You're not my nurse, you're my worst enemy
Avid to rob me of my dignity;
It's you that should instruct me in what's right,
And keep me safe throughout the day and night,
And so you praised yourself as pure and blameless –
But what are you? Despicable and shameless!
With your cruel nature, your lascivious eyes,
Your coarse behavior, and your specious lies,
You've dragged your good name in the dust, no one
With any shame approves of what you've done;
Your words spell death to me, I tremble now
Like the last leaf on an autumnal bough.

    You say that life has all too short a span,
That I should look for pleasure while I can,

But pleasure's less worthwhile than doing good,
And acting well, and living as I should;
Those who seek pleasure here will not be given
God's blessing and eternal life in heaven –
The wise say that this world is best regarded
As being like a toy that's soon discarded.
And so dear nurse you have no need to fret
On my account, to swindle, swear, or sweat,
Since I won't hear the foolish words you say
Or follow your advice in any way –
I'm not a child deceived by colored toys,
I'm not a bird that's startled by a noise.
And when you told me of his declaration
I heard it as an evil incantation:
Don't say such things, don't try to make me sell
My sweet soul to the demons thronging hell;
I have renounced this world, and made my soul
Subject to wisdom's capable control –
Whatever happens, God is better than
Ramin and devils and your Khuzestan.
I will not forfeit life in paradise
By listening to your infamous advice;
Both this world and the world you've never seen
Are lost to you: for what? For Prince Ramin!"

Now when the nurse saw Vis's furious face
And heard her talk of heaven and God's grace
She searched within her scheming heart to find
Some means to soothe her charge's troubled mind:
Her demon did not rest, but wondered how
Vis and Ramin could be united now,
And how like fat and sugar they could be
Blended entirely and inseparably.
Then one by one the sly nurse recollected
All the old tricks and spells that she'd collected,

And when she spoke her voice was lovelier than
The frescoes at Noshad.[36] The nurse began:
"You're dearer to me than my soul, more blessed
And virtuous even than I'd ever guessed;
May you seek justice always, may you stay
Truthful and honored, wise in every way.
Why should I need or want, dear Vis, to grieve you?
What fear or greed could drive me to deceive you?
Why should I want to trick you? I'm not trying
To steal from you, why should I think of lying?
Ramin is not my brother or my son;
And can you tell me what it is he's done
To make me favor him, so that I'd be
His faithful friend and your sworn enemy?

       I only want one thing from life, that you
Find happiness in everything you do,
And that your reputation stay intact.
But I must tell you an undoubted fact:
You are a woman, not a demon, not
A fairy, houri, or I don't know what.
Viru has gone, and as for Mobad, well
He's been disposed of by a clever spell:
No one's enjoyed your body, no one can,
You've never truly slept with any man.
You've had no joy of men, you've never known
A man whom you could really call your own.
You've married twice, but each time you've moved on;
Both husbands crossed the river, and they're gone!
But if you want a man, I've never seen
A finer specimen than this Ramin:
What use is beauty if it doesn't bless
Your life with pleasure and love's happiness?
You're innocent, you're in the dark about it,
You don't know how forlorn life is without it.

Women were made for men, dear Vis, and you
Are not exempt, whatever you might do.
  The well-born women of the world delight
In marrying a courtier or a knight,
And some, who have a husband, also see
A special friend who's sworn to secrecy;
She loves her husband, she embraces him,
And then her happy friend replaces him.
You can have royal riches beyond measure,
Brocades, and jewels, and every kind of treasure,
But joy is something that you won't discover
Until you have a husband or a lover.
If you need riches it's to make you more
Attractive to him than you were before;
What use are all your red and yellow dresses
Unless they lead to kisses and caresses?
If you can see this, it was wrong of you
To slander me when all I said is true;
I spoke maternally, and as your nurse,
I'm trying to make things better now, not worse.
Ramin is worthy of you, and I've seen
That you, dear Vis, are worthy of Ramin:
You are the sun and he's the moon; if he
Is like an elegant, tall cypress tree,
You are a bough of blossoms in the spring;
If you are milk, he's wine.[37] In everything
You're worthy of each other's love, and I
Will never grieve again until I die
If I can see love mutually requited
When you and he are happily united."

And as the nurse spoke, at her voice's sound,
A horde of hellish demons crowded round,
And set a thousand traps, a thousand snares
Before her feet, to catch Vis unawares.

The nurse went on: "A noble woman spends
Her life in pleasure, with her special friends
Or with her husband; you sit here and sigh,
And weep your heart away, and moan and cry.
Your youth will soon be gone, and you'll have had
No time at all when you were young and glad;
How long will you stay grieving and alone?
You're not composed of brass, my dear, or stone."

And gradually the heart of Vis was stirred
And softened by the arguments she heard:
She felt herself assent, but did not let
Her tongue bear witness to her heart as yet.
Gently she said, "I shouldn't shout at you;
No woman can avoid a mate, it's true.
Women are weak and frail, though they delight
The noble heart of many a stalwart knight;
They have a thousand faults, the wisest way
Is not to trust the careless things they say.
Anger is in a woman's temperament,
But I should not have been so vehement;
The words I heard from you were like a dart,
Tipped with cruel poison, piercing my poor heart.
I'd heard harsh words from you, and this is why
I was a little harsh in my reply;
I should have held my foolish tongue instead,
I'm truly sorry for the things I said,
I should say nothing when I disagree
With things that people sometimes say to me.
Now what I pray for is that God protect me
From all the evil sins that could infect me,
That women's faults not stain me, that I seek
To keep myself from evil when I speak.
And while I stay alive may God ensure
My body is kept healthy, whole, and pure;

And may He see you're not among my friends
Since all your charges come to evil ends."

Day dawned, and in the predetermined place
Ramin and Vis's nurse met face to face.
Sadly she said, "Ramin, how long will you
Send messages that bring back nothing new?
You're seeking water in the midst of fire,
The wind can't be embraced by your desire,
The sea can't be encompassed in your fist,
And granite Vis continues to resist;
Accept that you will never share her bed
Or lay your head beside her lovely head.
Mountains will melt with love before her mind
Grows less impervious and less unkind;
A man who cries out to a mountain hears
An answering echo greet his waiting ears,
But Vis won't answer, and her nature's like
An evil scorpion that is poised to strike.
She didn't answer you, she swore at me,
And everything I tried – my flattery,
My guile, my stock of tricks – had no effect;
It was as if a wise man might expect
A drunkard to sit up and pay attention
To any good advice he'd care to mention.
Water will wear out iron before she'll take
Account of any pleas or plans I make."

Ramin felt like a partridge pinioned by
A hawk that plummets from an empty sky:
The world grew dark to him, and full of fear;
Hope had departed, and his death drew near.
He was a cloud when dreadful tempests start,
Rain filled his eyes, and lightning filled his heart.

His anger, and the scornful words of Vis,
Were arrow wounds that gave his heart no peace;
He wept and wailed, a hundred times he cried,
"Help me, agree once more to be my guide,
I've no one in the world but you, if I
Despair of you then I will surely die,
I'll tell the world my secret, and I'll sever
The bonds that fasten me to life forever.
If you will try, just once more, to explain
To jasmine-breasted Vis my grievous pain
I'll honor you for all eternity.
Perhaps her stony heart will grieve for me,
Perhaps a flickering flame of love will start
To burn within the lamp of Vis's heart;
Perhaps she will be sorry that she's shed
My blood like this and left me here for dead.
Both young and old are eager to possess her;
Give her my greetings, lovingly address her,
Tell her, 'You have my heart, and this is right,
Since conquering lovers' hearts is your delight;
You spill my blood, and I cannot object,
Since lovers whom you kill you resurrect;
You rule my soul and body, and I see
That you are worthy of such sovereignty.

    Take pity on my soul, and it will serve you,
My life will pass in striving to deserve you,
And I'll behave well – violence and abduction
Are not how I would set about seduction!
Many will love you, but you'll never find
A man as true as I am, or as kind,
And rest assured that if you're good to me
I will repay you with fidelity –
Shine like the sun on me, and you will learn
I'll be a faithful ruby[38] in return.

Grant me my life, and I shall live for you,
Willingly serving you in all I do,
And if one day you wish you were without it
Then take my life, and think no more about it.
But if your heart continues to ignore me,
And if you make it plain that you abhor me,
Then I'll despair of life and seek release
In death from my obsessive love for Vis:
I'll climb a crag, and cast my body down,
Or dive into the ocean's depths, and drown,
And then my blood will be upon your head
And God will give me justice when I'm dead;
You know as well as I do that it's true
God watches everything we say and do.'"

He wept so piteously the poor nurse felt
Her heart in sympathetic sorrow melt.
She went to Vis and sat in silence there,
Her heart distracted by Ramin's despair.
Then, once again, she strung the pearls of speech,
And spoke of him, and did her best to reach
Her charge's heart: "O moon of houris, queen
Of every beauty that the world has seen,
Adored by many men, both far and near;
I have to tell you that my shame and fear
Prevent my talking openly to you:
I fear Mobad, and all that he might do,
I fear men's ridicule, I fear they'll blame me,
I fear the life I'm leading now will shame me,
I fear that when I bid this world farewell
My final dwelling place will be in hell.
But then I think of Prince Ramin's sad tears,
And his wan face, and I forget my fears;
I hear his plea for help, I hear his cry
That he despises life and longs to die,

And Wisdom's eyes are seeled, and once again
My heart is wrung for all his grief and pain.
Oh, I've seen lovers with their hearts on fire,
Weeping and wailing, wretched with desire,
But I am sure that I have never seen
A lover who's as heartsick as Ramin.
And now I am afraid that in God's eyes
I'll be to blame if suddenly he dies;
Pity this wretch, dear Vis, do not demean
Your soul with blood by murdering Ramin;
What will it profit you to have him dead?
How will it help you if his blood is shed?
Who will you fly to then? You'll never find
Another youth with such an agile mind,
Not in a hundred years will you discover
So handsome and so mettlesome a lover,
Whose princely elegance seems heaven-sent,
And who's so charming and so eloquent.
I tell you, God has given you your beauty
For his sake, and to love him is your duty;
God made you like a houri in your grace,
In sun and shade God nourished your sweet face
For this one purpose – that you love Ramin,
That to his Khosrow you would be Shirin.[39]
Ramin – dear Vis, I swear this must be so –
Will be the only lord you'll ever know."

And as she swore, Vis gradually relented,
And bit by bit believed, and so assented.
She grew compassionate, and tender-hearted,
Her anger and her stubbornness departed
And in their place a loving kindness came:
A wisp of smoke curled upward from the flame.
Within her yielding soul, benevolence
Dawned slowly with a gentle radiance,

Until love's sun dispelled the lingering night
And filled the heavens with its glorious light.

It seemed at first as though she would depend
On cautious silence as her loyal friend:
She stared distractedly, and glanced around,
And looked now at the sky, now at the ground;
Shame made her blush like wine, then turn so pale
That all her vigor seemed to faint and fail;
And it was shame that made her body wet
With dripping, trickling, pearl-like drops of sweat.
Love, like a lodestone drawing iron, compels
Another's heart to answer to its spells;
Love cannot stay secluded in one heart,
A second heart must play an answering part –
The weight a donkey carries has to be
Distributed on both sides equally.
The nurse, who was a cunning sorceress,
Watched Vis and was aware of her success;
Her arrow had struck home, her hidden snare
Had caught its prey and held her spellbound there.

VIS SEES RAMIN AND FALLS IN LOVE WITH HIM

The country's nobles came to celebrate
In their king's palace Ram's auspicious date,[40]
And all the court was like a starry night
Glittering with splendor and suffused with light.
The goblets that they drank from seemed to shine
Like elegant narcissi filled with wine,
And everywhere conviviality
Mingled with courtesy and chivalry,
While in among these stars and planets one
Resplendent courtier glittered like the sun,
The rose-cheeked and narcissus-eyed Ramin,
The loveliest courtier whom the court had seen,

Whose curls were like black grapes, and whose complexion
Was grape juice that's fermented to perfection.
In stature like a cypress tree that grows
Near where an irrigation channel flows,
His mouth was small, his figure neat and trim,
And all the world admired and longed for him.
He sat among musicians and seemed drowned
Within the music's sweet, voluptuous sound,
While love and wine together made him weak
And brought a sallow pallor to his cheek;
His eyes saw only Vis, and in his mind
The scent of Vis was all that he could find –
Her face seemed lustrous as the wine, her scent
Like basil, strong and sweetly vehement.

Vis sat above him, on the second storey,
And lit the place she sat in with her glory
(The cunning nurse had taken special care
To calm all Vis's fears and hide her there,
And show her to a louver in the wall
Through which the scene below was visible).
"Look there," she said, "Now, have you ever seen
A man as wonderful as this Ramin?
Doesn't he seem immaculate to you?
Didn't I tell you that he's like Viru?
That's not a face, it's God's own masterpiece!
There is a courtier worthy of my Vis,
He fills the splendid palace of our king
With all the gorgeous happiness of spring,
There is the only man who's worthy of
My Vis's admiration and her love."

Vis gazed at him, and you would say she saw
Her soul's perfection there, without a flaw,

And as she looked the love she'd lavished on
Viru was instantaneously gone.
And then she asked herself, "How would it be
If I allowed Ramin to sleep with me?
O heart, what more should I expect of you
When you so easily forget Viru?
I'm here without my mother and my brother,
Why should I feed love's fire now for another?
I cannot bear the loneliness I feel,
How long I've suffered! I'm not made of steel.
I will submit then, since I won't discover
A finer man than this to be my lover."
These were her thoughts, and with a heartfelt sigh
She thought of all the days that had gone by,
But took good care that she did not reveal
The fevered love she had begun to feel.
She turned now to her nurse and said, "Ramin
Is just as you described, I've never seen
A finer man, he's handsome, and it's true
He's very similar to Prince Viru,
But he won't get what he desires: I might
Be like the moon, dear nurse, but this moon's light
Won't shine on him. I've no desire that he
Or I should undergo such misery:
For me I don't want shame and degradation,
For him I don't want longing and frustration:
I wish him well, and may he go in peace,
And never give another thought to Vis!"

But when she came down from the upper floor
She could not see the sunlight any more;
The demon love, before Vis could depart,
Had sunk his poisoned claws within her heart,
And quickly from her face and heart he stole
Color and strength, and wisdom from her soul.

At times her fancies took her by surprise
And conquered her, and blinded Reason's eyes;
At times she'd think, "My cruelest enemy
Could not desire a nastier fate for me,"
And then, "It's not as though no woman's ever
Thought love was worth her serious endeavor,
And if it's love for someone who's as fine
As Prince Ramin, why shouldn't he be mine?"
But then shame drove desire away, and made
Her feel she should be cautious and afraid;
She feared the world's contempt, that she'd be tried
And punished by the heavens when she died,
And thoughts of hell below and God above
Made her choose wisdom over thoughts of love,
Preferring freedom and nobility,
Reverence for God, and seemly chastity,
To love and all its ugly complications.
She'd free her heart from love's manipulations,
And swore that she would never lay her head
Beside Ramin, on an unworthy bed.

The nurse, who did not know that Vis's soul
Was struggling to maintain its self-control,
Went to Ramin and said, "Good news, my boy,
Your sapling touches heaven in its joy;
Our wild one's gradually becoming more
Receptive and less headstrong than before;
She doesn't argue like she used to do,
And I'm quite certain she approves of you."

Ramin was so entranced by what she said
He seemed like someone risen from the dead.
He kissed the ground, then brought himself to speak,
"Dear nurse, your skill and knowledge are unique,

My gratitude means more to me I swear
Than does the royal diadem I wear.
You've rescued me from death, may you be given
Rewards for all you've done by God in heaven,
I'll think of you now as my mother, who
I'll strive to satisfy in all I do,
My mistress whom I'll never disobey,
Whose every whim I'll serve in every way."
And as he lavished praise on her he pressed
Three purses of gold coins, a golden chest
Containing pearls arranged in six long strands,
Fine rings and precious scents into her hands.
At first the nurse said she could not agree
To profit from his generosity:
"I want no gifts from you, my noble lord,
To see you is an adequate reward,
I've wealth enough, and in your nurse's sight
You're like the sun's illuminating light."
But he insisted, and she said she'd take
A little silver ring, for friendship's sake.

THE NURSE RETURNS TO VIS

But when the nurse returned she came on Vis
Weeping as though her tears would never cease,
And instantly Vis saw the nurse approach her
She flew at her and started to reproach her:
She said, "It's God I want, and my good name,
Not Prince Ramin, and calumny, and shame;
Why should I even think of ugliness
That can procure me nothing but distress?
What will my family call me? How shall I
Ask God for His forgiveness when I die?
What shall I say? That one desire betrayed me
And found a hundred methods to degrade me?

You say Ramin is sweet – this might be so,
But heaven is sweeter than Ramin, I know:
And if Ramin is angered by my pride
What does it matter if God's satisfied?
How will Ramin's love help or comfort me
When I'm in hell for all eternity?
My days can turn to night, but I will never
Choose to destroy my life and name forever."

And when she'd heard her out the nurse became
As sly as foxes are when stalking game:
She said, "You are my soul's delight, dear Vis,
But when will all these moods and rages cease?
Make up your mind now! Round and round you turn
Like a revolving mill wheel or a quern;
Each time day turns to night it seems that you
Decide it's time you looked for something new;
You're one thing, then another, in a trice,
As unpredictable as throws of dice.
You're like a turquoise glittering with hints
Of I don't know how many hues and tints,
Or like an iron blade that rust defaces
With new spots every day in different places.
But you can't shirk God's will, you can't evade
The destiny the turning skies have made.
If you go on like this, I see that you
Won't be worth living with, dear Vis; it's true!
Stay here then, stay with your Mobad, while I
Will live in Mahabad until I die.
Demons could not put up with you, my dear,
And you're the only reason that I'm here,
But you despise me Vis, and every day
You call me to account in some new way.
I'll go and live with your dear mother then
And never have to face your moods again;

I swear by God and by I don't know who
That I have had enough of Marv and you!"

Vis answered her, "And why are you so keen
On everything to do with Prince Ramin?
You're hurting me, you're putting me in danger,
By giving your affection to this stranger;
How can you find it in your heart to see
Another person and abandon me?
You're like my mother, how can I survive
Without you? How will I remain alive?
Life has become so difficult and cruel,
And it is hard to live as Fortune's fool!
I'm separated from my home and mother,
From all my family and from my brother,
You were my refuge in this alien land,
From loneliness's agonizing brand
You saved me; now you too are tired of me
And making common cause with treachery.
But if you leave me in this way, your name
Will be a byword for disgrace and shame,
You'll throw your reputation in the river
Where you will see it swept away forever.
You'll find no medicine for your sorrow, none;
Nothing will heal the pain of what you've done!"

The wily nurse then tried another tack:
"You're on the right road now, so don't turn back;
Fate has decided for you, and what use
Is all this talk now? What will it produce?
Consider, concentrate your conversation,
Just give me one small piece of information,
When will you see Ramin? Say when and how
You'll welcome him, and that's enough for now;

Talk that goes round and round and on and on
Is of no earthly use to anyone.
      You must refine your speech, so that it seems
To be an answer to youth's sweetest dreams,
Then show the springtime of your chivalry
And harvest ripened fruit from pleasure's tree:
Enjoy your youth and rank and royal treasures
And spend your days in youth's tumultuous pleasures.
You're not a God or angel, you are clay,
Like all of us whose lives must pass away,
Desire and longing live in us, and you
Are not exempt, you feel their vigor too.
God made us so that nothing's lovelier than
What we as women feel when with a man,
And you don't know how vehemently sweet
The pleasure is when men and women meet;
If you make love just once, I know that then
You won't hold back from doing so again."

But Vis replied to her, "And I know heaven
Is sweeter than the joys that men have given;
If you would trick me and deceive me less
I could forget men and love's happiness.
But, as it is, my poor heart takes your part
And I admit desire lives in my heart.
And even if I didn't feel for you
I'd sympathize with all Ramin's been through,
And if this weren't the case Ramin could fly
Like some great hunting hawk about the sky,
Or bluster like the wind, and not come near me;
He'd find that he could never see or hear me.
You must ensure that nothing goes amiss,
That no one in the world can learn of this;
Think how Mobad is certain to react
If he suspects his honor's been attacked,

His anger's like a slashing sword if he
Hears any hint of hidden treachery,
He's like a lion if he can detect
A trace of mutiny or disrespect;
And if one day he ever thinks that I
Might be unfaithful, I will surely die.
Keep all this hidden, and we might devise
Some way to close Disaster's watchful eyes."

VIS AND RAMIN

ویس و رامین

Vis and Ramin meet

The first shoots of a sapling clearly show
How straight and tall the tiny tree will grow,
And similarly in the spring it's clear
What we can hope for from the coming year,
So the long course of love was plainly seen
When it began, for Vis and Prince Ramin;
They'd suffered greatly, but their happiness
Proved to be as intense as their distress.
The rust of spite besmirching Vis's heart
Vanished for good once they were not apart;
And, in the week they met, no one was there
To spoil the idyll they began to share.

Mobad led out his men from Khorasan
And set up his encampment near Gorgan;
Making for Kuhestan,[41] he took the way
That leads to Saveh and traverses Rey.
Ramin remained behind (his bold excuse
Was that he felt too sick to be of use);

His brother told him to assume the throne
And rule with equity while he was gone.
The king left Marv, traveling without his queen;
Vis stayed in Marv, and so did Prince Ramin.

And so it was that on the following day,
Immediately the king had gone away,
Vis sat, a vision of magnificence,
Of loveliness, and shifting tints and scents,
Upon her throne, within an audience hall
With golden pictures painted on each wall;
Three doors led to a garden, and three more
To private rooms reached by a corridor.
The splendid gold and jewels with which she shone
Made Vis appear as dazzling as the sun,
And all her loveliness and radiance
Made idols look like tawdry ornaments.
A thousand rosebuds opened in her face,
Her mouth was thirty stars' sweet hiding place,
The fragrance wafting from her was the scent
Of gardens when they're sweetly redolent;
The scent of Vis, the odors from the flowers,
Mingled to make a potent salve whose powers
Would hold back spirits on the point of death
And heal their wounds, and resurrect their breath.
The roses bloomed like Vis's countenance,
Their musky scent set off her elegance,
And like a swirling cloud from censers there
Sweet ambergris and musk filled all the air.
        Then, if you saw the palace, you would say
It seemed like paradise in every way
With Vis its houri, while her nurse knew well
The role of Rezvan,[42] heaven's sentinel,
Now fussing over Vis, and now hard pressed
To have the room and garden look their best.

She cleared the room of strangers, and when she
Felt sure she had secured their privacy,
When not another person could be seen,
She let in, from the rooftop,[43] Prince Ramin;
And, entering, he thought he had been given
A vision of the starry court of heaven
With Vis there as the moon. He saw her face
But could not credit its enchanting grace;
His sick heart felt such sudden pleasure then
He seemed an old man who'd grown young again,
Or you would say a corpse had come alive,
So eagerly did Prince Ramin revive.
His soul was like a desiccated plain
That's given up all hope of life or rain,
Till Vis's subtle scent convinced him he
Had drunk the waters of eternity;
The smoke that had beclouded all his heart
Began to clear and gradually depart.

    He sat by her and said, "Oh, you suffice
To show the promised joys of paradise,
You are the first of all magicians, Vis,
The first of ladies, and God's masterpiece;
You are a rose that's camphor white, whose scent
Is sweetly musky and magnificent,
An idol with a box tree's slender grace,
And tulips bloom in your bewitching face.
You are the sun in your bright radiance,
Happy the man on whom you turn your glance!
You are the moon in shining beauty Vis,
Making all darkness and all sorrow cease,
Scouring the rust of pain and misery
From souls made wretched by adversity.
Let me be one who waits on you, and then
I'll count myself the happiest of men;

The heavens would be my home if I could serve you,
And stand before you trying to deserve you."

Vis answered him with shame-faced reticence,
Coyly, and with seductive eloquence.
She said, "Young man, I see your chivalry.
This harsh world has dealt callously with me;
I've never known of grief like mine, disgrace
For me is now a sordid commonplace.
I've soiled my body's purity, and all
My faith and shame are now contemptible.
Two agents have reduced me to this state,
One is my nurse-companion, one is Fate.
My nurse's tricks and stories are to blame
For sinking me within this pit of shame;
She pleaded and berated me and swore
Until she got what she was aiming for.
        Tell me what you intend to do with me,
Are you my friend now or my enemy?
Will love be like a rose, that in a day
Opens and blossoms and then fades away,
Or like a jewel, a turquoise, that persists
And come what may still stubbornly exists?
The months and years will turn, and so will you,
And you'll regret the things love made you do.
If this is how your promises will be
Why this great show of grief and misery?
Why risk eternal shame for hopes that last
One day before they fade into the past?
A hundred years of pleasure here on earth
Would not suffice; their joys would not be worth
The rust that would corrode your soul, and make
You forfeit paradise for passion's sake.
And for one day of pleasure? No, restrain
Yourself, and spare your soul eternal pain."

Ramin replied, "O silver cypress tree,
Your Mahabad's the dearest place to me,
That has a mother in it like Shahru
Whose daughter's Vis, whose son is great Viru:
A thousand blessings on your land and name
And on the noble lineage you claim,
A thousand blessings on your mother who
Gave birth to such a heavenly child as you!
Happy the woman who's your noble mother,
Happy the man who calls himself your brother,
Happy your nurse, happy those mortals who
Contrive to spend a single day with you,
Happy whoever hears your name, or sees you,
Happy whoever as your friend can please you.
Marv's royal glory is that you reside here,
The king's is that he brought you as his bride here;
As for Ramin, my happy fame will be
Eternal if the sun will welcome me.
These ears have heard your voice, these eyes have seen
The beauty of your face; henceforth Ramin
Can see no sights but happiness, and hear
No sounds but celebration and good cheer."

Vis and Ramin then swore no force could sever
The love that bound the two of them forever.
Ramin spoke first: "I swear by God, and by
His sovereignty that rules the earth and sky,
I swear now by the sun, and by the light
The shining moon bestows on us at night,
I swear by Venus and by noble Jupiter,
I swear by bread and salt and flickering fire,
I swear by faith and God's omnipotence,
And by the soul and all its eloquence,
That while winds scour the wastelands and the mountains,
While waters flow in rivers and in fountains,

While night has darkness, and while streams have fishes,
While stars have courses, and while souls have wishes,
Ramin will not regret his love, or break
The binding oath that he and Vis now make;
He'll never take another love, or cease
To give his heart exclusively to Vis."

Vis promised love when Prince Ramin had spoken
And swore her promises would not be broken.
She gave him violets then and murmured, "Take
This pretty posy, keep it for my sake,
Keep it forever, so that when you see
Fresh violets blooming you'll remember me;
And may the soul that breaks this solemn vow
Darken and droop as these poor flowers do now.
Each time I see the spring's new flowers appear
I will recall the oaths we swore to here;
May anyone that breaks this oath decay
And wither as fresh flowers do – in a day."

And once these promises of love were given,
And they had called to witness God and heaven,
They lay beside each other telling tales
Of all their former sorrows and travails.
Vis lay beside her prince now, face to face,
The full moon lay in Prince Ramin's embrace,
And when Ramin affectionately placed
His gentle arm about her yielding waist
It was as if a golden torque should grasp
A silver cypress in its circling clasp,
And then Rezvan[44] himself could not declare
Which was the lovelier of this noble pair.
Their pillow smelt of musk, and jeweled bedcovers
Bestrewed with roses lay upon the lovers.

Now lip to lip and cheek to cheek they lay
And struck the ball of pleasure into play;[45]
So close together were their bodies pressed
That rain could not have reached to either's breast,
And Vis's heart was now a balm that cured
The agonies Ramin's heart had endured,
For every wound she'd dealt his heart before
He kissed her face a thousand times and more.
Now happiness emboldened him, and he
Placed in the lock of pleasure longing's key,
And felt his joy and eagerness increase
As he discerned the virgin seal of Vis;
Ramin pressed on and pierced this precious pearl,
And Vis was now a woman, not a girl.
When he withdrew the arrow, blood was seen
On wounded Vis, and on her Prince Ramin,
But though Ramin had wounded her she knew
A heartfelt pleasure and contentment too;
And now that their desire was satisfied
Their love grew deeper and intensified.
So for two months of luxury and leisure
They gave themselves to happiness and pleasure.

VIS AND RAMIN JOIN MOBAD IN THE MOUNTAINS

The king heard that Ramin had quit his bed,
And sent a message to the prince that said:
"I get no pleasure from my life without you,
I miss you, I think constantly about you –
Drinking my wine, at polo, in the chase,
I'm miserable if I don't see your face.
Come here and hunt with me, we'll spend our time
Cleansing our hearts of harmful rust and grime.
The countryside near Mahabad is green,
The moon and Venus rule this land, Ramin;

Mount Arvand's clothed in Byzantine brocade,
It's cast aside the ermine cap it made,[46]
Among its tulips and its roses sleep
Well-hidden goats, and flocks of mountain sheep;
Spring floods have so obscured these plains, you'd say
A cheetah needs a boat to catch his prey!
As soon as you have read this, hurry here
And spring will make your sorrows disappear.
And bring Vis with you, since I know that she
Pines for her absent mother's company."
Ramin received this letter from Mobad
And set out straightaway for Mahabad.

The bugles blared, Ramin remained light-hearted
As he and Vis triumphantly departed;
Mobad and all his court rode out to greet them,
Traveling along the road to Marv to meet them.
Immediately Vis went to find her mother,
And though she was ashamed to see her brother
Her heart rejoiced to be with them; but then
Heartache and sorrow came to Vis again.
She longed to see the face of Prince Ramin
And haunted places where he might be seen,
But all her glimpses of him were too short,
As he passed by, or with the king at court.
So for a week she longed for him, and peace
Abandoned the unhappy heart of Vis;
Betrayed by her desire's insidious power
Love did not leave her for a single hour.
How strong first love is! And, for Vis, Ramin
Meant more than even life itself could mean.

KING MOBAD LEARNS OF THEIR LOVE

Now King Mobad and Prince Ramin his brother
Hunted and banqueted with one another;

A month passed, and Ramin expressed the wish
To travel to Mughan[47] to hunt and fish.
Vis slept beside Mobad, and his desire
Burned like a brand that's heated in the fire,
But his embraces only aggravated
His wretched state and left him more frustrated.

In secret then, beset by doubt and fear,
The wet-nurse whispered in her Vis's ear:
"How can you lie here sleeping? Don't you know
Ramin is getting ready now to go?
He's traveling to Arman,[48] to hunt and fight,
To face our foes now as befits a knight;
His men know this, his tents and baggage train
Are moving, as we speak, across the plain.
The drums are beating and the trumpets blowing
To tell the moon and stars Ramin is going.
Go up on to the roof now, if you dare,
Be quick, or he'll have gone before you're there,
And then you'll see his face that's lovelier than
Brocades brought by a Chinese caravan.
Your heart will be his hawks' and cheetahs' prey,
It's you he'll hunt for while he's far away;
And now that he is leaving us we'll find
My soul goes with him, and your peace of mind."

By chance Mobad was not asleep, and heard
The furtive nurse's every whispered word:
Enraged he sprang up from the nuptial bed
And cursed the cowering nurse who quickly fled.
Then like a maddened elephant he roared,
"Bring me that hag, that crone, that filthy bawd,
That bitch who's worse than any loathsome cur,
And let her see what I've in store for her.

May hail storms flatten Khuzestan, that gave
The world this wanton witch, this shameless slave,
Who's taught her charges evil, who conspires
To shame her betters with her foul desires.
All Khuzestan brings forth is heretics,
Practitioners of lies and devils' tricks;
May no one make them welcome, or defend them,
Employ them in his household, or befriend them,
Or choose a nurse from them, and, God forbid,
Bring ruin on her house as Shahru did.
A lookout who is blind's of more use than
A children's nurse who hails from Khuzestan,
And those who follow crows will find they're led
To live in graveyards and among the dead."[49]
And then he turned to Vis: "This crone's to blame
For tricking you and ruining your good name;
You're willful, and your soul lacks common sense
Your eyes lack shame, your mind lacks reticence,
You've wantonly betrayed your marriage oath
And brought disgrace and ruin on us both.
Custom and faith are things that you despise
And you're contemptible in people's eyes;
Your actions won't be welcomed by your brother,
Or by your family, or by your mother –
You've shamed them, mortified them, one and all,
Making them wretched and despicable.
Destruction's wicked devils dwell inside you
Since you have had that evil nurse to guide you;
Children will dance as they're directed to –
That teacher showed you what you had to do!"

He had Viru brought in to him and said,
"Your sister needs to be more strictly led;
Put pressure on her, civilize her, tame her,
Punish her nurse a little, see you shame her,

Because if I'm to punish them I know
I'll go much further than I ought to go –
I'll hang the nurse, I'll burn out Vis's eyes,
I'll drive Ramin from Marv to exorcise
This sickness from my soul, and never say
His name again until my dying day."

Now see how jasmine-breasted Vis replied
To King Mobad's display of angry pride.
Fate washed her eyes of reticence, and she
Abandoned her habitual modesty;
She drew herself up from the royal bed,
And crossed her arms against her breasts, and said,
"You are a mighty king! Why should you fear
To punish me appropriately here?
All that you said is true, and you are right
To thrust my sins like this into the light.
If you desire to, banish me or bind me,
If you desire to, murder me or blind me,
If you desire to, have your men display me
Stripped in the marketplace, shame me or slay me,
But know that in both worlds Ramin will be
My life, my soul, for all eternity,
My heart's peace and my eyes' light, and my friend,
My love, my lord, forever without end.
And if I die for love of him, I give
My loving soul for him for whom I live;
Know I will not give up his love till I
Am forced to give up life itself and die.
And what are Mahabad and Marv to me
When set beside that slender cypress tree?
The sun and moon are in his countenance,
And hope and pleasure live within his glance,
Ramin is dearer to me than Shahru
And more essential to me than Viru.

I've told you all the secrets of my soul,
Now rage at me, or act with self-control,
But you can hang me and I will not cease
To love Ramin. I am your subject, Vis,
And I accept that I am ruled by you
And by my noble brother, Prince Viru;
I will not argue, should Viru decree
To have me burnt, or to imprison me,
And if, as you may do, my sovereign lord,
You end my life now with your royal sword
My name will live forever, I'll be known
As one who lived her life for love alone,
Throughout posterity I will be seen
As Vis who gave her soul for Prince Ramin,
And I would give a hundred souls to be
Remembered in this way eternally.

But if the lion lives, who'd dare destroy
His den, and kill his cubs, his pride and joy?
A thousand years might pass, and who would dare
To kill me, knowing Prince Ramin is there?
I have the ocean in my hands, what fire
Could make me shrink from seeking my desire?
You can divide us from each other when
You find you're capable of making men.[50]
I have no fear of death or pain, and you
Should think of what it is that you can do."

Hearing this speech Viru was horrified
And wished that hearing it he could have died.
He took Vis to his house, and privately
Reproached her for her infidelity:
"Vis, this was not an unimportant thing
To shame me in this way before the king.
Have you no decency to say you're glad
Ramin is with you now and not Mobad?

Why have you chosen him? What have you seen
That's so extraordinary in Prince Ramin?
What can he boast of? Pretty melodies,
Harps, lutes, and suchlike trivialities.
If he has any special competence
It's on the lute and other instruments,
But people never mention him unless
To comment on his rowdy drunkenness.
He pawns his clothes for wine, his friends are Jews[51]
Demanding money for his tavern dues –
I can't imagine what peculiar whim
Has made you want to fall in love with him.
But think of shame and heaven, don't indulge
In acts that it's degrading to divulge.
Why should you bring disgrace upon your mother,
And why should you embarrass me, your brother?
You have inherited a noble name,
Don't tarnish it by acting with no shame.
Don't give both worlds away for him, don't make
Yourself the devil's plaything for his sake;
You say Ramin is sweet, but heaven is far
More sure and sweet than mortal lovers are.
I've told you what I know, now make your peace
With God and with your husband. Farewell, Vis."

And as Viru berated her, Vis wept.
She answered him, "My brother, I accept
The truth of all you say, the noble tree
Whose fruit you've gathered here is honesty.
But now my soul has fallen in this fire
And wise advice can't cancel my desire;
My heart is broken and no man can mend it,
My love is fated and no words can end it.
Why lock the doors now to discourage theft
After the thief has robbed my house and left?

Ramin's love binds me now, nothing can sever
The love that I shall feel for him forever:
If you should say, 'Decide between these two,
Ramin's face and God's heaven,' I swear to you
I'd choose Ramin's face over heaven, since he
And his dear face are heaven itself to me."
Viru decided further argument
Was casting pearls in front of swine;[52] he went,
His heart suffused with grief, and left her to
Whatever conscience and her God might do.

When, like a golden ball, the sun rose high
Into the circle of the turning sky,
Mobad rode with his courtiers to the space
Where rival polo teams met face to face,
And struck a polo ball onto the field
To see which side could make the other yield.
Mobad reviewed his men and chose a score
For his team, while Viru chose twenty more:
Mobad chose Rafida and Prince Ramin,
While with Viru Arghash rode, and Sharvin,
And other noblemen agreed to ride
With Prince Viru, or on their sovereign's side.
The ball was put in play, and soon it rose
To Saturn's circle from their mallets' blows,
But all the back and forth was now between
Viru on this side and on that Ramin,
They put the other noblemen to shame
And with their skills divided up the game.

Accompanied by the women of the court
Vis went up on the roof to watch the sport,
But of those horsemen she saw only two –
Ramin on this side and on that Viru.

Now sick at heart, she frowned, her face grew pale,
She trembled like a cypress in a gale;
Like pearls on petals tears rolled down her cheeks.
The nurse said fulsomely, "Dear Vis, who seeks
To let the devil rule her as you do?
Why do you weep now, what's got into you?
Isn't the queen Shahru your noble mother?
Isn't your champion here Viru your brother,
Your husband King Mobad? Wasn't Qaren
Your honored father, and the best of men?
Aren't you acknowledged here as beauty's sun,
Aren't you the cynosure of everyone,
Queen of Iran and of Turan, admired
In both great countries, and in both desired,
The envy of the sun and moon, a queen
Whose lover is the handsome Prince Ramin?
And if you have a hundred griefs, when he
Is next to you they vanish instantly.
Why do you call on God, when he has given
You here on earth the wondrous joys of heaven?
What can you ask of God? What might he give
That could be sweeter than the life you live?
You've beauty, youth, authority, and wealth,
You have your lover, and you have your health;
This wanting more continually will bring
Your ruin, and you'll forfeit everything.
Don't do this, Vis, try to be satisfied
With all that Destiny and God provide.
Don't rage against the king, or vex Viru
With all the irritating things you do,
These drops will gather to a storm one day
And in their fury sweep us all away."

But cypress-statured, jasmine-scented Vis
Waited until the wet-nurse held her peace,

Then answered her, "Dear nurse, when will you tire
Of seeking water in the midst of fire,
And saying things that make no sense at all,
And recommending what's impossible?
Haven't you heard the adage that a fight
Seems easy when it's safely out of sight?
And there's that golden saying, 'No one knows
Or really cares about another's woes.'
You're like a rich man on his horse, while I
Must trudge on foot as you pass proudly by,
You're like a healthy man, while I must groan
And nurse my hideous sicknesses alone;
You have no notion of my pain. You claim
I'm lucky that I bear a royal name;
My husband is a king, you say, but he
Thinks only envious, evil thoughts of me;
He is a husband, but he's weak and old,
He's heartless, and cantankerous, and cold.
Viru's suspicious of me; oh, it's true,
There's no one who's as splendid as Viru,
But he's not there for me now, is he nurse?
To me, he's cash in someone else's purse.
And then there is the noble prince Ramin,
My handsome lover; but, nurse, you have seen
How glib he is; his wealth is blandishments,
A smooth tongue, and deceitful eloquence;
His words seem sweet, but put them to the test
And they're a bitter morsel to digest.
And now, a hundred times, I must discover
I have a hundred lovers and no lover;
Brother, husband, and lover – I've all three,
And all three are a burning fire to me.
I'm famous for my husbands, and my name
Is now a byword for love's grief and shame;

This husband and this lover both torment me,
Heartbreak and horror are the gifts they've sent me,
What is a golden bowl to me if I
Must fill it with my blood until I die?
    If Fortune had befriended me, Viru
Would be the only love I ever knew.
I'd live with him, and I would not have seen
These faithless friends Mobad and Prince Ramin,
One harsh as grief, seeking revenge alone,
And one as smooth as glass, as hard as stone;
One a dissembler, whose bland words and heart
Distrust each other and stay far apart,
And one whose callous words and heart agree
To act together in reviling me."

King Mobad returns from Kuhestan to Khorasan

How sweet the land of Khorasan: live there,
And let the world go by without a care!
In Pahlavi the two words "Khor," "asan"
Mean "Where the sun comes up"; throughout Iran
The sun comes up from Khorasan, and so
In time it came to bear the name we know.
How sweet this name is, its bewitching grace
Is suitable for such a lovely place,
Whose soil is fruitful and whose streams are clear.
As April's the most charming time of year
So Marv, of Khorasan's towns, is the best –
The spirit there feels pampered and caressed;
Its soil, and flowing streams, and limpid air
Would make you say that Paradise is there.
Now when Mobad came back from Kuhestan
And took up residence in Khorasan
He went up on his palace roof with Vis,
Like Solomon with Sheba's queen Bilqis.[53]

They sat there and looked out across the plain,
And as the king surveyed his lush domain
Its silver blossoms sparkling far and wide
Seemed like an image of his lovely bride.
He smiled and gently said, "Look, Vis, this place
Resembles in its loveliness your face;
Look at its orchards, gardens, vineyards, streams,
Its flowers and blossoms. Now, Vis, say which seems
More beautiful: your Mahabad or here?
To me the answer to my question's clear;
Marv is a place of beauty and delight,
As lovely as the starlit sky at night,
As though God, in creating Marv, had given
The earth a place men might mistake for heaven.
As Marv outshines your Mahabad, so you
Should understand that I outshine Viru;
I've many lands like yours, and in these lands
Many Virus submit to my commands."

But Vis was like a lion in her boldness
And answered him with calculated coldness:
"I wish you well of Marv, and good or bad
It's yours; if you delight in it I'm glad.
But Marv to me means anguish and despair,
I'm like a fawn here, trapped within a snare.
You wouldn't see me if I hadn't seen
The face of my belovèd, Prince Ramin;
What's Mahabad or Marv if I can see
Ramin's loved face, wherever I may be?
Deserts are gardens when he's there, and when
He goes they turn to deserts once again.
If it were not for him you could not say
That you beheld me, here, alive, today.
If I seem meek and ready to obey you
It's for my faithless prince, it's to betray you;

I can put up with thorns; thorns will disclose
In due course what we tend them for: the rose."

Bloodshot like blossoms then the king's eyes glared,
And saffron pale he gazed around and stared,
His heart glowed like a fire, his body shook
Like willow leaves reflected in a brook.
He longed to kill her, but good sense prevailed
And all his anger faltered and then failed,
Fate cast cold water on his rage, his knife
Could not deprive God's favorite of her life –
He stepped back from the lion, from the grim
Uplifted mammoth foot [54] that threatened him:
Vis too stepped back; see now how Fortune served her,
And shielded her from him, and so preserved her.
She was a treasure, hidden and unseen
By everyone, except her prince, Ramin.

Wisdom held back the king, but his voice broke
With pent-up rage and fury when he spoke:
"You're born from dogs, from noisome curs and bitches,
And you were raised by Babylonian witches,
My curses on the family of Shahru
And on the lands and wealth of Prince Viru,
Not one of you who's not a foul magician,
A loathsome devil who deserves perdition;
Snakes will give birth to snakes, and while it lives
Sour fruit is all a rotten fruit tree gives.
Shahru's spawned thirty brats in her foul den,
That's thirty brats by thirty different men –
Azarbad, and Farrokhzad, and your Viru,
Sasan, and Bahram Yal, and that Gilu,
There's Izadyar, and Gardan, and Ruin,
For girls there's you, Vis, Abnaz, and Shirin,

Born from a filthy dam and then what's worse
Raised by an evil and disgusting nurse.
And you are born from Jamshid's line, you claim,
If so you've stained your ancestry with shame.
Three roads are open to you now; take one,
Choose one of them, choose quickly, and be gone.
Go to Gorgan now, or to Damavand,
Or go to Hamedan and Nahavand,
But go, and may disaster follow you
And trouble dog whatever you may do,
And may you see a weary road ahead
Where you must beg for water and for bread;
May snow make every mountain pass defy you
May slithering snakes appear and horrify you,
May all your fruit be sour, may water which
You come on in your thirst be turned to pitch,
May lions haunt your path, and in the night
May ghouls be there until the dawning light,
May all the rivers that you meet be wide
And have no bridges to the other side!"

VIS RETURNS TO HER MOTHER

باز گشت ویس به مادر

VIS LEAVES MARV FOR KUHESTAN

Vis heard him out, and bowed, and in her heart
Rejoiced that she was able to depart.
She turned aside, and called her nurse, and said,
"Take this good news for me, go on ahead,
Say that I'm coming now to Queen Shahru,
Ask for a present from our king,[55] Viru,
Tell him his sister, his belovèd bride,
Is even now returning to his side;
Say that a glowing sun will soon arise
And shine on him from unexpected skies,
Tell him his loneliness is over, say
Two suns[56] from Khorasan are on their way.
Go to my mother for your next reward;
Tell her the moon's escaped its dragon lord,[57]
The dates are free of thorns, spring's vegetation
Is safe from winter and its devastation,
Good fortune has awoken from its sleep,
The precious pearl's been brought up from the deep:

Tell her I know that God has set me free
From King Mobad, and all iniquity."

Then she addressed the king: "My lord, may you
Meet with prosperity in all you do:
I wish you life eternal, joys unbounded,
And may you see your enemies confounded.
Marry a worthy wife, one you deserve,
A woman whom a hundred Vises serve,
One who surpasses me, and may you find
The sight of her strikes all your rivals blind,
A lamp in lineage and a shining sun,
Praised for her purity by everyone.
May you know greatness when you live without me,
May you be just when you don't have to doubt me,
Without you, may I live in honesty,
And know good fortune and felicity;
May all our days be prosperous and glorious
May all the world see both of us victorious,
And may we know such happiness and peace
That Vis forgets Mobad, and Mobad Vis."
She freed her slaves and handed back the key
That locked Mobad's imperial treasury,
And said, "Go, find a better treasurer,
A better spouse; I wish you joy of her:
May you be comforted when we're apart,
And may no further grief assail my heart."

Vis bowed before the king and then withdrew.
Immediately, the royal retinue
Was thrown into confusion; anguished cries
Resounded, tears filled all the courtiers' eyes,
It seemed when Vis announced that she would leave
All that the court could do was wail and grieve,

And weeping women crowded round to say
Farewell to Vis, and send her on her way.

The courtiers wept, but this was nothing to
The torment that Ramin was going through:
Now day and night he knew no peace or rest,
Each hour of weeping left him more distressed,
He wept for his poor heart, he wept for Vis,
And day and night his groaning did not cease.
He cried aloud, "Heart, what more will you do
To my poor soul that's been destroyed by you?
You've blackened all my days with grief and trouble,
You've bent the cypress of my body double;
You've known the bitterness of adoration,
The lover's life of sorrow and frustration:
You could not bear one day without her, how
Will you endure her endless absence now?
What bitter draughts of grief you'll have to taste,
What miseries will lay your body waste;
Prepare for pain, since separation's like
A vicious snake that lies in wait to strike.
She's gone, and where you fed on dates before
Thorns are your diet now for evermore –
Heart, you deserve to suffer, and the root
Of evil that you planted has born fruit.
And weep, my eyes; she's gone, and tears must be
Your only wares, your only currency:
Since it was you that saw her lovely face
And led me to be captured by her grace,
Now you must weep for separation's pain,
Now you must have your flowing teardrops stain
The roses of my cheeks, and leach away
The blackness from your pupils so that they
See nothing of the world – and this is right
Since only Vis was pleasing to your sight,

And it's appropriate that you'll be blind
As there's no other Vis for you to find.
If I am not to see her, may my eyes
Never behold the sun or moonlit skies,
I'll tear them from their sockets – if she's gone
What is there I could bear to look upon?
O Fortune, you're a lion, I'm your prey,
An onager that's wandered in your way;
A pleasant meadow seemed to stretch before me,
Where love would comfort me and reassure me,
But you lay prone there waiting patiently
To pounce and drag my love away from me;
Come, take my soul as well, I cannot use it,
What good is it to me? I'll gladly lose it!
You gave me all I longed for once, and then
Snatched all that you had given back again;
How cruel you are! You could not bear to see
Our joy in one another's company.
If Fortune's not unjust and envious
Why does it take back all it gives to us?"

And so Ramin soliloquized and wept
And in his heartsick anguish never slept,
Brooding on stratagems that might release
His mind from grief and bring him close to Vis.
He sent a message to the king that said,
"Six months I've weakly lain here, sick in bed,
But now my strength is coming back; I feel
That I grow sturdier and begin to heal.
For six months now my horses have been idle
And I've not seen a saddle or a bridle,
My cheetahs and my hounds have been asleep
Instead of coursing after mountain sheep,
It's six months since I saw my falcons fly,
Pursuing partridges about the sky.

My heart's grown tired of sloth; a man who lies
In bed all day is someone to despise!
Now if the king will give me his permission
I'll go out on a hawking expedition;
I'll go to Sari and Gorgan, and when
Six months have passed I will return again."

The king was too quick-witted to believe him,
And knew the prince was trying to deceive him;
He knew that it was not the court that made
Ramin grow faint and his complexion fade,
That hunting wasn't what he had in mind,
That Vis was all the prey he hoped to find.
He saw the message was a trick, a screen,
And gave an ugly answer to Ramin:
He cursed and swore and in his fury said,
"And may the world soon hear Ramin is dead!
May he set out and never reappear,
I'd rather have him die than come back here!
Tell him, 'Go now, do what you long to do,
And may bad luck and sorrow go with you;
May you meet mountain leopards, hissing snakes,
May your blood spatter stones and thorny brakes.
Vis loves Ramin, I know, Ramin loves Vis,
And you two think your love will never cease
Until in death you bid the world farewell
And sin will take the two of you to hell.
But listen carefully to what I say,
Take the advice I'm giving you today,
It tastes like bitter wine, but only try it
And you will see how you can profit by it.
In Kuhestan seek out a woman who
Is noble, virtuous, and who pleases you,
And marry her, and may your marriage be
A blessing to you both eternally.

Don't hanker after Vis; her lap will mean
A fiery dagger will dispatch Ramin;
I'll kill you both, I will not let my name
Be sullied by an evil brother's shame.
Listen, take seriously what I am saying,
A lion hunt is not the time for playing;
When clouds come, seek high ground – before the rain
Comes pelting down and inundates the plain."'

Now when Ramin received this message he
Swore by his hatred of all heresy,[58]
By all the radiant sun's refulgent light,
And by the splendid moon that shines at night,
By his devotion to the royal throne,
And by his sovereign's soul, and by his own,
That he would be obedient to Mobad
And never try to visit Mahabad,
Or see Vis, or endeavor to confer
With anyone who might be close to her.
He said, "You do not know, my noble king,
How I submit to you in everything
And that I would expect to lose my head
If I should deviate from all you've said."
This was the sugared message that he sent,
But all his words were false and fraudulent:
The moon-like Vis was his intended prey
And he was eager to be on his way.

RAMIN TRAVELS TO HAMEDAN TO BE WITH VIS

He left the city gates and left behind
Half of the grief that had unmanned his mind,
And as the breeze from Kuhestan caressed him
It seemed a heavenly scent that bathed and blessed him.
Happy the road for one who can discover
The way that leads directly to his lover,

Then all the hardships that the way discloses
Seem palaces, and gardens filled with roses,
And if the journey is a lengthy one
How sweet his lover's face looks when it's done!
So love impelled Ramin to undertake
This harsh task for its sweet conclusion's sake.

For her part, lovely Vis seemed withered now
A leaf that shrivels on a wintry bough;
Her Mahabad seemed like a loathsome place,
And straw-like pallor spread across her face;
She had no time for courtly elegance,
For splendid clothes, or jewelry, or sweet scents.
She could not eat or sleep, her soul's distress
Dispelled all hopes of joy or happiness,
None of the world's sweet pleasures now beguiled
He aching heart, she never laughed or smiled;
She saw a snake when she beheld her mother
And scorned the kindness shown her by her brother.
The dazzling daylight seemed a memory of
Ramin's bright countenance and tender love,
And night reminded her of his black hair
And eased the ravages of her despair.
She sat up on the roof, and night and day
Fixed her attention on the winding way
That led from Khorasan. "How would it be,"
She mused, " if dawn should bring a breeze to me,
And in that dawn a rider should appear
Making his way from Khorasan to here,
Tall as a cypress tree, a noble knight?
How would it be if I saw such a sight,
The noblest picture that was ever seen,
A splendid warhorse bearing Prince Ramin?"
And so she mused and grieved, and felt love's pain
Assail her heart and body once again.

And then one morning, as the sun's first rays
Lit up the landscape, her astonished gaze
Beheld a second sun beside the sun;
One came to cleanse the world of darkness, one
To cleanse his lover's heart of grime and grief.
Now as a sick man longs for some relief
Ramin pressed forward, till his arms embraced
His eager love, and they seemed interlaced
Like branches of a myrtle when it twines
About a box tree its meandering vines.
They wept for joy, and kissed in their embraces
The flowers and coral[59] of each other's faces.
They were like buds that open in spring weather
As walking hand in hand they turned together
And went into the house, where Vis declared,
"These royal rooms are mine, may they be shared
By you, my love; your search for jewels is over;
Your heart's desire is here, with me, your lover.
And may your heart know happiness, and peace,
And pleasure while you tarry here with Vis.
Wine will be yours, you'll toy here with my hair too,[60]
And you can go out hunting when you care to;
Hunting, I think, was why you came this way,
And, oh, how easily you caught your prey!
I am your deer, the pheasant that you aim for,
The cypress and the box tree that you came for;
Sit at the feet then of your splendid tree
And taste the happiness of hunting me.
We'll be together now, we'll banish sorrow,
And give no thought to what might come tomorrow;
We'll drink until the day's departing light
And lie in one another's arms all night,
Joy will be all we'll think of, and we'll live
To see what new delights our love can give;

We're young and fortunate, and we shall see,
And savor, Love's triumphant victory."

So seven months went by in which these two
Lived happily, and joy was all they knew.
Outside the winter had set in, and snows
Obscured the passes, and the hillsides froze,
But snug in Vis's rooms, the lovers spent
Their days in drunkenness and merriment:
Look how they lived, with not a moment wasted,
With not one jot of pleasure left untasted.

MOBAD LEARNS THAT RAMIN HAS JOINED VIS

Then King Mobad learned that, once more, Ramin
Had let his evil character be seen,
That he was now with Vis, and that they swore
Their mutual love would last for evermore.
("Eblis's[61] need for evil cannot cease,"
He thought, "nor Prince Ramin's desire for Vis;
If rabbits are transformed to lions he may
Grow tired of Vis, but not before that day,
When sparrows turn to hawks, he might discover
That he'd prefer to have another lover.)"
Mobad went in his anger to his mother
Complaining of the actions of his brother:
"Ramin is with my wife, this situation
Will utterly destroy my reputation:
Now tell me, is this right? Would anyone
Who's sensible defend what he has done?
How can two brothers share a wife? What shame
Is worse than this? He's ruined my good name!
I tell you this so that you'll comprehend
Just why my self-control is at an end;

Shame wouldn't let me tell you this before,
But I can't hide my trouble any more.
I'm telling you so that you won't berate me
When I have been revenged on him, or hate me:
I'll kill him, and your weeping eyes will be
Like clouds in spring that rain incessantly.
You're heaven and hell to me, but you can't blame
Your son now if he rids himself of shame.
Let Prince Ramin's blood wash my face, and then
It will be bright with honor once again."

His mother said, "What wise man would decide
To cut his hands off for the sake of pride?[62]
Don't kill Ramin; where will you find another
As necessary to you as your brother?
You'll have no ally when war comes, no one
To feast and drink with, when your brother's gone;
You'll take your seat with no one there beside you,
You'll be alone, with no advice to guide you.
You have no son to leave your kingdom to
And Prince Ramin must rule here after you,
Or, when God calls you, all your royal lands
Will fall into our rivals' greedy hands;
Isn't it better that Ramin should reign
In regal splendor over our domain,
So that our family will not cease to own
This country's royal revenues and throne?
Don't kill your brother; set the woman free –
Release her, and give someone else the key.
Beauties with silver breasts and musky hair
Can easily be met with anywhere;
Choose one, and with your heart give her the keys
That open your imperial treasuries,
So that in time a precious royal pearl
Will be the issue of this lovely girl,

And your auspicious union will bless
Your kingdom with an heir and happiness.
What princes do you hope that Vis might breed?
Granted, she claims descent from King Jamshid,
She has a royal lineage, this is true,
But then she has a hundred failings too.
Don't do this, calm yourself, and exercise
That moderation which makes mortals wise.
You'll find a thousand brides like Vis, why can't
You cut your heart off from this termagant?
And I've heard worse about her, I have heard
That since your recent falling out occurred
The brat has gone back to Viru, and they
Sit drinking wine together night and day;
That now she's happy, since she's got what she
Has always hankered after secretly.
Why do you persecute Ramin? Viru –
Not poor Ramin – has shamed and ruined you.
Ramin's in Hamedan because his heart
Can't bear that he and Vis should be apart;
Like you, he loves her; much good that will do him!
Vis acts as if she never loved or knew him.
But this is Vis, it's just her usual way,
She needs a different lover every day.
Her love won't last a month; she's beautiful,
But also wholly unreliable:
She's like a pretty rose whose charms won't last –
They flourish quickly and they fade as fast."

Now as Mobad sat listening to his mother
His heart relaxed a little toward his brother.
He raged at Vis, and at Viru; his face
Grew yellow at the thought of his disgrace;
He wrote then to Viru – his pen was like
A glittering scimitar unsheathed to strike.

He wrote, "Would you not say your attitude
To me is arrogant, unjust, and rude?
Whence comes this courage, this impertinence?
Who is behind your foolish insolence?
You are a fox, but now you act as though
You were a lion. You! Who wouldn't show
Resistance if a braying ass attacked you.
Who's put you up to this then? Who has backed you?
You're weak and worthless, yet you dare to seize
My wife as if we two were enemies:
I'm well aware that she's your sister too
But what's she doing in your court with you?
Where have you heard a wife can have a pair
Of husbands? It's as if a single hair
Should bind two raging elephants when they
Chafe uncontrollably to get away.
I haven't seen your city for a while:
It may be you've grown stronger, that your style
Is now more manly that it was before;
But I've not heard of any famous war
In which you've fought, of any petty king
You've conquered, and who's now your underling;
Of any enemies you've crushed, or lands
You've taken that submit to your commands,
Or towns that you've subdued. I haven't heard
From friends or enemies a single word
Of your accomplishments or victories.
And I suppose you know your family's
The kind that can't sustain its luck, that when
It's doing well it soon sinks down again?
It's like a barren mule, whose only pride
Is what it boasts of on its mother's side.
I've seen you hunting, and I've seen the show
You make then with your arrows and your bow,

I've seen you put your horses through their paces
Playing at polo, or in friendly races,
And I don't doubt you play the man at night
Among your women, safely out of sight.
But fighting's an entirely different story –
There, it appears, you're not so keen on glory,
There, like a woman, you turn tail and run,
Eager to get away from everyone:
A lion in Mahabad it seems; elsewhere
A cowardly fox can drive you from its lair.
Have you forgotten then the blows I gave you,
When you collapsed as if no help could save you?
Have you forgotten all my cavalry,
Savage as lions in their ferocity,
Like thunder in their charges? Groans and sighs
Still rise from Mahabad into the skies
From all the devastation that they wrought.
My sword and strength, the soldiers who once fought
To scour the world of all my enemies,
Stand ready still, to call on when I please.
Know when you read this letter then, Viru,
My sword's still thirsty for your blood and you.
I've heard of all your boasting, how you say,
'The king leapt like a lion on its prey
When I was drunk and fast asleep; if not,
If I'd been there, I would have foiled his plot,
He'd never have abducted Vis from me.'
Now that you're sober and at home we'll see
How well you fight. I've told you what I'll do –
I am determined to make war on you.
Give all your spies and scouts their marching orders,
Send out commanders to protect your borders,
Gather a massive army from Iran,
Azerbaijan, and Rey, and great Gilan,

Prepare your fighting men till I attack
And break their serried ranks, and drive them back.
Throw all your wealth away, you might as well,
I'll break your forces and they'll flee pell-mell.
They'll scatter on the wind, you'll fight in vain,
I'll turn your country to a level plain
Piled high with corpses, where a raging flood
Will flow, a Tigris of your people's blood:
And don't imagine I'll let you survive,
This time Viru will not remain alive.
Then like a dog I'll drag your Vis before
The soldiers who have triumphed in this war;
Unshod, unveiled, her public shame will be
A lesson for her in humility."

Immediately the messenger had gone
Mobad informed his court of what he'd done,
Then he and his imperial retinue
Made preparations to attack Viru.

MOBAD TRAVELS FROM KHORASAN TO HAMEDAN

At dawn the trumpets blared, and like an ocean
The mighty army trembled into motion,
As if the Oxus flowed from Khorasan
And took its winding course to Kuhestan,
And their encampment seemed to block the way
The moon took as the night encountered day.
They seemed a mountain on the move, that weighed
The earth down with the progress that they made,
Or you would say they were the massive wall
That Gog and Magog made impassable.
The messenger pressed on, always ahead
Of King Mobad, who followed where he led.

Viru received the letter, and he felt
The strength within his limbs dissolve and melt:
Blood filled his eyes, and to his clouded sight
The shining world became as dark as night.
He said, "What is this rubbish he's confessed to,
And who is all this blustering addressed to?
He takes my sister to his harem, then
When winter comes he throws her out again:
He hits us, and protests that he's been hit,
And makes two provocations out of it.
My sister is his wife, and yet you'd say
That she's his enemy in every way –
He doesn't care what miseries befall her
And doesn't send a letter to recall her.
He's in the wrong, and yet he turns on us;
How is this just? The man's ridiculous!
As for his boasts…he isn't brass or stone,
How dare he make these threats against my throne!
He brought his army here once and he knows
That I can give and take a warrior's blows;
I sent him packing then, and he became
A byword for embarrassment and shame.
Our battle wasn't secret, words won't change it,
What happened happened, he can't rearrange it:
I broke him once, his forces weren't so tough,
So why should he come here to huff and puff,
And make a fuss with this unseemly show?
Why should two warriors fear a broken bow? [63]
I've never heard of such a foolish tale.
I'm not afraid though, let *his* courage fail;
Wise men are well aware that fighting me
Is not to be embarked on carelessly."

VIRU SENDS HIS ANSWER TO MOBAD

The answer that Viru prepared to send
Was sweet at first, but bitter at its end.
He said, "Renowned and warlike sovereign, you
Can do whatever you desire to do;
But what have these desires brought? Consternation,
Grief, sorrow, and a ruined reputation;
You are a king, men hurry to fulfill
The slightest indication of your will,
And so your will should be a moderate one
With knowledge guiding everything you've done.
My lord, as our superior you should weigh
With care and custom all the words you say:
Wise men speak soberly, my lord, they seek
To further truth and justice when they speak.
You are more wise than other men, but still
Your heart's tormented by your vengeful will –
And we are allies, friends; it isn't right
For friends and allies to prepare to fight.
Well, you can say such things, but as for me
I can't regard you as my enemy.
You threw your wife out, you can't pin the blame
On someone else and ruin his good name;
There's no need for a letter, you can make her
Go anywhere you wish, so come and take her.
Tell me to send her home, and I'll obey,
I'll send her back to you without delay,
But, on my soul, since she arrived I've sat
With her three times I think, no more than that;
And as your wife's my sister why can't she
Associate with me, and sit with me?
Don't taint me with this evil accusation;
Consider carefully my reputation,
Let reason judge me fairly, and you'll see
Such evil things could not be done by me.

So much for Vis; I've told you what I can,
And you're aware that I'm an honest man.

   As for our wish to have a noble name,
Our shared desire for honor and for fame,
How many boasts you make of martial glory,
What flourishes you use to tell your story!
You're proud of Dinavar? I fought there too
More fearlessly and valiantly than you.
You say the selfsame sword you used to kill
Your enemies is at your service still –
But if your sword's of iron you can be sure
Mine's not of wood; I'm ready too for war.
Your sword splits helmets and chain mail, you claim;
With rocks and anvils my sword does the same.
You ask if I've forgotten your attack
That robbed me of my strength and drove me back;
I think this was a dream you'd hoped to see,
You never saw it in reality.
Your letter claims my exploits as your own,
Your foolish lies demean your crown and throne;
Boast all you wish, but if the army hears
Your letter's claims they'll answer you with jeers.

   Then you deride my father's lineage
As less than my maternal heritage,
But sense, and wisdom, and a fighting spirit,
Not the fine family name that we inherit,
These are the qualities that bring men fame;
When battle's joined, what good's a noble name?
Come then, and face me on the battlefield,
And you'll see soon enough who's forced to yield.
My sword will speak for me, and I won't say
A word of self-praise when we fight that day;
Lineage and boasting are worth nothing when
Army commanders field their fighting men.

Attack with courage now, not words, and we
Shall see to whom God gives the victory."

His messenger was soon confronted by
A forest of tall spears that thronged the sky,
And, like a cloud of kohl, dust filled the air.
He found Mobad and his companions there,
And when the king had read the letter through
He paused, as if uncertain what to do:
He'd thought Viru and he were rivals for
The love of Vis, and so had threatened war,
But as he read the missive through he felt
Remorse unman him, and his anger melt.
At once he sent a message to Viru:
"I see that ugly talk has slandered you,
You've put my anxious mind at rest, and I
Acknowledge that I trusted in a lie.
I've no need for my warhorse now, I'll ride
The horse of friendship till I reach your side,
And spend a pleasant month with you – so make
Your castle ready, for our friendship's sake,
And when the month is over you will be
My honored guest and stay a year with me.
Deliver Vis to me, and may you find
No enmity against me in your mind,
Since she's my sister now, and you're my brother,
And splendid Shahru is my noble mother."

Now when Mobad's reply had reached Viru
And countless gifts had come for Queen Shahru,
Rancor's cruel demon hid his ugly face
And friendship's roses opened in its place,
Kindness awoke and raised its sleepy head,
And concord's waters filled the riverbed.

Now sun-like Vis was given to Mobad
And every heart that witnessed this was glad;
A month passed with such pleasure that you'd say
The court was honoring their wedding day.
Wine, hunting, polo filled their time, and then
Mobad and Vis set out for Marv again.

MOBAD REPROACHES VIS

As King Mobad re-entered Marv, the sight
Of Vis beside him filled him with delight;
Her face was now his sun, her lovely tresses
Seemed like the scent that purest musk possesses.
But then one day he came to sit beside her
And started to reproach her, and to chide her:
He said, "You only stayed in Mahabad
Because Ramin was there, and you were glad
To be with him; but if he'd gone away
You wouldn't have remained there half a day."
And sun-like, silver-breasted Vis replied,
"Which charge should I reply to? You decide:
Sometimes you say that I was with Viru,
And being with him seems a sin to you,
Sometimes you say that I was with Ramin,
Which of these accusations do you mean?
But hell is not as hot as people claim
Or Ahriman[64] as ugly as his name,
A thief's a thief, but then men have to add
Their gossip too, and say he's twice as bad.
You know Viru is virile, young, and strong,
And loves to be out hunting all day long,
And when he's not out on the plain he spends
His time carousing with his closest friends.
Ramin's just like Viru, they were together
Through thick and thin, in every kind of weather,

Like brothers they were never seen apart,
Each the companion of the other's heart:
Youth loves the sweet society of youth
And has no dearer wish than this: in truth,
God fashioned youth as if it breathed the scent
Of heaven and the starry firmament.
For six months Prince Ramin and Prince Viru
Were bosom friends in all they wished to do,
Indoors and out, hunting or drinking, they
Shared everything they could in every way –
Ramin was like a brother to Viru,
And like a loving son to Queen Shahru.
Not everyone who's friendly hides within
His heart a secret hankering for sin,
Not all men are malicious and unkind,
Not all men have your mean, suspicious mind."

The king replied, "All this is excellent
If you and he are really innocent;
Ramin deserves my praise, and so do you,
If you can swear that all you've said is true."
And Vis replied, "Why should I hesitate?
A solemn oath would be appropriate.
An uncommitted sin cannot alarm me,
And swearing I am guiltless will not harm me:
Garlic I haven't eaten cannot make
My mouth stink, so I'm not afraid to take
This solemn, sacred oath that you suggest,
Don't be afraid, my lord, I'll pass your test:
An oath's like drinking water,[65] if one's sure
One's acts and thoughts are innocent and pure."

The king said, "This is how it ought to be,
An oath will indicate your purity:

Swear then, and you'll escape from all the blame
That's sullied and besmirched your noble name.
I'll light a blazing fire, and you will swear
Before our priests and nobles gathered there,
As musk and aloes wood diffuse their scent,
That you are guiltless, pure, and innocent.
And once you've sworn this oath your soul, dear Vis,
Will be exonerated and at peace,
Never again will I reproach or chide you,
Revile you, or abuse you, or deride you.
You'll be my world, my soul, my life; my land
Will then be yours to govern and command,
Since what is finer than when sovereignty
Is joined with innocence and purity?"

Vis said to him, "Do this, and make us both
Guiltless and pure by this momentous oath.
Nothing but harm can come to you while you
Call into question everything I do;
And certainly it's better to deny
Even real vices than believe a lie."
And so the king sent out a summons for
His nobles, priests, and counselors in war.

MOBAD GOES TO THE FIRE TEMPLE, WHILE VIS AND RAMIN FLEE TO REY

He gave more presents to the temple than
Could be computed by the mind of man:
Gold coins and jewels, orchards and mills, and stocks
Of grazing cows and sheep in countless flocks,
And mettlesome fine mares, and tracts of land –
All these were given now at his command.
He brought a flame lit from the temple fire
To where his men had built a massive pyre,

And as the sudden flame sprang up they stood
With aloes wood, musk, camphor, sandalwood,
To feed the blaze until it seemed to rise
And be a partner of the turning skies:
It was a golden dome, a wondrous sight
That shook with incandescent flakes of light,
A lovely woman in a crimson dress
Strutting and roaring, wild with drunkenness,
Splendid as when she meets her love, and burning
With all the heat of separation's yearning;
Filling the world with dazzling, brilliant light,
Banishing darkness and the shades of night.
But men and women had no notion why
The king had made these flames assault the sky.

Although not one of all the nobles who
Were in attendance on their sovereign knew
Why he had had this conflagration lit
Or who or what was to be burned by it,
High on the palace roof, Vis and Ramin
Observed the fire, and knew what it must mean.
"Look at the state of this pathetic man,"
Vis said. "Isn't it obvious that his plan
Is that we'll perish on this flaming pyre?
But why should we accede to his desire?
Come now, let's leave him here and let him be
The one who burns, in flames of jealousy.
His sweet words tricked me yesterday, but all
His wily stratagems won't make me fall:
I tricked him too, I told him I would swear
A hundred times and more to him that there
Was never any link of love between
The princess Vis and noble Prince Ramin,
And I repeated this till he believed
My story and was glad to be deceived.

And now he wants to show his people I'm
A woman who is innocent of crime.
'Pass through the fire', he says, 'and demonstrate
To all the world your pure and virtuous state,
And let the nobles and the peasants see
That they've believed a vicious calumny.'
But we should leave before he summons us;
Let him remain deceived and credulous."
Then she addressed her nurse: "What do you say?
How can we flee this fire and get away?
This is no time, dear nurse, to stand and fight,
This is a time for prudence and for flight:
You're expert at deception, what do you
Advise the two of us that we should do?
Where can we hide ourselves? Who will befriend us?
Where's there a prince and army to defend us?"
"How should I know?" the wily nurse replied,
"This knot is not so easily untied.
Your situation's risky, you'll require
God's help, and luck, if you're to flee this fire;
What's done is done, your only remedy
Is to depart, and quickly! Follow me."

Look at her cleverness: she had them bring
Gold coins and jewels belonging to the king,
Then, from the harem roof, she led them to
The bathhouse, where there was a secret flue;
Their hearts on fire with hope and fear, they went
Into the garden through this hidden vent.
Ramin soon scrambled up the garden wall,
Unwound his turban's length[66] and let it fall,
And grasping one end helped them up, and then
Helped each one down the other side again.
He jumped down after them, and dressed as they did,
So that his face was veiled like theirs and shaded,

As if the three of them were demons who
Deliberately hid themselves from view.
Ramin knew that a gardener lived nearby;
He sought him out and asked him to supply
Horses for all of them, and what he could
By way of armor, hunting gear, and food.
All he required was brought him, and as night
Came quickly on the three resumed their flight:
They rode from Marv toward the setting sun
Swift as the wind, unseen by anyone.
The arid wasteland where disaster waited,
The dragon's gaping maw that's never sated,
Was made by Vis's and Ramin's sweet faces
Into the loveliest of charming places,
And from their scent the desert seemed to be
A tray of perfumes in a pharmacy.
Now, to the lovers, all this barren waste,
The fierce simoom, the countless trials they faced,
Seemed like a garden filled with sweet delight
So dear to them was one another's sight.
So quickly time passed, they were unaware
Of sand and stones and burning desert air:
In China is inscribed, "Where lovers dwell
Is heaven, even in the depths of hell."
When lovers clasp each other, in their eyes
Rank ugliness is beauty in disguise,
Deserts are gardens, snowdrifts in their sight
Are orchards filled with pleasure and delight;
A lover's like a drunkard, joy and pain
Mingle and merge together in his brain.

Ten days and nights they journeyed on their way
Westward from Marv, until they came to Rey
Where Prince Ramin possessed a bosom friend,
A man whose riches seemed to have no end,

A generous, chivalrous companion whose
Appropriate name was "Fortunate" ("Behruz").
It was a moonless and a starless night,
The moon and sun were hidden from men's sight
As though the world were like a well in which
The air had taken on the hue of pitch,
As Prince Ramin sought out the splendid gate
Whose owner was well named as "Fortunate."
And when Behruz saw Prince Ramin, surprise
And disbelief stood in his wondering eyes:
"This is the finest sight I've ever seen,"
He said, "To have a guest like Prince Ramin!"
Ramin replied, "But, brother, do not fail
To hide my presence with deception's veil;
Tell no one that I'm here, let no one see
That you've a guest, and that the guest is me."
Behruz was chivalrous and said, "I'm sure
It's my good luck that's brought you to my door:
I am your servant's servant, and I live
To execute the orders that you give:
I will vacate my house if you desire it,
My home is yours as long as you require it."

And so the host Behruz, Ramin, and Vis,
Sat happy and secure, their minds at peace;
The shut door meant their hearts could open wide.
With wine the lovers rested from their ride,
Their days now passed in pleasure, and each night
Was filled with joy and mutual delight:
They drank their wine, then lay down face to face,
And drank wine in the midst of their embrace.
Vis like a splendid shining torch now lay
Within her lover's arms till break of day,
And slept till Venus rose, and music woke
Her gently from her sleep, and morning broke:

The last night's wine still lingered in her head
And wine was served her as she left their bed.
Ramin sat with her, it was he who'd made
The music that awoke her as he played
Sometimes a lute, sometimes a harp, and blent
In song his sweet voice with each instrument,
Singing of love in heart-delighting strains,
Dwelling on love's sweet pleasures and its pains.

He sang: *"We are two lovers who would give*
Our lives and souls to have each other live,
Our loyalty is worth kings' treasuries,
Our love impales the eyes of enemies,
And as we live in joy and happiness
They live in grief and torment and distress.
We cannot tire of love, nothing will make
Us leave the road we travel for love's sake,
In love we're like two lamps diffusing light,
Two gardens filled with blossoms and delight;
Our love brings only joy to us, since we
Have shown that we deserve love's victory.
How happy Vis is when Ramin is there,
A partridge by a hawk, a pretty pair;
How happy Vis is when she drinks her wine
And drunkenness and loveliness combine;
How happy Vis is with Ramin, how sad
The hopeless, broken heart of King Mobad;
How happy Vis is when she laughs, and when
Ramin's lips touch her open lips again;
How happy Vis is to be drunk, aware
Love is the faith Ramin and she now share!
Long live Ramin, since you have found a way
To hunt down Vis as your bewitching prey;
Long live Ramin, and may you never cease
To know love's joys with your companion, Vis;

Long live Ramin, since paradise is here,
Where spring flowers flourish all the livelong year;
Long live Ramin, since she you've sought and won
As your companion is the glorious sun!
A thousand blessings light on Mah, the place
Where moon-like Vis first showed her lovely face;
A thousand blessings on its queen, Shahru,
The mother of dear Vis and Prince Viru;
A thousand blessings on its king, Qaren,
Her father, whom we shall not see again;
A thousand blessings on her pretty wiles
That make the world the servant of her smiles!

Bring me a bowl, dear Vis, that's filled with wine[67]
As flushed as you, as delicate and fine;
When I take wine from you it cannot hurt me,
Vitality and strength will not desert me.
What makes me drunk with such desire for you?
Your face, your love, the wine? I wish I knew!
But this I know, that poison from your hand
Will give me life, not death: at your command
All joy and all contentment come to me,
And you erase all grief and misery.
My heart is like a casket, where I hide
A precious jewel, my lovely Vis, inside;
My arms are like a zodiacal sign
Within which, as its star, you reign and shine;
And may this radiant jewel, this glittering star,
Remain secure forever where they are;
And may my laboring hands forever nourish
The garden of your face and make it flourish.
How long will men recall our story's fame
And wondering wisdom marvel at our name!
Such beauty and such love deserve to be
Renowned and honored for eternity.

My heart, how much you've suffered and endured,
But love is here now, pleasure is assured,
You've found a heart that brims with equal love,
A face as radiant as the sun above;
Gaze on it then, adore it day and night,
And pass your time in sweetness and delight,
But see you arm yourself against your foes,
Since love consists of mingled joys and woes;
Where sweet dates flourish, painful thorns abound,
And where delight is, sorrow's also found.

Give all your soul for love, in all the earth
You won't find anything of greater worth;
Love is the meaning, the predestined goal,
Of all the world, and of the human soul.
Drink wine then, banish thoughts of pain and sorrow,
Since God will send whatever comes tomorrow:
It may be love will bring a better fate
Than you dare hope for, or anticipate."

So Prince Ramin drank wine and sang, while she
Delighted in his charming company.
But while Vis lived in joy and happiness
Mobad knew only suffering and distress,
And in his grief still cherished his desire
To have her undergo the trial by fire,
And with this trial of hers to break apart
The chains of doubt that bound his aching heart.
Now, as he vainly searched for her, the light
Of day for him was turned to darkest night;
He scoured the world for Vis, his heart aflame
With grief, suspicion, and a husband's shame.

The sun had darkened for Mobad since Vis,
In leaving, had deprived him of all peace,
His brother Zard, his trusted minister,
Ruled Marv, while he set off in search of her.
He chose a horse so swift it seemed to fly
As quickly as the clouds across the sky,
Sharp swords, and diamond arrows, and strong bows
Intractable as hearts of heathen foes;
And as he rode across the lonely plain
He murmured, "Vis, Vis, Vis," as if in pain.
He went through India, and through Iran,
He searched Byzantium, and all Turan,
And always asked for Vis, but found no trace,
No news, no sign of her in any place.
Now like a goat he climbs the mountainsides,
Now in the meadows like a lion he hides,
He is a demon in the desert sands,
A snake in marshy reeds; through countless lands,
Traversing trackless forests, dangerous seas,
Through arid plains, and mountain fastnesses,
For five long months he prosecutes his quest
Like someone madness won't allow to rest.
Cold pierces him, then he's assailed by heat;
He eats with anyone whom he might meet,
And dines on shepherds' milk, or he is fed
By travelers willing to divide their bread.
He hardly sleeps, his pillow is his hand,
His mattress is the unforgiving land;
For five months now the road across the plain
Is his companion, and his friend is pain.

He beat his head with stones, he wept hot tears,
And wandered on alone, beset with fears;

Weeping like rain clouds he cried out, "Alas
That such misfortunes ever came to pass!
I've thrown away my kingdom, all I own,
I'm left here powerless, broken, and alone;
I've squandered wealth and sovereignty, and all
For one who still remains unreachable.
The path I travel is so harsh and grim
At every step I seem to lose a limb,
And I've endured so much adversity
I feel my very soul's deserted me.
The wind's a fire that roars about my head,
The earth is iron everywhere I tread;
All that I see that's fine and wonderful
To me is ugly and contemptible,
And to my worn-out heart even the air
Seems poisoned and mephitic everywhere.
Age is not made for love, so how should I,
At my age, weep for love, and rage and sigh?
Love makes a young man old, and now I find
That in an old man it destroys his mind.
      I chose a heaven on earth, and oh, how well
I know that now she's gone I live in hell!
When I remember how she's treated me,
Her vicious cruelty, and her treachery,
I find I love her more, as though it were
Her faults themselves I loved, as much as her.
My heart is blind now to the world's delight,
Its loveliness is hidden from my sight;
Before I loved her I was strong, my eyes
Saw justly, I was capable and wise,
But now, in love, my foolish frailties mean
I see, and don't know what it is I've seen.
Alas for my departed reputation,
Alas for all my hardship and frustration!

The wind has mocked my struggles, and desire
Has filled my soul with everlasting fire.
Do men now wash their hands of me, and blame
My passion for the loss of my good name?
What does the world say? Do men think I'm mad
And say there's no one crazier than Mobad?
Surely I must be mad to wander here,
Among wild onagers and timid deer?
Why did I listen to an enemy
When she was mine at least, and lived with me?
And if I cannot bear to be without her
Why can't I yield to her, and cease to doubt her?
If I should ever see her face again
My seal and crown are hers, and she shall reign;
I'll bow to her, I'll be her slave, I'll make
Myself an abject servant for her sake;
And now I wear Love's earring[68] I'll comply
With all she asks of me until I die."

So five or six months passed; his strength was gone,
And still he forced his weakened body on,
But then he feared that he might die alone
Or that an enemy might seize his throne.
He thought he should return to Marv and cease
To prosecute his pointless search for Vis,
And live in hope that some day he might find
Some trace of her to ease his troubled mind.
So he retraced his steps to Marv, and men
Rejoiced that he was now their king again:
It was as if a mendicant had found
A heap of gold, or rain fell on parched ground.
The streets were filled with cheerful decorations
And pretty girls thronged all the celebrations;
So many coins and jewels were thrown away
The poor of Marv grew wealthy in a day.

Ramin writes to his mother, and Mobad hears of this

Now while Mobad had chosen to disown
His sovereignty, his palace, and his throne
To wander through the barren wilderness
And search for lovely Vis in his distress,
Ramin, who'd spent the months he was away
Concealed with his companion, safe in Rey,
Wrote to his mother, who seemed dressed in joy
To hear once more from her belovèd boy
(Since both the king of Marv and Prince Ramin
Were sons of this renowned and virtuous queen,
While Zard, Mobad's advisor and their brother,
Had, as I've heard, a Hindustani mother).
The wind of Mehregan[69] does not blow faster
Than this quick messenger sped from his master.
He entered Marv in secret; no one knew
That he'd arrived or what he planned to do.

Feeling herself abandoned and bereft
The queen had wept since both her sons had left,
But when she heard Ramin's swift messenger
Was now in Marv, her life returned to her.
The letter said, "Dear, good, and noble mother,
I'm cut off from the world now by my brother;
He wants to murder me, he's like a knife
That threatens to deprive me of my life.
His anger's fastened on both Vis and me,
And he's become our open enemy.
To me a hundred brothers can't compare
With one strand of my moon-like Vis's hair,
She gives me only pleasure, while his glance
Disdains me with contemptuous arrogance.
My life is sweet for me when I'm not near him,
And when I'm with him all I do is fear him.

Our parents are the same, so why should he
Act like the heavens and sun and moon to me?
I'm just as good as him; I'd make him yield,
And fifty like him, on the battlefield.
Away from hateful Marv my time is spent
In laughter, pleasure, games, and merriment;
But he's a cheetah[70] when I'm at his court
And I'm the deer he chases for his sport.
And this is not enough for him, to see
Me trapped and trampled by adversity,
He has to threaten us with fire as well;
And why? He's not the lord of heaven and hell!
But here I'm happy and I live in peace,
Content to drink my wine and be with Vis.
I've sent this secret message to ensure
That you won't fret about me any more;
The world's grief passes, and I'll see that you
Are kept informed of everything I do.
I'll go about the earth until I hear
The king's no more, and then I'll reappear;
When King Mobad vacates the royal throne
Fortune will help me claim it for my own,
His soul's not fastened to a granite mountain,
He hasn't bathed in life's eternal fountain.
And if he lives a while I'll bring him down
By force of arms and seize his royal crown.
I'll share the throne with Vis then; you'll soon see
The truth implicit in my prophecy,
And when the things I've written here come true
Tell me, 'There never was a man like you!'
Accept the greetings Vis now sends you, they
Are sweeter than a rose at break of day."

His mother read the letter through, and shed
Tears of delight and wonder as she read;

Mobad returned home on the following day
And she was then so happy you could say
She seemed to fly with joy: such is our fate
To vary constantly our human state.
Lucky the man who learns that while we live
Our joy and grief must both be fugitive:
See in your suffering that you don't complain
Since, when you call on Fate, you call in vain;
Know that your days of joy are nothing more
Than an illusory, brief metaphor.

HIS MOTHER TELLS MOBAD ABOUT VIS AND RAMIN, AND WRITES TO RAMIN

A week passed, and Mobad resumed the throne
But he could hardly bear to be alone;
When his advisors left, the demon thought
Deranged his mind as if he were distraught.
And then one night his mother questioned him,
"Why do you look so sorrowful and grim?
What makes you melt with grief? What troubles you?
Aren't you Iran's king, and Turan's king too?
And don't the world's lords bow to you, and pay you
Taxes and tribute, happy to obey you?
From Qayravan[71] to China's distant shores
The land, and all you need from it, is yours.
Why all this grief? What is it that you seek?
How can you bear your soul to be so weak?
An old man puts away the dreams of youth,
He cares for virtue, righteousness, and truth.
Age and white hairs protect a man, and he
Forgets the sins youth sought so avidly –
In you though, as you age, desire grows stronger;
My poor heart can't endure this any longer!"

The king replied then, "Mother, you might say
My heart's my enemy in every way;
From all the world I chose a woman who
Gives me no rest whatever I might do;
If I advise her she pays no attention,
She treats my love with scornful condescension,
She's made me search six months for her, she's made me
A mass of misery since she's betrayed me;
My soul despairs that I must live my life
Deprived forever of my longed-for wife:
And I've no heart for war now, only Vis
Can comfort me and make my sorrows cease.
Should she return I'll happily confer
My seal ring and my royal crown on her,
And I'll obey the orders of my love
As surely as I bow to God above:
I will forget her sins, and all my pain,
I'll never mention them to her again.
As for Ramin, I wish him well: he'll be
My brother and a bosom friend to me."

And when his mother heard this you would say
Fire fastened on her grieving heart that day:
Her tears were pomegranate seeds[72] upon
Her saffron cheeks, so withered now, and wan.
She clasped his hands in hers, "Swear you'll abide
By all that you've just said to me," she cried,
"Swear you won't spill their blood, swear now that Vis
And Prince Ramin can flourish here in peace,
Swear it, swear you won't threaten them or harm them,
Swear that your sudden rages won't alarm them;
Because I've news of them, news that I'll share
With you, as soon as I have heard you swear."
Now joy transformed the features of the king
That opened like a tulip in the spring,

Before his mother's feet he bowed his head,
And kissed her hand a thousand times, and said,
"Rescue me, Mother, from the flames of hell,
From this cruel agony in which I dwell;
Command me, and my head won't pull away;
My heart submits to you; I will obey."

He swore then by their faith, by wisdom, by
The puissant God who rules the earth and sky,
He swore by those whose souls had gone before
And would be honored now for evermore,
He swore by fire and water, earth and air,
By knowledge, by the justice that men share,
That he would never seek to harm Ramin,
That Vis should live with him and be his queen:
His private quarters would be hers at night,
And she would be his solace and delight;
Her former sins would be forgotten, he
Would treat her with respect and dignity.
As soon as King Mobad swore he and Vis
Would live in amity and be at peace,
His mother sent an answer to Ramin
Recounting everything she'd done and seen.
More valuable than jewels, and much more sweet
Than sugared dishes when men sit to eat,
Her letter said, "My darling, listen well;
A mother's orders are both heaven and hell,
If you defy my words you can be sure
That hell will be your home for evermore –
As soon as you have read this, hurry here.
Life will return to me when you appear;
My eyes are blind with weeping, and believe me
I feel my soul is ready now to leave me.
My soul's lamp gutters, and my heart encloses
Only the remnants of spring's withered roses:

My face is in the dust[73] until I see
The splendor of your face restored to me.
It's you I long to glimpse, since all the earth
Has no one dearer or of greater worth.
The king too pines for you, and you would say
Grieving has made his body waste away;
He saw your value when you'd gone, and spent
His time in voluntary banishment
Wandering the world; what pains and miseries
Mobad endured, and what indignities!
Now he's returned, and seeing you will give
His sorry soul the strength again to live.
He's sworn a solemn oath that you will be
The partner of his power and majesty,
His favorite brother, and his first delight,
As precious to him as his soul and sight;
And as you rule in public Vis will reign
Within his private quarters once again.
She'll be his queen, you'll be a mighty lord
Commanding all his kingdom with your sword;
He'll find no fault with anything you do
But, like a father, he will comfort you.

      And you, for your part, should not be afraid,
Or angry, or suspect you'll be betrayed.
You might have wealth, but living among strangers
Depletes your riches and is fraught with dangers;
Since you can rule in Khorasan, why should
You go elsewhere to seek your livelihood?
This country's like a paradise men say,
And God has made you from this country's clay;
Now you're the ruler here, how can you face
The thought of living in another place?
Strangers must worry about everything
And what is sweeter than to be a king?

A mine of jewels waits here for you, so why
Seek other jewels beneath another sky?"

Quick couriers took this answer from the queen
And bore it straightaway to Prince Ramin,
Who asked for news of her, and of Mobad,
And read the words she'd written, and was glad.
As soon as he had learned about the oath
That promised peace and safety to them both
Ramin and Vis set out for Marv from Rey:
Ramin rode, while his comely lover lay
Inside a litter like a pearl that's set
Within a splendid royal coronet.
So lovely was her face, so sweet her scent,
The way seemed musk and tulips where they went,
And though the litter hid her from men's sight
She seemed a full moon shining in the night.
Gently the loving, dewy air caressed her,
A thousand pearls of glistening starlight blessed her.
For five, six months she'd lived at ease, away
From pallid moonlight and the garish day –
Pure as a water drop, she'd grown to be
As lovely as a slender cypress tree.
For every grace she'd had, a hundred more
Had now been added to the peerless store,
And when the king beheld her beauty he
Forgot the world, and power, and sovereignty,
And as he saw more loveliness in Vis
He felt his love proportionately increase.
His grief departed; this demonic creature
Seemed to take on a sweet, angelic nature,
And once again they gave themselves to joy,
Counting the world as nothing but a toy,
Possessed of all that happiness requires
And nourishing with wine the heart's desires.

The love of King Mobad, Ramin, and Vis
Now seemed to banish grief and promise peace;
Amity was restored, rancor was driven
Out of their hearts, and past sins were forgiven.
One day the happy king sat down to dine
Holding a crystal goblet filled with wine
As ruby red as Vis's blushing face
That shone beside him with bewitching grace.
He summoned Prince Ramin, and sat him there,
And looked with pleasure at the lovely pair.
While Vis's comely face seduced his sight
Ramin's harp charmed his hearing with delight;
The prince played with such skill you'd say he'd make
Stones float on water for his music's sake,
And Vis flushed like a rose as Prince Ramin
Sang of the troubles that his heart had seen.

"O wounded heart," he sang, "this too will pass
And you're not made of stone or burnished brass,
Do not despair, or quarrel with your friend,
Or show your anguish, since this too shall end.
Let wine and music charm you, and beguile
Grief from your heart, and comfort you a while.
Let wine lay sorrow's dust, since if you live
Sorrow's not everything that Fate can give;
This selfsame Fate that you complain of must
Ask pardon from you, and at last be just.
For many a day you will rejoice, set free
From all this anguish and anxiety –
And if the world has changed your state, it too
Must change again, as you have had to do."

Wine weakened wisdom in their monarch's head.
"Give us a love song, something sweet," he said,
The tender song that Prince Ramin began
Would lift old sorrows from the heart of man.

He sang: "*I saw a walking cypress tree,*
I saw the full moon and she spoke to me,
I saw a garden in the spring, a site
Worthy of love's attentions and delight,
I saw a rose there so magnificent
You'd say that heaven was in its hue and scent,
A rose to comfort you in your distress,
A rose to share your joy and happiness.
I gave my heart to it and said that I
Would be the gardener there until I die.
I walk among its tulips day and night,
The springtime's blossoms open in my sight,
While those who wish me ill are forced to wait
Glued like its knocker to the garden gate.
Why should the jealous envy me? God gives
His just desserts to everyone that lives:
Heaven deserves the moon, so God has given
The shining moon's magnificence to heaven."

Hearing this song, Mobad forgot his pain
And felt his love for Vis revive again.
Hoping that drunkenness would scour away
The rust that eats existence day by day
He asked Vis for a cup of wine: she said,
"Great king, may blessings rain upon your head,
May victory and joy crown all your days
May all your acts be worthy of our praise;
Today it's right that we should drink to you
And call down blessings on the deeds you do,
And it would also be appropriate
For my dear nurse to share our happy state –

Since no one loves you so wholeheartedly,
And she should join us here, if you agree."
The nurse was duly summoned and assigned
A seat before the couch where Vis reclined.
The king declared, "Ramin, you serve the wine,
Friends serving wine is an auspicious sign."
Ramin was happy to comply and went
About the court dispensing merriment;
He drank too as he served, and soon he felt
The wine had made his inhibitions melt.
As he gave Vis her wine he whispered, "Take
This wine, dear angel, for affection's sake;
Drink it with pleasure now, since wine will nourish
The fields where love is sown and make them flourish."
Her heart rejoiced, and – as she hoped – unseen
By King Mobad, she smiled at Prince Ramin.
She said, "May Fortune guide you, may the field
You cultivate in love's fair country yield
A handsome harvest, and may you and I
Know ever greater love until we die.
Choose me, and no-one else, within your heart
As I choose you, and may we never part:
Rejoice in me as I rejoice in you,
Remember all our love, as I shall do,
May both our hearts be mines of joy, while fire
Consumes Mobad's with sorrow and desire."

It happened that Mobad had overheard,
Despite their caution, every whispered word,
But kept his heart controlled, and outwardly
Acted with self-restraint and chivalry.
Mobad addressed the nurse, "You serve the wine,"
And to Ramin he said, "You should confine
Yourself to love songs, they spread happiness:
Take up your harp; sing more, and chatter less."

So while the nurse poured wine, Ramin poured out
All of his heart's affliction, love, and doubt.
The song he sang was subtly sweet and fine,
May you sing such a song when you drink wine!

He sang: *"The pain of separation's made*
My face take on a sickly, yellow shade;
May wine restore its ruddy hue, and may
Wine scour my soul's corrosive rust away –
So that my enemies perceive no sign
Of all my sorrows hidden by the wine.
Her face has made me drunk, and day and night
Wine is the solace of my helpless plight –
I give myself to wine continually
In order to forget my misery;
What comfort can compare with wine, that heals
All of the sorrows that a sufferer feels?
But still, it seems, my love is well aware
Love's fire has branded me with love's despair,
And that, though I can fight with lions, I
In love's encounters must consent to die.
O God, who knows the grief I suffer here,
As you make night depart and day appear,
May you disperse these sorrows in my heart,
And bring me joy, and make my grief depart!"

His voice together with his harp's sweet tones
Were piteous enough to soften stones,
And all the love he'd thought to hide away
Seemed to be obvious now and on display,
Since hearts that are ablaze must twist and turn
And show the anguished grief with which they burn.
Love joined with drunkenness, and these two fires
Were fed by youth's impetuous desires:
How could Ramin show calm and resignation
When placed in such a perilous situation?

Clutching his harp, young, drunk, in love, to see
His love beside another – how could he
Continue to prevaricate and hide
The wild emotions that he felt inside?
Just as when water rises it will ooze
Around whatever barriers men use,
So love cannot be cabined or confined
By admonitions or a clever mind.
Drunk now with wine, Mobad in triumph led
Vis to his night apartments and their bed,
And in his room Ramin lay down alone
Upon a bed that seemed as hard as stone.

Mobad's heart ached; he loved and hated Vis
And, in his cups now, he berated Vis.
He said to her, "Alas that not a trace
Of love accompanies your lovely face:
You're like the springtime of a fresh young tree
Whose pretty blossoms are a joy to see,
But whose sour fruit is bitter fare to eat.
To see you and to hear you, Vis, is sweet
But bitterness mars everything you do.
I've never known of anyone like you;
Though I've seen brazen women here and there
I've not known anyone who could compare
With you for shamelessness; I've never seen
A woman act as you do with Ramin.
The two of you sit opposite my throne
And carry on as if you were alone!
But bitter is the fate that lovers find
And bitterness has always made them blind;
A hundred others can be there but they
Think no one sees the things they do and say,
And some small clod of earth they sit beside
Will seem a crag behind which they can hide:

And this is you two lovers, unaware
Of how your shamelessness makes people stare.
But Vis, don't be so impudent with me,
Impudence makes a friend an enemy:
Your king might be a donkey, but don't ride him,
Don't publicly abuse him and deride him!
Kings are like fire, or so the proverb says,
And fires can flare up in a sudden blaze:
Wild lions and elephants don't dare attack
Where flames erupt and threaten to strike back.
Don't think the sea will always be at rest,
Look at it when its combers plunge and crest;
Don't be so brazen, Vis, this wall you trust
Will, at my anger, crumble in the dust.
I've suffered much for love of you and known
The bitterness of being left alone;
How much must I endure before you cease
To twist this sword within my vitals, Vis?
Stop treating me so ignominiously
Since your disdain harms you as much as me.
    But if, one day, you free me from this chain,
And show me love, and pity all my pain,
I'll treasure your sweet love; for happiness
I'll give you everything that I possess,
Then Khorasan and Kuhestan will be
Your provinces, beneath your sovereignty,
And you will be a sun diffusing light
Within my private chambers every night.
I'll see the world through your eyes, you alone
Will be the mistress of my seal and throne;
You'll rule this land, and I will be content
With nothing more than clothes and nourishment."

When stubborn Vis had heard him out she felt
Her heart within her burning body melt,

And soft compunction that she had distressed him
Sweetened her answering words when she addressed him.
She said: "May nothing now, in any way,
Divide me from your presence for a day:
My bond with you, my lord, is sweeter than
Such bonds could be with any other man.
I place my eyes beneath your feet, the earth
You tread upon is of far greater worth
Than Prince Ramin to me; my lord, believe me
I take no joy in one who would deceive me;
You are the sun to me, why should I find
The pallid moon more pleasing to my mind?
You are the rivers and the mighty seas,
All other kings are but your tributaries,
You are the sun, all other kings adore you
And strew the way with opening flowers before you.
If I deserve to serve you, may I be
Yours now, my lord, as you belong to me;
And don't imagine I intend to leave you,
Complain to you, or break my oath, or grieve you;
Your love's my soul to me and, as you know,
When once the soul goes life itself must go.
The past is past my lord, from now on I
Will strive to keep you happy till I die."
Mobad felt pleasure and astonishment
That Vis could be so kind and eloquent.
A sweeter, softer breeze than blows in spring
Seemed to revive the spirits of the king,
And as he fell asleep, weighed down by wine,
Hope sprang up like a sprig of eglantine.

But while Mobad slept Vis lay thinking of
Mobad, and then Ramin, and all their love;
As she was thinking she had never seen
A man who could compare with Prince Ramin,

She heard a noise come from the roof above.
It was Ramin, made wretched by his love,
Whose passion had persuaded him to rise;
Patience had left his heart, and sleep his eyes.
The night was overcast and dark, as though
It were a soul consumed with hopeless woe,
And from the winter clouds that gathered there
Snow fell like camphor[74] through the gloomy air.
Clouds veiled the shining moon and hid from sight,
Like Vis's face when veiled, its lovely light;
The air wept that the moon could not be seen
As Vis's absence drew tears from Ramin –
To him the moon occluded by such gloom
Was like Vis hidden in her husband's room.
He sat down on the roof's edge, and the dart
Of hope was lodged within his wounded heart.
His love transformed the snow to wondrous roses,
The darkness to the light that dawn discloses,
The roof to palace halls, the sodden earth
To silks and satins of unequaled worth;
And though Vis was not there he was content
That in his mind he could recall her scent.
What keener pleasure do you know of than
When love's afraid that some malicious man
Will chance on what is happening, and discover
Who the belovèd is and who the lover,
When she will be despised, and he will say
The scandal is another Judgment Day?
Although the night was dark and cold, Ramin
Was unaffected by the wintry scene –
The fire of love burned in his heart, wet snow
And rain could not abate its ardent glow,
A hundred rivers there for every drop
Could not have made his blazing passion stop,

And all his tears together with the rain
Threatened a storm to inundate the plain.
His burning heart and soul now sought release
For all their passion with a song to Vis.

He sang: *"Oh, is it right that you're abed*
While snow and rain pour down upon my head?
Squirrel and ermine make a cosy cover
Where you lie warm beside another lover,
While I wait here alone, trapped in the mire
Of love, and grief, and comfortless desire.
You sleep, and have no knowledge of the fears
A lover feels, or of his desperate tears!
Fall, snow, upon the fire within my heart,
Since suffering's right when lovers are apart,
And if I sigh the force of my desire
Will burn the clouds and earth with raging fire.
Blow, winds, about the earth, let Vis's hair
Lift from her pillow, twisting in the air,
Drive sleep now from her lovely eyes, and make her
Start from her bedding; jolt the world and wake her!
Convey my song into her ears, explain
My heartbreak to her and my hopeless pain,
Tell her my wretchedness, and let her know
I sit alone here in the wind and snow
Where even enemies would pity me –
And may my plight provoke her sympathy."

Vis heard a movement, and became aware
Of Prince Ramin's voice in the wintry air:
Love welled up in her anxious heart, and she
Dispatched the nurse to him immediately,
And till the nurse came back again you'd say
Impatience drained poor Vis's life away.

Quickly the nurse returned, said what she'd seen,
And brought a lovelorn message from Ramin:
"My love, you're drunk on lovers' blood, you're tired
Of all the passion that you once desired;
What have you drunk that you should now neglect me?
Why do you scorn my love now and reject me?
I am the man you saw, so why aren't you
In love and faithfulness the Vis I knew?
You're in brocade and fur, I'm in the snow,
Pleasure is yours while grief is all I know,
You live in happiness and I in sadness,
You live with luxury and I with madness:
Is this what God decreed? Your happiness
And comfort, my affliction and distress?
May it be so then! May you always find
Comforts to ease your body and your mind,
Since you're too delicately made to bear
The torments that accompany despair.
It's I who suffer, I who must behave
With all the resignation of a slave.
Enjoy yourself, since joy's your due, my queen,
But know the sufferings of your slave Ramin:
My captured heart can never now work loose
From your black, musky hair's encircling noose,
And in the night's dark watches that I keep
My heart's deprived of rest, my eyes of sleep.
Scrambling on walls and rooftops, I adore you,
I'm like a madman in my longing for you;
Don't wreck my hopes, turn night to day, allow
Your lover to take refuge with you now,
(What sweeter refuge is there than to hide
Safe from the winter at a lover's side?)
Show me your splendid face, show me you love me,
Spread your hair's musky shadow now above me,

And let the silver of your breasts be pressed
Against the golden contours of my chest,
Since gold and silver have no greater grace
Than when they're seen together in one place.
My love for you has made my poor heart stray
Into a pit of grief; don't turn away,
Don't laugh at my afflictions now, don't tear
The veil of patience that obscures despair,
And with the dagger of your tyranny
Pierce my poor soul, and then abandon me.
If you will give me hope I swear that I
Will be your willing slave until I die."

As soon as Vis heard Prince Ramin's lament
Her heart seethed like a vat where grapes ferment.
"Nurse, you must use your skills for me," she said.
"How can I leave Mobad alone in bed?
We're ruined if he wakes and looks for me.
There's only one solution I can see:
You'll have to take my place beneath the covers,
You two must lie there, side by side, like lovers.
Just turn your back on him; he's drunk, the wine
Means he won't know your body's form from mine;
Besides, they are alike; he might, it's true,
Caress you, but he'll never know it's you.
Given the drowsy, drunken state he's in
How could his touch distinguish skin from skin?"
She made the nurse lie in her husband's bed,
Then seized the chamber's lamp, and quickly fled
Up to the roof, on fire to see her friend,
Where, with a kiss, she made his sorrows end.
She tore away the fox and squirrel fur
That might have sheltered and protected her,
Baring her silver bosom to the rain;
And, as she shed her clothes, she shed the pain

That had oppressed her heart. In spring you've seen
Narcissi next to roses – so Ramin
Lay next to Vis, so Jupiter might lie
Beside the full moon in the evening sky.
Their cheeks brought tulips to the earth, their scent
Perfumed with musk the starry firmament;
The dark clouds parted, and the stars came out
To watch what these two lovers were about –
Whispering secrets now, and happily
Delighting in each other's company.
They'd lay their heads on Vis's arm, and then
On Prince Ramin's, and then on hers again;
They were like wine when it is mixed with milk,[75]
Or satin thrown together with fine silk,
Or two snakes twined together – and what bliss
Can equal lovers twined as one like this?
Cheek against cheek, lip against lip, they lay
Consumed with kisses and sweet amorous play,
So closely bound no hair could pass between
The bodies of fair Vis and Prince Ramin.
Playing together, and in greedy sips
Sucking the sugar of each other's lips,
These happy whispering lovers passed the night
In secrecy and mutual delight.

Meanwhile Mobad, as yet still unaware
That his belovèd was no longer there,
Awoke and touched the woman at his side.
No slender cypress lay there, but a dried
And withered reed; how could a bent bow be
Mistaken for an arrow? How could he
Not tell the nurse from Vis? Who could mistake
Sharp thorns for softest silk? Now wide awake
He roared like thunder, seized her hand, and said,
"What demon are you, lurking in my bed?

Who put you here? Who laid you at my side?
How is it I've a devil for a bride?"
He called his servants, crying out for light,
For lamps and torches to dispel the night,
Then said again, "What kind of thing are you?
What is your name? Tell me, who are you? Who?"
But all this while the nurse said not a word,
And all his shouts for torches went unheard
By everyone except Ramin, who kept
A wakeful vigil while his lover slept,
Kissing her lips (rubies and sugar met),
Weeping above her (jewels made blossoms wet),
And thinking of the dawn when all the pain
Of separation would be theirs again;
And sweetly, to himself, within his heart,
He sang a song of how they'd have to part:
"O happy night, driving all cares away!
To others night, to us the sweetest day,
And when day comes to others with its light
That day for me will be the darkest night!
Now dawn draws near; prepare yourself, my heart
To feel the pain of separation's dart –
How sweet this work would be, if assignations
Did not lead on to heartsick separations!
Evil is all you know, O world, since when
You give us joy you snatch it back again;
How pleasant your first wine tastes! So we think,
But then we see it's poison that we drink.
How evil was the day love's sweetness first
Entered my hopeful heart; may it be cursed!
I launched my skiff then on the waves, and thought
I'd welcome all the storms my journey brought –
But when I'm with her my uneasy heart
Fears for the time when we must be apart,

And when we're parted, I can't bear the pain
I suffer till I see her once again.
O God, I know that there is no one who
Can help my heart, in all the world, but you!"

So the prince sang, and made his sorrow more
By wistful thoughts than it had been before.
He saw sweet sleep had snatched his love away,
And on their mutual pillow where she lay
Pink pomegranate flowers were gently spread,
And hyacinths were clustered at her head.[76]
But now the king's cries reached him, showing he
Had stumbled on their tricks and treachery,
And quick as fire Ramin began to shake
His lover till she sat up wide awake:
"Quickly," he said, "be on your way! Alas,
The evil that we feared has come to pass!
The wine put you to sleep, but as you slept
Thank heavens I remained awake and wept,
Weighed down by grief that we would have to part,
Sorrowing for you in my hopeless heart:
I feared one evil, and a worse one's here –
I heard the king shout and I thought my fear
Would make me faint, I felt so frail and weak.
But now my heart revives, I hear it speak:
'Go, pull your foot out from this mire,' it says,
'Go down and end your wretched brother's days,
Cut off his head!' I swear, my love, you'll see
His blood means less than does a cat's to me!"
"Ah, not so fast," Vis said, "caution requires
That you pour Wisdom's water on these fires;
The day will come, and no blood need be spilled,
When all your heart's desires will be fulfilled."
Then like an onager that darts away,
Fleeing the lion who's tracked her as his prey,

She sped down from the roof to trick the king;
Now watch how well she managed everything!
She stole into their room and made her way
To where her ranting, drunken husband lay.
"You're mauling my poor hand," she said, "so please,
For a moment, take my other hand to squeeze."
He heard her voice and didn't understand
That he'd been tricked; he dropped the nurse's hand
(She sped off from the shameful trap) and said,
"But why have you lain silent in our bed?
You set my heart on fire with worry, why
When I asked questions didn't you reply?"
Once Vis was sure the nurse was safe she found
New courage in her heart and stood her ground.
She cried, "For months and years my enemy
Has kept me here and made a slave of me;
I can go straight, or twist round like a snake,
It doesn't matter: any route I take
It seems that I've gone wrong, they're all the same
Because it's always me who is to blame!
I pray that no poor woman ever find
The man she's married has a jealous mind,
Because she'll soon see that her jealous master
Is always on the lookout for disaster;
I'm sleeping in my husband's bed, and he
Begins insulting and accusing me!"

Mobad expressed remorse and said, "Dear Vis,
Don't think my love for you could ever cease;
You are my life and sweeter than my life,
My guide to happiness, my dearest wife.
It was the wine that did it! Why did I
Not swallow spears instead of wine and die?
But it was you that plied me with the wine
So this misfortune's all your fault, not mine.

Vis, may I never prosper if I doubt you:
Forgive me, Vis, I cannot live without you.
Drunks sin because wine makes them ignorant;
They should be pardoned when they're penitent.
As sleep will close a person's weary eyes
Wine closes sense and makes a man unwise;
As water washes clothes, sincere repentance
Will mitigate the guilty sinner's sentence."

Then Vis, the sinner, deigned to hear his pleas
And to acknowledge his apologies.
But so it is in love – the lover must
Humble himself and bow down in the dust;
When his belovèd sins it's he who pleads
For her forgiveness for his sinful deeds,
When she refuses to forgive him he
Redoubles his requests' intensity.
The master bows in love before his slave,
The lion in love forgets how lions behave
And turns into a fox that seeks to hide
The rage and fury that he feels inside;
A lover's fury's blunted by his love
Now matter what his lover's guilty of.
Let no one plant the tree of love, whose shoots
Grow into poisonous and bitter fruits.

RAMIN COMES TO VIS IN THE DEVILS' FORTRESS

آمدن رامین به در دیلان شیروسیس

MOBAD LEARNS OF AN ATTACK BY THE ROMAN EMPEROR AND MARCHES TO MAKE WAR ON HIM

This is the custom of the world, to hate
The progeny its processes create,
Summoning and dismissing in a day,
Bestowing gifts and snatching them away;
Its bitterness and sweetness are allied,
Blessings and curses spring up side by side,
Night's twinned with day, riches with poverty,
And joy's the partner of catastrophe;
There is no happiness without distress,
No triumph that's not joined to wretchedness.
Read now this tale of Vis and her Ramin,
In which the world's ways can be clearly seen,
Giving now pleasure, now adversity,
Their faithful friend, and then their enemy.

No sooner had Mobad acquitted Vis
Than both of them were ambushed by Eblis,[77]

Who dowsed the lamp of love and violently
Uprooted Happiness's noble tree.
Mobad learned that the emperor of Rome,
Forsaking both his treaties and his home,
Had chosen evil ways, deceit, and lies:
Thinking to raise his head above the skies;
He'd marched on Persia, and destroyed both land
And livelihoods beneath Mobad's command.
A mob of refugees appeared at court;
They heaped dust on their heads, and wailed, and sought
For justice from the king, for some defense
Against the emperor's malevolence.
Mobad, responding to their wretched state,
Resolved to fight, and so eradicate
The weeds that were about to overwhelm
The cultivated orchard of his realm.
He wrote a letter to his chieftains then,
Summoning them to muster fighting men
And bring them to his palace; in due course
These levies made so huge a fighting force
Marv's spacious plain appeared to be too small
To welcome and accommodate them all.
A tucket sounded as the signal for
The king of king's departure to the war;
His progress was an autumn wind that left
Marv a stripped garden, dreary and bereft.

As he set off he thought again of Vis
And how his mind was never now at peace
Because she loved Ramin so much, and how
These lovers' hearts seemed twinned together now.
"She ran away from me before," he said,
"And left me wretched and as good as dead;
It's best I keep her under lock and key,
The grief I suffered then exhausted me.

Once was enough; I couldn't bear the pain
If I found out she'd fled from me again.
A man who's sensible, who heeds advice,
Doesn't get bitten by the same snake twice;
Hobbling a camel's much less hard to do
Than finding one that's wandered off from you."

As all these fears and fancies filled his head
He called his brother Zard to him and said,
"I love you as I love my life and sight,
Say if you've seen or heard of any knight
Who's done what Prince Ramin has done to me,
Making me loath my life and sovereignty.
I burn in fire, I have no hope or peace
Because of him, and Vis's nurse, and Vis.
I'm in their hands, these sorcerers control me,
And nothing now can cure me or console me –
They have no fear of prison or of chains,
Of God's decrees, or hell's eternal pains;
What can be done with fiends who've no idea
Of what men mean by modesty and fear?
They act just as they wish, no shame restrains them,
No fear of scandal or disgrace detains them.
I might be king of kings, but I've not known
A man with greater troubles than my own;
What use is being powerful and rich
When daylight is to me as black as pitch?
While I give justice to the world, my cries
For justice rise unheard into the skies,
And I, who've made so many plaintiffs quake,
Now bow and tremble for a woman's sake.
        But my injustices spring from my heart
That loves my enemy, and takes her part –
The world's allied with her, and longs to spill
My blood to satisfy her evil will;

A hundred seas can't wash away the shame
That clings to me and blackens my good name.
Here is a woman whose infatuation
Has dimmed the sunlight of my reputation –
She waits on one side for me; on the other,
His dagger at the ready, there's my brother
Watching for when the opportunity
Presents itself for him to murder me,
And I've no notion of what Fate will send
Or how the life I'm living now will end.
My soul seems lost, suspicious fears possess me,
Day follows night, and still my doubts obsess me;
Why should I seek out enemies in Rome
When enemies are lurking in my home?
Why shut the door against a rising tide
When all the water's coming from inside?
Now, in old age, affliction's come to me
And wiped the world out from my memory.
But I must fight, and leave Vis here, who'd break
Through brass and iron for her prince's sake.
　　　I see I have no choice but to ensure
That Prince Ramin comes with me in this war,
While Vis remains in Devils' Fortress, where
Her wailing will give vent to her despair.
With Vis immured and Prince Ramin away
These two can't settle on a trysting day.
The Fortress will be under your command,
My heart knows you'll rule justly in this land,
And I don't have to tell you, 'Be on guard!'
But double all of your precautions, Zard:
Watch these two witches [78] well, Ramin is sly
And who knows what deceitful tricks he'll try!
My journey will be lengthy, and my aim
Is that these battles will augment my fame,

But if Ramin should visit Vis I'll see
Not fame but shame attach itself to me.
Two hundred build a house up, wall by wall,
But one's enough to make the building fall –
Three sorcerers live in my home, and they
Play more tricks than a thousand devils play,
You've seen how their deceitful wiles destroy
All my heart's hopes of happiness and joy;
Their spells have ripped my name to rags, they've torn
To shreds the cloak of patience that I've worn.
A man who's drowning in mid-ocean knows
One third of all my agonies and woes."

Zard said, "You're wise my lord, the words I hear
Are more exalted than the lunar sphere,
But don't torment yourself like this, such sadness
Can only lead to maladies and madness.
What is this woman that you weep for her,
And groan and moan? She'll be my prisoner;
If she's an Ahriman of magic, she
Will still be weak and pliable to me.
No wind will reach her in that sheltered place,
The sun and moon won't shine upon her face,
She'll be alone; she won't see anyone
Till you return with all your battles won.
As misers hoard their gold, so I'll protect her;
As nobles honor guests, so I'll respect her."
Mobad and seven hundred warriors brought
Vis to the castle that would be her court.

The Devils' Fortress:
Ramin learns what has happened to Vis

The Fortress soared above a crag so high
It seemed a mighty tower that touched the sky:

Hard as an anvil stood each stone that made it,
No file could smooth such granite or abrade it;
So wide, it seemed that half the world was there;
So tall, it towered into the upper air;
The moon and stars were like the burning light
Shed by this massive candle in the night;
To stand there was to be the confidant
Of moonlight and the starry firmament,
And when Mobad brought Vis it was as though
A second moon lit up the world below;
The fortress seemed a censer, Vis's face
The fire that glowed in that restricted space –
The charming mole upon her cheek became
A fleck of ambergris within the flame:
The prisoner's beauty made the prison shine
Like gardens where spring's blossoms intertwine.
The king then locked five massy doors upon
Vis and her nurse, and sealed them one by one,
The royal seals were ratified by Zard
Who was to be the prisoners' watchful guard.
A hundred open coffers filled with treasure,
Provisions for a hundred years of pleasure
Awaited them; it was a wondrous scene
That only lacked one thing for Vis – Ramin.

Mobad returned to Marv, to make plans for
His army and its journey to the war.
He led an iron mountain, every man
Was braver and more mighty than Bizhan,[79]
And all were laughing, joking, as they went
Except Ramin – whose passionate lament
Unmanned him, and whose feverish heart was like
A partridge when a falcon's talons strike.
The dust of longing made his visage grim,
Silk and brocade seemed like harsh thorns to him;

His soul despaired of Vis and, broken-hearted,
He wished his body and his soul were parted.
Restless by day and sleepless through the night,
Weary and wounded in his wretched plight,
Communing with his heart he softly said:
"What is this love, that fills me with such dread,
That never yields, or weakens, or grows less,
From which my heart has known no happiness?
Since love's been my companion I've not seen
Good Fortune shine for me. Luck's left Ramin!
If once it stuck cruel thorns into my heart
It's now lodged there a mortal, poisoned dart.
She's separated from me now, what peace
Or patience can I know, deprived of Vis?
I've been unfaithful to our love – when I
Saw that she'd gone from me I did not die,
How stony-hearted I've become, how strong,
That I can live without her for so long!
Better to be without my soul than see
The world without her face to comfort me;
My friends, what state is worse than to prefer
Death to a wretched life deprived of her?
My soul and sight were hers, without her I've
No wish to see the world, or stay alive."

So he complained of how his fortunes went
And inwardly began a new lament:

"Sigh, heart, since you're in love. No judge can force
Desire's injustice to reverse its course!
Who pities lovers? Who is moved or cares,
In all the world, when one of us despairs?
It's just if I complain, since they have felled
The sapling of my happiness, withheld
The sun that shone for me in heaven's vault,
And now her absence fills my wounds with salt.

Oh weep your tears, my eyes; I'll never see
A day of greater grief or misery,
And it is just that you should cry a flood
Of bitter tears commingled with my blood.
Why do tears waste away my cheeks, when rain
Restores the withered plants to life again?
Grief's melted my poor heart, that's left its trace
As trickling tears upon my sallow face.
It's wrong for men to weep, but when delight
Is snatched from me like this, to weep is right."

The king returned; Ramin was now assured
Of Vis's state, and where she was immured,
But knowledge of her brought him no relief –
New pain was piled on pain, and grief on grief;
The dust of longing dimmed his face, and then
A storm of tears would wash it clean again.
The song he sang was touchingly sincere,
The kind that hopeless lovers love to hear:

"I'm now a lovelorn man whose friend's departed,
Who curses Fortune, and who's broken hearted.
My love's become a captive, and you'd say
It's me those brazen walls have locked away.
Go to my love, sweet breeze, convey to her
My plaint: 'A hundred fires, dear prisoner,
Burn in my heart for you, and in my mind
Your image and your voice are all I find,
One robs me of my sleep, the other's taken
The world from me and left me here forsaken.
Though I were made of iron this agony
Of longing for your face would weary me,
And if my endless sorrow could be split
Each man on earth could take his share of it.
I am so weak, so faint, so scant of breath,
That life is less desirable than death;

And who can cure me, who can heal my heart,
When you're my medicine, and we're far apart?"'

Ramin was such a sorry sight from sighing,
So wasted now, so worn away with crying,
That seeing him his ancient enemies
Would have felt pity for his miseries.
Within a week his body was laid low,
The silver arrow was a golden bow.[80]
Wailing with grief as though a poisoned dart
Had lodged within his lacerated heart,
Prone in a litter, Prince Ramin was brought
To great Gorgan, where King Mobad held court.
Before Mobad, the chieftains one by one
Declared, "Ramin's your brother and your son;
In all the world, my lord, you'll never find
The equal of his body or his mind,
No horseman's like Ramin; would that we all
Had such fine subjects at our beck and call!
Blunting the teeth of your adversaries,
A lion, a mammoth, to your enemies,
A brother like Ramin is worth far more
Than countless hordes of men equipped for war;
But now he's close to death – the man you saw
Is like a withered flower, a puny straw.
If you were angry with him, you forgave him,
Forget old grudges now and try to save him.
A lengthy journey can be hard enough
On men whose bodies are robust and tough,
Think what it is for travelers racked with pain!
Ramin is sick and weak; let him remain
A month, till he grows stronger, in Gorgan,
Then let him travel back to Khorasan;
It may be he'll recover once he's there,
Drinking its water, breathing in its air;

If this land's poison for him, that may be
The antidote for all his misery."
Mobad agreed to implement their plan
And left Ramin behind him in Gorgan.

As soon as King Mobad had gone, the grief
And pain Ramin had felt found some relief;
His saffron cheeks took on a healthier flush
Rivaling the ruddy Judas blossom's blush,
The bent bow of his body, freed from pain,
Was now a noble box tree once again,
His avid longing to see Vis became
An arrow in his heart, a flickering flame.
Mounted upon a swift Tocharian horse
He left Gorgan alone, setting his course
For Khorasan; and like a nightingale
He sang a song that told a lover's tale:

"Without you, Vis, I've no desire to live,
No longing for the joys the world can give;
And seeking you I fear no enemy,
Not if the world itself contends with me,
Not if snakes fill the highway and oppose me
Not if a hundred iron walls enclose me,
Not if foul monsters lurk in dank morasses,
Not if wild leopards throng the mountain passes,
Not if the grass turns into blades of iron,
Not if the sands become a raging lion,
Not if the wind is like a harsh simoom,
Not if the thunderous clouds pronounce my doom
And hurl down swords and stones against me here;
I swear upon your soul I'll show no fear,
I swear I won't retreat, and if I do
It's not a man who is in love with you.
If fire surrounds you I will gladly cast
My wondering eyes within the fiery blast,

If I must face a lion's maw to see you
My sword will bandy words with it and free you.
Swords will not keep me from you, or the flash
Of vivid meteors, or the thunder's crash."

When Vis learned that Ramin had gone, dawn's light
Became as dark and drear to her as night.
His absence spread a saffron hue upon
Her cheeks where once pink Judas blossoms shone,
The tears she wept displayed their trickling trace
Like jewels upon the amber of her face.
Absence now fashioned all her face from gold
But it was shining jewels her lashes sold.
Her hennaed hands beat at her cheeks and made
Their roses darken with the violet's shade;
Her gown was blue[81] as if she mourned the dead,
Her sweet complexion was a tulip-red,
But as she scored her cheeks the blood dripped down
Giving her face's color to her gown,
And in the same way her repeated blows
Made her bruised face the color of her clothes.

She wept and wailed and cursed their separation
And cried out to her nurse in desperation:
"I've sacrificed my life to love, my youth
To lovers' promises of faith and truth:
I thought we'd be together and achieve
All that the heart can hope for or believe –
Fate tore our promises, and us, apart
And absence rent the veil that hid my heart.
My love, when you were held in my embrace,
I went to sleep in an enchanted place,
But now you've filled my bed with thorns, and taken
Sweet sleep from me, and left me here forsaken;

You've snatched sleep from my eyes and left me tears.
And now my heart is always filled with fears
Because you'll join the battles to beat back
Our enemy's malevolent attack,
Because your face as splendid as the moon
Will feel the sun's force when it shines at noon;
Because the windblown dust will hover there
And settle on the blackness of your hair;
Because you'll wear no crown now, and instead
An iron helmet will enclose your head;
Because the lute and wine cup that you know
Must yield their places to a warrior's bow;
Because your lovely body that has worn
Brocades and softest silks since you were born
Must now be clothed in armor's strength and feel
The hard abrasions of unyielding steel,
And as your flower-like eyes have wounded me
Your dagger now will wound your enemy.
Why when you spoke to me did I not hear you,
Or, when you left, not hurry to be near you?
Perhaps the dust made musky by your scent
Would have been blown against me as I went.
But, as it is, my wounded heart's your friend
And travels with you to your journey's end,
Cherish your friend as you go off to war
And do not harm or hurt her any more;
It's sweet when noble souls act well and make
Kind gestures to their friends for friendship's sake.
Be kind to me, Ramin, and don't disgrace
The sun-like splendor of your lovely face;
Remember me, my lord, since it is right
For kings to sometimes see a beggar's plight;
You saw the smoke that rose from my desire
And now beneath the smoke you see the fire.

How trivial other pains appear to me
Now that I've known this abject misery!
I feel a tempest in my soul arise,
I weep a flowing Oxus from my eyes.
My heart's a letter filled with pain, its seal
My sallow face that shows the grief I feel;
Read there my grief, Ramin, read there the flood
Of agony which I have sealed in blood."

And as Vis stormed and wept for sorrow's sake,
Writhing and twisting like a sinuous snake,
The nurse's heart was wrung for her, but she
Could only recommend one remedy –
Patience. "Resign yourself to this, dear Vis,
Patience will triumph when your sorrows cease;
Patience will bring you all that you require,
Patience will lead you to your heart's desire,
Let patience be the simple seed you sow
And from this seed your happiness will grow.
Hear what your nurse says, Vis, hear and repeat,
'Patience is bitter, but its fruit is sweet.'
God is the only medicine for your pains
And only He can free you from these chains:
Call on your Maker now for help, and see
You act towards everyone with charity,
It may be He will help you, and the fire
Lit by your foes will suddenly expire.
Be patient; this is my advice to you;
I know of nothing else that you can do."

Vis said, "Who can be patient when she burns
Within a fire whichever way she turns?
Haven't you heard the words a mourner said
To one who heaped advice upon his head?

'My friend, however many you might throw,
Walnuts won't fasten on a dome, you know.'[82]
My lover's gone, and everything you say
Is like a bridge that leads another way.
What do you understand of what I feel?
Another's pain and grief are never real!
You tell me to let patience be my guide;
How simple, when one's watching from outside!
You're like a horseman, nurse; what can you know
Of all a man on foot must undergo?
You've patience in abundance, I have none.
Hunger's ridiculous to anyone
Whose belly's full; but if you had my grief
Your lamentations would surpass belief.
'Be patient,' but you never make it clear
How I'm to do this now my heart's not here:
A lion who has no heart can easily
Be bested by a fox's trickery.
Do you think I want to weep like this and live
Afraid of all the sorrows Fate can give?
Who would seek out her own misfortune, nurse?
What wise man puts himself beneath a curse?
You dug this pit for me, and with your wiles,
And specious prattling, and persuasive smiles
You flung me in its darkness. Now you sit
And glibly sermonize beside the pit,
Saying I ought to pray, that God will find
A way to ease the sorrows in my mind;
But though it's easy to throw felt in streams
Getting it out is harder than it seems!"[83]

RAMIN COMES TO VIS IN THE DEVILS' FORTRESS

Ramin returned to Marv and saw that where
The cypress had once grown the plot was bare;

The palace's apartments were bereft
Of happiness and blossoms, Vis had left.
Her musky hair, the roses of her face
No longer made the rooms a wondrous place,
So that this site of former happiness
Seemed like a pit of horror and distress;
The very rooms and walks looked broken-hearted,
As if they wept that Vis had now departed.
Once he perceived the absence of his friend
It seemed Ramin's sad tears would never end;
He wept as though a pomegranate's skin
Had split to weep the myriad seeds within,
As if a wine cup had been overfilled
And from its rim red droplets coursed and spilled.
In rooms and gardens then he laid his face
Against the ground in each deserted place,
Singing as though he were a nightingale
Bewailing his lost love, to no avail:

"O palace, once a lovely partridge made [84]
Its happy home within your pleasant shade;
You were a canopy of stars, and one
Within your heavens was the shining sun
Gilding the earth, diffusing balmy scent
That sweetened all the airy firmament.
In every chamber then soft lutes were played
And sweetly sung to by a lovely maid;
Your men were lions devoted to their duty,
Your women onagers of grace and beauty.
The moon and stars have gone, the lions too,
The splendid onagers who honored you,
The warriors and their mounts, the white and bay,
Have all vacated you and gone away.
You're not the place I knew, the place I've seen,
Now you resemble me, the wretch Ramin!

The world's a witch whose selfish sorcery
Has ruined you as it has ruined me –
From you it's taken pleasure and your queen,
And all his heart has longed for from Ramin.
Alas for days gone by, for fleeting hours
When sweet delight and happiness were ours!
I can't believe that I will ever reign here
Or that such pleasures will return again here,
But one sweet day of happiness outweighs
The heartache of a hundred desperate days."

When he had sung his fill and seen the sun –
For which he looked to no avail – had gone,
He left the castle gates and made his way
To where he knew the Devils' Fortress lay.
The road was barren, mountainous, and grim
But seemed like blossoms and sweet flowers to him;
He traveled day and night, since in his soul
He'd little patience now, or self-control.
He reached the walls at night, and under cover
Of darkness managed to approach his lover;
By day the lookouts missed him, and at night
The darkness kept him safely out of sight.
Ramin was artful, and was well aware
Of where exactly Vis was hidden there;
No archer could be found in all the earth
Who equaled Prince Ramin in skill and worth;
He loosed a poplar arrow in the dark,
Which flashed like sudden lightning to its mark,
And said, "Four-feathered, soulless bird, I send
You as my envoy to my dearest friend,
And though your usual mission is to sever
I send you to unite two friends forever."
The arrow flew as Prince Ramin intended,
Over the walls, down through the roof, and ended

Its flight by Vis's lion-footed bed.
The nurse saw where the arrow shaft had sped
And quickly then, as soon as she perceived it,
Scurried across the chamber and retrieved it;
She was so overjoyed it seemed the night
Before her wondering eyes was filled with light.
She brought the shaft to Vis and said, "My dear,
Look at the splendid arrow that is here,
This is a message from Ramin you know,
Released from his prodigious, brazen bow;
It bears his mark, look here's his noble name,
And it is feats like this that win him fame.
Sorush[85] is in the devils' dwelling place
Filling its darkness with his radiant grace,
Good fortune's sun has brought a new tomorrow
Dispelling our long night of pain and sorrow;
Your heart's desire will sit down here beside you,
Nothing you long for now will be denied you."

Vis saw his name, and took the shaft, and pressed it
Against her heart and cheek as she caressed it.
A thousand times she kissed it as she said:
"O dearer than the eyes within my head,
You wound all other mortals, but to me
You are my wounds' long-sought for remedy.
You are the envoy of his noble hand;
And may I always wear you on a band
About my neck: rubies will ring your head
And unpierced pearls will be your notch's bed,
My lovely breasts will be your silver quiver,
And may that quiver please your lord forever.
A hundred shafts like you have pierced my heart
Since Prince Ramin and I were forced to part,
But when you came you drove them out again
And rescued me from all my heartfelt pain;

I never saw an arrow that could heal
The woes that other arrows make us feel,
Of all the messages that I have seen
None was as sweet as yours from Prince Ramin."

Ramin dispatched his arrow on its way
And devilish thoughts began a fearful fray:
"Where is my arrow now? Will love prevail?
Or, God forbid, will all my efforts fail?
If Vis knew of my state surely she'd find
A hundred ways to reassure my mind."
Then he addressed himself: "Heart, have no fear
Of any enemy you'll meet with here;
Be ready to risk everything, and go!
I swear by God, who rules the world below,
The sun and moon, the blue revolving sky
Whose color gives us hope, I swear that I
Will not turn back, I swear by God above
That I shall find a way to reach my love.
If iron walls oppose me filled with fire
That burns as fiercely as my wild desire,
If poisonous demons in the moat waylay me,
If men like leaping lions try to slay me,
If vipers top the walls, and those within
Are wizards steeped in sorcery and sin
With crag-like arms and lightning claws, whose breath
Is venom-laden and delivers death,
Courage will rouse my heart, and I will break
Their doors and walls wide open for love's sake.
My heart won't fear their snakes or sorcery
God's glory and my strength will succor me;
I'll rescue Vis, and even Time and Fate
Before my dagger's point will fall prostrate,
Courage will kiss my hands when he's aware
How many warriors' necks I've broken there;

While life is mine I swear I'll never cease
In all I strive for to keep faith with Vis.
A world of enemies will not alarm me,
Zard and Mobad can never hope to harm me –
I'm Saturn[86] to their pride, and I'm the sea
To any fire they might oppose to me;
We're of one royal seed, but swords will show
Who's worse, who's better; and the world will know."

On this side Prince Ramin stood lost in thought,
On that Vis waited, captive and distraught,
Repeating his sweet name as if to greet him,
Her mind preoccupied with how to meet him;
Her face on fire, she feverishly tried
To think of ways to bring him to her side.
The wily nurse said, "Fortune favors you,
The heavens approve of everything you do;
It's winter now, and all the world is white,
The guard sits shivering in his cell all night,
Shunning the cold that comes with snow and ice,
And venturing on the roof no more than twice.
The way is clear, and since the roof's not guarded
Your patience and your plans will be rewarded.
Somewhere out there, not far from us, Ramin
Waits in the darkness, silent and unseen.
He's been here with Mobad so often, all
The stones are known to him in every wall;
He knows the castle's ramparts and escarpments
And he's aware we're in the royal apartments.
Embedded in one wall's a bathhouse where
The ovens' fires give off a dazzling glare –
Open its doors and make the fires burn bright
So that Ramin sees day replace the night;
He'll climb up to the wall then, never fear,
And soon enough I'll have him safe in here."

They did as she suggested, and her skill
Reduced the castle's devils to her will.
Ramin looked up and saw the burst of flame
And recognized exactly whence it came –
He knew the blazing fire that burned above
Was lit by Vis and signified her love.
No clambering mountain sheep was ever seen
To climb as nimbly upwards as Ramin
As if he'd sprouted wings to reach the glow
That shone like gold upon the world below.
But so love is, that makes its votaries
Ignore all obstacles and injuries,
And take on all the hardships they might meet
To make itself accomplished and complete.
      No hindrance keeps it from its longed-for goal,
A lion's a fox, a journey is a stroll,
A desert's like the garden of a king,
A mirage like sweet jasmine in the spring,
And lions' lairs are fragrant gardens where
Male peacocks strut and proudly take the air;
A sea confronting love's a little river,
A mountain peak is like a trivial sliver.
Desire gives courage to a man, he seems
Indifferent to the world and all its dreams.
The heart becomes desire's best customer,
And this is why there's no controlling her –
She sells off peace and wisdom to acquire
The means to make a bargain with desire.
Desire knows neither good nor bad; the mind
With wisdom in it says desire is blind,
Since if desire knew good from bad why would
It purchase bad by selling off what's good?

Ramin now reached the wall, and from above
Vis glimpsed the figure of her dearest love;
She and the wily nurse together made
A rope of forty lengths of fine brocade,
Twisted and doubled, expertly and thickly,
And Prince Ramin ascended it so quickly
He seemed a royal falcon taking flight
And perching on the rooftop in the night.
One goblet now held mingled milk and wine,
The moon and Venus were a single sign,
In one sweet plot a pallid lily grew
Beside a blushing rose's ruddy hue.
Gold intertwined with jewels, Ramin with Vis,
As musk is melded into ambergris;
Rose water blent with honey now, as sweet,
You'd say, as when true love and goodness meet;
December's moon was now so clear and bright
It seemed a summer's not a winter's night.
Rubies touched rubies, two hearts were at peace,
And kisses made all lamentations cease;
Two splendid gardens, two brocades, combined,
A box tree and a cypress intertwined.

Then, happily, the two of them descended
To Vis's chamber, where their sorrows ended;
In golden goblets raised by silver hands
They pledged themselves to love and love's commands.
At times two corals kissed, at times they lay
Recounting sorrows that had passed away;
Ramin described to her how broken-hearted,
How sick with grief he'd been, since they had parted,
And Vis then told Ramin of everything
She'd suffered in her marriage to the king.
Demonic darkness seemed to shroud the night
From fish [87] to moon there was no sign of light,

But where Vis sat beside her prince Ramin
Three kinds of conflagration could be seen.
One from the fireplace there in Vis's room,
Where tongues of coral flickered in the gloom,
One from the wine, whose cheerful glowing fire
Proclaimed good fortune favored their desire,
One from the lovers' cheeks (as though their hair
Were black smoke rising from the furnace there).
Three faithful friends,[88] secure now and alone,
Sat safe within their chamber, locked in stone,
They had no fear of enemies, no fear
That obstacles to pleasure might appear,
No fear that they would have to separate
And once again bewail their lonely state.
A night like this means more than lifetimes spent
Deprived of love and joy and merriment,
How sweet their union was, with what delight
These happy lovers passed this longed-for night!
And when Ramin beheld his Vis's face
He sang a song, which for its plangent grace
Would have laid waste a lovely houri's heart:

"What does it matter if you've had to part
From your belovèd? If you've had to bear
Unhappiness, dear lover, and despair?
Joy will not come unless through desperation,
Fame will not come untried by tribulation.
You dive through seas, but then the pearl you gain
Is more than recompense for all your pain;
She went from you, my heart, but your distress
Has been transformed to joy and happiness –
I told you to be patient, that the end
Of absence is the presence of your friend.
Winter will turn to spring, and night to day,
And you will find the longer you must stay

Absent from her, the sweeter union
Will be when she is ultimately won.
Delight's more pleasing when pursuit requires
Trouble and toil to realize our desires:
I burned in hell's harsh flames, and now I see
The houri of this heaven welcome me,
Whose face has made December's cold and ice
Resemble all the flowers of paradise.
I planted faithfulness, and my reward
Is that my happiness is now assured;
Faith was my guide, and so the world has been
Firm in its faithfulness to Prince Ramin."

Vis heard his song, and poured out wine to raise
A brimming goblet in her lover's praise;
She said, "I drink to faith, I drink this wine
To one whose heart and hope and sight are mine,
Ramin, who's more than sovereignty to me,
Who's dearer than the eyes by which I see;
I look on him as other men look on
The glorious heavens and the shining sun.
I'm his until I die, and I will serve him,
Faithfully striving always to deserve him;
If I drank poison in his name, it would
Do nothing to my heart and soul but good."
She quaffed the wine, and then in thirsty sips
Drank down a hundred kisses from his lips,
And just as many sugared kisses followed
Each of the many draughts of wine she swallowed.
How sweet to drink red wine when love is there,
To have your lips caress your lover's hair,
And as the bowl is sipped your two mouths meet
And wine's astringent draughts taste strangely sweet.
Ramin lay drunk upon his lover's breast,
On musk and silver now he took his rest,

Drowsing, voluptuous and irresolute,
On pomegranate blossoms and their fruit.[89]
For nine months Prince Ramin was fed upon
Sweet rubies and sharp garnets, mixed as one –
And if the garnets of the wine deprived him
Of manly strength, her ruby lips revived him,
While in his bed moonlight and roses lay
Caught in his arms until the break of day.
So these two passed the night, and as dawn broke
They called for wine as soon as they awoke;
While Vis received the cup, their chamber rang
With Prince Ramin's voice as he sweetly sang:

"Wine is blood red and scours the rusty heart
Making its weariness and grief depart,
Returning to the pallid, careworn face
Its ruddy hue and customary grace.
Longing is pain, and wine will cure this pain,
Anguish is dust, and wine's its cleansing rain,
If sorrow's present, red wine will remove it,
If joy is present, red wine will improve it;
Wine burns away all suffering, while desire
And joy blaze up more brightly in its fire.
Good fortune's mine now, and my head reposes
On hyacinths and musk, lilies and roses,[90]
Her sugared wine-red lips are sought by mine,
The garden's rose blooms red as ruby wine.
My horse is mettlesome and will not tire
When ridden on the highway of desire;
I am the royal hawk who flies so high
He hunts the splendid sun across the sky,
Partridge and pheasant need not fear my flight,
My gaze is fixed upon the full moon's light;
My joy's a lion, brazen-clawed, whose prey's
The silver onager his skill waylays.

I've doffed the crown of Wisdom, and my feet
Tread cheerfully down Pleasure's bustling street;
No hour will pass me by devoid of wine,
No hour will pass when pleasure is not mine.
All the year round my love will yield to me
Sugar and musk to fill a treasury,
I'll need no roses when her face is there,
I'll need no scents when I've her musky hair.
This place is heaven where nothing is denied me
And its celestial houri sits beside me;
The sun and moon now serve me here, why then
Should I not drink my wine, and drink again?"

In gentle words more sweet than sugar he
Addressed Vis, saying, "Dearest, hand to me
A cup of wine as flushed as your complexion,
As heartening as the fire of your affection;
We'll never see a sweeter time, your face
Will never be more spring-like in its grace,
Why should we not rejoice, dear Vis, and bless
With happiness this day of happiness?
Come, let us sit, and drive away all sorrow,
And leave tomorrow's troubles to tomorrow;
Come, let us seize the day, which will not last
And won't return again when it has passed.
You've no desire to lose me, I believe you,
And I, dear Vis, have no desire to leave you;
This then is love, this is fidelity,
This is the life that's shared by you and me.
If God has willed this, then we must expect
To live the life that we cannot reject.
They walled you up, imprisoned you, while I
Lay sickening in Gorgan and like to die,
Yet God has brought me to this heavenly place,
And you and I now sit here face to face:

Who could do this but God, who needs no aid,
Or help, or anything that men have made?"

These two now gave themselves to mutual bliss
And nine euphoric months went by like this:
Tipsy at times, at times quite drunk, and when
The wine's effects wore off they'd drink again.
They needed no provisions from elsewhere,
Food for a hundred years was hoarded there;
The thorn of absence that had so distressed them
Was now plucked out, and countless pleasures blessed them;
Ramin's heart never tired of love, and Vis
Longed only for their passion to increase.
Their bodies were as one, together they
Thoughtlessly drank and slept their time away,
Now with the wine cup raised, now with their faces
Laid cheek to cheek in amorous embraces;
Joy filled their hearts, and wine's sweet influence
Persuaded them to love and somnolence.
The castle's door was barred, as was the door
To all the sorrows that they'd known before,
The wine jar had been broached, its seal was torn
As were the vows of chastity they'd sworn.

As yet the world was still quite unaware
That these three lived in joy together there,
Except the foreign princess, Zarin-Gis,[91]
Who knew Ramin had joined the nurse and Vis.
Of splendid lineage and beauty, she
Was so adept at spells and sorcery
That by her potent magic she could make
A tulip blossom from a metal stake.
When Prince Ramin returned to Marv, and went
Loudly bewailing his predicament,

Ransacking all the royal rooms and halls,
Pacing around the palace gardens' walls,
And found no faintest scent, no slightest trace
Of his belovèd Vis in any place,
Pouring a Tigris from his eyes, as he
Searched for some sign of her, and desperately
Ran back and forth like someone who's insane,
Seeking his love and seeking her in vain;
Then, when he left the town in frantic haste
And took his weary way across the waste
Leaving a trail of blood[92] as though he were
A wounded warrior or a prisoner,
And tugged his stalwart stallion's reins to ride
Up the defiles that split the mountainside,
As if he were a leopard scrambling there
To meet its mate within their rocky lair;
Such depths and heights he scaled, it seemed he fell
As low as Joseph captive in his well,
Till he'd ascend again and ride as high
As Jesus when he rose into the sky;
All this was known to wily Zarin-Gis
Who knew the medicine for his grief was Vis,
Who knew he wept for her, who knew his sadness
Was but a sign of love's tumultuous madness,
Who knew he traveled hard and long to find
The medicine that would soothe his troubled mind.

KING MOBAD RETURNS VICTORIOUS FROM HIS WAR AGAINST ROME AND GOES TO VISIT VIS IN THE DEVILS' FORTRESS

Now King Mobad returned in triumph home
Victorious from his battles against Rome;
Arran,[93] and all Armenia's noble land
Submitted willingly to his command,

The Turkish lords and Roman emperor sent
Tribute and taxes to his government,
And in his happiness and triumph he
Seemed doubly drunk with joy and sovereignty.
His crown and banners split the sky, his throne
And armies made the leveled hills [94] his own:
From every king and country he had brought
Suppliants and captives to his royal court,
And they confessed the power that victory brings
As if he said, "I am the king of kings."

But when he entered Marv, mourning supplanted
The celebrations he'd decreed and granted;
He heard the words that Zarin-Gis now said,
Fire flared up in his heart, smoke filled his head.
At first he sat there, seething in his heart,
Then sprang up, raging, ready to depart
And sent a message to his chieftains they
Should soon be ready to be on their way.
War drums were beaten at the palace door
Summoning his soldiers with their martial roar,
As if their groaning asked the king in vain
How many miles they'd march across the plain,
Just as the bugles' shrill cries seemed to mean
They wept for captive Vis, and her Ramin,
As if they knew the sweet love they enjoyed
Would turn to bitterness and be destroyed.
The king now longed to put Ramin to death,
But half his army'd hardly yet drawn breath,
Or lifted off their helmets, or drawn rein
After their year's laborious campaign,
And half were on the road still, not yet home
From King Mobad's offensive against Rome.
Unwillingly his soldiers made their way
To where the site of Devils' Fortress lay:

One said, "And now it seems Ramin's the reason
We're always marching, in and out of season,"
Another, "Well, we won't get any peace
While we've to keep Ramin away from Vis,"
And one, "A hundred emperors in Rome
Would give our king less grief than Vis at home."
Now like a scudding cloud the king made haste
Across the mountains and the desert waste;
The army's dust – swirled up into the sky
Like some black, baleful demon riding by –
Was sighted by a watchful fortress guard,
And news was quickly passed to noble Zard,
"Our mighty king's returned victorious,
And unannounced will soon be here with us!"
Confusion reigned, as when a gusting breeze
Plays sudden havoc in a clump of trees:
Zard had no time to welcome him or greet him,
Or have a fitting escort go to meet him,
But swifter than an arrow of Arash[95]
Mobad was in the fortress in a flash.
The fury in his eyes was from the blaze
Of anger in his heart – the wrathful gaze
He fixed on hapless Zard made Zard feel like
A tulip when the winds of winter strike.

"Worst of my woes," Mobad cried, "God preserve me
From you two brothers and the way you serve me!
A dog will show more loyalty than you –
Dogs can be loyal enough, but not you two!
I don't know under what malignant star
The stuff was formed that made you what you are –
One like a devil for his sorcery,
One like an ass for his stupidity!
Guarding a cowshed's all you're fit for, Zard,
How did you think you could be Vis's guard?

And I deserve the miseries I've seen –
I chose a dumb ox to outwit Ramin!
You sat outside the locked doors, while inside them
The lovers sat, and nothing was denied them.
You think that you've fulfilled your duties, do you?
That all you've managed is a credit to you?
But in your ignorance you never knew
Ramin's in there and ridiculing you,
And who knows what delights he now enjoys
While you're outside here, making all this noise!
The whole world knows of this, except for Zard;
What a disaster you've been as her guard!"

The noble Zard replied, "Your majesty,
You came with happiness and victory,
Don't let some idle gossip now mislead you,
Or Ahriman[96] deceive you or impede you.
Aware or unaware, you are our king,
And, good or bad, can swear to anything,
Kings rule the world, and aren't afraid to say
Whatever they might wish, in any way.
If what you've said turns out to be untrue,
Who here would dare to point that out to you?
You say my soul has sinned, but I can't see
How this has anything to do with me:
You took Ramin with you; how could I know
What you did then, or where he'd choose to go?
He's not an arrow or a bird to fly
Swiftly away from you across the sky,
And how was he supposed to penetrate
These fortress walls or get beyond its gate?
Look at the seals you set on every door,
Look, they're unbroken still, and furthermore
A year's dust lies upon them, undisturbed.
So why, my lord, should you be so perturbed?

This fortress stands upon a mountainside,
Its stone and brazen walls stretch far and wide,
Its bolts are all of iron, its seals of gold,
The nearby roads are endlessly patrolled
By watchful warriors spying out the land,
On every rooftop guards and lookouts stand:
Ramin could know a thousand tricks, but these
Sealed doors would outwit all his strategies;
And if he'd somehow opened them, then how
Could he replace the seals before us now?
You majesty, don't let such nonsense fool you,
Be sensible, my lord, let Wisdom rule you!
Don't say these things, which Wisdom would maintain
Are of less value than a barley grain."

The king said, "Zard, why do you set such store
By seals and bolts and padlocks on a door?
A strong lock's fine, if you're aware of it,
If you can be there to take care of it;
But, in a castle, watchful guards are worth
More than the strongest locks and chains on earth –
Even God, who set the heavens, stationed there
His shooting stars as guardians of the air.
The doors are locked from this side, but behind
These doors it's 'Out of sight is out of mind'!
Who knows what evil people throng that room?
Who knows who's in there doing what to whom?
A pretty belt's of no significance
Unless it's holding up some kind of pants!
Buckle your belt as tight as you can make it,
But with no pants to wear you're still stark naked!
What use are all my seals on doors when Zard
Turns out to be a weak and worthless guard?
All of my reputation, all the fame
I've gained this year, you've ruined with this shame;

My fame was like a noble castle which
You've smeared with ignominy's filthy pitch."
He railed at him a while, then drew the key
Out from his boot, and threw it furiously
At Zard and said, "Take it, open the door
That like this key's of no use any more."

The nurse had heard the king's voice loudly speaking,
And now she heard the door's great hinges creaking:
Then like the wind she ran to Vis and cried,
"The king has reached the castle, he's inside,
An evil star now rises, sorrows crowd
Above us like a lightning-riven cloud,
From Envy's mountain, waters thunder down
To make a roiling flood in which we'll drown.
And now you'll see a dragon's wrath prevail,
Wrath against which our sorceries must fail;
You'll see a fire to burn the world, the sight
Of its black smoke will turn the day to night."
Their one hope was the cloth, which they unwound
To let Ramin down till he reached the ground,
Where like a mountain sheep he turned and fled,
His soul consumed with fear, his heart with dread.

Weeping and wailing on the mountainside,
Within his grieving, lovelorn heart he cried:
"What is it that you want from me, O Fate?
You make despair and grief my constant state,
My fortune in your hands is desolation
You wound me with the sword of separation,
You try my soul with torment and distress,
You turn my pleasures into bitterness.
My thoughts are like a caravan that's scattered,
Whose order and coherence has been shattered;

My soul is like a noble tribe whose members
Have all dispersed, whom no one now remembers.
I was like kings who rule from golden thrones,
Now I'm a goat that scrambles over stones;
The rocks turn red as blossoms from my tears,
Their granite splits, a yawning cleft appears.
The partridge moans with me at dawn, as though
We were two voices blended, high and low,
I take the treble part, and he the bass –
Two singers come together in one place.
My groans out-thunder thunder – mine arise
From burning fire, his from the smoky skies:
My eyes out-weep the clouds – their rain is drops,
My tears are like a sea that never stops.
My heart and heart's belovèd were once one –
My heart and heart's belovèd are now gone.
Earth was my heaven; now I'll never find
Peace in this world to solace my sad mind."

And when Ramin had paced the mountainside,
And like a weeping cloud had stormed and cried,
His sorrow wearied him, and soon he found
Exhaustion made him sink down to the ground.
He sat, and wept, and as a cloud disperses
Its raindrops, so Ramin wept tears and verses.
He sang alone, as lovers find relief
In singing songs that tell of love and grief:

"My love, you cannot know my inmost heart,
The bitterness of life while we're apart;
A little partridge caught within a snare
Would weep in sympathy for my despair,
For my distress that I'm unable to
Discover any word or news of you,
That I don't know what horrors now befall you,
What fears beset your sweet soul and appall you.

Grief is my fate, but may you never see
The least misfortune, Vis, or misery!
Were I to list your beauties one by one
I'd surely die before the list were done;
I have good cause to weep! Since so much beauty
Is lost to me now, weeping is my duty!
I say a hundred prayers to God that I
Shall see you once again before I die,
But now, without you here, I feel such sorrow
I doubt that I can live until tomorrow."

Now that Ramin had got away, Vis saw
Herself as caught within a dragon's maw;
She ran distractedly about the place
Beating her silver fists against her face,
Tearing out locks of hyacinthine hair,
Clawing her rosy cheeks in her despair.
Her hair's thick scent of musk and ambergris,
Her fiery cries and sighs that would not cease,
Hung in the air, as if the fortress were
A burning censer that imprisoned her.
Wildly she beat her breasts, and tears of blood
Poured from her eyes in an unending flood.
Her heart was glowing iron, a white-hot blade
That's worked and hammered when a sword is made;
She snatched her necklace off, and jeweled light
Scattered across the floor like stars at night,
She tore her golden garments from her back
And like a mourner dressed herself in black –
And all this grief was for her absent lover,
Not for what King Mobad might now discover.

The king came in and saw the lovely rose
Of Vis's face disfigured by her blows,

And then he saw the coils of rope they'd made
From forty lengths of silk and fine brocade
Lying in front of her, its knots still tied
(The wily nurse had scuttled off to hide).
Vis sat upon the ground, the silks she'd worn
Ripped from her body, thrown aside and torn;
She'd yanked her hair out, heaped dust on her head,
Clawed at her arms, so that they bruised and bled,
And all the while her eyes ran with a river
Of desperate tears as if she'd weep forever.

The king exclaimed, "Ah, Vis, you're demon-born,
I curse you in both worlds,[97] you're devil's spawn!
You flout God's laws and man's, and you despise
Whatever punishments I might devise;
You face my chains and prisons without fear,
The good advice I give you, you don't hear.
Tell me what you deserve! What should I do?
What can I do but do away with you?
Your head's so full of sorcery and lies
This mountain and this fortress in your eyes
Are like a plain where you're at liberty
To come and go and feel completely free;
If you went up to heaven you'd find some way
To fool the stars and lead them all astray.
Chastising you's no good, nothing can chain you,
Your promises and pledges don't restrain you;
How much I've tried! I've punished you and then
Been kind to you, and tried, and tried again!
You're like a wolf who preys on everyone,
A demon whose foul tricks are never done;
You're like a jewel to look at, but within
You're broken earthenware, you're filth and sin;
Alas that such a form should be allied
With such foul faults and wickedness inside!

I've kept my anger in, I've counseled you,
I've told you, Vis, 'Be careful what you do;
Don't hurt me in this manner, Vis, or I
Will see to it that you will surely die!'
But you ignored me, and the crops you've sown
Will be your harvest now they're fully grown.
Yes, you're as splendid as the heavens above,
But I've no hopes I'll ever gain your love.

    I won't try kindness now or clemency –
Your faults are there for everyone to see;
I thought you were the moon, but you're a snake,
Seeking out evil ways for evil's sake.
I won't pursue your love now, I foreswear it,
I won't go on like this, I cannot bear it –
I'm not a man of iron, or brass, or stone,
And all the days I've spent with you alone
Were so much wasted time – you don't respond,
I might as well paint pictures on a pond!
And giving you suggestions is as vain
As scattering seeds upon a salt-sown plain;
When wolves become good shepherds, Vis will be
A woman known for her fidelity.
You're like sweet sherbet, but I've drunk my fill
Of cloying sweetnesses that make me ill,
And now I'll give my heart to abstinence
And plant the noble sapling of good sense.

    But since I've had no joy of you, and you
Make bitterness my lot by all you do,
I'll break the vows and promises I made you –
As you have broken yours – till I've repaid you.
I'll make you long for death to intervene
To end your anguish; you'll forget Ramin.
He won't be singing for you as before,
You won't be drinking with him any more;

His songs sung to the harp, your simpering smiles,
His playing for you, your lascivious wiles
Are over, Vis; what I'm about to do
Will make the granite mountains weep for you.
Your mutual love's my bitterest enemy,
Your kisses and caresses tortured me,
But now I'll be revenged on you, and sever
My heart's ties to the two of you forever.
If I have any wisdom, what has made me
Play host to enemies who have betrayed me?
It's acting like a man who sleeps beside
A thicket where he knows that lions hide;
An enemy within the house is like
A snake inside your collar poised to strike!"

He strode to her before she could resist
And grabbed her musky locks within his fist;
Dragging her from her couch,[98] he whirled her round
And threw her sprawling headlong to the ground.
He tied her arms and hands, as though she were
A thief he'd caught, and took a whip to her,
And in his fury started to chastise
Her breasts, her back, her buttocks, and her thighs,
And soon his violent blows began to mar
The camphor of her flesh with cinnabar.[99]
Her skin was like a pomegranate's skin
That splits to show the scarlet seeds within,
Or like a crystal goblet when it glows
Brimful of crimson wine, and overflows,
Or like a silver slope on which are found
Rubies and garnets scattered on the ground,
And all her many wounds now ran with blood
As if her body were the Nile in flood.
Then, when he found the trembling, cowering nurse,
The beating she received was even worse –

He rained blows on her shoulders and her head
As if he hoped that she'd be left for dead.
The beaten women both lost consciousness;
Their blood lay on them like a flowered dress,
Like rubies set in silver, like the glow
Of crimson gillyflowers where lilies grow,
And no one knew if when the dawn arrived
The two of them could say they had survived.
He locked the door on them, expecting they
Could hardly live to see another day,
And all the world now grieved and wept as one
For all the torments they had undergone.
Mobad then chose another man to guard
The fortress gates and walls, in place of Zard.

He stayed a week in Marv; regret obsessed him,
Anguish at everything he'd done possessed him.
"What smoke is this," he said, "that clouds my mind,
That's made my world end and my senses blind?
What rage is this, that's turned upon my wife
Who's dearer to me than my soul or life?
I might be king of kings, but sovereignty's
Made me the plaything of my enemies.
Why should I vent my rage on someone who
I've loved so wildly and so long? And you,
My heart, why have you now turned out to be
My own most violent, ruthless enemy?
Why should I set upon what's all my own,
And burn the harvest of the seeds I've sown?"

Ah, lovers, anger's there when you forget
Tomorrow comes and with it comes regret,
And foolish actions done today will make
Tomorrow like a venomous, cruel snake

That feeds upon your heart and poisons you.
True lovers though, whatever they may do,
Should not let anger overcome desire –
They'll be the ones to suffer in its fire.
How can a lover be enraged, when he
Can't even bear her absence patiently?
Love will not smile for him unless he shows
That he can bear the worst of Fortune's blows;
He loves his lover's faults, and uses them
To show he loves her, and excuses them.

Shahru weeps before Mobad

Now when the king of kings returned alone
And, without Vis, assumed the royal throne,
Shahru, confronting him with moans and wails,
Scoring her visage with her hennaed nails,
Demanded audience and said, "Dear Vis,
Sweet balm that makes your mother's sorrows cease,
Soul of my soul, why has Mobad not brought
You with him here to grace his royal court?
What has that devil done? Where are you, where?
What dreadful horrors now confront you there?"
Abruptly turning to Mobad she cried,
"Why is my Vis not seated at your side?
What's your excuse? Where is that sun at noon?
Why are these stars deprived now of their moon?
She made your private rooms a heaven at night,
A garden of sweet pleasure and delight,
Now heaven has lost its houri, and you're faced
Not with a garden but a desert waste.
Hand over Vis to me, or else my tears
Will be a river till she reappears,
I'll moan till mountains moan in sympathy,
And share my endless grief, and mourn with me;

The seas will weep for me, and you will know
That all the world has now become your foe.
Show me my Vis, or I will drag you down
And see you lose your royal throne and crown."

And as Shahru wept, King Mobad wept too;
He said, "Whether you weep or not, Shahru,
Or think me good or evil, I have done
A deed that will be shunned by everyone,
Something that I've not done before, which I
Will never do again until I die,
Something that dims my glory, brings you shame,
And ruins what is left of my good name.
If you should see your Vis now you would see
That lovely form, that noble cypress tree,
Prone in the dust, weltering in blood and grime,
While Youth and Beauty mourn this wicked crime:
The sunlight of her face is smirched with mud,
And all her hair's like rust now, caked with blood."

When Queen Shahru had realized what he'd said
She slumped down to the ground as if struck dead,
Then writhed there like a snake; grief's piercing dart,
Shot by the world and Fate, transfixed her heart.
She cried,[100] "O world, you've stolen my sweet girl,
What sage said you should steal my precious pearl,
And thrust her in the earth like looted treasure?
Does she give you the happiness and pleasure
That once upon a time she gave to me?
Why, when you saw that heavenly cypress tree,
Did you uproot the tree that you had planted,
Whose life was life that you yourself had granted?
A tree won't grow again when once you fell it,
When ambergris is buried you can't smell it.

O earth, devourer of mankind, how long
Will you gulp down the beautiful and strong,
The princes and the kings, the beauties who
Are both engendered and destroyed by you?
Don't those that you've devoured before today
Suffice you? Must you snatch Vis too away?
I fear her silver body will be hurt,
For silver tarnishes when smeared with dirt;
Why does my star not set, when my dear jewel
Is in the earth now, and invisible?
In gardens now no cypresses will grow
Since my sweet cypress tree has been laid low,
And in the heavens no moon will shine at night
Since earth eclipses her once splendid light,
But stars still shine, and there the Pleiades
Seem gathered to observe my miseries.

    My cypress tree, my moon, who shall I find
Like you to comfort my distracted mind?
To whom shall I now tell my wild distress?
From whom can I seek justice and redress?
He's killed the world itself in killing you,
And worse than either he has killed me too,
And doctors brought from all the world won't know
The remedies to cure my hopeless woe.
You had no equal here, and now, my love,
You've joined your angel in the world above;[101]
In taking you, Death took my hopes; the earth
Will not provide another of your worth –
Where shall I find your dignity and grace?
What other girl could ever take your place?
Who's worthy of your jeweled accoutrements,
Who could I deck with your magnificence,
The patterned silks of all your lovely gowns,
Your necklaces, your earrings, and your crowns?

And who'll dare take the news now to Viru
That Death, for all your tears, has taken you?
My sunlike Vis has gone, and I remain
To seek her, and to call her name, in vain.
May Ghur [102] and Devils' Fortress be destroyed,
May they be wasteland and an empty void,
For there my moon was murdered, and the din
Of devils' laughter celebrates their sin!
But everyone shall know that Vis's blood
Will be requited with an answering flood
Of blood I'll weep, and blood I'll spill of those
Who were my Vis's stony-hearted foes,
Though one drop of my Vis's blood's worth more
Than flowing Oxuses of others' gore.

     Ah, Marv, the jewel of Khorasan, don't flatter
Yourself that Vis's blood's a trivial matter:
Ghur's mountains feed your flowing watercourses
But blood now pours from their polluted sources,
And you'll see soon enough, within a year,
Blood in the ditches and the gutters here.
Those mountain slopes from which your streams are fed
Will bring disasters down upon your head;
You'll see more swords and spears, more enemies,
Than there are leaves upon a forest's trees,
Mobad won't reign for long, a storm will bring
Deserved destruction to this worthless king,
The east and west will muster men to take
Revenge on you for lovely Vis's sake,
Their horses' hooves will trample you, and leave
Destruction here for you to mourn and grieve –
The world's destroyed by what Mobad has done,
The world is ruined now that Vis has gone.
That ruby's gone, now nothing will compete
With sugar, nothing else can be as sweet;

That box tree's gone, now gardens have the chance
To boast of their tall box trees' elegance;
That musky hair is gone, now ambergris
Smells good again since it's discounted Vis;
Those cheeks are gone, tulips revive again
On every mountainside and every plain,
Spring was so jealous of her, but this year
Spring will not hesitate to reappear.
Alas for Vis, the princess of Iran,
Alas for Vis, the mistress of Turan,
Alas for Vis, the love of Khorasan,
Alas for Vis, the moon of Kuhestan,
Alas for Vis, belov'd of emperors,
Alas for Vis, the moon among bright stars,
Alas for Vis, that moon of eloquence,
Alas for Vis, that cypress of sweet scents,
Alas for Vis, that sun diffusing light,
Alas for Vis, your mother's sole delight.

Where are you now, dear lovely child, ah, where?
Why did you leave me here in such despair?
Where should I look for you? What pleasure dome,[103]
What garden, or what palace is your home?
You filled our pleasure dome with heavenly light,
You made our gardens like the moon at night,
You made our palace porticoes appear
To be the very crown of Saturn's sphere.
If I see tulips in your absence they
Are like a brand that burns my heart away,
If I see lovely roses they resemble
A yoke that weighs me down and makes me tremble,
And when I see the moon I look at it
And see a loathsome snake within a pit.

I don't know how to live without you, Vis,
The streams of blood I weep will never cease;

Ah, woe, that Fate has forced me to behold
Your death, my child, now that I'm weak and old!
If granite mountains bore such agony
They'd shatter into pieces instantly,
And if the sea's depths felt such grief, the shock
Would turn them to a landscape of dry rock.
Why was this luckless baby born to me?
Why did I wed her so disastrously?
When I was old was not the proper time
To bear a child, and it was like a crime
To give her to that treacherous nurse to rear her!
Why did I let that loathsome devil near her?
I'll go to Devils' Fortress now and cry
My wretched life away until I die,
The sighs that issue from my burning heart
Will split its stones and tear its walls apart.
Why did they take my lovely houri there,
A place where devils throng the fetid air?
I'll hurl myself from that high mountainside
And they can all rejoice that I have died.
I have no joy in life since she has gone,
And why, deprived of joy, should I go on?
No, I'll die there, this will be right and just,
That my dust mingles there with Vis's dust.

    But first Mobad must suffer, smoke must rise
Into the air from his tormented sighs –
My lovely Vis must not lie prone and dead
While someone else is welcomed to his bed;
The leaves are falling – shall he celebrate
Their fall with wine,[104] forgetting Vis's fate?
I'll rouse the world, I'll stir up everyone,
They'll hate him when I tell them what he's done,
And to the wind I'll say, 'When Vis's hair
Lifted and tumbled in the moving air,

You bore her scent about the land, now take
Death to her enemies for Vis's sake.'
And to the moon, 'You were so jealous once
Of shining Vis, who shared your radiance,
Now help me spill the sinful blood of those
Who've proved to be my Vis's evil foes.'
And to the sun, 'You were the crown upon
My Vis's head, or like a jewel that shone
In Vis's splendid crown, and you and she
Were one in beauty and in sovereignty,
Now shine on those who were her friends, and leave
Her foes in darkness to lament and grieve.'
And to the passing clouds, 'Each time you broke
You rained down jewels as Vis did when she spoke,
She was a cloud that rained munificence
And lightning flashed out from her laughing glance –
Now bring a storm down on her enemies
And flood them for their foul iniquities.'
I'll bow my face down to the earth and pray,
'All-suffering God, how long will you delay
Before you strike this tyrant who has made
Oppression of your suffering slaves his trade,
Whose rule each day proceeds from bad to worse,
Whose sovereignty's a universal curse,
Who's like a sword that thrusts, and cuts, and slashes,
A slavering wolf that gnaws, and tears, and gashes?
Render me justice, Lord; destroy his reign,
Let nothing of his wealth and power remain,
And as this tyrant's wrecked my happiness,
Wreck his, and let him suffer my distress.'"

MOBAD ANSWERS SHAHRU

When King Mobad had listened to Shahru
He feared her, and he feared her son, Viru.

He said, "You're dearer than my eyes to me,
And I have caused you untold misery;
You are my dearest sister, Queen Shahru,
My brother is your noble son, Viru;
Vis is my love, sweeter than life or sight,
Than wealth, or sovereignty, or martial might:
I love that loveless woman more than I
Love life itself, for her I'd gladly die;
If she'd not acted so unjustly I'd
Have had her every whim and want supplied.
I hid her state from you, the things I said
Exaggerated, you have been misled.
How could I kill her when I've plainly shown
Her life is dearer to me than my own?
Her brand is in my flesh, and I adore her,
I am her prisoner, let me die before her.

     Don't strike, amidst your loud laments and shrieks,
Your silver hands against your golden cheeks –
I'll send for her, Shahru, I cannot bear
To leave her in her pain and anguish there;
I don't know how she'll treat me now. Oh, why
Should I deceive myself with such a lie?
Of course I know, I know it all too well,
She'll make my wretched life a living hell,
What bitterness she'll make me drink, what pain
She'll force me to endure! And she'll remain
Just as she was before: I know I'll see
Nothing from her but tricks and treachery,
I know that for as long as she's my wife
Torment will be the business of my life.
But all the agonies I suffer start
Within myself, within my faithless heart,
That seems another's heart, that won't obey me,
That is, you'd say, determined to betray me,
All happiness has been forbidden me

A hundred times, it's under lock and key.
Ah, may no child be born who will inherit
The restless torments of my wretched spirit –
My heart won't give me even one day's peace,
So why should I expect as much from Vis?"

Mobad then said to Zard, "Be on your way
To Devils' Fortress now, brook no delay –
See that you take two hundred cavalry,
Go like the wind, and bring Vis here to me."
Within a month Zard had returned, and brought
Vis back with him to the imperial court –
Her body was still bruised, as though she were
A trapped and wildly struggling onager
Who hurts herself while vainly, valiantly,
She kicks and tugs and plunges to get free.
And during all this month, heartsick Ramin
Lay low in Zard's house, hidden and unseen;
Zard spoke on his behalf, trying to save him,
Until eventually Mobad forgave him;
Ramin's ripped cloak of Fortune was now mended,
And all the king's impetuous rage was ended,
Demonic anger hid its ugly face
And love and kindness blossomed in its place.
Pleasure returned, roses and eglantine
Bloomed in the gardens as they sipped their wine;
Cool, balmy breezes welcomed and caressed them
And they forgot the pains that had possessed them.

Neither our joy nor sorrow will remain,
Both will return to nothingness again;
Live with what joy you can, since joy ensures
Intensity to life while life is yours,
And since our days on earth must end tomorrow
Why should we seek unnecessary sorrow?

MOBAD ENTRUSTS VIS TO THE NURSE

سپردن ویس به دایه

Mobad entrusts Vis to the nurse, and Ramin enters the palace gardens

Mobad came back from Sari and Gorgan,
One Sunday night in spring, to Khorasan,
And had a rampart built, a new defense
Around his palace's circumference,
And then had brass and iron render all
The palace walls themselves impregnable;
Alani[105] locks of Indian steel, with keys
Of Roman make, secured the entrances,
And on the windows iron bars made sure
That every opening there was now secure.
Now that no breath of wind could penetrate
Beyond the palace walls or doors or gate,
He set gold seals upon each door, then handed
The keys to Vis's nurse, whom he commanded
To guard them well. He said, "I've seen from you
Ruses and wiles and lies in all you do,
You could teach demons tricks and treachery,
But try this time to act with chivalry.

I'll be in Zavol for a month; take care
To keep my palace guarded while I'm there,
I've set these golden seals, see they remain
Just as they are till I come back again.
I've given you my keys, so now for once
Prove that you're worthy of my confidence.
This time I'll trust you, see that you obey me,
If you know right from wrong you won't betray me,
I'm testing you, act well and you'll soon see
How richly you'll be recompensed by me.
I'm adding to my grief, of that I'm sure,
By testing what I've tested here before,
But I have heard resourceful men attest
That of all guardians bandits are the best."

Mobad chose an auspicious time and day
And set out with his soldiers on his way;
When they pitched camp tumultuous thoughts of Vis
Left him with not a single moment's peace,
And all the glories of his royal reign
Tasted of bitterness and parting's pain.
Ramin was with him but stayed out of sight
And doubled back to Marv again that night.
As evening fell, and it was time to dine,
Mobad inquired for him, to share his wine,
And when they said, "Ramin has gone," he knew
Exactly what Ramin now meant to do –
Ramin would see his love, and treachery
Was all that he, Mobad, would ever see.

Ramin approached the palace gardens' gate
And found it firmly locked; the hour was late,
And using night and darkness as his cover
He scaled the wall and quickly scrambled over.

Now sick at heart he paced the walks, on fire
With love and longing and renewed desire;
Impatience filled his anguished heart and head
As, moaning in love's agonies, he said:
"My dearest love, my Vis, whom jealousy
Has jubilantly snatched away from me,
Climb to your roof now, see me clutch and tear
The clothes about my heart in my despair.
This night seems like an ocean where I'm drowned,
Whose endless depths and shores cannot be found,
My tears are pearls and coral, and the trees
That sway above me seem like moving seas;
The tears I weep now, and the blood I shed,
Deepen these pomegranate blossoms' red,
But what can tears avail me when you know
Nothing of all my agony and woe?
One sigh of mine could utterly consume
This palace wall by wall and room by room,
But how can I do this when she is here,
And she too in that fire would disappear?
If fire so much as touched her skirt its flame
Would sear my soul with misery and shame.

        Your eyebrows' bow has shot your glances' dart
And pierced, dear Vis, the armor of my heart;
Fortune has parted me from you, but I
Shall see your lovely image till I die.
Sometimes you leave my eyes deprived of sleep,
Then fill them with my tears, and make me weep;
Why should I sleep if you're not here beside me?
Why should I live if you're not here to guide me?"
But, when he'd wept a while, sleep overtook him,
He lay down on the ground, and sense forsook him;
Now eglantine and lilies were his bed,
And box trees towered above his sleeping head.

This thundercloud of grief, this heart that made
Hell seem as gentle as a garden's shade,[106]
Now slept a while among the mingled scents
That breathed of Vis's charm and elegance.

But, while he slept, within the palace walls
Vis scored her cheeks, pacing the rooms and halls.
She sensed Ramin was near, and wept, and acted
Like one whom grief and madness have distracted,
And cried out to her nurse in misery,
"Oh, take this heavy weight of grief from me;
Open the doors, and let my soul catch sight
Of that resplendent sun on this dark night.
My fate's as black as night; he's drawing near,
It's but a step now, nurse, I know he's here,
But all these doors are locked, and you could say
My love is sixty parasangs[107] away;
Alas, a lengthy path that's harsh and hard
Is easier than one that's blocked and barred.
Ah, nurse have pity on me, bring the keys,
Open these doors now, nurse, I beg you, please!
Oh, I was born to grief, love's longings chain me,
You don't need doors and shackles to detain me!
Why wound the wounded? And why lock the door
On one whose heart is locked for evermore?
I'm caught within his curls, his musky hair
Has chained my soul to longing and despair,
Look where his stature's silver arrow lies
Lodged now immovably within my eyes!"

The nurse replied: "Now no one, Vis, will see
Your nurse act any way but honorably;
When someone like our king instructs me to
Be careful that I keep an eye on you

How could I open all these doors? You're mad!
How do you think I can oppose Mobad?
No, I don't think a thousand armies can
Successfully oppose that splendid man!
Besides, he had me swear I'd keep you here;
Don't tell me I should break my oath, my dear.
You can desire Ramin a hundred times
More than you do, I won't abet your crimes.
The king's not half a parasang away –
Perhaps he's testing us, Vis, who can say?
I'm sure he won't stay where he is all night,
He'll be back here before the morning light.
Mobad will hurt us if we hurt him, Vis,
This mischief we've been up to has to cease!
Think of the proverb wise men love to say,
'The wrongs we do return to us one day.'"
The nurse paused, and her heartfelt rage so moved her
She turned from Vis, to show how she reproved her.
When she resumed she said, "My dear, you should
Act well to King Mobad, be meek and good;
Restrain yourself tonight at least, control
For now the hope and longing in your soul,
Then later on do all you want to do.
Tonight I fear what he might do to you!
For now obey me, be discreet and wise,
And pray that we can blind the Devil's eyes."

The nurse left; Vis, however, could not rest
But paced the rooms, and wildly beat her breast,
Seeking for some way that she might discover
Up to the roof, from where she'd reach her lover,
But not a chink or cranny could she find.
And so, on fire with love, she searched her mind,
Trusting her wits to give her inspiration
And show how she might save the situation.

Within the palace courtyard[108] was a tent
That towered up to the starry firmament;
It was secured by ropes, and in each rope
Vis spied an answer and a source of hope.
She slipped her shoes off, leaped, and seemed to fly
As if she were a falcon in the sky
(A squall of wind snatched at her ruby crown,
Which, as she caught the rope, went tumbling down;
Her necklace snapped, its glistening pearls were scattered,
Her earrings fell and in their fall were shattered).
      She leaped again, and gained the roof, then ran
To where she knew the garden wall began.
There she secured her veil; grasping one end,
She jumped, on fire with hope to find her friend;
But, as she fell, her clothes snagged on the wall,
And though soft vegetation broke her fall
Both of her feet were hurt. The dress she'd worn,
Her tunic and her pants,[109] were slashed and torn;
She loosed her belt and let the tatters go,
And she was naked now from head to toe.
Barefoot, she ran to every corner of
The shadowy garden searching for her love;
Her feet now flowed with blood, her eyes with tears,
As she bewailed her fate and voiced her fears:
"Where shall I find his lovely face again?
Where shall I find that springtime among men?
I shouldn't run so pointlessly, since night
Will not reveal the sun's resplendent light.
But you, O morning breeze, if you can take
Some pity on me now for friendship's sake,
If you can pity wretches, pity me,
A woman struck down by adversity!
I grant that you traverse the world, but you
Don't bleed as my poor feet are forced to do,

Your road is not so long, the ways you tread
Don't bring such sufferings down upon your head!
Show me where I might find that man who's made
Despoiling girls like me his stock in trade,
Thousands there are whom he's defiled and hurt,
Whom he'll abduct, degrade, and then desert;
He's left so many thousands broken-hearted,
And used them, and indifferently departed,
While they're consumed in separation's fire,
In flames of hopeless longing and desire.
Ah, look what love's reduced me to! What sadness,
What shame and hardship, what despair and madness!
A hundred trials and troubles now assail me,
And all my fortitude and patience fail me.
But take my message to that man whose face
Is praised by everyone in every place;
Bring my cheeks' petals his sweet musk, and bear
My scent to his curled hyacinthine hair.
Address him, 'Spring of gardens, worthy of
All happiness, all pleasure, and all love,
Dear heart-bewitching sun whom all adore,
Whom even Beauty bows herself before,
You've lit a fire within my soul, you've made me
Haunt roofs and doors in darkness, and betrayed me;
I'm heartbroken, and you don't comfort me,
Desperate, and you withhold your sympathy.

Fate makes me wander shelterless and weeping,
Fate makes me sleepless while the world is sleeping;
Why, if I'm human, must my life be so
Unlike the lives of others whom I know?
Here, in my wretchedness, I curse my fate,
My luckless life, my mind's distracted state!
Ramin, you called me to you and I'm here,
But where are you? Who is it that you fear?

Why don't you come to me, and ask me how
I have endured your absence until now?
If I see moonlight, not your face's light,
The moon will be a pit, a loathsome sight;
If I smell musk, and not your musky hair,
Musk will be dust, and I'll embrace despair;
If I taste sherbet, not your sugared lip,
I swear it will be poison that I sip –
Since what are musk and sugared drinks to me?
You are both love and love's sweet remedy.
Your locks' black snakes have bitten my poor heart,
My wounded soul is ready to depart,
My medicine is your lips, my sun your face,
But now you've disappeared without a trace
And I am left alone on this dark night,
Deprived of you and your reviving light.
My friends and foes both pity me; can you
Not pity me, Ramin, as others do?'
    Where are you now, O moon? Why don't you rise,
A silver mirror in the eastern skies,
And flood the mountaintops with light, and see
The hundred sorrows that encompass me?
The world's corroded iron, it's filth and rust,
Desire's betrayed me, and its vows are dust;
My heart has gone from me, my love's departed,
And we're two lovers, lost and broken-hearted.
Come to my aid, O moon, bestow your light
To guide me through this dark and fearful night –
My love's a moon like you; without his face
The world to me's a dismal, dreary place.
Oh, pity me, dear God, grant me the sight
Of these two shining, glorious moons tonight –
One with its solitary radiance,
One with its glory and magnificence;

One in the turning skies that shines alone,
One who becomes the saddle and the throne."

When half of night's dark army had passed by
The moon rose shining in the eastern sky,
A silver boat upon a sea, a charm
That glittered on a dusky houri's arm.
Now, as the air grew clearer, Vis's soul
Began to reassert its self-control,
And then she saw her lover lying there,
With violets clustered in his violet hair,
With faintly blushing roses held in place
Beneath the pressure of his rosy face.
The moon and Vis looked down, spring's musky breeze
Played in the blossoms of the garden's trees;
But it was Vis's scent that woke Ramin.
He looked around him at the moonlit scene;
Her jasmine breasts, her cypress stature, shared
The flowery bed on which he lay. He stared,
And started up, and clasped her to his chest,
And, oh, how eagerly his hands caressed
Her curls' sweet ambergris, so that two scents
Mingled their sweetness and magnificence;
Her ambergris and his sweet musk were one,
The full moon was united with the sun.
Like jasmine plants their bodies intertwined,
Or two brocades a tailor has combined,
Like milk and wine, like lilies placed beside
The pomegranate blossoms of springtide.
Their faces lit the darkness, and they lay
As if surrounded by the light of day,
A thousand nightingales filled all the night
With tales of their affection and delight,
The tulips smiled on them, the roses drew
New beauty from them and a livelier hue.

Now as love's mutual secrets passed between
The lovely Vis and her loved Prince Ramin
What joy they gave each other! But the field
That's sown by lovers' happiness must yield
To Time's cruel sickle; soon the ugly face
Of dawn drew near, so that their trysting place
Seemed like a spot where animals are branded.
Why should you think the world is evenhanded?
Why do you listen to its blandishments
And treat its pledges with such confidence?
No man's unhurt by it, no man survives
The shameless way it deals with human lives.

MOBAD GOES TO THE GARDEN WHEN HE HEARS OF RAMIN'S ABSENCE

Mobad learned that Ramin had gone, and pain
Transformed itself to hatred once again.
He fought a battle in his heart all night:
"How long must I endure this wretch's spite?
While there's one person left alive, my name
Will be a byword for disgrace and shame;
I've let this ghoul destroy my reputation,
I've made a banner of my degradation.
Vis may be like the sun, or like the heaven
That those whom Fortune blesses will be given,
But she's not worth this weight of misery,
This black despair, this hopeless agony.
Yes she's as sweet as roses, but desire
For sweetness has destroyed me in its fire;
And yes her lips are nectar, but their taste
Has poisoned me and laid my spirit waste;
Yes she's a houri in her loveliness,
But she's a demon too and pitiless.
To seek her love's like trying to wash away
Clay from a sun-dried brick that's made of clay;

It's to drink poison, thinking it might prove
To be a honeyed draught of joy and love.
Why should I try what I've already tried
And make myself still more dissatisfied?
Why ask a devil to behave with kindness,
Or seek for sight from one who's cursed with blindness?
Why ask a bear to cherish and befriend me,
Or hope a ghoul will nourish me and tend me?
And why ask Vis for love or sympathy,
Or that accursèd nurse for loyalty?
I left a thousand locks in her safekeeping,
My heart was dazed, my intellect was sleeping!
I threw musk to the whirling winds, I made
A wolf the guardian of my lamb's stockade;
I chose as fools choose, and like them I sit
Grieved by my choice now, and regretting it.
Ah, I deserve this, I've been deaf and blind,
I've exiled Wisdom from my heart and mind
(Wisdom whose lessons should have guided me),
And I've not seen what I could plainly see.
If I go back, my army will discover
That I'm quite certain Vis is with her lover;
What will they call me then? Already they
Despise my weakness, to a man they'll say
I'm not a man! And they'll be right to treat me
With such contempt, when women can defeat me."

Till dawn the king's thoughts wandered in a maze
That led a hundred contradictory ways:
At times he said, "I'll try to hide this shame,
My actions mustn't tarnish my good name."
At times, "What's it to me if everyone
Gossips about the things I've said and done?
I must go back!" Now Wisdom was his guide,
And now the demon of his injured Pride;

At times his mind was water, bright and clear,
At times a smoky cloud of rage and fear,
But gradually his Anger won the field,
And captured Wisdom was compelled to yield.
The shining moon arose; Mobad retraced
His steps to Marv in ignominious haste.

He found his castle locked, and had to wait,
Until the nurse arrived, outside the gate.
She showed him every bolt was still intact,
The locks untampered with, the seals uncracked –
All just as they had been when he departed.
Now reassured, and suddenly light-hearted,
Mobad went in – to find that he'd been shown
A locked but empty cage; the bird had flown;
And though the necklace's strong clasp was sound
Its pendant jewel was nowhere to be found.
He turned upon the nurse, "Where is my Vis?
When will your devilish machinations cease?
Where have you spirited my wife to now?
How did you get her through locked doors, nurse? How?
The locks are here, but where is she? She might
For all I know have gone to spend the night
With King Zahhak in Damavand,[110] since she's
His equal with her tricks and treacheries!"
He whipped the nurse, and as his anger rose
She fainted from the violence of his blows.
He searched the rooms, and ransacked every place
Where Vis might be, but turned up not one trace
Of where she'd gone, until at last he found
Her veil, and saw her slippers on the ground
(Who could have guessed she'd used the guy ropes of
The courtyard's tent to lead her to her love?).

He burst into the garden, and the night
Was lit up with his servants' torches' light;
Vis saw them and her heart, distraught with love,
Trembled and fluttered like a frightened dove.
"Get up, my love," she whispered to Ramin,
"The king is coming, you must not be seen!
Hurry, my love, you can't stay here with me,
Darkness approaches with those lights you see,
Mobad is here, he's like a lion who
Has lain in wait till he can leap on you.
Go now, you must escape, while I await
The shameful blows that are my wretched fate;
I wish that all your woes could light on me
While you knew only joy and victory!
May God be with you, go, and I will bow
Before the flood that must engulf me now.
My fate's a tale that everyone now knows –
One kiss from you, from him a hundred blows!
Thorns guard the dates I long for, and distress
Awaits me in the midst of happiness."

Ramin's heart felt so weak and wan you'd say
He'd fainted and his life had drained away;
He seemed a soulless statue, every limb
Grew slack, his strength and will deserted him;
He pitied Vis, and was so loath to part
It seemed an arrow had transfixed his heart.
Unwillingly he rose, and felt he went
From danger to a worse predicament;
The king was like a snare, but separation
From Vis was like a pit of desolation,
And if he fled the dangers of the snare
The pit awaited him, and black despair.
When lovers are conjoined no enemy
Can seem as cruel as parting seems to be

(Together they are sure that they can master
Any privation, sorrow, or disaster).
May no one love as wildly as these two;
May nothing separate them if they do.

Ramin now fled from Vis's side as though
He were an arrow speeding from a bow;
Then, like a nimbly scrambling mountain sheep,
He scaled the garden wall, and with a leap
Was on the other side; just as the snare
Closed in on him, Ramin had fled elsewhere.
But jasmine-breasted Vis lay moaning, sighing,
Gripped by an anguish that was worse than dying;
This moon of beauty's soul was tossed between
Exhaustion and her longing for Ramin.
She laid her head upon her silver hand,
Her fingers shone like fishes brought to land
Within the intricacies of her hair,
As if she'd cast her curls to catch them there;
And on her hand were hennaed loops and swirls
As black and labyrinthine as those curls.
        As soon as King Mobad discovered her
He harshly kicked her, but she did not stir;
Ramin had left, and in her grief she lay
As though her spirit too had slunk away.
The king sent men to every corner of
The palace grounds to find her hidden love;
They scoured the garden but could find no trace
Of any living soul in any place
Except for birds, whose pretty melodies
Resounded from the branches of the trees;
They searched the trees themselves, and carefully
Parted the foliage of every tree –
They looked a hundred ways for Prince Ramin
And only saw that he could not be seen,

And since they did not know their prey had gone
Their futile, unproductive search went on.

Mobad addressed Vis: "Well then, tell me how
I should behave. How should I treat you now?
I fitted fifty bolts, made doubly sure
I'd barred the windows, and locked every door,
And left you here. And in a single night
I find the bird I left has taken flight –
Nothing I do is able to detain you,
No stratagems or iron can restrain you.
Wisdom's as far from you as is the sphere
Of sacred heaven itself, but lust's as near
As is your soul to your disgusting mind.
        Your ears are deaf to me, your eyes are blind,
And wisdom's pearls to you are like a pan
For cooking given to a starving man,
Or shoes to someone like a fuller whose
Wet feet have neither need nor use for shoes.
If I advise you, Wisdom will, I know,
Abandon my poor soul and simply go;
Besides, advising you is an abuse
Of language since it's of no earthly use.
How could I calculate the wrongs you've done
To me by tallying them one by one?
If I'm to number your iniquities
I'll have to count them off in centuries.
You're like Bimashi,[111] Vis, since you reject
Whatever pathways Virtue might select,
You cut off Virtue's head, and tear apart,
As soon as you locate it, Virtue's heart;
You loathe all Righteousness, and where you find her
You cruelly gouge out both her eyes to blind her.
You might be visible, but all the same
You are a demon, Vis, in all but name,

You might be beautiful, but you are still
Possessed of an ignoble, wicked will.
I've known of no one, Vis, who is more shameless,
And this to me, whose love for you's been blameless.
It seems as though some devil's said to you,
'Heaven is yours if evil's all you do,'
May you, your nurse, that paramour you cherish,
And all your cronies and companions perish!
You're like a plague – I swear, Vis, that it's licit
To take your life, and if I do who'll miss it?
I'll kill you now, my sword will set you free
From your sick self; here's your soul's remedy!"

With that he wound her hair about his wrist
And grasped his deadly sword within his fist;
His sword blade glittered like bright silk, her hair
Was braided musk – whoever saw a pair
(A silken sword, a noose of ambergris)
Like these two weapons of Mobad and Vis?
But as he raised his silken sword to sever
The full moon from its cypress tree forever,[112]
To cut the rose and scatter in the mud
The fragile petals of her crimson blood
(Vis brooded on Ramin still, and ignored
The glittering menace of her husband's sword),
Zard intervened and said: "Your majesty,
May you live prosperously and happily
As all your friends would wish – but, if you kill
Your noble wife, in doing so you'll spill
The one effective medicine for your pain;
A severed head will not grow back again.
　　How many days must yield themselves to night
Before the world brings forth another sight
As lovely as her face! And when you think
Of Vis's radiance your heart will sink,

You'll twist and turn in torments of despair
As blackly serpentine as Vis's hair.
You'll never find her equal, or be given
A houri who's as sweet as her in heaven,
And you'll have quantities of tears to shed,
But they'll be worse than useless when she's dead.

You've tried to live without her once, and I
Don't think you're eager for another try;
Though, if this wretched color pleases you,
Then dip your other hand in – dye it too!
But I saw how you were when she departed,
How wild love made you, and how broken-hearted,
So that you wandered in the plains where deer
And asses passed you by and felt no fear,
Or on the seashore, or in reed beds where
You lived with lions in their marshy lair.
Have you forgotten how distressed you were,
As I was too for you, from love of her?
Recall the solemn oaths you've sworn, my lord,
Think what will happen if you break your word;
Think of the honor that you owe Shahru,
Think of Viru's long loyalty to you.

Yes, Vis has sinned before, but here, today,
You have no evidence she's gone astray;
And if she's slept here, well it's not unknown
To sleep in gardens and be quite alone!
If she's had someone with her, tell me how
He's got away from us, where is he now?
This castle's ramparts reach the Pleiades,
Strong, iron bolts secure its entrances –
No bird could overfly the ramparts here,
No demon make these barriers disappear;
Perhaps Vis chose this pretty place to be
Alone and pensive in her misery,

And now you want to aggravate her pain
By branding an existing scar again?
Question her, punish her according to
The things she says, and how she answers you;
But if you stab Vis with that sword, you'll feel
The wound as well, and it will never heal."

With winning words Zard managed to assuage
The king's contempt for Vis, and all his rage.
Mobad cut curls from Vis's musky hair
And seemed content to leave the matter there,
Then took her by the hand and gently led
Her back into the palace where he said,
"Before God, Vis, how were you able to
Get past the barriers that imprisoned you?
You're not an arrow, or a bird to fly
About the further reaches of the sky!
How did you get into the garden then?
Sometimes I think you're not like mortal men,
I think that you know magic, that you've made
Demonic tricks and spells your murky trade;
It must be that you know such secrets well
If you can bring off such a tricky spell!"

And lovely, jasmine-breasted Vis replied,
"I know that God is always at my side;
What do I care for your malevolence
When God protects me with his providence?
He saves me from your sword when you would slay me,
And when you steal from me He makes you pay me;
You lessen what I am, while He increases me,
And you imprison me, while He releases me:
When you declare that I'm your enemy
It's God you're really fighting with, not me.

He tears up all you sew, and what you sow
He slashes so that it will never grow;
You lock me up, then bring me to your bed,
You rage at me, then flatter me instead,
But God does not allow you to restrain me,
He breaks your locks, He will not let you chain me.
You are my king, Mobad, my enemy,
And He's my solace in adversity;
God helps the helpless, God befriends all those
Abandoned to the mercy of their foes.
Heartsick and suffering in your rooms, I cried
For God to comfort me and be my guide;
I told Him of your cruelty; as I wept
Worn out with grief and misery I slept.
      Then, in my sleep, an angel dressed in green,[113]
The loveliest being I have ever seen,
Appeared to me; he caught me up and flew
Down to the spot where I was found by you.
He took me to the garden from your room,
He freed me from that overwhelming gloom,
And not a hair of mine was hurt; my bed
Was eglantine, I'd lilies at my head,
And there beside me lay Ramin;[114] his face
Lit up the garden with its radiant grace
As whispering secrets then we spent the night
In mutual joy and passionate delight
Until our shared desire was satisfied
And we lay gently sleeping side by side
Where eglantine and roses grew around us,
And joy and happiness and sleep had found us.
But when I woke from that sweet sleep the sight
Of you destroyed my briefly won delight;
As if you were a savage lion you roared,
Like flashing fire you shook your glittering sword.

Believe me, doubt me, but I give my word
That I have said exactly what occurred,
However unexpected it might seem
An angel came and helped me in my dream;
How cruel you are! You know you can't condemn
A person's dreams, or what goes on in them!"

The moon-faced beauty lied, Mobad believed her
And asked her to forgive him that he'd grieved her;
He gave the nurse and Vis new gifts, he plied them
With clothes and jewels, and nothing was denied them.
The king and Vis put by their ancient feud;
In ruby wine their friendship was renewed.

So Adam's offspring live, and put away
The happiness and grief of yesterday.
Why should you grieve for what's gone by? Forget!
Why brood on things that haven't happened yet?
Grief won't bring back the past, and all your scolding
Will not prevent the future from unfolding.
Enjoy a hundred years of victory
But one day's all your lifetime here will be;
Whatever riches you might hope to win
One day alone is yours – the day you're in;
The best course is to look for pleasure, to
Enjoy the single day that's given you.

IN THE PALACE GARDENS MOBAD HOLDS FESTIVITIES AT WHICH A MINSTREL SINGS

One day in spring, when all the world was glad,
As lovely as Karkh's gardens in Baghdad,[115]
When deserts flowered like gardens, and the sight
Of pretty girls filled gardens with delight,
As if they were like pagan temples where
Men bow before the lovely idols there,

When silver blossoms drifted from the trees
And fluttered in the musk-diffusing breeze,
When all of nature seemed to be arrayed
For courtly festivals where minstrels played,
Whose harps were voices of sweet nightingales,
Whose flutes were ringdoves' moans and plaintive wails,
Where bold narcissi passed the wine around
And drunken violets nodded to the ground,
Where boughs were like jeweled crowns, where charm and grace
Rivaled the fabled Layla's[116] lovely face,
Where earth shone emerald green, and tulips made
Bright topaz of the mountain's granite shade.
The earth was heaven, as gorgeous as a bride,
Where Vis and King Mobad sat side by side;
Next to them, on their right, sat brave Viru,
While on their left sat radiant Shahru;
Before them sat Ramin, the warrior prince
Whose like has not been seen before or since,
And next to him a minstrel sat, whose art
Delighted every listener's mind and heart.
The wine went round continually, which made
For wine-red faces as the minstrel played;
He sang a strange and unfamiliar piece
That told obliquely of Ramin and Vis;
Consider now the minstrel's song with care
And you will see the meaning hidden there.

THE MINSTREL'S SONG

"Upon a mountaintop I saw a tree
That rose into the sky's immensity;
The shadow of this tree of unmatched worth
Covers the provinces of half the earth,
Its beauty's sun-like, and the world believes
Good fortune lives within its fruits and leaves.

There at its feet a stream, intensely bright,
Shines with a priceless pearl's refulgent light;
How sweet its waters are, and where they flow
Hyacinths, violets, and wild tulips grow!
A strong young bull is grazing there, the kind
That brings Gilani buffalos[117] to mind;
He drinks the limpid water, and devours
The springtime grass and thickly clustered flowers.
May this sweet stream flow on as I have sung,
The tree stay fruitful, and the bull stay young!"
The king exclaimed, "Well done, and no mistake!
You're singing this for that young prince's sake,
Beneath the cover of your pretty lays
You're hinting at Ramin's malignant ways."
Vis took a hundred gold rings[118] from her hair
And gave them to the minstrel sitting there,
And said, "Now sing a song in praise of me,
But sing it so the meaning's plain to see,
Sing of our love, which Mobad says you've hidden.
Sing openly. Now, do as you've been bidden."

Once more[119] the skillful minstrel played, once more
He sang the song that he had sung before,
But this time as he sang he interwove
A gloss that told of their illicit love:
The fruitful tree with its inclusive shade
Was King Mobad, whom half the world obeyed;
Its leaves were glory and its fruit was fame,
Its roots were power, its top his noble name;
The shining stream was Vis, his splendid queen,
Her smile the limpid water's pearl-like sheen,
The flowers that grew with such bewitching grace
The myriad beauties of her lovely face;
The bull was Prince Ramin, who sometimes drank,
And sometimes grazed upon the flowery bank.

"May heaven," he sang, "augment the shady tree
So that it thrives for all eternity;
May fate ensure the stream forever plays there,
And may the bull forever drink and graze there."

The minstrel ended his description of
The lovers and the story of their love.
The king sprang up in rage, in one hand shone
A poisoned knife, the other closed upon
Ramin's young beard. "Now swear," he cried, "swear by
The sun and moon as they traverse the sky,
That you will never more show love to Vis,
That all your courtship of my wife will cease.
Swear this to me, or I shall cut your head
Clean from your trunk and leave you here for dead –
My shame has made me lose my head; God knows it!
It's you who's done this, your behavior shows it!"
Ramin said, "By the moon, by God above,
And by the stars, I'll not renounce my love;
In this world and the world to come I swear
As others face the sun in prayer,[120] my prayer
Will always be to her belovèd face,
I will not turn from her in any place;
She is the sweetness of my soul, and I
Cannot renounce her while I live or die."
The king then cursed Ramin, and with his knife
Lunged at him to deprive him of his life,
But Prince Ramin grasped both his wrists (you'd say
A nimble lion made a fox its prey)
And threw him to the ground, and pried the hasp
Of his sharp Indian dagger from his grasp.
Mobad was tipsy, wine had quite bereft him
Of strength and consciousness, and both had left him;
His mind could not take in what Prince Ramin
Had done to him, and he forgot the scene.

How drunkenness and love drive Wisdom out,
And in its stead bring misery and doubt!
If he had not allowed these two to hurt him
Evil could not have made Delight desert him.

Behgui advises Ramin

The sun rose, and the air grew clear and bright
As if it were a sword reflecting light,
And all the earth turned yellow then as though
Crushed saffron shone there with its golden glow.
There was a subtle and experienced man,
The best astrologer in Khorasan,
Whose name was Behgui,[121] and this made sense
Since he possessed unrivalled eloquence.
He sat with Prince Ramin now night and day
Trying to sluice the prince's grief away;
He'd say, "One day you will be king, desire
Will furnish you whatever you require,
The tree of fortune will bear fruit, you'll be
The first in all the world for sovereignty."
When he arrived that morning he perceived
Ramin's tears, and how desperately he grieved.
He said, "Why these low spirits? What's upset you?
Be happy now! What can there be to fret you?
You're young, and you're a prince; what more can you
Require now, in addition to these two?
How long will you let love and passion fool you,
And twist your suffering soul, and have grief rule you?
You've vexed your soul so much that she will be,
When you meet God, your angry enemy;
Why, whilst you live, should you not make the choice
To give yourself to pleasure and rejoice?
If God's will does not change, if His commands
Are absolute, and fate lies in His hands,

Why should one grieve so vainly? Or take fright
At things that time has yet to bring to light?"

Weary and sick at heart, Ramin replied,
"The truth of what you say can't be denied,
You see the world, and what you say about it
Is all too true my friend, and I don't doubt it;
But when the heavens' cruelty's all we're shown...
A man's heart isn't iron, or a stone,
That he can turn to pleasure for relief
When he's tormented by unyielding grief.
How much does one poor body have to bear?
How long can one poor heart endure despair?
The world has more unsavory tricks than we
Have strength or patience or tenacity.
Rain falls in every life, I know, but I've
Endured a tempest to remain alive;
There's not one day that passes but I feel
Fate brand me, and the scars will never heal.
Whenever joy is promised me, a snare
Is certain to be lurking somewhere there,
And if I'm crowned with roses every bud
Conceals a thorn to prick me and draw blood;
I never drank down wine and did not find
A draught of poison following on behind.
With such a fate and such a life, who can
Pretend that he's a happy, carefree man?
Given that I was shamed last night, berated,
Attacked, degraded, and humiliated,
The best course open to me is if I
Forget about advice and simply die."
And then he told Behgui everything
That had occurred between him and the king,
Of how, in front of Vis, Mobad had blamed him,
And raged at him, and threatened him, and shamed him.

He said, "I'd rather die than have to face
The bitter degradation and disgrace.
I can put up with anything, but don't
Ask me to bear such shame, because I won't."

Now hear how Behgui replied (and may
You give a similar reply one day).
When Prince Ramin had had his say, and shed
His tears, and wailed a while, Behgui said,
"How you complain about your fate! Should you,
A lion, whine about what jackals do?
But weep and wail, Fortune will come again
Returning joy will banish all your pain,
Still, for as long as longing haunts your heart
These agonies you suffer won't depart.
You shouldn't fall in love if you can't bear
The miseries that lovers have to share.
Didn't you know when seeds of love are sown
Grief is the harvest once its shoots have grown?
That when you're plucking roses one by one
A thorn might scratch your hand before you're done?
You're like a merchant who's made love his trade:
Sometimes a loss, sometimes a profit's made,
But you thought only profits would accrue,
That losses couldn't hurt or threaten you;
You thought you'd have a fire without the smoke,
But love is not a pastime or a joke.
The man who sows this field is anxious, worried,
The sowing, growing, reaping can't be hurried;
You thought you'd sow love's seeds, and in a trice
You'd have a houri straight from paradise,
You didn't know how much you'd suffer here
Before your longed-for harvest would appear.
    How many times I've told you not to take
Such burdens on your body for love's sake!

Love's like a raging sea, no wise man would
Think sailing there could come to any good,
Love in the heart is like a raging fire,
What pleasures are there in a burning pyre?
While Vis remains your friend Mobad will be
Your stubborn and relentless enemy;
So tell yourself you'll suffer shame and grief,
That hardships borne will bring you no relief,
That all your body will be racked with pain
And sorrow will become your heart's refrain.
A mammoth's your opponent in this fight,
Who knows if you can overcome his might?
A raging lion is leaping from his lair,
And who knows how your lion heart will fare?
You're all at sea without a ship, you think
You'll find your royal pearl before you sink,
But who knows how all this will end for you,
What good or bad the heavens portend for you?
You've built a house where sudden floods arise
And heedless fools are taken by surprise,
How carelessly you sleep there, as if sunk
In lethargy like someone who is drunk,
But winds will blow and storms will come one day
To sweep both you and your frail house away.

     A hundred times you've stepped into love's snare
And luck has always helped you, but beware –
One day you won't escape, your soul will find
That it's forever captured and confined,
And then your shame will shame your present shame
And you will only have yourself to blame,
What shame do you know worse than this, to be
Confined to hell for all eternity,
Where you will suffer, overwhelmed with grief,
And your regret will never find relief?

But, if you can, take my advice, and learn
That patience has to be your first concern:
There is no strength or heroism like
Patience when parting comes and sorrows strike;
If you will but be patient, you can start
To cleanse the rust that eats into your heart.
If you can find a lover far from here
And not set eyes on Vis now for a year,
You won't be sorry that you've had to lose her,
You will forget her and what made you choose her.
When conquering love subdues a sickly lover
No medicine makes his wretched heart recover
Like Absence can; then, certainly, you'll find
That out of sight is truly out of mind,
And there'll be many days you won't recall
The lineaments of Vis's face at all.
    Events confront a man and they demand
That he react; this might be sword in hand,
With cash, with learning, with some kind of plot,
With tricks or intrigues or I don't know what,
But now this problem has confronted you
It's clear you've no idea what you should do.
You are a byword; in your brother's eyes
You're someone to disparage and despise,
When commoners or courtiers drink they name you
As someone worthy of contempt; they blame you
For all of your behavior, which they say
Has grown unchivalrous in every way.
'What is the point of such a wretched creature,'
They ask, 'who shames his brother by his nature?'
If Vis had been the sun and moon in heaven,
The sweetest prize that Wisdom could be given,
All that the soul could hope for or require,
All love could ever long for or desire,

Ramin should still have known that sense and duty
Prevented him from coveting her beauty.
May any love or happiness we cherish
That brings an evil reputation perish,
For when a name is soiled a hundred seas
Won't wash away its foul impurities;
The soul endures forever and its fame
Is bound up with its good or evil name.
And has Ramin no friend who can advise him
Not to do things that make the world despise him?
A wise friend's better than a jewel, you'll find
No fiefdom's worth more than a friendly mind.

    Your heart has had its fill of Vis, the tree
Of love's rewarded you abundantly,
And let a hundred years pass, she won't change,
She'll still be Vis, not someone new or strange.
You know her, so take heed of my advice:
She's not a houri come from paradise,
She's not the moon, and there are thousands who
Are lovelier and far more fit for you.
How can you spend your youth, your life, in thrall
To one girl and not see the rest at all?
If you find someone else, you'll soon discover
Your heart no longer wants Vis for a lover;
You've had no basis for comparison
And this is why Vis seems a paragon,
You haven't seen the moon yet, which is why
You think your star the center of the sky.
Drive out this love, from which your heart has grown
So weak and tired, and strike out on your own!
From China, and from India, every land
Lies under your and King Mobad's command,
And to the west your potent sovereignty
Stretches as far as Rome and Barbary:

Our Khorasan is not the only place,
Vis doesn't have the only lovely face,
So go to other lands, and everywhere
Discover silver-breasted beauties there,
Review them all, compare them all, and soon
You'll find a lover lovelier than the moon,
A pretty girl whose charming face and smiles
Will make you quite forget Vis and her wiles.
      Enjoy your life and wealth, and while you can
Grasp at the pleasures that are given man.
It's time for you to make peace with your brother,
So that once more you'll honor one another,
It's time for you to turn to chivalry,
To feasting, war, and knightly dignity,
It's time for you to seek magnificence
By living justly, under providence.
You are a prince, so act like one, and cease
To hang around that wretched nurse and Vis,
Who have destroyed your royal reputation
And bring you only anger and frustration;
For years you have pursued them; change your story,
Pursue bright honor now, and princely glory.
Your friends are out there seeking noble names
While all you've sought is love and silly games,
How long can such behavior be defended?
It's time your trivial, joking days were ended!
What demon was it cast his spell and made you
So dully weak and wanton, and betrayed you?
Because it is a devil and a traitor
Whom you now serve, and not the world's creator;
I fear the end you're headed for will please
No one at all but your sworn enemies.
      But listen to my words, they'll show you how
You can escape the griefs that crush you now,

Wisdom will come from woe, pleasure from pain,
Comfort from grief, you'll be Ramin again.
If you're not sated with the life you're seeking
You cannot hear me and I've not been speaking!
But I'm an onlooker, all I can do
Is see your struggles and encourage you."

And all the while that Behgui addressed him
Ramin was silent as if grief oppressed him;
You'd say he was a donkey, one who sticks
Deeper in mud the more he strains and kicks;
His face turned tulip red at the attack,
Then saffron pale, and then a pitchy black.
He said, "It's true, all that you've said to me,
My heart's become my soul's sworn enemy.
I heard your words, I heard them, and I'll start
This moment, now, to turn against my heart.
You'll see, I won't be lust's slave any more,
I shall not be as I have been before.
Tomorrow I shall go to Mahabad,
I'll be a wild ass, free, unfettered, glad;
But I won't look for pretty lovers there,
Why should I look for scandals and despair?"

MOBAD ADVISES VIS AND REPROACHES HER

While Behgui was talking to Ramin
The king of kings was talking to his queen.
He talked so wisely and so well she felt
The stony heart within her yield and melt.
He set each point out one by one, and then
Painstakingly repeated them again.
He said, "You are the spring of love, your face
Is beauty's sun, unrivaled in its grace;
What pains I've suffered through my love for you,
What miseries your cruelty's put me through!

How long I've loved you, and how much you've sinned
By throwing my good fortune to the wind;
What evils are there that you've not committed?
What good deeds can you claim that I've omitted?
But I'm the world's king, Vis, and you're the queen
Of all the beauties that the earth has seen,
So let us rule now as good friends, and try
To live in happiness until we die.
You'll rule within the house, while I will be
The outward symbol of our sovereignty.
I'll have the name, but if the truth be known
You, Vis, will be the power behind the throne.
I give you every orchard, every town,
Each site of any splendor or renown,
Each upland filled with flowers, each flowery plain,
To be a place where you can live and reign.
My ministers are yours, and all my court,
And all of this I know falls far too short,
Since you deserve to reign here, to dispense
Our justice, and receive men's reverence.
And, as I love you, all men will obey you,
Who'd dare defy your orders, or betray you?

     My darling, listen to my words, I love you,
I wish you well, nothing for me's above you.
My soul is not like yours, I'm not suspicious,
My nature isn't false, or surreptitious;
My soul loves kindness, everything I say
Is wholly true, my love, in every way.
If you will but incline your heart to me,
And stop this dicing with dishonesty,
You'll have the mighty kings of every nation
Bowing before your threshold in prostration,
But if you go on as before, Mobad
Will be the bitterest foe you've ever had.

Ah, fear my deadly anger, dearest, fear it,
Since even fires are fearful to come near it!
How can you see your noble brother's face
Darkened with shame because of your disgrace?
If you had dealt more justly with Viru
I would have dealt more temperately with you;
But since you don't care for your valiant brother,
Your ancestors' good name, your noble mother,
I know that I can't hope you'll ever love me,
Not if the sun and moon should shine above me
And be my kingly crown. Don't fight with Fate,
Don't argue with me or prevaricate,
Just tell me which grows in your heart – the tree
Of friendship, or of bitter enmity?
Love's worn me out with longing and frustration,
And I have had my fill of moderation;
From now on Vis, to question you I'll stand
Before you with a drawn sword in my hand.
Ah, but my secret's out, and everyone
Now knows the wretched truth of what you've done!"

Vis answers Mobad

As Vis took in his admonitions she
Trembled and shuddered like a cypress tree,
Then said: "O mighty lord of all this land,
Your wisdom's greater than Mount Damavand;[122]
Your heart's accustomed to endure distress,
Your hand to scatter bounteous largesse.
God's granted you all that a sovereign needs,
Sunlike abilities, illustrious deeds,
And Fortune favoring you in each endeavor;
So may you live and reign, my lord, for ever!
Your fame is like the sun's, your royal orders
Are like God's law and recognize no borders.

My lord, you are aware the heavens display
A new face every hour of every day,
And that the consequences they attest
Are done at God's divinely just behest,
That He it is who has apportioned all
The world's realities, both great and small,
And that until the world's end He will be
The arbiter of every destiny,
That every being in the world fulfills
The ends that its divine Creator wills.
For better or for worse, it is His pen
That writes the fates of individual men;
No knowledge now can redirect our state
Or bravery rewrite our destined fate,
And when they contemplate the lives they've led,
The deeds Fate's given them, the words they've said,
Weakness and wonder equally condemn
The subtlest and the stupidest of men.

  If I am pure or foul, it's His decree
That's formed my nature; He created me,
And ever since my earthly life began
I've grown according to His destined plan.
I didn't say, 'I don't want happiness,
Please give me pain, and heartbreak, and distress.'
When I was born, sorrow was given me,
And I was brought up to adversity.
I didn't say, 'Please give me sallow skin
To show the sufferings of my heart within.'
And always when I said, 'I'm happy,' I
Found happiness to be a foolish lie.
What can I do if this is how Fate treats me,
If heaven hates my spirit and defeats me?
My heart's in mourning, and I've lost my way
As though some ghoul were leading me astray.

I'd gladly let a lion overpower me,
And tear me limb from limb, and so devour me;
Would that my nails could score my wretched heart,
Would that my teeth could rip my soul apart –
Would that I'd neither soul nor heart, since they're
The source of all my sorrow and despair!
Not for one day do cooling breezes blow
To ease my heart's intolerable woe,
Not for one day does happiness relieve
My wretched soul's necessity to grieve.
My life's a chaos, all I do is weep,
Whatever luck I had's now fast asleep,
Why should I look for love, why should I care
For love that's brought me scandal and despair,
That's made you execrate me and chastise me,
That's made my noble family despise me?
My secret's out, my foes all know of it,
To me the world's become a loathsome pit;
What use is love in such a situation,
Or longing in the midst of desperation?
And I'm a byword for disgrace, I know it,
The murmurings I hear about me show it.

But these same murmurings have shone new light
Into a soul that's been as dark as night,
They've opened up a door, they've shown my heart
That she and Wisdom should not live apart;
I've seen that love at last will mean that I
Will live in hell both here and when I die.
Love's like a fathomless, uncharted sea
Immeasurable in its immensity,
And if I traveled there forevermore
I know I'd never see its further shore,
If I'd a thousand Noahs' souls, I'd fail
To salvage even one to tell the tale.

Why should my wretched soul and I contend?
Why should I spill my blood to no good end?
Why should I not take your advice? Why should
I not turn now to everything that's good?
From now on if you see me injure you
Loathe me, and then decide what you must do.
If Prince Ramin becomes a lion he
Still won't possess the strength to conquer me,
And if he haunts my rooftop as a breeze
He won't scent Vis, for all his flatteries;
If he's a sorcerer he'll never find
A charm or spell to undermine my mind.
    Now, before you and God, I will not break
This oath I make for our affection's sake,
If you accept me, let this be a sign
That I am yours now just as you are mine –
And let your heart rejoice; from now on I
Will be like sugar to you till I die,
And you will find my mouth exhales the scent
Of truth and honesty, and sweet content."

The king heard words he'd never heard before,
And kissed her lovely eyes and cheeks, and swore
That he would love her, praise her, cherish her
And keep her safe whatever might occur.
The two now parted, and the words they'd spoken
Brought happiness; grief's army had been broken.

RAMIN LEAVES VIS AND TRAVELS TO GURAB

In early morning we already know
If there's to be a day of rain and snow;
The air turns dark, the world's bewildered by
The clouds that whirl about the windy sky.
A man feels lassitude in every limb
Before a raging fever seizes him,

And Fate will give some previous intimation
When she effects two lovers' separation.

Ramin was sick of sorrow, weary of
The days and nights he'd spent pursuing love,
Of always being trapped in snares that shamed him,
Of always hearing wagging tongues that blamed him,
And so he sent a message to Mobad
Asking that he be sent to Mahabad
To take charge of the royal armies there;
"My body aches here, and the change of air
Might free me from this weakness that I feel
And give my maladies a chance to heal.
I think that I can cure my body's ills there,
There's splendid hunting in the plains and hills there,
I'll catch the finest quarry, never fear –
With cheetahs I'll hunt mountain sheep and deer,
With hawks I'll bring down partridges and quail
And when you need my presence I won't fail
To hurry back to court at your behest."
Mobad was pleased, and granted his request,
And sent the royal seal for Kuhestan,
As well as that for Rey and fair Gorgan,
To Prince Ramin who, now he was to rule,
Ceased acting like a wastrel and a fool.

He went to see Vis, with the notion they
Would bid farewell, and he'd be on his way,
But when he took his place upon the throne
Vis waved him off and said, "The king alone
Can sit there; if you think that you are fit
To seat yourself where only he should sit
Perhaps you think that you're his equal too?
Perhaps some foolish demon's tempting you?

It's far too soon to think of such a thing;
Remember, you're a subject, not the king!"

Enraged, Ramin rose, muttering curses on
Both Fate and Vis and all that they had done,
He said, "Oh, foolish and inconstant heart,
Realize that this is where your troubles start!
What woes you underwent for Vis, and look
How she repays you for the pains you took!
May no man hope for woman's love: we know
That in the wastelands roses cannot grow.
A woman's love is like a donkey's tail,
Don't try to make it longer then, you'll fail!
Tug it, measure it, but it's just the same.
        A demon tempted me, but I'm to blame.
I thank God that I've woken up; my mind
And eyes can see now, they're no longer blind
To what is virtue, what is vice, to what
Is beautiful and good, and what is not.
Why did I waste my youth, and let my life
Be buffeted by storms, and endless strife?
Alas for my past days, alas that I
Saw hope spring up within my heart and die!
The end's in sight though, I'll no longer grieve,
Here is the perfect cause for me to leave;
This cold reproach of hers has chilled my heart
And strengthened my decision to depart,
Her words are worth a hundred jewels, they show
Quite plainly that it's time for me to go.
Why should I be affronted then if she
Reproaches me and so releases me?
Go then, my heart, go while you're able to,
Run from this shameful fate, be off with you!
Go, before anger means there's blood to spill;
Go! If you don't go now, you never will."

As though sharp pepper fretted an incision,
He turned and turned, writhing with indecision.

When jasmine-breasted Vis saw all his pain
Affliction's javelin pierced her heart again,
And she regretted her harsh words, her scorn
That made him seem so helpless and forlorn.
Then from the royal treasury she brought
A hundred chests, and thirty more, all wrought
From seasoned leather, with designs in gold,
Filled with bright cloths, a wonder to behold,
Cloths made in Shushtar, China, and the West,
With colors that dissolved and deliquesced,
With various scenes as lovely as the spring
And worthy of the wardrobe of a king.
She dressed him royally then, in tulip red,
And wound a crimson turban on his head;
And in the turban's every twist and fold
The ruby threads were intertwined with gold,
As if they showed a pallid lover who
Lay next to his belovèd's rosy hue.
Ramin and Vis clasped hands, and walked once more
Within the garden as they'd done before,
Two lovers linked together for a while,
Able to tease each other and to smile;
At first they laughed again, and then their fears
Of separation's pains provoked their tears,
And Vis's tear-stained, blood-smeared face resembled
A blood-soaked dinar as she wept and trembled.
     Her agate lips were turquoise now, her eyes
Wept like a thousand clouds in rainy skies,
Her musky, hennaed nails scratched at her cheeks
Disfiguring her flesh with bloody streaks.
She cried: "My faithless love, my heart's delight,
Why have you turned my days to darkest night?

Oh, this was not the vow you made to me
On that first day! And have fidelity
And love so weakened in your heart that now
You're sated with me, and forget your vow?
I'm Vis still, with the same fair, sun-like face,
The same sweet breasts and cypress-slender grace;
What have you seen from me but love? And so
What's made you suddenly decide to go?
If you have found a newer love than me
Don't cruelly cast your old love in the sea.
Ramin, don't leave me here, don't put me through
The pain of knowing I'm deprived of you,
Ramin, don't leave me to my enemies'
Despicable desires and promises.
Ramin, don't do this; if you ever leave me
And break your faith with me, Ramin, believe me
You will regret what you have done, and when
You come back here you won't see me again.
You are a wolf now, then you'll be a sheep,
You're haughty now, but then you'll wail and weep;
You'll whimper like a harp's high notes, and place
Beneath my dusty feet your humbled face.
You'll taste what I have tasted, and I'll make
You suffer as I've suffered for your sake;
I'll be as arrogant as you have been,
And see you get back what you gave, Ramin."

Ramin replied, "God knows I love you, Vis,
You know the love I feel for you won't cease –
But I'm afraid of what my foes will do,
The whole world hates me now because of you:
Even my shirt seems angry with my back,
Deer look like leopards waiting to attack,
And every little fish within the sea
Seems an immense leviathan to me.

A goblet handed to me makes me think
That someone's giving me a poisoned drink,
And dreams of dragons, swords, and desperate fights,
Of lions and of leopards, fill my nights.
I fear that King Mobad will secretly
Contrive my death and so dispose of me,
And when I'm gone, Vis, there'll be no one who
Will love you in the way that I've loved you,
When once they take my soul, I'll be at peace,
I won't care for Ramin then, or for Vis.
     But wouldn't you prefer that I survive
To be your lover while I'm still alive?
And pregnant night draws near, who knows what sorrow,
What happiness, might yet be born tomorrow?
It may be that a year will pass and then
We'll meet and be together once again,
And after separation's fearful night
We'll live in an eternity of light.
     Though pain has been my fate I trust that I
Will find an end to pain before I die –
Through months and years of endless agony,
I still expect the day of victory.
My god's the god of justice; every man
Will live in hopes of justice while he can,
Hoping that pain will pass, that he'll be given
In recompense the happiness of heaven,
And while I live I'll hope that I can say
The sun's my partner once again, one day.
Fate's made me suffer in my life, it's true,
And all this suffering's been for love of you,
But this will pass, I know, and I am sure
My heart will fill with happiness once more.
Fate locks its doors before they're opened wide;
While blizzards block the wintry mountainside,

New growth is stirring; soon fresh flowers and trees
Will waken with the spring's caressing breeze."

And jasmine-breasted Vis replied, "I know
That everything you're telling me is so,
But Fate's against me, and I don't think when
My lover's left me that we'll meet again.
I fear that in Gurab you'll see some girl
As sweet and pretty as a precious pearl,
Slim as a cypress in her elegance,
Fair as the full moon in her radiance,
A moon diffusing musk, a cypress tree
That bears sweet jasmine flowers; and as for me,
I'll be forgotten then, you will prefer
To give your faithless, fickle heart to her.
Don't go now to Gurab, Ramin: I feel
Your heart will turn there like a waterwheel;
You'll see so many beauties there you'll lose
Your heart to them and not know which to choose;
When they reveal their lovely faces they
Are used to stealing hopeless hearts away,
Just as the gentle winds of springtime tear
The petals from a rose bush till it's bare.
As onagers and deer become the prey
Of cheetahs and of lions every day,
So you'll be trapped within the devious snare
Of their bewitching eyes and lovely hair.
If you'd a thousand hearts, and every one
Were like an anvil, by the time they'd done
You would have lost them all. If you'd the skill
To make wild demons truckle to your will,
Still you would not know what you ought to do
To make sure that they could not capture you."

And radiant Ramin replied, "My love,
If I were circled by the moon above
And if she wore the shining Pleiades
In lieu of glittering chains and necklaces,
The sun her crown, Canopus at her waist,
Venus her bracelet, if her speech were graced
With every ornament of eloquence,
Her acts with magic and magnificence,
If her sweet kisses were a draught to give
Renewed robustness and the strength to live,
Her cheeks a source of endless sorcery,
Her eyes a way of wanton wizardry,
Her glance a means to give youth to old men,
Her lips to bring the dead to life again,
I swear upon your soul, my love for you
Would never lessen but be always new,
That such a heavenly woman would be worse
In my eyes and for your sake than your nurse,
And that despite her beauty and her throne
My love would be for you, and you alone."

They kissed then, and a thousand times they laid
Cheek against cheek still, while their poor eyes made
Two running rivers as they said goodbye
And fiery sighs ascended to the sky.
The ground was like the sea of Oman there
From all the tears they wept in their despair,
The air was like the burning breath of hell
From all their sighing as they said farewell.
Two desperate souls, they were becalmed between
The sea and hell,[123] and when at last Ramin
Mounted his horse, preparing to depart,
This tore the veil of patience from her heart,
And Fate now bent Vis like a pliant bow;
Her noble stature bowed itself as though

She were a bow to shoot Ramin and send
Him like an arrow to his journey's end.
The arrow sped off tipped with blood; the bow,
Bent and bereft, remained, and could not go.

Vis wept and wailed then in her desperation,
"Patience deserts me with this separation;
Fate sends you on your way, Ramin, while I
Am thrust by love into a pit to die,
And I'll remain bereaved here every day
That you, my darling, keep yourself away.
I curse my fate – one moment I am crowned,
The next I'm flung down weeping on the ground;
My little heart is forced now to contain
Grief to fill sixty parasangs[124] of plain.
I've wept an ocean with my wretched eyes,
My grieving soul's a hell of burning sighs,
How can sleep touch my eyes, or patience dwell
Within the confines of a soul in hell?
When was an ocean space for moderation,
Or hell a place for quiet contemplation?
The worst fate I could wish an enemy
Is that he be identical with me."

Ramin rode from the court, and all the sky
Rang with his brazen trumpets' martial cry;
His horse sent up a cloud of dust, its rain
The horseman's tears as he traversed the plain.
He had been hurt by her, but how much more
His aching heart now suffered than before!
He writhed with grief, the dust of parting lay
Smeared on his features as he rode away.
A lover has no patience in his heart,
Especially when lovers have to part;

The man who leaves his love, and can discover
Patience within his heart, is not a lover.

RAMIN TRAVELS TO GURAB, AND MEETS WITH GOL,
AND FALLS IN LOVE WITH HER

Although his brother'd granted him command
And stewardship of an extensive land,
Deprived of Vis, Ramin's heart seemed to be
A floundering fish that longs to find the sea.
He toured his appanage's far-flung borders
And saw that everyone obeyed his orders,
Ensuring that in every state and town,
He raised the good and brought the evil down.
In Sari and Gorgan[125] he reconciled
The tame and trusting with the fierce and wild,
The wolves were shepherds to the mountain sheep,
The eagles let the game birds safely sleep,
And in Amol his banquets seemed a sign
The very streams and rivers ran with wine.
His justice meant that men could day and night
Devote themselves to pleasure and delight,
And fearful of his sword the lion lay
Beside the onager to drink each day.
He billeted his troops in Isfahan;
In Rey and Ahvaz, Baghdad and Gorgan,
In every town, throughout the countryside
The carpet of his reign spread far and wide.
The world was like a man who has expended
His strength on struggles that, at last, have ended,
So that he sleeps, and feels he has been given
The comforts and the happiness of heaven,
And nobles raised their wine cups in their hands
Sure that prosperity had reached their lands.

Ramin now traveled to Gurab, a town
Where local gentry, men of great renown
Like Rafida and Shapur, entertained him
And with their hospitality detained him.
Each dawn they went out hunting, at midday
They turned to wine to while their time away,
And so the prince's busy days were spent
In hunting and in tipsy merriment,
Now seeking lions with his spear and bow
Now sipping wine where pretty roses grow.
But, in the midst of all this pleasure I've
Described for you, his grief remained alive;
And drunk or sober, still his poor heart trembled
From all the pain within it, and resembled
A ripened pomegranate's skin when it
Is filled with flesh and seeds and longs to split.
And when he hunted there, for every dart
That pierced his prey, love's arrow pierced his heart,
And when he left his friends each night he wept
An ocean of salt tears before he slept.

This was his state, until one day by chance
He saw a woman of such radiance
It seemed the sun was shining in his heart.
Her splendid beauty had no counterpart,
She rode as if she were a bandit who
Would steal his captured heart before he knew,
A tyrant, and as lovely as the spring,
In stateliness and splendor like a king.
Her kisses would revive the soul, her face
Was like a flowering garden in its grace,
A garden where sweet sugar could be found.
Her locks seemed magic as they curled and wound
This way and that, as though they had been set
To mimic letters of the alphabet.

Her lips would cure all sicknesses, and were
Sweeter than any honeyed elixir;
Her mouth was like an agate, and beneath
Its redness gleamed the silver of her teeth;
Her eyes were like an archer from Abkhaz,
Her locks curled like a scorpion from Ahvaz,[126]
Her cheeks were like brocade brought from Shushtar,
Her little lips like sugar from Askar,
One like a rose musk touches, one a line
Of pretty pearls that have been steeped in wine.[127]
Jewels glittered in her hyacinthine hair
As if the Pleiades were scattered there;
Her curls were like chain mail, it was as though
An armorer had made her eyebrows' bow,
And stone and adamantine steel would start
To soften sooner than her callous heart.

  The cypress's and box tree's stature were
No match for all the grace bestowed on her;
The color in her cheeks was said to be
"Pink pomegranate flowers from Barbary,"
And, in the same way, men were said to call
Her ringlets "Snares to hold men's hearts in thrall."
Her cheeks were wine and milk, or blood and snow,
Her mouth was honey hiding pearls below.
Her silver limbs were visible and then,
Beneath her silks, invisible again,
As fishes flicker in a stream, revealed
And in a flash as suddenly concealed.
Her head was crowned with musky hair, on which
A gold crown fitted, fabulously rich
And studded with bright jewels; thick ringlets fell
In tumbling glory to her feet pell-mell,
Black as the spirit of a sorceress,
Laden with scents in every curl and tress.

Her nape and ears beneath her lovely hair
Glowed as though roses or brocade were there,
Sweet-voiced, coquettish, proud, she would delight
The heart, and melt the strength, of any knight.
A garden could be glimpsed in her sweet face
Where roses shone with lilies in one place –
The moon and Pleiades were seen to glow there
As if they too were flowers, content to grow there.
God made her lovely, and her loveliness
Was heightened by the splendor of her dress;
Her body was brocade, brocade she wore
Rendered her even lovelier than before,
The beauty of her face was ornamented
By maquillage and artfully augmented.
She wore so many jewels she seemed to be
A mine of gemstones, or a treasury,
Her gown so glittered with bright jewels and pearls,
Such precious perfumes wafted from her curls
A parasang away the light and scent
Were still intensely bright and redolent.
In loveliness like youth and sovereignty,
In sweetness like life's love and energy,
In beauty like a garden at springtide,
And like a wild doe in her sprightly pride.
Around her eighty girls, from China, Rome,
From India and every distant home,
Were clustered like an eglantine that twines
About a cypress tree its clambering vines,
Or like the Pleiades when they're nearby
As the full moon ascends the evening sky.

When Prince Ramin perceived this cypress tree,
This moving moon, this living idol, he
Was like a man who's dazzled by the sun
And feels his trickling tears begin to run;

His legs grew weak, he stared in consternation,
And dropped his arrows in his admiration.
He could not credit what he saw: the moon?
A breathing idol? Or the sun at noon?
"Or is this heaven?" he pondered, " and is she
A heavenly houri come to welcome me?
A Chinese painting? Or a noble queen?
She is the loveliest sight I've ever seen:
A cypress whose delights could never cloy,
A strutting pheasant on the plains of joy,
And all these maidens are an army she
Commands with royal might and sovereignty,
Or they're the stars the shimmering moon is given
To wait on her when she presides in heaven."

And while he wondered what this sight might mean
The silver cypress tree approached Ramin,
As casually familiar, and as bold,
As though they'd known each other from of old.
She said, "Your majesty, you're famous here;
Your presence makes our Mahabad appear
As lovely as the moon.[128] The night draws on,
There is no reason why you should be gone;
Dismount, and spend the night with us; you'll find
Our friendliness will soothe your troubled mind.
I'll bring you musky wine, as clear and bright
As blazing fires to while away the night,
I'll bring wild fenugreek, wild violets too,[129]
Violets that smell as sweetly as you do,
And from the hills I'll bring you game to eat,
You'll dine on francolin and partridge meat,
While from our gardens I will bring you posies
Of candid lilies mixed with crimson roses;
I'll see the banquet you receive is made
As richly wondrous as a fine brocade.

Thus do we treat our guests, and you will be
As precious now as is my soul to me."

Illustrious Ramin replied, "But you
Must tell me what your name is first, and who
Your family is, if you're unmarried, or
Your silver body has been spoken for.
What is your name? And what's your family tree?
And do you think that you could marry me?
If someone asked your mother for your hand
What is the bride fee that she would demand?
Your lips are sugar, honey, what's the price
You think they'd sell for? Would my soul suffice?
If you consider that it would, I swear
The price is cheap for such delicious ware!"
That houri of bewitching elegance,
That image of Sorush's radiance,[130]
That shining sun replied, "There is no shame
In answering one who wants to know my name,
No one's kept in the dark about the sun,
Its reputation's known to everyone.
My mother's called Gowhar, my father's name
Is Rafida, and in Gurab their fame
Is known to all; my brother's sword commands
Azerbaijan's unruly borderlands.
And, since it happened I was born below
A bush on which sweet, fragrant roses grow,
My mother called me Gol;[131] on both sides then
I come from families of illustrious men;
My father's from Gurab, my mother's clan
Originally comes from Hamedan.
Since my complexion is as pink as roses
And since my scent's the scent a rose discloses,
And everything about me's roseate
And petal-like, it's quite appropriate

That they have named me Gol, a rose; and I
Am princess here, as all will testify.
My mother's passed her beauty on to me,
My nurse has brought me up in luxury:
My neck's like crystal, and my breasts combine
Silver, soft ermine, and sweet eglantine.[132]
But I'm surprised, my lord, you didn't know me
Since I know you; you needn't tell or show me!
You are Ramin, the brother to the king;
To you, your Vis's love means everything,
Here though you're happy, you've no wish to court her?
You're happy as a fish deprived of water!
And you'll forget her beauty, and be glad?
First separate the Tigris from Baghdad!
When Ethiopians are no longer black
Your soul will get its health and vigor back.
That nurse has put a spell on you, she chains you,
Her magic's locked you up and still detains you;
You can't leave Vis, Ramin, and you can't take
Another love; you can't, for Vis's sake.
So stick to her alone, in fact and name,
Continue as each other's cause for shame;
You've shamed the king, and everything you do
Makes God himself ashamed of both of you."

And hearing this Ramin now cursed the ways
His heartfelt frenzy had usurped his days;
He was a byword in the world's eyes, one
Whom every passerby heaped scorn upon.
Again he spoke, with soft, persuasive force,
Luring her heart from its determined course.
He said: "Dear sun, dear moon, dear cypress tree,
Don't laugh at one who's seen such misery,
But pray instead to God that he may find
Health once again for his unhappy mind.

God's actions are unknown to his creation;
Fate keeps us in a state of subjugation;
Don't blame me for my life, who knows but Fate
Has written that this had to be my state?
And why bring up what's over now, since men
Can never make the past come back again?
If you'll take my advice, Gol, you won't dwell
On what is gone; no, bid the past farewell,
Dear radiant moon, and look on what's before you;
Choose me, dear moon, take me, and I assure you
You'll be my castle's sunlight, and your face
Will be like springtime caught in my embrace.
Give me my heart's desire, and I shall give
Your heart's desire to you, Gol, while I live;
The generous king, the radiant moon, will be
Joined each to each in mutual amity –
You'll be my shining moon, and I, your king,
Will name you as the queen of everything
I'm lord of in the world; and if then you
Require my life of me you'll have that too.

    As soon as you have pledged yourself to me
I swear by honor and by honesty
That while the world about us still contains
Its empty deserts and high mountain chains,
While the Oxus and the Tigris are in motion
Wending their way down to the mighty ocean,
While fishes live in flowing streams, while night
Gives darkness to us and the sun gives light,
While heaven's sun and moon have radiance,
While noble cypress trees have elegance,
While breezes blow on mountains, while wild deer
Graze in the upland meadows without fear,
So long shall I be yours, you mine, and we
Will live with love for all eternity.

No other love will know my arms but you,
And I'll forget the love I thought I knew:
I had no sweeter love than Vis, but I
Renounce her in this world and when I die."

That shining sun, that radiant rosebud, said,
"Ramin, there is no need for you to spread
These magic snares of yours to capture me;
I won't be tricked or trapped so easily.
If I desire your company, Ramin,
It's not to be your powerful, honored queen,
To have your milling troops at my command,
To own the wealth and castles of your land.
Please me, and I'll be yours, my lord: I'll serve you
And, as your servant, labor to deserve you.
If you can feed my love with love, and stay
Faithful to me, Ramin, in every way,
You will not find another lover who
Will love and honor you as I shall do.
What's Khorasan to you, my lord? Stay here,
And live in happiness, set free from fear.
Vis is a sorceress, leave her Ramin,
How can you love Mobad's appointed queen?
She might have loved you, but forget you've known her;
She's someone else's, you can never own her!
Swear you won't look for love from her, or send
Her messages, or greetings through a friend;
If you swear this, two bodies will combine
With one soul shared between them, yours and mine."

Ramin said little in reply; instead,
To show that he'd accepted all she said,
He took her hand in his, and quickly led her
To Rafida's – her father's – house to wed her.

A hundred goblets of bright jewels were flung
Before their feet, the castle walls were hung
With rich brocades, the floors were redolent
With ambergris's sweet, luxurious scent.

RAMIN AND GOL

لامین و گل

A summons brought the country's noblemen,
And jewels and pearls were scattered once again.
According to the customs there, Ramin
Swore Gol alone would be his wife and queen.
"Until my body renders up my life,"
He said, "the sun-faced Gol will be my wife,
I will foreswear Vis and her evil ways
And any other beauties men might praise.
My heart is tired of other loves, and I
Want only Gol beside me till I die;
Rose-scented Gol's my heart's delight, I'll make
Gurab my dwelling place for her sweet sake.
Why look for lilies, or the stars at night,
When I've a rose here, and the full moon's light?"

Gol sent out messages inviting all
Her family to the coming festival,
From Rey and Qom, Gorgan and Isfahan,
Arran, and Kuhestan, and Khuzestan.

From frontiers noblemen of great renown
Came to Gurab, and kings from every town
Filled all the court, whose private rooms were soon
Crowded with beauties lovely as the moon,
And when the full moon was bestowed upon
Ramin, his joy was shared by everyone.
For forty parasangs rich decorations
Were seen in honor of the celebrations,
On every side small groups of revelers sat
Passing the time with wine and friendly chat –
So many hands held brimming wine cups there
The plain seemed filled with tulips everywhere.
When day broke music sounded far and wide,
From every stream bank, every mountainside;
When darkness came the wine cups that men held
Glowed in the night, and darkness was dispelled;
Like agate stones the mountains shone and glowed,
And honeyed waters in the streambeds flowed.
The plains were filled with so much pleasure then
That onagers rejoiced and copied men,
And in the mountains wild sheep were instructed
In how wine-drinking parties are conducted.
It seemed the desert wastelands had been made
Kharkhiz with musk, and Shushtar with brocade,[133]
It seemed the birds there had been turned to flutes
Or singing instruments like harps and lutes,
And that the flooding hillside streams were filled
With all the wine that had been poured and spilled –
Its scent hung like a cloudy vapor there
And all the dust was wine-washed everywhere.
Now for a month there were no separations
Of rank or gender in the celebrations,
Men, women, peasants, lords hunted as one
And drank together when the hunt was done.

At times they held a lute, at times a spear,
At times they drank, at times their heads were clear,
They'd sit to polo then they'd sit to dine,
They'd sport with lances then they'd sport with wine,
They'd chase deer from the mountaintops and then
They'd chase grief from the heavy hearts of men;
They'd chase wild mountain goats, and sheep, and stags
Down to the desert from their rocky crags,
Then dogs and cheetahs chased wild deer and asses
Up from the desert to the mountain passes.
Such grief and care pervade the world! But there,
For one month, men knew neither grief nor care,
A world of lovers mingled day with night
Reveling in joy and mutual delight.
Nobles bestowed gifts with a generous hand,
Musicians were in limitless demand,
And every singer's subject was the same,
Praise of Ramin and his auspicious name.

They sang: "*Ramin, may you live happily,*
Eternally, and free from misery!
All you have wished for has achieved fruition,
Here you've achieved the bourn of your ambition;
Desire has been fulfilled, your noble name
Will now enjoy perpetual praise and fame.
You came to hunt, and what a prey you found here,
Gol is the precious prey you've run to ground here;
It is the sun you've caught, and at your side
The rosebud Gol blooms as your lovely bride;
Now Gol's beside you, and your creed will be
Belief in Gol for all eternity.
Heaven's roses cannot rival Gol, who grows
Within your heart now as a fragrant rose,
And in December's cold she'll be there too,
A thornless rose to warm and comfort you.

Who knows of any rose like yours, that shows
A cypress grace, yet still remains a rose?
Now where you go your rose is always there,
In gardens and in castles, everywhere.
Live happily with her, whose petals will
Survive both summer's heat and winter's chill,
A rose whose thorn's a musky curl, whose dart
Enchants and never hurts your happy heart,
A rose two scorpions safeguard, while a pair
Of bright narcissi watch like sentries there,[134]
A rose whose color speaks of youth, whose scent
Brings life itself and heavenly content,
A rose whose scent is musk, whose petals' hue
Is like red wine to warm and comfort you,
A rose an angel planted here and nourished,
A rose Rezvan[135] then watered till it flourished,
A special rose that's worthy of the name,
A rose that puts all other flowers to shame,
A rose that spreads about herself a snare
Of ambergris that hovers in the air.
Now may this lovely rose be always seen
Gracing the noble hand of Prince Ramin,
And may his other hand forever clasp
A goblet of red wine within its grasp;
May victory be theirs, and may they live
With all the pleasures that the world can give!"

GOL IS ANGERED BY RAMIN'S WORDS

A month of music, drinking, celebration,
Of parties, polo, hunting, recreation
Went by at last; and all the noblemen
Who'd gathered at the court went home again.
In Gurab's citadel the happy pair
Rested and reveled now without a care,

And lovely Gol was once again arrayed
From head to foot in splendor by her maid.
Now that this moon was even lovelier
Eyes wept when they so much as looked at her;
Her locks were lustrous, thick, and black as jet –
With musk her maid now made them blacker yet,
Her deer-like eyes were made more dark and wide
With careful kohl her skillful maid applied,
Who plucked her eyebrows, tucked her curls in place,
And chose bright jewels to complement her face.[136]
Her heady perfume was the scent of roses,
The fragrance an unfolding bloom discloses,
Her moist mouth promised life, and from her eyes
Youth trickled down her cheeks in tears and sighs,
While on her hands the henna's loops and swirls
Clustered as thickly as her tumbling curls;
She seemed a cypress tree bedecked with gold[137]
And hung with jewels, a marvel to behold.

When Prince Ramin beheld her lovely face
That blossomed with an opening rose's grace,
Her starry earrings in her dark hair's dusk,
A lustrous cloud that rained down pungent musk,
Her cheeks like tulips, and her scented hair
That curled like ambergris coiled tightly there,
Her necklace of bright pearls that lay like drops
Of rain on lilies when a shower stops
(Or, if day's light could show us stars, they lay
Like stars upon her breasts' resplendent day),
Her smiling ruby lips, so small and neat,
Attar of roses could not be more sweet,
He said, "You are Gurab's bright moon, your name
And beauty put the moon herself to shame,
You bring my soul such happiness and peace –
How closely, dearest, you resemble Vis!

Your lovely lips, your silver body, you
And she are like an apple cut in two!"
Gol was enraged by what she heard, and said,
"Evil lives in your heart and in your head,
Is this how courtiers talk? Is this the way
Princes behave? Are these the words they say?
As for that Vis, may evil fortune strike her,
And may the world henceforth produce none like her,
She and that nurse of hers, that hag who's made
Witchcraft and sorcery her evil trade;
Those two have made you so self-satisfied
That you're a byword for your loathsome pride,
And what will pride bring? Nothing – which is what
The girls who fall for you will find they've got;
That nurse has made you such a simpleton
That you won't hear advice from anyone!"

Ramin writes a letter of complaint to Vis

And when Ramin saw that he'd caused offense
Look what he did by way of recompense.
In front of Gol, he took up silk, and dipped
His pen in musk,[138] and in so doing slipped
The sword of cruelty from its sheath, and made
A havoc of his old vows with its blade.
This faithless lover wrote to Vis, who'd been
Steadfast and faithful to her prince, Ramin.

He wrote: "Dear Vis, oh, all too well you know
The sufferings I have had to undergo,
And all for you; God and the world both blame me,
And everywhere men mock me when they name me;
Some hate me, some berate me – everywhere
My name's synonymous with love's despair.
How would it be if my two eyes could see
A single person who approved of me?

You'd think my love was hatred from the way
Both men and women curse me every day –
They hear my name and move in to attack,
Their slanders rip my jerkin from my back.
Such ugliness has smeared my reputation!
Love for me now's a foul abomination,
It's like a sword that hangs above my head,
A stealthy lion watching where I tread.
    No joy's been mine since I caught sight of you;
Where are the gentle breezes that once blew,
Before I'd seen you, in my poor parched heart?
How much I've suffered when we've had to part,
How copiously my eyes have wept a flood
Of desperate tears commingled with my blood;
And how much worse it was to meet, when I
Feared that my mind and soul would surely die!
When have I not despaired and, broken-hearted,
Wept like the Oxus for you when we parted?
When has my heart not known a world of pain
When once we two contrived to meet again?
But 'mind and soul,' what do they matter when
I had no shame, no fear of God or men?
You saw me in my youth, before love seized me,
How strong I was, how life provoked and pleased me,
How leopards were like timid deer to me,
Leviathans like fishes in the sea.
Each time a little breeze was set in motion
I wasn't in a turmoil like the ocean,
My anger would intimidate a lion
Or smash a sword that had been forged from iron,
And when my hawk flew up, the moon in fear
Trembled and wavered in her turning sphere.
    The steed of my desire could not be caught
By any plodding care or anxious thought,

My hope glimpsed distant prospects, sweet content
Galloped beside me everywhere I went.
Pleasure was mine, my brimming treasury
Was filled with jewels of joy for all to see,
In gardens of delight, you'd say Ramin
Was like a box tree, flourishing and green,
And when Ramin fought on the battlefield,
He was sharp steel that forced his foes to yield.
My mountain rocks were gold; and pearls, not sand,
Gleamed on the streambeds of my native land.
Then, later on, you saw what I became,
The weakest of the weak, consumed with shame;
The cypress tree of youth grew curved and bent,
The full moon, that had ruled the firmament,
Became a minor star; fate and love's trouble,
Or so it seemed, seized me, and bent me double.
Love touched my heart with fire, immediately
Joy fled a hundred parasangs from me,
Love drove out Wisdom, forcing her to roam,
Without recourse or choice, away from home.
Then everyone took up his bow, to aim
Their scornful arrows at my wretched shame,
But love had kindled such a conflagration
I didn't need their scorn as confirmation!
I was so drunk with my desire for you
I didn't need you, Vis, to beat me too.

  I send you many greetings, but my love
For you is something that I'm weary of,
So let me tell you now how happily
My days go by, how well Fate's treating me.
Vis, since I left you I've become a king,
Able to have my way in everything;
I washed my heart in patience, then I tried
To find myself a pleasing, perfect bride –

And what a rose I find that I've been given,
A rose whose scent now keeps me here in heaven,
Who's next to me whatever might betide me,
Who blossoms for me, who lies down beside me,
So that my pillow's pressed now by her head,
So that her form sleeps next to me in bed,
And her dear presence gives me such delight
She is more sweet to me than soul or sight.
Gol is my wife, and for eternity
The sun and moon mean nothing now to me;
Because of Gol the castle where I live
Has all the pleasures flower-filled gardens give,
And she now brings me thrice more happiness
Than you once brought me horror and distress –
My soul and body would have split in two
If I had ever seen such joy from you!

    I pity my poor wounded soul when I
Recall the wretched years that have gone by,
The patience I displayed (that did not save me),
The way I drank the poison that you gave me.
I did not know the world, I made a show
Of happiness while wallowing in woe,
I'd lost my way, I was a worm whose fare
Was vinegar, while I was unaware
That honey could be mine. But now I've woken,
My drunkenness is gone, my sleep is broken;
I've smashed disaster's chains, and I am free
Of the foul dungeon that imprisoned me.
Now to rose-scented Gol I plight my troth,
Wisely, in noble words, I've sworn this oath –
By God, by knowledge, faith, and hope, and by
The shining sun and moon that cross the sky,
That face to face, as long as I have life,
I'll live with faithful Gol, my loving wife;

From now on Marv is yours, and King Mobad,
The shining moon is mine, and Mahabad.
That hundred years when pleasure was denied me
Are less than one week's joy with Gol beside me,
Don't watch the road for me, find other ways
To spend your weary years and months and days;
Long roads, long days, will keep us far apart now,
The need for you has left my needy heart now,
And patience now will benefit you more
Than caravans of gold brought to your door."

He placed his gold seal on the document
Which was complete, and ready to be sent,
And gave it to his squire, and told him he
Should ride with it to Vis immediately.
The squire rode like the wind, he rode so fast
He entered Marv before three weeks had passed;
Mobad heard tell of this, and had him brought
Into his presence in the royal court,
And took the letter, and could hardly credit
The sentiments he found there when he read it.
He handed it to Vis and said, "You'd better
Read your Ramin's good news, dear, in this letter;
I'm sure your eyes will sparkle when you learn
Ramin's gone picking roses out of turn.
He's married now, let's wish him joy of it;
It seems he's left you roasting, on a spit."

Vis's reaction to Ramin's news

Even before the letter had been read
The squire's arrival'd filled her heart with dread,
His very presence there in Marv had made her
Suspect that Prince Ramin had now betrayed her,
And when Mobad passed her the letter she
Felt in her heart the fires of jealousy.

Her blood boiled in her, but she took good care
To hide her feelings from the courtiers there,
Her smiling lips were tulip red, although
Her anvil heart winced at the hammer's blow –
She seemed a heaven of joy, no one could tell
That all her soul burned in the fires of hell.
She hid her pain with laughter, just as shame
Will make a person try to run who's lame,
But still her face turned sallow, since she knew
That what the worthless writer wrote was true.
She said, "I've prayed for this, my enemies
Will find no one requires their calumnies,
And you, my lord, from now on might not be
So keen on slandering and suspecting me!
Great news! I'll set aside some gemstones for
Our temples, and give money to the poor;
Ramin is free from grief now, so am I,
And all that gossip's shown to be a lie.
I've not a care in all the world, my lord,
I'm not afraid now of your frowns or sword.
I've never known real joy, or lived without
Discomfort, and distress, and dread, and doubt –
But now, while I'm still young, I'll live at ease,
Without a care, and do just what I please.
If I have lost the moon, I have the sun,
The sun is what's desired by everyone.
So, I won't see Ramin again! My sight
Sees only you, you are my heart's delight."

These were her words, but nothing that she said
Matched what was in her heart and in her head.
The king left; fever gripped her, and you'd say
Her soul rose to her lips to fly away,
Her heart within her breast was fluttering like
A dove's heart when a falcon's talons strike,

Like dew on yellow flowers, an icy sweat
Broke on her flesh and made it cold and wet;
The cypress was a trembling willow tree,
Her eyes wept rubies and she could not see,
She clutched her golden torque and used it to
Beat at her breasts till they were black and blue,
She bowed down to the ground, her ringlets swept
The household dust around her while she wept,
She writhed in dust and cried amidst her sighs,
"What arrow's this that's pieced my wretched eyes?
What fate is this that's turned my days to night?
What day is this that kills my soul with spite?
O nurse, dear nurse, run to me now and see
This storm of grief that's overwhelming me,
That's hurled me headlong from my golden bed
And strewn with thorns and stones the way ahead.
Do you already know, or must I say
The grief Ramin has given me today?
He's married in Gurab, and now he's sent
A letter telling me of the event,
He says, 'I've plucked a rose, that's far above
All other flowers that anyone might love.'
What will men say of me in Marv? Ah, they
Should mourn with me and weep their hearts away!
How can I save my soul? Help me to find
Some remedy to soothe my desperate mind,
How could I hear such news? Oh, would that I,
Before I heard it, had contrived to die!
I want no gold, no jewels, I want no mother,
No soul or life, no livelihood, no brother,
Ramin is all I want, Ramin has gone,
And so what pleasures now await me? None.
Ramin's my soul, what is a body when
It knows it will not see its soul again?

I will confess my sins, I'll beg, I'll pray
For God himself to help me in some way,
I'll give my fortune to the poor, I'll plead
For God to grant me this one thing I need,
I'll pray to God that Prince Ramin may yet
Suffer remorse and passionate regret,
That he may come back here one night of rain,
His body wet and worn out, racked with pain,
Trembling and weak as I am, sick at heart,
His heart like mine was when we had to part.
Hurt by the cold, hurt by his grief, he'll sue
For love and mercy then from me and you,
And on that day he'll understand the way
That he's behaved to you and me today.
God give me vengeance on him, make him feel
The wounds I've suffered that will never heal."

The nurse replied to her, "This has to cease,
It isn't right for you to grieve now, Vis;
Cleanse your heart's rust, give up this fretful violence,
Scour your heart clean with patience, stillness, silence,
Let your poor body rest, and slowly start
To stop this torture that torments your heart,
Don't hurt your soul like this, stop all this strife,
Death would be better than your present life.
You've clawed your face so much, yanked so much hair
Out of your lovely head in your despair,
That heavenly face of yours is uglier than
The nauseating face of Ahriman.
So, you're demanding more from life, but why?
To live, to nourish your sweet soul, not die
(And when at last the world is quit of you
May I, Mobad, and Prince Ramin die too!).
All men are wild with love at first, but when
They're sated, Vis, all men move on again;

If that Ramin is tired of you, whose beauty
Even the sun would bow to as a duty,
He'll tire of Gol; to her, now, he's like wax –
He'll be a sword that slashes and attacks.
And let him see a thousand moons, not one
Will have the light that radiates from the sun;
This Gol might be a moon, she might be sweet,
But she's not worth the dust beneath your feet;
Your foot's sole's lovelier than her face, her smell
Is ranker than the dust it treads as well.
Ramin had lost you and I can't accuse him –
And if he took a wife, well, I excuse him;
A man who can't find good wine can't be blamed
For drinking dregs! He shouldn't be ashamed."

"I lost my youth in longing," Vis replied,
"Dear nurse, you know this, you were at my side.
Women must have a husband or a lover,
And I have neither that I can discover,
Oh, I've a husband, but he hates and hurts me,
And I've a lover, yes, and he deserts me.
It's I who ruined Vis, my wealth is lost,
I looked for profit and ignored the cost,
For silver I threw gold away, somehow
I find I'm left with neither of them now.
Don't tell me to be patient, nurse; fires burn
My bed, patience is something I can't learn;
My pillow burns, my mattress burns, desire
Sits like a demon laughing in the fire,
And if my soul were brass or granite, still
No patience could subdue my stubborn will.
Enough of patience, don't suggest it nurse,
It's measuring the wind[139] or something worse;
No one can cure my ills, and no one knows
Of any way to free me from my woes.

What of this courier, nurse, who's shot a dart
That's lodged itself within my breast and heart?
From Prince Ramin this speedy courier brought
A letter scented with sweet musk to court,
And he'll take back poor Vis's blood-stained dress.
Oh, how I weep now for my heart's distress!
Ah, lovers, you who nourish love, I reign
Today as princess of love's wide domain,
And out of kindness to you now I'll give
Advice to you on how you ought to live;
If you will listen, my advice is free,
So take this friendly counsel now from me.
Look at me now, hear of my wretched state,
Abandon love, and so escape my fate,
Look at me now, learn from me now, be wise,
Ignore your worthless lover's sighs and lies;
Don't plant love's sapling in your heart, you'll rue
The day when it demands your life from you.
If you don't know my fate, look on my cheeks –
The bloody message that I've scratched there speaks,
It says, 'Within my heart love lit a fire,
And when I beat it out the flames beat higher.
I soaked the world with weeping, but the flood
Could not put out the blaze within my blood;
What eyes are these, that weep and never sleep?
Whose tears won't quench love's burning when I weep'

    I kept a sparrow hawk once, for a whim,
Oh, how I petted him and pampered him!
My wrist was where he perched throughout the day,
At night I tethered him near where I lay;
And when his baby down began to go
His full-grown feathers made a splendid show.
He learned to soar up from my wrist, to fly
And chase wild flocks of doves about the sky,

I thought he'd hunt for me, and that he'd be
A friend who'd stay with me, and comfort me.
Then suddenly he spread his wings, took flight,
And soared into the clouds, and out of sight,
And now I'm weary, worn out with despair,
Searching for some small trace of him, somewhere.
Alas for my heart's hope, for all my grief,
From which, alas, I've never found relief.
I'm like a caravan that travels on
In hopes of finding what's forever gone,
My friend has gone, my heart has gone, and I
Without my friend and heart must surely die.
I sleep on mountain rocks because of him
Whose heart's as hard as mountains, and as grim;
My heart is lost, to find it I would give
In gratitude the soul by which I live,
But I am she whose faithless friend deserts her,
Whose fortune rages at her heart and hurts her.

     Ah, nurse, you've murdered me without a knife,
You sowed love's seed in me and took my life.
You were my blind guide, and I'm in this pit
Because of you, now get me out of it!
It's you that's caused me all this grief and pain,
It's you that has to make me well again!
Off to Ramin with you, be on your way,
And take this message: word for word now, say,
'You faithless wretch, treachery's all you know,
The bow you've strung's an evil ruffian's bow,
You've blinded righteousness, you've made men's lives
A brackish waste where nothing good survives;
Your scorpion nature means you're sure to sting
All you encounter, men, rocks, anything,
Or you're a snake whose fangs are venomous,
A ravening wolf who's sly and treacherous.

It's in your evil character to break
The vows you were so eager once to make,
But though you've hurt my heart (God knows that's true!)
Still I can't bring myself to act like you
(Since "Think no ill" and "Do no ill" defend us,
Our bad acts hurt us, and our good befriend us),
But, if you have renounced my love, then shame
On you when lovers meet and say my name!
How evilly you've acted to me now!
Yes, you've forgotten that sweet flattering vow,
Which was a crimson tulip meant to charm me;
Beneath the flower a black snake lurked to harm me.
But if you've found a new love, then so be it –
Have what you want, as quickly as you see it!
But don't make me despair now, why dispense
With silver now you've gold? Does that make sense?
You've dug a channel in Gurab,[140] but why
Should you allow the old one to run dry?
You needn't raze your house in Khorasan
Because you've built a house in Kuhestan.
You've planted roses, does this therefore mean
Your box tree's[141] been uprooted now, Ramin?
Keep both of us, your lover and your wife –
May both of us bring sweetness to your life!'"

Vis spoke and wept; you'd say her weeping eyes
Were opening clouds in springtime's rainy skies.
The nurse's heart contracted at the sight,
She cried, "Dear Vis, dear springtime of delight,
Don't thrust me in this fire, don't sprinkle more
Rose water on those blossoms[142] than before,
I'll go now to Gurab, I won't delay
For rest or sleep or food along the way;
I'll try to save you, Vis, I'll intervene
And see what can be done with Prince Ramin."

At dawn she set off; Marv was the bent bow
That sent her speeding where she had to go,
An arrow shot from Marv in Khorasan
And hastening to Gurab in Kuhestan.
No sooner could the borderlands be seen
Than she came face to face with Prince Ramin;
The faithless prince was hunting, round him lay
The slaughtered carcasses of all his prey –
His lion rage had forayed far and near
And brought down onagers, wild boar, and deer.
His men had spread out like a castle wall,
Driving the prey before them, great and small
(So many arrows lodged in them you'd say
They'd sprouted wings, straining to fly away),
Dogs dashed across the plain, hawks thronged the air,
The tumult of pursuit was everywhere,
The stones were stained with blood, and fleeing deer
Scrambled in narrow passes, wild with fear;
And, as she watched, the nurse too felt her heart
Pierced by this faithless prince's fateful dart.

Then, seeing her, Ramin did not ask how
Her journey there had been, or Vis fared now;[143]
Instead he cried, "Foul devil that you are,
Foul-minded, born beneath a vicious star,
A hundred times you duped me, tricked me, made me
As foolish as a drunkard, and betrayed me –
And here you are again, you ugly ghoul,
Thinking you'll once more make Ramin a fool!
But you won't see my dust, my reins won't be
Grabbed by you this time quite so easily;
Go back the way you came, nurse, go now, leave me,
Your being here's a waste of time, believe me,

And say to Vis, 'Ramin says, "What can you
Still want from me, what more is there to do?
Doesn't the horror that you've made suffice you?
Since you first let your lustful heart entice you
Your crimes cannot be counted, and your name
Is now synonymous with sin and shame;
It's time that you repented, time you swore
That henceforth you'll act well and sin no more.
We threw our youth away upon the wind,
Both of us did this, Vis, and when we sinned
We dragged our reputations in the dust,
And gave up this world and the next for lust.
And why? Our lust met only with frustration,
Our noble names with scorn and condemnation.
If you still wish to go on as before
I cannot travel with you any more,
Think, if we love a hundred years, what will
The end of love be? That we've nothing still?"'
Tell her wise sages have advised me now:
As God's my witness, I have made a vow
By all that's best here, by the turning sky
And by the radiant sun and moon, that I
Will have no contact with her now unless
I do so in a way that God can bless.
Until I'm king, and so can claim her, she
Must not expect to see or hear from me –
At that time, when I'm king, we'll meet again;
Who knows how many years must pass till then?
I'm the proverbial donkey, 'Wait until
The grass grows, donkey; then you'll eat your fill!'[144]
What tumbling streams will have to flow away
Before Ramin can hope to see that day,
And how long can such hopes be justified
For someone with a husband at her side?

The sun would darken, nothing could maintain it,
If only hope existed to sustain it,
And, oh, how passionately I lament
The futile hopes in which my youth was spent;
Alas for all I planned, for all I missed,
All that remains is wind within my fist.
  My youth was like a peacock in its pride,
Its strength was Arvand's[145] granite mountainside,
I was a glorious springtime garden then,
A cynosure, a byword among men;
But love's harsh winds soon blew there, and defaced
My springtime's loveliness, and laid it waste.
Roses revive with each returning year,
But my lost spring will never reappear;
That time has gone, those days are gone, I cast
My life upon the winds, my youth has passed.
If autumn could be spring again I'd be
Young once again, youth would come back to me –
But don't waste foolish words, nurse, now; old men
Don't look to have their springtime back again!
Go, and tell Vis, 'A husband is the best
Good luck with which a woman can be blessed;
God's given you a husband who's the sun,
Whose luck outshines the luck of everyone;
Honor his star, don't let its radiance dim,
And keep your mind off every man but him.
If you can do this you'll know happiness,
The world itself will shine with your success,
I'll be your husband's brother, he'll be king,
The world will be your slave in everything;
Here you'll be honored, when you die you'll be
A soul who dwells in bliss eternally.'"

He turned in fury from the nurse. To her
The plain was prison, she its prisoner,

She'd heard no warmth from him, she'd seen no kindness;
She journeyed back now as if struck with blindness –
Her sorry soul was filled with dark despair,
Sick beyond medicine or a doctor's care.
But if the nurse was ill with grief and dread
From brooding on the things Ramin had said,
Look at the lovely Vis, when suddenly
She found her friend was now her enemy;
She'd sown good faith, her harvest was rejection,
Cruelty was his response to her affection.
The nurse came back, tears flooded from her eyes,
Dust smeared her face, her heart heaved bitter sighs;
Sweeter than sugar were the words she'd taken,
She brought back daggers – Vis was now forsaken.
A black cloud broke above Vis, all its rain
Was poisoned spears and agonizing pain,
Now, from afar, lightning struck Vis's heart,
She felt the roses of her cheeks depart
Within the fierce simoom that blew around her.
The fetters of catastrophe now bound her,
And all her heart was riven by the sword
Of cruelty wielded by her absent lord.

VIS BECOMES ILL BECAUSE RAMIN HAS ABANDONED HER

What grief assailed her heart and soul as she
Fell on her bed, a toppled cypress tree.
Her sallow face upon her pillow lay
Like yellow flowers that shrivel and decay,
While noble women crowded round her bed.
"The evil eye has wounded her," one said,
Another cried, "No, it's a witch's spell."
Erudite doctors could not make her well;
One said, "It's black bile." One, "I don't agree,
The symptoms look like yellow bile to me."

Astrologers then came from every town
As well as sages, men of great renown;
One said, "The moon's in Libra now," and one,
"But Saturn's course through Cancer has begun,"
And sorcerers and mountebanks were there
Helpless and hopeless in their shared despair –
One said, "An evil glance has injured her,"
Another, "Fairies make these things occur."
Not one of them could understand what ailed her,
None of them knew the grief that had assailed her.
Vis's poor heart was burning for Ramin,
While King Mobad's heart writhed for his sick queen;
Her tears were pearls on roses, his a flood
Of salty water mingled with his blood,
And when the weeping king at last departed,
Her cries left all her courtiers broken hearted:
"O lovers, why will you not look on me
And learn your lesson from the grief you see?
Entrust your hearts to no one; if you do,
What horrors and what sorrows wait for you!
Look on me now, look from afar and fear me,
You'll burn in my fierce flames if you come near me!
Whence comes this heart-destroying fire I feel?
From my cruel friend, whose heart is flint and steel![146]
I showed my lover my poor heart and said,
'For you this heart is pierced, for you it bled.'
Who knows how cruel he was, and how his crimes
Within my soul increased a hundred times?
He took my joy, he took my heart from me,
And now this friend's become my enemy.
What kindness is there that I did not do
For him when our sweet friendship was still new?
Gladly I let my hopes and fears depart
And told him all the secrets of my heart.

I planted faithfulness, why should I reap
This endless grief that makes me rage and weep?
I said sweet words to him, why should I hear
His evil curses, his contemptuous sneer?
But since my fate so hates me, why should I
Blame others when I suffer here and sigh?
I fought my fate, but what can glass alone
Achieve when it is battered by a stone?
As one whom Fate has spurned I lay my head
Upon a pillow filled with grief and dread.
What's left for me but death? And death is right
For one who finds herself in my sad plight;
My love prefers another love, and I
Should have my soul prepare herself to die."

She called her scribe, Moshkin, to her, and told
Him all the secrets of her heart; of old
He'd been her confidant, kept privy to
All that Ramin and Vis had suffered through.
"Tell me, Moshkin," she said, "if you have seen
A lover who's more faithless than Ramin;
I thought I'd see my nails sprout hair before
He'd act like this and break the oath he swore;
I did not know that roaring flames can turn
To running water as they flare and burn,
Or that the vapor from sweet nectar can
Condense to poisons that could kill a man.
You've seen my goodness and nobility,
How well I carried off my sovereignty –
Now both are gone, I've neither; in the end
I'm scorned by both my enemy and friend.
I'm hardly queen now, and I cannot claim
A place among the good now, to my shame;
Given what I've become, I have no right
To seek to exercise a sovereign's might.

For years, Ramin was all I sought – my health,
My heart, my soul, my honor, and my wealth,
I sacrificed them all for him. I wooed him,
Longing to be beside him I pursued him,
And then I wept and wailed in consternation,
When I was forced to face our separation.
Now, if I had a thousand lives, I'd make
Quite sure not one was wasted for his sake.
His folly hurt me once, but this attack
With one blow toppled me and broke my back,
He's lopped off limbs and branches in the past,
And now he's cut the whole tree down at last.
Oh, I've been patient when before he's hurt me,
But not now he's decided to desert me;
This time he's wounded me so viciously
That patience is impossible for me.
Cruelty's his sword, and absence is his spear,
One's pierced my heart, one's cut my head off here,
And how can I be patient when my head
And heart are gone, and I've been left for dead?
What could be worse, Moshkin, than how he's acted?
He's found a wife, his former vow's retracted,
He sends a letter to me saying, 'I've
Planted and picked the prettiest rose alive,
And all the other flowers I've known now mean
Nothing at all to noble Prince Ramin.'
And then he sends my poor nurse packing when
She takes my message to that worst of men,
You'd say till then he'd never even seen her
Or she'd attacked him! Why should he demean her?
But here I'm on my deathbed, and I see
Death's fatal dagger drawing near to me.
Now dip your pen in musky ink, Moskhin –
Prepare to write a letter to Ramin.

Look at my icy sighs, my fevered brow,
See you record them in my answer now.
No better scribe than you are can be found,
You know how fluent letters ought to sound;
If you can bring him back again here, I
Will be your willing slave until I die –
You're wise and eloquent, I'm sure you can
Impress an inexperienced young man."[147]

VIS'S LETTER TO RAMIN

ناموسربه رامین

Vis's letter to Ramin asking for a meeting

The wise Moshkin submitted to her will
And made the whole world musky[148] with his skill,
Writing from noble Vis, the heartsick queen,
To fortune's lordly favorite, Prince Ramin.
He wrote on Chinese silk, and used a piece
Of musk brought from Tibet, the ambergris
Was from Nasrin, the pen within his hand
Had been devised in Egypt's distant land,
Its case was aloes wood from Samandur,
The sweet attar of roses came from Jur.
All Babylon itself could not produce
The magic that this scribe now put to use;
Like Vis's face the silk was smooth and fair,
The ink as sweetly smelling as her hair,
The pen was thin, as Vis had grown now since
She'd suffered such ill treatment from her prince,
Her scribe's bejeweled and sugared words were wise
And powerful as the magic in her eyes.

He wrote of God first, God who is alone,
Then of their vows, and of the love they'd known:
    "From an uprooted, fire-scorched cypress tree
To one that flourishes, alive and free,
From an eclipsed and ever-darkened moon
To one that shines now like the sun at noon,
From a poor garden plot where nothing grows
To one where springtime's sweetest blossom blows,
From an emaciated, withered bough
To one whose fruit's the starlit heavens now,
From an abandoned, worked-out, empty mine
To one where all the world's jewels seem to shine,
From one whose western daylight's almost done
To one who greets the newly risen sun,
From one whose ruby's been plucked out, cast down,
To one whose ruby's set within a crown,
From one whose flowers the dusty wind's destroyed
To one whose flowers are cherished and enjoyed,
From one whose pearlless sea has shrunk and dried
To one whose pearl-filled sea's a flowing tide,
From one whose darkened fortune's stream is salt
To one whose fortune's sun the heavens exalt,
From one whose feverish love's grown overbold
To one whose love was warm and has grown cold,
From one whose anguished soul endures distress
To one whose soul knows luck and happiness,
From one whose sight is clouded with disgrace
To one whose glory radiates from his face,
From one who's like worn cloth whose colors fade
To one who's like a sumptuous brocade,
From eyes that never sleep and always weep
To eyes that never weep and sweetly sleep,
From kindness from a faithful, constant friend
To callous treachery that has no end,

From the sad moon who's lovelorn and alone
To the world's king in splendor on his throne
I write this letter now, so sick at heart
I pray my flesh may die, my soul depart.
    I melt within the flames of separation
While your life's one continuous celebration,
I guard the treasures of fidelity,
While you're oppression's evil deputy.
Now, in this letter, I would have you swear,
By friendship, love, and all we used to share,
By every secret whispered confidence
And by the fact that we were lovers once,
By all the years of friendship we have seen,
By love itself, I charge you now, Ramin,
To read this letter to the very end,
So you may know the fortunes of your friend.
    Know then, the world will turn, and turn again,
Bringing us health at times, at others pain,
Bringing us happiness, and grief and strife,
Bringing us death when it has brought us life,
But this world's good and bad will end, and we
Will see the world of God's eternity;
All that will last of us will be a story
While God alone lives in eternal glory.
The world will come to read our story, men
Will know its ugliness and sweetness then;
You know which of the two of us did wrong,
To whom the sins of lust and fraud belong.
You saw my blameless state, my purity,
And for my beauty's sake selected me.
I was a dewdrop, pure and innocent,
A little tulip, sweet and elegant.
No man but you enjoyed me; don't forget
The world had cast no dust on me as yet,

I was an onager, you'd say, who knew
Nothing of what men's snares and traps might do,
You set the trap for me, you laid the snare
Before my wandering feet, and caught me there.

You tricked me and misled me then, and now
You've tried to abrogate our mutual vow;
I found you were a hypocrite, I find
That treachery is all that's in your mind.
You say you've sworn that you will never see
Your Vis again for all eternity,
But didn't you once swear to me that I
Would be your only love until you die?
Which of these oaths should I believe is true?
This one or that one then, which of the two?
Your vows veer like the wind, your oaths flow on
Like streams of water and are quickly gone –
Now wind and water are great things, but they
Can't stay in one place for a single day!
You're like a cloth shot through with silver thread,
It's one hue, then another hue instead;
Or like a gold coin journeying through the land
By constant passages from hand to hand.

Who have you known for love like me? If you
Won't stay with me, who will you stay with? Who?
Look at your evil deeds, all that you've done
Has meant our noble reputation's gone.

First, you seduced another's wife, the shame
Of this besmirched an honored family's name;
Second, you swore an oath that you then broke,
And spoke fair words, and lied too as you spoke;
Third, you betrayed your faithful lover who
Had never hurt or harmed or injured you;
Fourth, you insulted one who loves you more
Than all the world and whom you still ignore.

I am still Vis, Vis of the sun-like face,
Whose tumbling hair still curls with musky grace,
I am still Vis, whose glance is like the spring,
Whose steadfast love will outlast everything,
I am still Vis, the moon when she is full,
I am still Vis, whose mouth's delectable,
I am still Vis, whom every beauty blesses,
I am still Vis, queen of all sorceresses,
When you were Solomon, I was Bilqis,[149]
I am still Vis, I am still Vis, I'm Vis!
    I can find better lords than you, but you
Won't find my like, whatever you might do.
Whenever you reject me, you will learn
How harsh your Vis can be when you return;
Ramin, don't do this, you'll regret it, Vis
And Vis alone can make your sorrows cease;
Ramin, don't do this, Gol will soon disgust you,
But Vis will turn away then and not trust you;
Ramin, don't do this, you are drunk, that's why
You broke your oath to me with this new lie;
Ramin, don't do this, when sobriety
Returns you won't have either Gol or me –
Ah, how you'll whine and grovel then before me,
Your faced pressed in the dust, how you'll implore me
To take you back again, but you will find
None of your pleas will alter Vis's mind.
    You tired of my sweet lips, and I know you
Without a doubt will tire of Gol's lips too;
If you can't play love's game with me, Ramin,
Who can you play it with? What could love mean?
Don't lovers say, 'To say "I love, but I
Could not love Vis" means you deserve to die'?
But let this warn you when all's said and done:
You have a rose now, but your garden's gone,

You have the moon that shines for you at night,
But you have lost the sun's life-giving light;
You love your Judas tree, but can't you see
You lost your orchard when you gained this tree?
Have you forgotten all that bitterness,
That wild desire, that passionate distress?
If you but dreamt of me, Ramin, you thought
You were a king with all that kingship brought,
If you were dying and you caught my scent
Your health returned and every sickness went;
But that's what thoughtless men are like, Ramin –
Their hearts forget the joys and griefs they've seen.
And then you sigh, 'I've lost my youth,' and cry
'Alas for all my life that's now gone by.'
I lost my youth in loving you, I lost
My life in faithfulness, and at what cost!
You seemed so sweet, a sugar plant – I'd sow
My plant and nourish it and watch it grow,
And it would yield me sugar when it grew;
But bitterness is all I've seen from you!
When I consider all that I have done,
When I remember all I've undergone,
And all for you, fire rages in my brain,
I weep an Oxus for my pointless pain,
What hardships I've endured for you, Ramin –
And why? I've seen from you what I have seen!
You dug the pit, my nurse pushed me inside it,
Then sat herself down happily beside it;
You brought the wood, my nurse set fire to it –
And I was burnt just as my foes saw fit!
I don't know whether I should rail at you
Or her more; you're to blame, but she is too.
     But though I've seen your cruel unfaithfulness,
And felt your brand, and suffered such distress,

Though you have lit this fire within my blood,
And left me like a donkey stuck in mud,
Though you have made me weep without relief
So that I seem an Oxus formed from grief,
My heart still won't allow me to abuse you
Before God's throne; ah, no, Vis can't accuse you!
Oh, may it never happen that I see
Your suffering, since your suffering tortures me.
But now I'll write ten sections of this letter
So that, Ramin, you'll understand me better;
And, writing them, the very pen will run
With blood before this anguished letter's done.

THE FIRST SECTION:
ON THE SORROWS OF SEPARATION

If I'd the heavens to write on, and were given
As many scribes as there are stars in heaven,
And if my endless inkwell were the sky,
And if my ink were night itself, and I
Possessed as many pages as I'd wish,
As numerous as leaves or sands or fish,
And if these scribes wrote all I tried to say
Laboring on till Resurrection Day,
They could not tell – upon your soul I swear –
Half of the wretched terror and despair
That separation brings; when you're not here
Sleep too decides it's time to disappear,
And I'm in such a state my enemy
Relents, and is my friend, and pities me.
I weep for comfort then, as though to tire
A fire by damping it with yet more fire –
I lay dust with more dust, I try to cure
My pain with more pain than I can endure.
I sit alone with grief when you desert me
While you rejoice with one who longs to hurt me,

I weep to see the halter in her hands
And you so biddable to her commands.
Although it seems to be a conflagration
Nothing but patience burns in separation;
No one can sleep in summer's heat, so how
Could I sleep in the fire around me now?
I am that cypress tree your absence killed
Exactly as my enemies once willed,
And humbled now I lie upon my bed
While my companions crowd about my head;
They've come here to inquire and sympathize,
But I have disappeared before their eyes,
I've grown so thin they joke, 'She can't be found,
Perhaps she's gone off to our hunting ground!'
My wayward grief, my longing for Ramin,
Has so destroyed me that I can't be seen.

    Before, my cries showed I was here, but I
Have grown so weak now that I cannot cry –
If Death should come and sit here for a year
I swear he wouldn't find me, I'm not here;
This is my profit then when you forsake me –
I've grown so thin that Death himself can't take me!

    My sorrow's like a rugged mountain chain
That I traverse with misery and pain,
And if I'm patient with this pain may I
Find no relief from it until I die,
But how could anything like patience dwell
Within a heart that now resembles hell?
And what else could be found within a heart
From which its own blood hastens to depart?
(It's wrong to say the soul's composed of blood –
My soul's still here, my blood though's left for good.)[150]
My love, when we embraced I seemed to be
A bough of blossoms on a noble tree;

It's right I burn now, since men burn dead wood
That bears no fruit or flowers, and does no good.
All joy left when you left, now neither peace
Nor you remain available to Vis,
And joy will not return again till you
One day decide that you'll return here too.
My destiny has turned on me, you'd say,
The heavens hate me since you went away,
My days are like a lawless army when
Its general has abandoned all his men,
Or they are like wild, panic-stricken deer
A cheetah chases, filled with grief and fear;
And if I fall to weeping, this is right –
It isn't wrong to weep in such a plight.
I have no friend, pain is my only friend,
No tasks to do, but love's tasks never end.
        You were my life, I know without you I
Will find no joy on earth until I die.
You sowed love's seeds within my heart, now give
A little water to them, let them live.
Look on my face once more, and say no face
Is sallow now like mine, in any place,
Ah, if you were my bitterest enemy
You would relent a little, seeing me;
Despite your faithlessness, your cruel suspicion,
You'd weep for me if you saw my condition.
They say to me, 'You're in a dreadful state,
You need a doctor's drugs to put things straight.'
In my case though the doctor's caused the pain
And it will last till he comes back again,
And I will look for you while I endure it
Since only you, Ramin, know how to cure it.
I'm not yet hopeless that one day I'll see
The shining sun rise here again for me,

And if your sun-like face returns, its light
Will bring an end to this unhappy night.
Old enemies forgive me, why can't you?
If they can do it, surely you can too?
Why shouldn't you be good and kind to me,
Rather than be my bitterest enemy?
If you can read this through and still refuse me,
The world will know how cruelly you abuse me.

THE SECOND SECTION:
ON REMEMBERING THE BELOVÈD
AND SEEING HIM IN DREAMS

My love, you took my heart with you; you went
And left me by myself here to lament.
My heart's your hostage, and I let her go
Because, Ramin, I wanted to you to know
I lack the heart for joy; wherever you
Decide to go my heart will be there too;
She's like a patient seeking health, and how
Can she love others when she's with you now?
And how can you forget her when she's there,
Your intimate companion everywhere?
Although her bitter sufferings make her doubt you
Life is still sweeter with you than without you;
What does it matter if you once waylaid me,
Then ignorantly hurt me and betrayed me?
I can forget the things you did before
And simply prize your loyalty the more,
I'll be so dear and good to you, you'll see
Your cruelty, and the love that's still in me.

When you were faithless to me you'd deride me
By claiming I'd a heart of stone inside me –
For love and faithfulness of heart I do,
My heart's eternal granite, yes, it's true,

And this is why my love will never falter,
It's based on solid stone that cannot alter,
And if my little heart were not so strong
My love for you could not have lived so long.
My heart sipped wine from your sweet lips, and I
Am drunk with love until the day I die;
Drunk now I see the moon, and say that it
Is certainly a dark and noisome pit,
I see the rising sun and think I've seen
The radiant countenance of Prince Ramin,
Or if I glimpse a lofty tree I say
'How tall and strong my lover seems today!'
I kiss the spring's first tulips and address them
As though they were your cheeks while I caress them,
I think the wild flowers' scent upon the breeze
Is your sweet scent, and in my reveries
I say, 'I know his body's scent so well,
He's on his way here now, that's his sweet smell!'
I see your face in dreams, so why when we
Are wide awake are you so cruel to me?
In dreams you are so kind, awake you leave me,
You lie to me, you trick me and deceive me;
Uncalled, you come to me when I'm asleep,
But will not come however much I weep
When we're awake. What does it matter though?
I dream of seeing you so long ago,
Of seeing you again; I long for you,
Remember you…whatever I might do,
Desiring you, unable to forget,
By night, by day, my eyes are always wet.
I trick myself imagining you're here,
Happy to have you suddenly appear –
Can there be happiness in such despair,
As when a bird is happy in a snare?

You'd say my mother must have prayed one day
That all I longed for should be kept away,
But I'm so deep in love I'm happy to
Accept the glimpses dreams provide of you –
How drunk my wretched heart must be to bless
Such sorrow with the name of happiness!
This is what Fate has granted me, to see
Your face in dreams, not in reality.
Would that my eyes could sleep then and not weep,
Would that I saw your image in my sleep.
But since I saw you, dearest, I've not slept,
All that I've done since then, my love, is wept,
And look now at the difference made by Fate
Between two different kinds of sleepless state:
One cannot sleep for love and love's sweet madness,
One cannot sleep for sorrow and for sadness.

     How would it be then if a century
Of sleeplessness proclaimed my constancy?
I've planted constancy, my sleepless eyes
Will nourish it with heartfelt tears and sighs,
My constancy's a jewel, it can't be mined
So simply from love's depths where it's confined.
Oh, if I ever seize you how I'll shame you,
How men will then disparage you and blame you!
My heart's kept faith with you for love's sweet sake,
You've broken faith with me; your heart will break.
If God's our judge, my suffering won't be bootless,
My constancy in love will not prove fruitless,
He'll bring my love to me, quickly he'll clean
Grief from my heart and give me back Ramin.

THE THIRD SECTION:
ON SEEKING A NEW BELOVÈD

Full moon, where are you now? Why do you hate me?
Why do you seek my blood, and execrate me?

May you have anyone you wish, but I
Want none but you, both now and when I die.
They say to me, 'Why do you weep and moan,
And long for one who's left you here alone?
A new love drives the old out, why not find
A sweeter love to occupy your mind?'
They do not understand, a thirsty man
Will always look for water while he can,
Rose water might be sweeter, but it's streams of
Pure water, wholesome water, that he dreams of;
And when a viper bites a man they treat
Him with the antidote, not something sweet –
Sugar's delicious, but it's useless when
One has to deal with sick or wounded men.
My enemies are happy that they've made me
Bereft of Prince Ramin, that he's betrayed me,
But now he's lost to me, now I can't see him,
No one supplants Ramin, no one can be him;
Think, if my hand were severed, could I face it
To have a hand of gold and jewels replace it?
You are my sun, you usher in the day,
Day will not come to me while you're away;
I was a shell when you were here beside me,
You were my precious pearl then, lodged inside me,
Now that this pearl no longer lies within me
May no pearl lie with me again, or win me –
No shell receives a second pearl, no new
Young love will ever substitute for you,
Though all the world might change, you will discover
One thing will not, the pure soul of your lover.

      The soul's a thousand things to you, it's one
To me, and one that cannot be undone;
I cannot look elsewhere for love, no moon
Will shine as brightly as the sun at noon.

I have not bathed my body since you went
So that my face and hair would keep your scent –
And as my love has been, so may it be,
No other lover will rejoice in me!
My love's a caravan that won't depart
From where it's lodged within my wretched heart,
And till it travels on there is no space
For other wayfarers to take its place.
My body's like a hair now I'm alone,
Absence has made my weary heart a stone,
Given such stony ground, why should I sow there
New seeds of love? No shoots or fruits would grow there.

    My love, you're far from me, but still your light
Illuminates my senses and my sight,
Don't try to lose me now, since Fate has sent you
No love as fit as Vis to complement you;
If I'm the last month of the turning year
You are the first – the two of us appear
Together then, or we're an image in
A mirror looking at its mirrored twin;
You're cruelty's partridge, I'm grief's mountain where
You proudly strut, so we're a perfect pair;
Your mouth's a shell where bright pearls can be seen,
And all my tears are like the sea; Ramin,
I don't know why you've grown so tired of me,
What shell has ever wearied of the sea?
Or you're a cypress, and my eyes provide
The stream that you should plant yourself beside;
Or we are flowers, you're red and I am yellow
(Joy makes you glow and sorrow makes me sallow),
So come to me, since gardens have more grace
When red and yellow mingle in one place.

    My love, my soul is worthless without you,
Without my soul the world is worthless too;

My body cannot sleep, my heart though seems
Always asleep and wrapped up in its dreams.
They say to me, 'Go, take another love;
He has a star, you take the moon above.'
But I have had no luck with love; why should
I try what's never done me any good?
This love that I've experienced with you
Is quite enough; I can't try someone new.
I hate this dye upon my hand; should I
Submit my foot then to the selfsame dye?
I planted constancy; what did I gain
That I should yet again endure such pain?
I sowed love's sapling once – let that suffice me,
I've written love off now – it can't entice me;
I've quenched lust's fire within my heart, I bow
Before whatever Fate awaits me now.
        Say I'm a bird, whose nickname once was 'Clever' –
That was before both feet were snared forever;
Say I'm a merchant sailing on the seas,
Seeking out splendid jewels and rarities –
The tale is longer than you might expect
To tell you how my voyaging ship was wrecked,
Nothing was salvaged, nothing could be found
And now I'm terrified I'll soon be drowned –
I call on God to help and comfort me,
To rescue me from this horrific sea,
And if I find my way back to the shore
I promise that I'll go to sea no more.
Now you've abandoned me, I've sworn that I
Will not seek love again until I die;
I'll give my heart to none but God, both now
And in the world to come: this is my vow.

If it were not for infidelity
How dear the day of parting could still be!
Parting is harsh, but there's a sweetness when
Two lovers hope that they will meet again,
And lonely melancholy can be sweet
When lovers are assured that they will meet.
Meeting can bring its troubles – truculence,
And quarrels, silly sulks, and arguments,
And then there is that bored satiety
Which is the bitterest fruit of passion's tree.
　　But parting brings us hope that in the end
We will be reunited with our friend,
So when my poor, impatient heart complains
Of loneliness and separation's pains,
I say to her, 'Dear heart, it makes good sense
That suffering will receive its recompense;
This is December's cold you're suffering through,
But April's warmth and joy will come back too –
What is a year's grief if you know that for
An instant you will see his face once more?
And when you drink together for a day
A century of suffering fades away.
　　Dear heart, you need a gardener's carefulness,
His constant toil and caution, nothing less!
You've seen how when a gardener plants a rose
He's eaten up with worry till it grows,
How he can't sleep, how day and night he's there
Watering and pruning it with fretful care,
Weary and pricked by thorns – all this is duty,
Done to ensure his rose's future beauty.
You've seen how one who keeps a nightingale,
In hopes its melodies will soon regale

His eager heart with sweetness and delight,
Proffers it seeds and water day and night,
And makes its pretty cage so cunningly
Of precious aloes wood and ivory –
All for the moment when the bird will start
To trill its song, and so delight his heart.
You've seen how one who voyages overseas
Becomes inured to dreadful miseries,
And how, deprived of food and sleep, he braves
The onslaughts of tempestuous winds and waves,
And how among their fierce contending strife
He fears now for his goods, now for his life –
All this is borne, and gladly, for the sake
Of future profits that he hopes to make.
You've seen how one who digs for jewels resigns
Himself to endless anguish in the mines,
The sleepless nights and restless days he spends
Are filled with wretchedness that never ends –
He's always lugging iron and stone about
Striving to get the gems he prizes out,
Hacking and hewing, hoping to unearth
A jewel that's of inestimable worth.

Hope and desire pervade the world's existence
And it is vain to offer them resistance,
And while the sun and moon still rise, believe me,
Hope and desire for you will never leave me.
Within my heart the tree of love, for me,
Is like a flourishing, green cypress tree:
Its leaves don't wither in the summer's heat,
Or turn to yellow in the cold and sleet,
It's always trim and green and fresh, you'd say
Unchanging spring sustains it every day.
But in your heart the tree of love is like
Deciduous trees when autumn's tempests strike,

Stripped naked, leafless, fruitless, with each limb,
Where blossoms opened once, now gaunt and grim.
My hope is that the springtime will restore
The greenery of love to you once more,
That leaves and flowers of faithfulness will grow
To clothe the bareness that your branches show.
But I see all my hopes of your affection
Thrice canceled in your obdurate rejection:
You are a cloud withholding rain, and I
A thirsty shoot that's shriveled now and dry;
You are a grasping miser, I a poor
Shunned mendicant who's begging at your door.
I weep, weeping's my only occupation,
What could be worse, or show more desperation,
Than to be one whose business is to be
Always in tears, weeping incessantly?
I'm like a sick man at the point of death
Who grimly hopes for health with every breath;
I'm one who wanders in the world, a stranger
Who pines for home, who's sneered at and in danger,
Who sits beside the road, with but one task –
To ask for news of you, and ask, and ask.
     Men say to me, 'Vis, hope for him no more,
Despair can't bring you what you're hoping for,'
'I'll always hope for him,' is my reply,
'I'll hope, and hope, and hope, until I die.'
My love, my hope for you cannot be shaken
Until that moment when my soul is taken,
Since love for you drove patience from my heart
This hope is in me and will not depart.
I burn, but I'll survive this cruel desire,
Since hope's sweet waters cool its raging fire –
If hope should leave me I would not survive;
Within an hour I would not be alive.

I've seen you when you weren't so high and mighty,
So angry, so coquettish, and so flighty;
I've seen you when the anguish of your sighs
Darkened the moon as she traversed the skies;
When you were like the highway's dust, when all
Your enemies rejoiced to see you fall;
When hell burned in your soul incessantly,
And tears flowed from you like a surging sea
(And when your weeping lessened one could say
Only a Tigris flowed from you that day).
But now you're grander than Jamshid,[151] your pride
Brags that the sun and you sit side by side!
Have you forgotten those days when you wooed me,
And desperately desired me, and pursued me?
Ah, but you won me, and my love assured you
Of how extravagantly I adored you,
And you forgot your former agony
And cruelly looked for ways to injure me.
Why are you cold to me, when you're so sweet
And courteous to everyone you meet?
Pride is your due, your splendor justifies you,
But you can't prize yourself more than I prize you –
I love your pride, Ramin, and you will see
How kind I'll be, if you are kind to me.
But though your face is like the spring, and though
Your cheeks are where spring's sweetest roses grow,
Spring tarries here for no one, and the day
The world bestows on us it takes away:
Don't draw your bow against your friends; a blow
From Fate can suddenly destroy your bow,
And don't use up the arrows in your quiver
Against someone who worships you forever.

My love, my heart's like roasted meat, desire
Has turned it night and day within love's fire –
Let the fire blaze then; but, my love, take care
It doesn't burn the heart you've roasted there!
　　　Ah, don't humiliate me now, don't do
These shameful things I've never done to you.
Don't torture my poor heart, my love; aren't we
Made from one earth, from one humanity?
When it was you who grieved and wept and sighed
I did not act with such exalted pride.
How can a friendship flourish or minds meet
In such an atmosphere of self-conceit?
And isn't it enough that we're apart
Without this further torment for my heart?
You're not a God: you're human, just like me,
So why should I endure your tyranny?
You think yourself the sun at noon, and yet
When night approaches you will surely set.
Would that I had a heart like yours, as black,
As ignorant, as ready to attack –
The happy lord of such a heart will make
A world of victims suffer for his sake.
Your face is like a garden in its grace,
Your heart is like a craggy, barren place,
Alas for me now, that your heart should be
Like iron in its infidelity!
The absence that you seek I will not seek,
The cold words that you speak I will not speak,
You're faithless, but my faith will never tire,
I bring you water though you bring me fire.
My mother bore me to be faithful, you
Were born for cruelty and to be untrue;
　　　But it's my foolish heart that's injured me,
In your deceit she looked for loyalty –

You made a target of her; let the dart
Be shot then from your eyes into my heart!
Shoot now, and let them raise their cry, 'But why
Should she seek danger out and choose to die?'
Arash[152] was a great archer, so men say,
The arrow that he shot sped all the way
From Sari's plain to Marv, but every hour
You shoot a hundred arrows with such power
They fly here from Gurab and only cease
Their flight within the wounded heart of Vis;
So you've outdone what Arash did before,
Adding a hundred parasangs or more.
You've made so many cruel pursuits your own
That you must have a heart that's made of stone –
You've made my face an Oxus with my weeping,
My heart a miser who's intent on keeping
His hoard of grief and sorrow since you left
Your lover here, abandoned and bereft;
And strangest is that I am still alive –
I must be made of iron to survive!

     They say my weeping's worn me to a hair,
That I have been destroyed by my despair.
But don't they know that rain like this must bring
Within its train the advent of the spring?
It may be that my tears, like April rain,
Will bring my lover back to me again;
As I would greet the spring with flowers, I'll greet
My lover with my heart's love when we meet.
If God will let this happen, I will cast
My soul before him when we meet at last –
How welcome that sweet day will be! I'd buy
Two hundred souls to give Ramin if I
Could do it – if each soul I purchased cost
A hundred souls, I'd think those souls well lost!

O my belovèd, when you went away
What orders did you leave? You didn't say.
You took my heart with you and felt no pity
That I was left here in this strangers' city;
You rode away, and I remained here grieving
Like a sick patient when her doctor's leaving.

I know you never think of me, that you
Are faithless, cruel, in everything you do,
That you've no fear of God, and that you take
No interest in the wretches you forsake,
That you don't say, 'How is that girl, is she
Drowning in waves of blood and missing me?'
Is this then faithfulness and love? That I,
Without your knowing it, should grieve and die?
Without you here I don't know what to do –
Should I cry *to* you, or *because of* you?
Your absence brings such endless pain to me
It seems that death's my only remedy.
(And love and joy don't mix, who can discover
In all the world a single happy lover?)
Although it angers you when I complain
I want you to be conscious of my pain –
How can you have the heart to injure me,
Your friend, as though I were an enemy?
And wasn't it enough then to desert me?
Ah, no, you took another love, to hurt me;
I had to hear of this, I had to see
This further proof of infidelity,
To know you sit with her now and despise me,
To know that this is why you ostracize me.

Aren't you Ramin, who recklessly admired me,
Who desperately and thirstily desired me?

Aren't I still Vis, in all the world your one
Desire, your only hope, your radiant sun?
Aren't you Ramin, who died without me, like
A withered leaf when winter's tempests strike?
Aren't I still Vis, who gave you life again
And made you the most fortunate of men?
Aren't you Ramin, for whom I was so sweet
You used for kohl the dust beneath my feet?[153]
Aren't I still Vis, your soul's companion who
Once made the world a joyful place for you?
Why am I what I was, while you have changed?
Why are we now so different and estranged?
Why do I love you still, while you now hate me?
What have I done that you should so berate me?

    Leaving is hard, although perhaps for you
It wasn't such a dreadful thing to do,
Since you had scorned my love. But then I know
That you were drowning in a sea of woe;
Your heart sought out another love, it's true,
But what's a drowning man supposed to do?
He makes a grab for hope where he can find it –
There's no surprise in that, why should I mind it?
And many men, faced with a toothsome spread,
Might choose to dine on vinegar instead.

    If being with me was like wine and laughter,
Then losing me was like the morning after;
You're drunk, your head is spinning, wine distracts you;
It's natural that its heady scent attracts you.
And if your headache comes from wine, why then
Drinking more wine's the only regimen![154]
But first love's like one's soul, and if you find
New love, don't leave your former love behind –
Cherish your new love, see that you don't hurt her,
But love your old love too, and don't desert her.

Love is like precious jewels, put to the test
It's always found the oldest are the best;
New jewels can lose their color, then they're worth
No more than ordinary stones or earth,
And it's the same with love – new love can falter,
Its glittering colors all too quickly alter.
    I will not find another love like you
Who wounds my heart with everything you do,
You will not find another love like me
Who loves you with unchanged fidelity;
I can't withdraw my heart from you, and you
Can't proudly cast me off for someone new
Since you're the moon and I'm the sun of love,
Eternal partners in the heavens above;
Don't pride yourself on all your shining light,
Your wandering in the darkness of the night.
Your light's from me – it's mine! – and though you leave me[155]
You'll always travel back to me, believe me.
My stony-hearted love, come back again
And save both you and me from further pain,
And I shall be to you, when you are mine,
Like knowledge to the soul, or milk to wine.
Your leaving locked my soul, the only key
To open it is your return to me;
Don't be ashamed of all you've done, but start
Once more to cherish love within your heart.
What does it matter if you felled the tree
Of all our friendship and fidelity?
You felled it; you can graft the broken shoot.
A grafted tree bears more, and sweeter, fruit.

Come weeping clouds of spring, learn from my eyes –
It's there the nature of true weeping lies,
A single shower would flood the world if you
Could weep as copiously as I now do.
I weep so much, but I'm ashamed that I
Can't weep a hundred times as much: I try,
My grief deserves it, but I'm not so strong
That I can weep so freely for so long.
      I weep both tears and blood, and when these two
Have all been wept what's left for me to do?
That day that neither tears nor blood arise
To brim my weeping eyes, I'll weep my eyes –
My eyes are good for seeing you and when
They can't see you I won't need them again.
My tears will make this plain a sea, my groans
Will crumble into kohl its hardest stones.
May God forgive my eyes' incessant tears!
But they're the friends whose friendship perseveres,
Not like that traitor Patience, who's defected,
Or my hard heart by whom I'm now rejected.
We look for friendship in adversity
But all my friends have now deserted me –
Patience will not support me, and my fate
Is what's responsible for my sad state.
      My heart is trapped in trouble – who befriends her?
This is the message absent Patience sends her:
'O heart, I am a slip from heaven's tree,
And deep in hell is where you planted me;
You're fire and smoke and everything I dread,
So I precipitately turned and fled.'

Dear heart, you brought this on yourself, and we've
No right to carp at Patience, or to grieve;
Patience soothes every agony, but in
The case of lovers Patience is a sin,
So let me sit here while she quits this place,
And I shall never have to glimpse her face.
You brought me peace, Ramin; you've gone, and Vis
Deserves now neither Patience, hope, nor peace;
To be content, now you've abandoned me,
Would be a sign of my disloyalty.
For one who has love's business in her head,
Two hundred souls aren't worth a crust of bread.
This is how love must be, what love must mean,
This is the way a lover's loyalty's seen;
You know my heart and soul are yours, that you
Can treat them any way you wish to do;
And since you cause me pain, you can be sure
The worse you are, the more I shall endure.

How sweet those days were when you lay beside me,
My lover then, when nothing was denied me,
When Fate was sleeping and few fears constrained us,
When Fortune woke and many hopes sustained us!
But that's the turning world's way – to destroy
With Time's sharp sword each momentary joy.

It cut you from my eyes, which wept a flood
Of constantly cascading tears and blood
(A wounded body bleeds, and this is why
Now that you've left me it is blood I cry);
Weeping's become my friend, you went away
And sorrow set up house in me you'd say –
In sympathy with me my neighbors keep
A weeping vigil for me when I weep,
And cry for me to pity them and end
My lamentation for my absent friend,

Saying, 'Many's the lover we have seen
But none as wild as you are for Ramin.'
He's left me here, as shepherds might move on
From fires they warm themselves at, then they're gone;
He's left me like a house belonging to
A man who's gone away for somewhere new –
And it was not enough that he should leave me,
Ah, no, he's found another love to grieve me,
And, if I weep now, this is just and right
Since he's responsible for my sad plight.
My heart accuses me, 'You weep and groan
So much you're like a song's incessant drone!
And why? Because your lover's found a new
Friend somewhere else, whom he prefers to you?
But don't you see, your lover is the sun,
And that the sun's desired by everyone?
At times he's near, at times he's far away,
To everyone in turn he brings the day.'
     O my sweet love, if I could tell you how
Profoundly, desperately, I miss you now!
I'm like a mother who has lost her child,
Who dashes here and there, distracted, wild
With all the myriad worries that distress her –
Two hundred Damavands[156] of grief oppress her!
A thorn could pierce my heart and I'd remain
Unmoved by it and unaware of pain –
How can it comfort you, how can you bear
To cause me such vexation and despair?
     But still, for all the sorrows that I've seen,
I can't complain to God of you, Ramin;
Ah, no, I fear the fate that must await you –
My heart is hurt, Ramin, but cannot hate you.
But since you've gone my wretchedness compels me
To say to you the message longing tells me:

'Without me, may you forfeit joy; may I,
Without you, forfeit life itself, and die.'

THE EIGHTH SECTION:
ON ASKING FOR NEWS OF THE BELOVÈD

My heart is branded by my hopes and fears,
My wretched state's apparent from my tears,
My body's wasted to a hair; despair
Has made my world as black as musky hair;
My dreary days are dark as any night,
My nights are utterly deprived of light –
My eyes will only glimpse the morning when
They see your soul-bewitching face again.
Now, since your caravan has gone, I wait,
A patient sentry watching at a gate,
Scanning the road for you as though I were
A zealous guard or customs officer!
When caravans arrive here, none get through
Until I've questioned them for news of you,
Asking, 'Who's seen my faithless love, whose mind
Has learned one lesson – how to be unkind?
Who's seen that martial moon-like face, the one
God made to steal the hearts of everyone?
Who's seen that rogue whom every lover knows,
Who stirs up trouble everywhere he goes?
And have you news of whether he has more
Or less love in his heart now than before?
And have you heard of how he thinks of me?
With kindness once again, or enmity?
Will he keep faith with me? And will he meet me?
And if he does, how can I hope he'll treat me?
How does he talk about me with his friends,
His enemies? Might he soon make amends

For his neglect of me? Does he despise me,
Or does he once again begin to prize me?
And does he think of me, and wonder how
One who has thought of him for years fares now?
Is he inquisitive to find out whether
I still have hopes that we shall be together?'
      Whether or not he asks about my plight
I ask how he is faring, day and night.
But he's the same man I've already seen,
He's still the same hard-hearted, cruel Ramin,
The same sweet-scented, handsome knight – a man
Who looks for blood and spills it where he can;
Though even if his hard heart wishes me
Injustice, wretchedness, and misery,
I wish him joy, and pray he will be given
An endless sanctuary from harm in heaven.
When I hear anything of my Ramin
I feel that once again I am a queen,
And since he's seen my dearest love, I prize
The bringer of such tidings like my eyes –
And if he says, 'I saw him happy,' I
Am glad to give my soul to him and die;
I love him for my lover's sake, his face
Eases the pangs of absence and disgrace.
The winds from where Ramin lives are to me
Dearer than life itself could ever be,
And when the wind smells sweet I know it means
That health and happiness are now Ramin's –
That hyacinthine scent is from his hair,
His lips and cheeks diffuse into the air
These scents of wine and roses. Sadly I
Heave from my wretched heart an icy sigh
And whisper to the wind, 'Dear breeze of spring,
It is the sweet scent of his hair you bring;

Tell that tall cypress when you see him he
Still holds his slave here in captivity.
You please me with the perfume from his hair,
But you're unjust to scatter it elsewhere,
And does he know my sleepless desperation,
The grief I suffer in our separation?
With windy sighs and weeping eyes my pain
Has turned my body into wind and rain.

     Is he like me, or has he now decided
His heart's affection for me was misguided?
And is he overjoyed to hear my name
Or filled with anger, and disloyal shame?
Dear breeze, take him my message now, and say
In taking him Fate took my life away –
Tell him that kindly lovers will disown him
For his forgetting all the love I've shown him;
Ask him if this is loyalty, that I,
While he survives, should waste away and die?
And say, "You're chivalrous to everyone –
Is this how deeds of chivalry are done?
I've seen a thousand hearts that cruelty's bruised,
But none misused as mine has been misused.
What evil's worse than this – that you repay me
For all my love with hatred, and betray me?
You never ask for news of me, or give
My wounded soul new hope that it might live,
Or try to ease the pangs of separation
With letters telling of your situation.
I don't know how your heart fares, but I know
My own is crushed beneath a weight of woe,
And that I'm forced to live without you where
My enemies delight in my despair.
I watch the road, I listen at the door,
As if in prison here for evermore –

But birds can fly, and now my suffering heart
Will emulate their soaring and depart;
Your peacock pride and comeliness, my love,
Have turned my heart into a fluttering dove."'

O love, full moon, tall noble cypress tree,
Whose body's heaven, whose curls have captured me,
How long will you mistreat me? Ah, Ramin,
Alas for all the suffering that I've seen!
Now by your callous soul I conjure you
To know my grief and read this letter through.
I dipped my pen in heart's blood to explain
The record of your wrongs and of my pain –
'The record of your wrongs,' I say, and when
I write your deeds blood trickles from my pen!
When I remember your unfaithfulness
And how you left me here in my distress,
The seven members of my body [157] scorch
The pen my fingers write with like a torch,
And I'm so weak and helpless that I then
Drench with my flowing tears the moving pen.
Now, in this state, I force my pen to write
The story of my soul's unhappy plight.
    Look at these letters, [158] every dot you see
Is heartfelt blood that has been wept by me;
The ink's as black as is my wretched fate,
The curves repeat my bent back's suffering state,
The circling letters are the world that jails me,
The broken letters are my hope that fails me.
Would we were drunk and happy once again
Like letters twined together by a pen!

But cruelty's now your only stock-in-trade,
I'm trapped within the cul-de-sac you've made
(It's like a curved, enclosing letter's shape,
A bowl-like form from which there's no escape);
I tell myself I'm here, I can't evade it –
I doubt though that you even know you've made it!
       This letter opens with an invocation
To God, the lord of us and all creation,
Who opened wide the door of love for me
And filled my spirit with fidelity.
It's Him I turn to now, begging Him to
Second my words and intercede with you,
And, if you recognize Him, may you start
To show some pity to my friendless heart –
I'll find no finer advocate, no better
Or more persuasive plaintiff than this letter.
Once it was you who begged, who sued for grace
To kiss the pomegranates of my face,
I brought my head into your snare, I met you,
You sent me many messages, I let you,
So why should you draw back your bow at me?
Think of our years of love and loyalty!
As you read this, remember when you thought
I was the wolf, and you the sheep I'd caught –
But you escaped my wolf claws, now it's you
Who plays the wolf observing what I do.
Remember when my love seemed like a snake,
And Fortune slept for you; now you're awake,
And you're the snake who gradually draws near
While I lie sleeping and defenseless here.
       Now, as you read this, ask if you have seen
Anyone's grief to equal mine, Ramin!
I'm still that friend who was so dear to you,
Who pleased you once and felt so near to you,

I'm still that friend who knew such joy with you,
Who loved to flirt, and joke, and toy with you;
And I'm reduced to writing this, resigned
To all the grief that's wrecked my peace of mind,
And here, where I was queen, my evil fate
Has humbled me to an ignoble state.
(Oh, learn from my example if you've sense,
Look at me here and see love's consequence,
Look at me if you're wise, and do not sow
Love's seeds within your heart, or let them grow.)
My love, this should be a sufficient shame
For you, that all the world abhors your name –
If someone reads this letter, what will he
Say about us, and how you've treated me?
He'll say, 'May God forgive this faithful child
Who sought his love so long and was reviled,
May God destroy this brute, who showed no trace
Of decency, whose life was a disgrace!'
      My letter's coming to an end, although
I've much to say still, as you surely know –
But I've complained enough, although I've said
A thousandth part of what is in my head,
And all my words won't bring me satisfaction
Since chiding you, I know, brings no reaction.
Instead of wasting foolish words on you
I'll turn to God himself, that's what I'll do,
I'll cry my cause before His palace gate
(No chancellor will say I'll have to wait),
It's Him I'll ask for light, not you, and end
By being His, not your, devoted friend.
The door He's shut He'll open, and I'll ask
No other being to perform this task;
I'll cut my heart off from the world, and He
Will be the best and only friend for me.

My fiery heart, my choking soul, my face
Made sallow now with sorrow and disgrace,
My withered body wasted to a hair –
At dawn I bow them in the dust in prayer;
And, as I pray, my raucous, rending cries
Resound beyond my palace to the skies.
I weep like clouds when winter ends, my groans
Are like a mountain partridge's harsh moans,
I seethe in anguish like a stormy sea,
I tremble like a windswept cypress tree.
My tears have trickled to the fish's back,[159]
They wash the night till it's no longer black,
And with the torment of my heartfelt sighs
The moon forgets her path across the skies.
    Such fires I sigh the rising sun's afraid
To climb the east, and daylight is delayed,
My soul exhales such sorrow it's as though
A black cloud blotted out the land below.
    Weeping and wretched, and worn out with pain,
Dust-smeared I call on God, and call again,
'Great lord, great world creator, God who gives
Its destiny to every life that lives,
Friend to the wretched and abandoned, who
Hastens to comfort those who call on you –
It's you alone, My Lord, I will confide in,
Yours is the love and friendship that I'll hide in:
You know how hurt my soul is, You know how
I must be careful who I talk to now.
When I must talk, I'll talk to You and place
My soul within the purview of your grace;
You'll cleanse my soul of grief, You'll free my heart
From Fate that keeps Ramin and me apart.

Oh, soften his hard heart, let love's warmth make
It soft and pliable, for Vis's sake,
Remind him of our ancient love, and fill
His heart with love's sweet kindness and good will,
And let him bear at least a little of
This mountain weight of grief I bear for love.
Then use your power to bring him here before me
Or take me to him where he can't ignore me.
Block off the road that's caused us all our pain,
Open the road for us to meet again.
And till I glimpse his radiant face, oh, see
That it's unhurt by hate or enmity –
May love for me be all that hurts him there,
Despair for me be all of his despair!
And if I'm not to see his face, I've no
Desire to stay here in the world below,
I won't require a soul again, and you
Can give mine to Ramin – let him have two!'
    O dearest love, tell me, how long must I
Complain to you like this, and groan, and cry?
I'll say no more here, though I could, I know,
Increase a hundred times this tale of woe:
A few words can suffice, a small expense
Can yield us profits of great consequence.
I've said what I've endured; and it's between
Your God and you what you do now, Ramin!
If I told mountains what you've done to me,
Their very stones would weep with misery,
They would condemn your hardened heart, each stone
Would show more chivalry than you have shown;
My drunken heart was granite long ago,
Your steel heart smashed it with a single blow.

Greetings to that tall tree whose leaves conceal
Within its shape a center formed from steel,
Greetings to that red jewel whose facets hide
Thirty unblemished pearls arrayed inside,
Greetings to those narcissus eyes whose light
Deprives me of my sleep throughout the night,
Greetings to that full moon whose course has made
My fortune's moon eclipsed by sorrow's shade,
Greetings to that fair garden, which has left
My house of patience ruined and bereft,
Greetings to that green fir tree branch, which shows
How fruitlessly my withered branch now grows,
Greetings to that sweet rose whose smiles ensure
My constant weeping here for evermore,
Greetings to that wild, wanton tulip who
Has brimmed my weary eyes with morning dew,
Greetings to that brash rogue whose ruses keep
My mind from any kind of restful sleep,
Greeting to that brocade's bright mysteries,
To that pale moonlight, and the Pleiades,
Greetings to that fair, flower-like cypress tree
Whose beauty wounds my heart continually,
Greetings to those sweet curls whose scent has made
Merchants of musk give up their pointless trade,
Greetings to those bewitching eyes whose glance
Has made me look on food and sleep askance,
Greetings to those bright cheeks whose charming fire
Has filled my soul with trouble and desire,
Greetings to that full moon whose loveliness
Has left me weak and senseless with distress,
Greetings to that renowned deceiver who
Deprives my heart of all it might pursue,

Greetings to that sweet rose whose heady scent
Has filled my months and years with discontent,
Greetings to those tight curls whose antics shame me
So much that even in Shiraz they blame me,[160]
Greetings to that coy grace, that charming chin
That's made my life a tale of shame and sin,
Greetings to glory, to that radiance
That's left me with this sallow countenance,
Greetings to that resplendent treasury
That's made a pastime of oppressing me,
Greetings to that refulgent sun that's given
The world more beauty than the sun in heaven,
Greetings to that sweet rose, which is so fair
That roses shed their petals in despair,
Greetings to that tall cypress tree whose scent's
Stronger than jasmine's in its vehemence,
Greetings to that great lord of victory,
Greetings to that bright moon of tyranny,
Greetings to that brave knight, that noble king,
Greetings to one who's envied by the spring,
Greetings to one who is my world, my truth,
Greetings to one who loved me in my youth,
Greetings to one I wish success forever
Without whom both my eyes flow like a river,
Greetings beyond all count and numbering,
More than the endless bounty of the spring,
More than the deserts' countless grains of sand,
More than the raindrops drenching sea and land,
More than the plants that spring up constantly,
More than the beings of the land and sea,
More than the days the two worlds have been given,
More than the stars that fill the vault of heaven,
More than the seeds in every last location,
More than mankind in every generation,

More than birds' feathers, hairs on every pelt,
More than all words that scribes have ever spelt,
More than your thoughts, and my anxieties,
More than all faiths and creeds and pieties,
I wish you joy for all eternity
And wish myself your love and loyalty.
     May you find happiness, and may the light
That shines from you illuminate my sight;
A thousand times I wish, and wish again,
That great good fortune may be yours. Amen!"

VIS SENDS AZIN WITH HER LETTER TO RAMIN

Moshkin used all his knowledge, skill, and wit
Fashioning the letter till he'd finished it.
He wrote with musky ink, his sharpened pen
Suffused the pages with its scent, and when
Vis took the pages written with such care
She rubbed the letter with her musky hair,
So that a parasang away its scent –
Mixed with her dress's – was still evident.
She called Azin to her and said, "Azin,
I love you as myself; till now you've been
My trusted slave, from now on you will be
A brother and a counselor to me;
I'll manumit you, and you'll be my friend,
My confidant, on whom I can depend.
I'm going to send you to Ramin, a knight
Who's dearer to me than my soul or sight,
You're like my son, and he's my lord – no one
Is dearer than one's lord is, or a son.

Fly like December's winds, be on your way,
Fly like an arrow to him, don't delay;
I'll watch the road for you to reappear,
I'll count the days and hours until you're here,
And, as you ride, make sure you stay unseen
By friend and foe until you reach Ramin.
        Give him more greetings than the stars in heaven,
Call him a breaker of the oaths he's given,
And say, 'Scoundrel, your cruelty and your crimes
Have made me taste my death a hundred times;
Oh, you've forgotten now the oath you made me
Two hundred times, before your heart betrayed me;
That oath was like a passing breeze, a shower
Of sudden April rain that lasts an hour.
You've hurt my heart in ways that enemies
Don't stoop to in their bitterest rivalries;
May all your evil exploits be repaid you
Where no one hears your clamor or can aid you.
You think that it was me you hurt? I swear
It was yourself you destined for despair;
Those who keep tally of our choices make
Your evil soul their target for my sake,
They register our actions as we do them
And see that fitting punishments pursue them.
Why look for love from enemies? Why leave
Your friends alone here to lament and grieve?
It's like a slavering dragon gnawing me
To think that you should choose this enemy;
Who will you find like me to make you glad?
Where will you find a king like King Mobad?
A place as sweet as Khorasan? A city
As safe as noble Marv is, or as pretty?
Have you forgotten all I've done, Ramin?
And all the many kindnesses you've seen

From King Mobad? While he was called our king
You, in reality, had everything!
His wealth was mine to use as I saw fit,
Which meant that you could pocket all of it:
You had your pick of fine accoutrements,
Of countless kinds of royal magnificence –
Your horses were the best, the belts you wore
Surpassed in splendor any seen before,
While all your multicolored clothes were made
Of silks from China and the best brocade.
Your wine was ruby red, glowing like Mars,
Your servants were as lovely as the stars,
And I was their resplendent sun, whose charms
You fondly clasped within your eager arms.

    This was your heart-enchanting sweet condition,
This was your heart-delighting high position –
You threw all this away. For what? For dross!
And where's your profit from this evil loss?
Profit? Not only have you realized none
All of your capital has also gone.
Fate snatched a fortune from you, your existence
Is now a desperate scrabble for subsistence –
Ah, what a fool you are if you can't see
How you've exchanged your wealth for misery!
You gave up many things for one, you sold
For worthless lead your stores of precious gold,
Exchanged pure gold and silver for a crass
Disgusting world of worthless iron and brass.
In place of luxury you've indigence,
In place of pearls you've trashy ornaments,
In place of musk you've dust and dirt, in place
Of glory you've discomfort and disgrace.
How can you be intelligent if you
Injure yourself in everything you do?

That rose of yours won't last; why bind your heart
To something that is certain to depart?
Is one rose better, or a garden where
A myriad moon-like roses scent the air?'"

Azin heard all his princess had to say,
Bestrode his horse, and set out on his way.
His mount was mountain-like, in speed and force
More like a mighty whirlwind than a horse,
A flood among the mountains, on the plain
A nimble demon nothing could detain,
A leopard in the hills, while rivers made him
A sinuous fish – no obstacles delayed him.
His rider rode so easily he seemed
To be a man who slept and sweetly dreamed;
He crossed the desert as a pen will write,
As quickly as a bird's impatient flight.
Not pausing to dismount and eat, or rest,
But pushing always onward in his quest
And strenuously avoiding all delays,
Azin was in Gurab in fourteen days.

Vis laments her separation from Ramin

When Vis dismissed her messenger, Azin,
She wept and wailed in anguish for Ramin,
And any man who reads her sorrow here
Will feel his heart destroyed by grief and fear.
"Where have those precious days gone now," she cried,
"When you, my sun, were seated at my side?
My sun has gone, and what could reassure me
I'll ever see his light again before me?
My eyes weep rivers when I think of how
Sunlight and moonlight have both left me now.

(Why is the world so dark to me if they
Have not abandoned me and gone away?)
Pain's worse in darkness, and in darkness I
Bemoan my sorrow here, and weep, and sigh.
I thought that if I did no evil, none
Would come to trouble me from anyone;
I did none, and so why is it that Fate
Has left me suffering in this wretched state,
As though new caravans of sorrow came
Each hour to fill my heart with grief and shame?
And as a pomegranate splits when it
Is filled with flesh, so too my heart must split.
No sun shines in my heart, no breezes blow there,
Dark clouds and weeping floods are all I know there;
My face is sallow gold, as constant showers
Will make a plain a mass of yellow flowers.

     Love taught my tearful cheeks the writer's art,
Their sad calligraphy spells out my heart.
Love lit a fire within my heart, and burned
My heart herself, and everything she'd learned;
I pity my poor heart for all that she
Has had to suffer from love's tyranny,
And it was surely this distress that made her
Act with the lack of knowledge that betrayed her.
How evil love has proved to be! In truth
It's robbed me of my heart, and soul, and youth,
And, if I brought love here, my punishment
Has been the tortures that I underwent,
This brand that sears my heart, whose scar will be
An emblem known for all eternity.
You are the arrow's shaft, my love, and I
The bow from which the arrow has to fly;
Now I'm bent double like a bow, and when
The arrow's gone it does not come again.

Recalling you, I curl up in despair
As tightly as the curls of your sweet hair,
And when I think of separation's pain
I shiver like a sparrow in the rain.
    I've given you my heart, although I've seen
The way you've broken faith with me, Ramin!
How could you bear to grieve my heart, to hurt her,
To break your word to her, and then desert her?
Wasn't she like a loving mother for you?
A nurse, whose one concern was to adore you?
Seeing the world as you desired to do,
Fearing the evil eye would injure you?
Wasn't your glance the solace she was given?
Wasn't your face her sun and moon in heaven?
Wasn't your stature like a cypress for her,
A lovely box tree flourishing before her?
When did she ever choose dark violets over
The violet, musky curls of her sweet lover?
Or suck on candied sugar when your kiss
Beguiled her lips? What was more sweet than this?
Why do you treat my soul with treachery
And spill my body's blood so pointlessly?
Am I not Vis, that Vis whose face's light
Was once your sun by day, your moon by night?
Wasn't your love my dearest friend, your scent
The breeze that filled my being with content?
Didn't I weep when I was left alone,
And lay upon my heart a massive stone?
Didn't my face turn sallow, and my tears
Display your cruelty and my anxious fears?
Isn't it true that in this world no one
Delights or saddens me as you have done?
    Before I loved you I was known to you,
And, if you say I've changed since then, it's true.

I'm not the Vis you witnessed then, I know;
I was an arrow then, now I'm a bow,
And beatings from my flailing fists have made
My face's pomegranate blossoms fade,
My cheeks are now like water lilies fed
And moistened by the tears my poor eyes shed.
I cry out in my sorrow and distress
Like wine grapes crushed beneath a heavy press,
Weeping my tears as clouds weep springtime's showers,
Dampening the earth and nourishing its flowers.
My eyes are tulip red, the moisture there
Is like the brimming dew of my despair;
My tree of troubles is bereft of fruit,
And all my hopes are cut off at the root.
My heart's my enemy; ah, pity me,
Turning for succor to an enemy!
Look what a fool I am, to seek for aid
From one by whom my honor's been betrayed –
I would not sense within me this sedition
If she weren't cruelly seeking my perdition;
She's stubborn and on fire, and this makes sense
Since fire should punish disobedience.

  Oh, weep, my heart! Here, on this earth, you're in
The hell allotted to you for your sin,
Fate has ensured you'll burn for endless years
While I, through those same years, shed endless tears,
And how could such a life be sweet when I'm
All water and you're burning all the time?
I'll weep an ocean, and I'll set afloat
Upon its breaking waves a little boat,
My sighs will swell its sails, which I shall make
Out of my bloodstained clothes, for sorrow's sake,
And since these winds and waves are both from me
They'll show my little ship no enmity,

And I'll be like a fish whose life is spent
Always within its watery element.
    I've sent my love a letter wrapped inside
One of my tunics that my blood has dyed;
Perhaps he'll read it, and perhaps reject it,
Acknowledge all my sorrow, or neglect it,
Forgive my talk of love…or even send
A message asking me to be his friend.
Nothing is worse for lovers than when they
Must watch for letters day by weary day;
Those blissful days when I was with my lover,
Those days of mutual happiness, are over!
Now we must talk in letters, and it seems
If I'm to see him it must be in dreams.
I've lived to see this day, to fall from grace
To this despicable and wretched place.
Why did I not drink poison when my state
Was happy, and die blessed and fortunate?
If at that moment Death had taken me
I'd not have seen the days I now must see;
Better to die while in the midst of bliss
Than to endure a piteous life like this.
    Ah, world, this is your constant way, to treat
With your contempt those broken by defeat,
Raining down yet more grief, like stones, on those
Already rendered wretched by your blows.
Breezes don't bring his scent now to delight me,
What have I done to them that they should slight me?
I see the blossoms of the spring have made
Earth's dust into a sumptuous brocade,
But spring can't come to me as long as he
Who is my soul remains away from me;
The very dust now shows that spring is here,
But in my heart no springtime can appear."

After some time with her, Ramin's desire
For Gol began to waver and to tire:
Joy's springtime withered, and the boisterous gale
Of his impulsive love began to fail;
Affection's bow was broken, and he knew
The arrows of his love had snapped in two.
The bright brocade of happiness grew dull,
The spring was muddied and undrinkable.
Gurab seemed like a goblet to Ramin,
Filled with a drink both brackish and unclean.
Gol's love had been like wine for him, and he,
While sober, drank this wine incessantly
(So drunkards drink, their hearts desirous of
Glasses and goblets of the wine they love,
But finally the heart grows stupefied
And finds that its desire for wine has died;
When we're replete with drink, and crapulous,
Even the best wine can taste poisonous).
Ramin and Vis had been too long apart
And weariness had settled on his heart.

He and his friends rode out one day to see
The world in all its springtime finery,
It was a sight to soften his distress,
A Chinese painting in its loveliness:
He glimpsed sweet tulips, heard the melodies
Of nightingales complaining in the trees,
And all the land glowed like brocade, a scene
Of red and purple, yellow, blue and green.
And as they rode, it happened then, by chance,
A little girl of heavenly elegance
Handed him violets;[161] and his heart was broken,
Remembering his oath, and Vis's token.

She'd sat upon her throne that day, her face
As lovely as the full moon in its grace,
And, giving him her gathered violets, she
Had murmured, "Keep these, and remember me;
And always, when spring's violets reappear,
Recall the promises you've made me here."
And then she'd cursed whoever thought to break
The oaths they'd sworn there, for affection's sake.
Ramin grew desolate with grief, and night
Obscured the world and dimmed his failing sight
(The world did not grow dark, it was his eyes
That darkened from his heart's smoke-laden sighs);
He wept more tears than all the clouds that bring
A flooding downpour to us every spring,
And in his heart he felt love's fire increase
The more he brooded on his absent Vis.
Now you would say the sun of love moved free
From all its clouds of doubt and enmity,
And as the clouds dispersed and darkness ceased
The sunlight's warmth took hold there, and increased.

Ramin reproaches his heart

He left his band of knights and moved apart
While love renewed itself within his heart.
Distraught now, he dismounted, and he felt
His face grow pallid and his courage melt,
And for a while he cursed the wretched state
That had been forced upon his soul by Fate,
Blaming with every breath his heart, whose fires
Seared his unhappy soul with its desires,
Crying, "Heart, heart, you're like Majnun,[162] who leaves
His friends and enemies, and raves and grieves,
Grieving at home, grieving when friends are there,
Grieving alone, abandoned to despair.

How long, my heart," he cried, "will you resign
Yourself to drunkenness bereft of wine?
You're like a drunkard who can't separate
What he should love from what he ought to hate,
Mirage or garden, autumn or the spring,
To you they've all become the selfsame thing,
You sleep wrapped in brocade or on the earth
And foolishly find both of equal worth;
Cruelty is loyalty for you, and lust
Becomes a wisdom that one has to trust;
You're weak, you break your promises, you're dyed
With every color that you've ever tried!
All of the evils of the world surround you,
All of the sorrows of the world confound you,
The door of hope has been shut fast upon you,
Your only friend's Disaster – she won't shun you!
You came here to Gurab and said, 'I'm free!'
But you're not free for all you claimed to me;
I was the drunken fool who trusted you,
Led by the winds your foolish fancies blew.

      You told me, 'Take another lover now,
Forget Vis, you can disregard your vow,
Don't be concerned for me; no, this won't hurt me;
If I don't see her, patience won't desert me.'

      I took you at your word, and look I've taken
Another love, and Vis is left forsaken,
And now you drown me in your grief, and spurn me
As all the fires of separation burn me.
Wasn't it you who said, 'Leave Vis, and go'?
And now you torture me for doing so!
Who said, 'Patience sustains me,' and whose rages
And wild impatience nothing now assuages?
How I regret obeying your commands!
Why did I place my bridle in your hands?

Since all your wisdom did is show me how
Hopeless and hapless you and I are now.
    I thought that you'd escaped from grief; I see you
Tangled in grief from which no ruses free you –
You're like a bird that seeds have lured inside
A snare a hunter's taken care to hide.
You broke faith with my soul, my enemies
Now toy with her and taunt her as they please;
Why did I listen to your words and do
The foolish things commanded me by you?
But I deserve this state, I am a fool,
And fools deserve despair and ridicule.
It's right that grief's my constant counterpart,
I snuffed the candle burning in my heart;
It's right that sorrow's mine, I felled the tree
Of my good fortune and prosperity.
I'm like a deer whose hoof's caught in a snare,
A fish that's hooked and tugged into the air;
With my own hands I dug this fearsome pit
And threw the hopes I'd cherished into it.
How could Vis hear excuses from Ramin?
Ah, what a thoughtless, shameless fool I've been!
Cursed be the day I planted love, then slew
With separation's sword the joy I knew!
But since the day that love has been my master
My wretched days have only known disaster –
Now among heartless strangers, now insane
With exile's grief and separation's pain.
Good Fortune shuns me, and may no child be
Born to such luckless grief and misery!"

Now when Ramin withdrew, leaving behind
His friends, to face the torments in his mind,
Prince Rafida came after him, and saw
The secret sorrows of his son-in-law;

And self-absorbed, as lovers are, Ramin
Was unaware his anguish had been seen.
Gol's father listened to him, then approached him,
And stood there as he questioned and reproached him.
"Bright lamp of all our noblemen," he said,
"You look like someone mourning for the dead;
What pleasure is there that God hasn't brought you?
What demon of unhappiness has caught you?
Why brood on useless things, and why complain
Of absent happiness and present pain?
Aren't you Ramin, the best of knights? The one
Whose brother, King Mobad, reigns like the sun?
And though you are a champion whose name
Already garners more than kingly fame
You are a young man still; Ramin, what more
Could you desire? What are you hankering for?
Don't be ungrateful for the state you're in,
Only despair can come from such a sin;
If you insist that silken pillows hurt
Perhaps you would prefer to sleep on dirt?"

Ramin replied, "A healthy man can't know
The agonies that sick men undergo,
And I forgive your saying I complain
Of useless matters and imagined pain.
There is no pleasure that could be more sweet
Than cherished friendship when companions meet,
There is no pain more bitter than when they
Accept that one of them must go away.
Cloth shrieks when it is torn, and vines weep tears
When they are cut with pruning knives or shears,
And I'm not less than they are if I care
That all my boon companions live elsewhere.
Gurab's your town, your family's here, you've grown here;
You're not like me, a stranger and alone here.

An exile might become a king, but he
Still hungers for familiar company.
The world means friends to me, that's all, and they're
The medicine that will cure me of despair;
Joy can be very sweet, but in the end
A hundred joys mean less than one loved friend.
At times I envy you, as you come back
From traveling on some road or desert track,
When all your household hurries out to meet you
And then your wife and children rush to greet you,
And you and they rejoice as they surround you
As if they were a loving chain that bound you,
And all the milling crowd of your relations
Mobs you with welcoming congratulations.
But as for me I've no one here, no one,
No friend, no precious confidant, no son.
  I was like you, I'd not a single care
When all my friends and relatives were there;
How sweet those days were when my family
And all my dearest friends surrounded me!
How sweet those days were, when disaster meant
The trials and tribulations love had sent,
When only her narcissus eyes destroyed me,
When only her red tulip lips annoyed me.
Such pain was a delicious provocation,
A time of tipsiness and sweet flirtation;
How sweet her cruelty was, how sweet to bite
My lips with mingled anger and delight,
How sweet her chiding of me was, how sweet
Her modesty when we contrived to meet.
If in a week she once unveiled her face
And let me glimpse its heart-bewitching grace,
She made a prisoner of me there and then,
A slave, who'd no wish to be free again.

How sweet to count our kisses, and to swear
Two hundred times the oaths we swore to there;
How sweet to groan and every day complain
Two hundred times to God of all my pain,
How sweet to be so changeable, to sigh
And then to laugh in triumph by and by,
And then to change again and take her part
Whispering two hundred blessings on her heart.
At times I'd tumble her thick curls, and make them
Disordered and disheveled, sweetly break them,
And then I'd take her fingers as she faced me
And link them round me so that she embraced me.
Those were my happiest days, and yet I thought
That I was wretched, desolate, distraught;
I feared the roses in her face could harm me,
I feared her sweet narcissus eyes would charm me
(Although why anyone at all should be
Afraid of flowers is still a mystery;
Besides, the rubies of her lips repaid me
Whenever her narcissus eyes waylaid me,
And if her curly hyacinthine hair
Entrapped me in its labyrinthine snare,
The pink, sweet-tasting blossoms of her face
Were there to rescue me from my disgrace).
Love was my only business then, the wiles
My lover practiced were my only trials,
And why should I or my poor heart complain
If we'd no other business than such pain?
This was my life; on pleasure's polo field
Each of my mounted rivals had to yield.
Banqueting, hunting, quaffing copious wine,
And counting kisses, all of these were mine;
And health was mine as well, although I said
That I was sick with love and nearly dead.

But life has moved inexorably on
And I complain that those complaints have gone,
And I am wretched when I think of how
All of love's wretchedness has left me now."

The hunt was over; Rafida returned
And told his daughter Gol what he had learned.
"Ramin has planted hatred here," he said,
"Though it's your love that he has harvested;
He opened up his heart to me, laid bare
The inmost secrets he's kept hidden there.
Gol, even if you trust him, and endeavor
To touch his heart, to treat him well forever,
He'll be a snake still, as a snake he'll bite you,
He'll be a wolf still, as a wolf he'll fight you
(We can pour sugared water on their roots
But bitter trees will give us bitter fruits,
And no refining processes, alas,
Can make pure gold from copper or from brass;
Boil pitch a hundred times, it's black as night,
It's never going to turn a milky white).
If this Ramin were just and virtuous he
Would not have acted so dishonorably
To Vis and King Mobad; he's lived his life
In such a way you should not be his wife;
His heart is fickle, and his evil nature
Makes him a lion-like and savage creature.
Because he was the only man you'd seen
You ignorantly fell for Prince Ramin,
But seeking love from him's a foolish fault –
It's planting roses on a plain of salt!
Why did you marry such a worthless cheat?
How could you hope such poison would be sweet?

But what's the point of my reproaching you
When Fate decides on everything we do?"

Ramin, returning from the hunt that day,
Appeared to be the hunt's heart-stricken prey –
A frown was knotted where his eyebrows met,
Cascading tears had left his cheeks still wet,
And at the evening banquet you'd have said
He was a man whose life and soul had fled.
Rose-scented Gol, whose face was lovelier than
All of the idols ever carved by man,
Whose youthful form was tall and cypress slim,
Who flickered like a flame, sat next to him,
As lovely as the moon when she is new
(A moon where tulips and white lilies grew);
And, like Arash's arrows,[163] flaming darts
Sped from her cheeks to pierce the courtiers' hearts.
But jasmine-breasted Gol was as unseen
As jewels are by a corpse, by Prince Ramin;
His body was beside her sitting there,
But it was clear his mind was all elsewhere –
He'd sigh distractedly, and groan, and then,
Lamenting his lost love, he'd sigh again,
Thinking that no one else there could perceive
That all he did was groan and sigh and grieve.
Now in his heart he said, "What is more sweet
Than banquets where young friends and lovers meet?
And yet to me this scene of revelry
Is sadder than a funeral obsequy.
My dearest love believes my days are spent
In thoughtless happiness and merriment,
Since she can have no way of knowing how
Heartbroken and regretful I am now.
She says, 'I know Ramin is weary of
My longing for him, and my constant love,'

She does not know my state here, left alone,
And lacking all the friends I've ever known.
She says, 'My faithless lover's happy to
Abandon my embrace for someone new,
To sit beside another love, and break
His hopeful heart with passion for her sake,'
She doesn't know that since I left her there
I curl up like her curls in my despair.
     Tell me, What has Fate written on my brow?
What will my heavenly star do with me now?
What will I see from that sweet cypress tree?
What will that speaking moon spell out to me?
There is no tyranny that's as malign
As hers has been, no suffering like mine;
I'm humbled to the ground with all my woes,
I'm iron beneath my sorrow's hammer blows,
I bear such panniers of grief that I
Am like a donkey laboring till I die.
But now I'll leave here, and I'll seek the ground
Within which my resplendent jewel is found,
I'll find the sovereign remedy to cure
All of the sorrows that I now endure –
Since leaving her has brought me all this pain
I'll seek her out and see her once again.
How strange this is, to find a remedy
By seeking out what caused my malady!
But she is all my joy and all my grief
And she alone can bring my soul relief.
Why should I fight my fortune now and run
In fear from what I'm certain must be done?
Why should I hide my illness from my nurse
Since doing this can only make it worse?
I can't be cautious now, I can't refrain
From telling all the world my heartfelt pain;

What use is caution, when I'm almost dead
And longing's waters rise above my head?
    I'll go to her and say what I must say
To cleanse the rust that eats my heart away,
Though I'm so sick I don't know now if I
Shall see her face again before I die.
I'll set off for the city of my friend,
And if I die before my journey's end
At least I'll die approaching her; they'll make
My grave there, where I perished for her sake,
And all the world will know the nature of
The sorrows of Ramin, who died for love.
Travelers who see my grave will pause and sit
And murmur prayers and blessings over it,
And say, 'Here lies a traveler killed by love,
May he be blessed, and loved, by God above' –
(Travelers will honor travelers, since they see
Their own in one another's misery).
If I were killed by enemies my name
Would be dishonored by disgrace and shame,
But if I'm killed by love my fame will spread
Throughout the world long after I am dead.
Lions and mammoths quaked and fled before me,
And routed armies quailed with dread before me,
But absence from my friend has done to me
All I have done to every enemy.
None of my enemies could trap me yet,
What trapped me is the snare my lover set,
And Death could not have found me were it not
That absence was the ambush in her plot.
    But if my journey is to stay unknown,
I'll have to travel this long road alone;
If I should make my journey with a guide,
And reach Marv's gates with someone at my side,

Mobad would know, he'd publicly reproach me,
And then make certain Vis could not approach me.
Besides it's winter, and I'm terrified,
Snow's silver mines block every mountainside,
Floods hide the plains, and every creeping thing
Has slunk away till the return of spring.
Marv will be snowbound now, its cypress trees
Shrouded in glistening camphor canopies;
I don't know how I'll find the strength to go
Alone through such a world of ice and snow,
And harder than the season and its dangers
Is that, for Vis now, she and I are strangers.
She'll show no mercy to me, she won't meet me,
She won't appear upon her roof to greet me,
She'll shut her door on me, she won't come near me,
And when I make excuses she won't hear me;
Despairing, broken-hearted, I shall wait
As lifeless as the knocker on her gate.

    Alas for all I had, my noble name,
My chivalry, my weapons, and my fame,
Alas for my fleet horses, for the press
Of friends with whom I shared my happiness,
Alas for glory, sovereignty, and for
The mighty forces I once led to war!
I cannot turn to them, I cannot ask
For them to help me in this fearsome task –
I don't fear swords or spears, the enemies
I face are neither Roman nor Chinese;
I fear her sun-like face, my enemy
Is my poor, fevered heart's timidity.
How can I fight my heart? How can the door
To manliness be forced ajar once more?
Sometimes I say, 'O heart, how long will you
Persist with tears whatever I might do?

Men's hearts delight them, but from you I gain
Nothing but burning, melting, endless pain;
You flare with fire, and then dissolve and weep,
Cheating my days of joy, my nights of sleep,'
No palaces, no gardens gratify me,
Indoors and outdoors, neither satisfy me,
Horse racing on the plain does not attract me,
Polo with troops of friends does not distract me;
I don't ride out to war to seek my name
By fighting and acquiring martial fame,
I don't seek pleasure with young men when they
Feast and carouse and drink the night away,
I don't consort with courtiers, or prefer
One girl to others and make love to her.
Where music once disarmed me with delight
Mockery's all I hear now, day and night.
In Kuhestan, Kerman, and Khuzestan,
Tabaristan, Gorgan, and Khorasan,
The story of Ramin is told and sung –
My name's in every mouth, on every tongue.
Listen, you'll hear them singing of my pain
By every river and on every plain;
Youths in the cities sing about my shame
And shepherds in the country do the same,
Women at home, men in the market, sing
The selfsame words about the selfsame thing.
 My hair's turned white with waiting, but no sign
Has reached my heart that hope might yet by mine,
And how can sense, and sleep, and patience stay
Beside me when that houri's far away?
I'm sallow as a gold coin, I'm as weak
As patients are when they can hardly speak,
I can't run fifty feet, my fingers lack
Even the strength to pull my bowstring back,

And every time I try to ride you'd say
My weak waist's on the point of giving way;
My back's like wax, it's soft and pliable,
My fist feels puny, as though made of wool.
I don't take cheetahs out to watch them leap
Upon the fleeing backs of mountain sheep,
Or send my hawks up now to watch them fly,
And wheel, and bring down woodcock from the sky.
My horse outran gazelles, now it's unable
To rouse itself enough to leave its stable;
I never try my strength with wrestlers, or
Drink with my friends till I can drink no more.
While fortune favors my contemporaries
(Who ride, or take part in festivities,
Go hunting in the foothills, or discover
The beauties of a garden with a lover;
Whose minds are fixed on study, or who live
For all the carnal pleasures life can give)
The world holds nothing for me, and I keep
My heart here, like my luck now, fast asleep.
  I'm like a messenger who, night and day,
Stays in one place and cannot get away,
I'm standing water in a well that time
Through months and years has mantled with its slime.
I take no pleasure in this world, and in
The next I will be punished for my sin;
In both worlds now, love's sword has severed me
From happiness for all eternity.
How long, my heart, will you augment love's fire
And melt me in this skillet of desire?
O heart, you've taken these absurdities
Beyond all reason and all boundaries,
You've slain me with my sorrow, and while I
Am murdered by you, you refuse to die;

You're like harsh poison, and this love has made you
Forfeit both worlds for nothing and betrayed you:
May no one have a heart like mine – so dull,
So drunk, so stupid, so contemptible!"

Ramin reproached his heart, but also fled
From all it told him, like a hen whose head
Has been cut off, whose torso jerks and flops,
And dashes here and there until it drops.
He felt so sad there in the feast that night
He ran out, like a coward from a fight;
Men brought his horse to him (a Rakhsh[164] you'd say,
Whom phantom wingbeats sped along its way).
Ramin set off for Khorasan, like one
Who knows where he is going, and is gone.

AZIN REACHES RAMIN WITH VIS'S LETTER

Sweet eastern wind, which seems to blow from where
A myriad lovely roses scent the air,
Kharkhiz, Gheisur, and Samandur bestow
Camphor and musk upon you when you blow,
And when a lover's longed-for scent augments
The vivid sweetness of your mingled scents
The fragrance that you bring is sweeter than
All of the perfumes ever made by man.
To Prince Ramin, no roses could compete
With Vis's scent, or be as soft and sweet,
And constantly he said, "I know full well
No rose or eglantine has such a smell,
It's Vis's scent! What blessèd wind is this
That brings me news and promises of bliss?"
These were the thoughts that occupied Ramin
When, in the distance, he espied Azin
And, urging on his brindled horse, made haste
Across the intervening desert waste.

The smiling messenger dismounted from
The mammoth-bodied horse on which he'd come
And kissed the ground before Ramin, who caught
The rosy, musky scents his presence brought –
But no, not musk and roses filled the air,
The heady scent of Vis herself was there.
How welcome now Azin was to Ramin,
How noble now Ramin looked to Azin,
As if, in pleasant springtime's balmy weather,
A box tree and a cypress grew together.

They tethered both their horses then and found
A patch of comfortable, grassy ground
To sit upon; and, when they'd sat, Azin
Questioned his prince on all he'd done and seen,
Then handed him the letter, still inside
The folded tunic Vis's blood had dyed.
Ramin became an onager, you'd say,
Who sees a lion has marked him for its prey –
His trembling legs and hands became so weak
He dropped the letter, and he could not speak;
At last he grasped it, read, and wept as though
His flooding tears would never cease to flow.
He'd touch her tunic to his heart, then place
The letter's words against his tear-stained face,
He'd smell the musky pages as he read,
Then kiss her tunic's stains where she had bled,
And all the while, amidst his cloudy sighs,
Diamonds and rubies rained down from his eyes,
While from that weeping cloud a lightning dart
Struck a new conflagration in his heart.
He'd cry and sigh, and then he'd scream and yell
As if he were a demon come from hell;
Then he grew silent for a little space,
And sprawled headlong upon his tearful face.

As he revived (his opening mouth now seemed
Like a dark shell, within which white pearls gleamed)
He said, "I sigh for my sad fate that's sown
This tree of grief, that's left me here alone,
That's cut me off from that sweet cypress tree
Whose palace plot is where I long to be,
That's severed me from that sweet sun whose light
Illuminates her palace through the night,
That will not let me see her now, or hear her,
Forbidding me forever to come near her.
But if I don't see Vis, at least I see
This blood-stained tunic she has sent to me,
And if I cannot hear her voice, I've read
This written record of the words she said;
This tunic gives my soul a sense of peace,
My spring returns now with these words from Vis."
Then he composed an answer lovelier
Than silks sewn by a skilled embroiderer.

Ramin's answer to Vis

His letter was addressed, "To Vis, whose face
Is lovelier than an idol's in its grace,
Who is a sun and moon of sweet delight,
Whose skin is jasmine scented, lily white,
Who's like an idol fashioned cunningly
From moon-like silver and pure ivory,
Whose matchless loveliness is praised as far
As China, who's adored in Qandahar,
Who is the spring itself, and springtime's roses,
The spring's full moon, the gardens she discloses,
A silver column, a tall cypress tree,
A palace made from glass and ivory,
Who is sweet wine, a drug that will suffice
To cure all ills, a draught of paradise.

Sweet rose, pure pearl, imperial silk, bright gem
That's worthy of a royal diadem,
Sun of the palace walks, moon of the night there,
Star of the pleasant kiosks of delight there,
Bough of the palace gardens, may you be
Blessed with all glory now eternally,
And may there be no life for me if I
Must live without your presence – may I die!
I do not hope to see your face, or hear
Your voice again that is so sweet and clear.
I know I've wronged you, and I fear that you
Might do to me what enemies would do;
And though I didn't sin I cannot claim
That it was you that sinned, you're not to blame.
But it was you who drove me out, who prayed
For heartless Separation's evil aid.
In love, Vis, you were quick to tire, you told me
To do just as I wished, you wouldn't hold me!
This wasn't what I'd thought your love was worth –
I had imagined heaven, I found the earth.
You knew the house I'd built was still, for me,
A house of love built for eternity,
And, oh, how quick you were then to destroy
That house which gave me such delusive joy!
The guilt is yours, although I'm penitent,
And say you're guiltless and quite innocent;
You rule me, I obey, my heart endures
All you command it to, since it is yours.

     My love, I'm absent from your side, it's true,
But I have left my hostage heart with you –
How could I shake your yoke off, when your breast
Houses my heart within it as a guest?
It is as if, upon your soul I swear,
I'm in a dragon's jaws when you're not there.

My sallow cheeks declare the pain my heart
Must undergo as long as we're apart –
They are my witnesses, their testament's
Confirmed by my poor eyes' improvidence;
These witnesses and their wise friends should be
More than enough to make you pity me.
My cheeks are sallow now as gold, my eyes
Are bloodshot with my tears; you'll recognize
That all they say of my despair is true
When I can show their wretchedness to you.
Honesty's all you'll see from me now, Vis,
My honesty won't falter now or cease:
Once you were cruel, cruelty was your reward,
Be faithful now, and I will keep my word.
You hurt yourself, and now you're sorry for it,
Your cruelty's over now and I'll ignore it;
I will begin our love again, I'll start
Our tale once more and offer you my heart –
It's you I know, it's you I love, no one
Can ever hold my heart as you have done.
My heart's corroded by your cruelty's rust,
I'll scour it off, my eyes will buy the dust
You tread upon, and though your love might falter
My love will not diminish, Vis, or alter.
        Why should I flee your face, why should I flee
That light that is the sun itself to me?
Why should I turn away from your sweet hair?
Where could I find the musk that I find there?
Men hope for houris and for heaven, and you
Are both my houri and my heaven too;
And, if I suffer for my love again,
Nothing is won without its share of pain.
Come, we shall count the world as wind, and let
The days gone by be over, and forget.

Be with me now as gold and wealth are one,
I'll be with you as sunlight's with the sun;
Be with me now as redness is with wine,
As scent belongs to roses you'll be mine.
I wield a poisoned dagger, you a glance
That pierces hearts with its cruel radiance –
If we unite our weapons there will be
No one who dares to be our enemy!
While oceans last and rivers run I send
Greetings and blessings to you without end.
I write this at the roadside, which is why
I've made so short an answer here, but I
Will follow swiftly after it and break
A hundred bonds if need be for your sake.
I'll come as quickly as an arrow flies
When it is shot across the empty skies,
I'll come as quickly as a stone when it
Is dropped into the darkness of a pit."

The letter was completed, and Azin
Sped like a gusting wind from Prince Ramin.
Ramin came after him with all the haste
Of polo players when the ball is chased –
Both rode for Khorasan, and neither thought
A moment of the trials the journey brought.
Two arrows flying with a single flight,
There was a day between them, and a night.

VIS LEARNS THAT AZIN HAS RETURNED FROM RAMIN

Though love's made up of endless injuries,
The soul's despair, the body's miseries,
It has two happy moments (even so,
Both bring their own ordeals to undergo);

One's when a letter comes, what's even better
Is when the lover comes who sends this letter,
Since no one feels such anguish in his heart
As lovers feel when they are kept apart.

As drought-parched, dusty pastures thirst for rain,
As patients long for drugs to dull their pain,
So jasmine-breasted Vis sat night and day
Where, like a lookout, she could watch the way
That would in time, she trusted, bring Azin
Back with an answer from her love, Ramin.
When she caught sight of him it was as though
Sweet April breezes had begun to blow,
Or you would say that when she saw Azin
She was a Chinese or Egyptian queen.
Then piece by piece Azin recounted how
Ramin's love-longing was far greater now,
And as a proof of all he said he'd seen
He handed her the letter from Ramin.
Oh, wonderful, her actions were the same
As his had been when her sweet letter came!
A thousand times she kissed it, then she pressed it
Against her heart, against her eyes, and blessed it;
Her sweetest kisses sweetened it, she blent
Its fragrance with her musky ringlets' scent,
And when she read his words you'd wager she
Was now beside herself with ecstasy.
She read the letter, then she kissed it, then
For two days read and kissed it yet again;
And while she chafed and waited for Ramin,
Her confidant and ally was Azin.

She made her face more lovely, and with care
Wove stems of roses in her musky hair,

And next, among their pretty petals, set
A precious, jewel-encrusted coronet –
And seeing all this splendor you would say
The shining moon had crowned the sun that day.
She dressed in silk brocades whose elegance
Rivaled the heavens themselves in radiance;
Perfection shone out from her lovely face,
Spring was embodied in her body's grace,
Her musky locks' sweet fragrances could give
A myriad perfumers the means to live,
The soothing balm of her sweet lips could free
A myriad patients from their misery;
Her face would ransack young men's hearts, her hair
Reduce the souls of lovers to despair.
Her tumbling ringlets fell below her waist,
As though a swarthy African embraced
Her body's slender form and held within
His clasp the Chinese pallor of her skin.
She was supremely lovely, as if made
From musk and sugar, petals and brocade;
She was a paradise of tints and scents,
All kindness, charm, and sweet benevolence.
This silver moon, so lovely to behold,
Had turned as sallow now as yellow gold,
Her beauty was made captive to desire
Who held her hand in love's tormenting fire.
Impatience was a fever in her blood,
And happiness a donkey mired in mud,
Absence a knife that cut her to the bone,
And grief the army she must face alone.

She posted lookouts then, and ordered sentries
To watch the city's alleyways and entries;
And paced the palace roof, more skittish than
A seed that's sizzling in a frying pan,

As she surveyed the highway to discover
Some distant sign of her approaching lover.
Night came, but not the moonlight that she sought;
She was so restless then, and so distraught,
You'd think the rich brocades she lay on were
A thorny bush that itched and prickled her;
As dawn came on, exhaustion overtook her,
She closed her eyes, and consciousness forsook her.
She slept a while, then started up, and screamed
As though a devil'd struck her while she dreamed,
Her nurse embraced her tightly then, and said,
"What evil nightmare's working in your head?"
And, as a willow gives a windswept shiver,
Or as the sun's reflected in a river,
Vis trembled and replied, "Nurse, have you seen
Or heard of love like mine for Prince Ramin?
I've never known a night like this, when I,
A hundred times, felt sure that I would die,
And my embroidered mattress seemed to be
A mass of snakes and scorpions stinging me.
My fortune's black as night, and in this night
That lovely moon Ramin's my only light,
And darkness will depart when his fair face
Shines with its light upon this wretched place.
I dreamt his face shone moon-like in the dusk,
His fragrant hair filled all the world with musk,
He took my hand, and with the rubies of
His sugared lips he said to me, 'My love,
I come to you in dreams because I fear
Your watchful enemies are waiting here,
They guard you from me, Vis, and they will make
Quite sure I cannot come when you're awake;
But though they keep us from each other they
Cannot forever keep my soul away.

Show me your face, my love, and let me see
The loveliness that has tormented me.
Don't be afraid, embrace me, and we'll meet
Like milk and wine, and what could be more sweet?
Make my chest fragrant with your locks, and make
My lips sweet with the kisses I will take.
Your heart has been like stone, now let it seek
For love and loyalty, and when you speak
Speak kindly to me, Vis; your angry ways
Were a mistake, since as the proverb says,
"It's goodness of the soul that makes good creatures,
And not the prettiness of goodly features."'

Why should I not show my distress when I
Have seen him in my dreams, and heard him sigh
And speak so sweetly? Now, while we're apart,
Why should I not feel sorrow in my heart?
And every man alive now would excuse me
If he saw how the heavens above abuse me!"

RAMIN REACHES MARV AND VIS

Greetings great Marv, the seat of kings, the seat
Of all that's pleasing, comforting, and sweet,
Greetings great Marv, pleasant in everything
In summer, winter, autumn, and the spring;
And how can anyone who's once lived there
Begin to think that he might live elsewhere?
And if his lover's there, how could he face
The thought of living in another place?
This was Ramin's case on both counts, since he
Had left both Marv and Vis so suddenly
(No love is like first love, and there is no
Place equal to the place in which we grow).
Ramin reached Marv and to his wondering eyes
The land appeared to be a paradise;

The very grass seemed fair as cypress trees,
The flowers all camphor and sweet fragrances,
The boughs were lovely houris, and you'd say
Rezvan[165] had opened heaven to him that day.
Now all his soul was like an April vine
Of youthful, newly budding eglantine.

As he approached, a lookout saw Ramin
And ran down to inform the nurse he'd seen
Their noble prince, on horseback, drawing near.
Her heart delivered from its grief and fear,
The nurse ran instantly to Vis[166] and said,
"The medicine comes to raise you from the dead;
The royal leopard saunters in his pride,
The lion advances with his kingly stride;
A splendid breeze, pursuing its reward,
Announces the approach of springtime's lord;[167]
Love's fruit has ripened on the burgeoning bough,
The mine of union has been opened now;
The roof is bathed in morning's eastern light,
Buds blossom in the purlieus of delight;
A glorious hope has come, the news is here
That soon your happy lover will appear.
Can you not see that night has turned to day,
That spring has come and winter's gone away?
That happiness's boughs are flourishing
And grief's boughs wither in the coming spring?
That all the earth is pretty as brocade,
That fragrant breezes fill each verdant glade?
Sweet moon, rise up now from this bed of pain,
Open your eyes and see the world again!
Your night was dark, as dark as your black hair,
The morning, like your face, is bright and fair;
Grief's rust is scoured away, and all the earth
Is filled with genial happiness and mirth.

Ramin's face makes the whole world smile, the air
Is musky from the fragrance of his hair,
And his auspicious coming will make one
The lovely moon, the radiance of the sun.
Rise now, and see your lover, and you'll say
It is the moon's child who has come this way
To stand, and ask for audience, and sue
For mercy and forgiveness now from you.
You have a wounded, he a broken, heart
And closed doors kept the two of you apart;
Open the door now to your love, and give
His soul-enchanting hopes the means to live."

Vis said, "The king's asleep; for now, disaster
Lies safely hidden with its sleeping master,
But if he wakes it's certain that we'll be
Quickly embroiled in a catastrophe;
Do something, nurse, contrive a way to keep
Our secret from him, see he stays asleep!"
The nurse intoned a spell, and you'd have said
That King Mobad lay not asleep but dead,
Or that he was a drunkard who'd passed out
After a long and heavy drinking bout.
Now moon-like Vis peered from an aperture
To see if Prince Ramin would come to her,
And felt love's blossoms opening in her when
She saw his radiant sun-like face again
But kept her features under firm control
And hid the turmoil seething in her soul.
It was Ramin's great horse that she addressed:
"O mountain-bodied mount, I once caressed
You like a son, so why then did you hurt me,
Break faith with me, and treacherously desert me?
Did I not dress you in magnificence,
A silken bridle, golden ornaments,

And make a silvered, marble manger for you,
And all the year set sesame before you?
Why did you leave me then and choose a manger
That's far from me, belonging to a stranger?
You don't deserve my kindness, I can see,
When I consider how you've treated me.
No, you deserve the manger that you sought –
You know the catalogue of woes it brought!
Those that don't merit dates get thorns instead
Just as a wretch deserves to lose his head."

Ramin replies to Vis

Now when Ramin saw all her pain, and heard
The poison gathered in each bitter word,
His anguished soul poured forth a thousand pleas,
Regrets, excuses, and apologies.
He said: "O springtime of all love, O sun
Who steals and holds the hearts of everyone,
Glory of kings, sweet paradise of love,
Fair, radiant rival to the moon above,
Loveliest of beauties, morning star, the light
Of sunny daytime and the moon at night,
Whitest of lilies, richest rose of all,
Goddess I love, who holds my heart in thrall,
Why do you seek my blood so ruthlessly
And turn your lovely face away from me?
I am Ramin, your soul's equivalent,
And you are Vis, my soul's admonishment;
I am Ramin, your servitor Ramin,
And you are Vis, my heart's acknowledged queen;
I am Ramin, love's wretchedness and glory,
And all the world now knows my lovelorn story;
And you are Vis, moon of all loveliness,
The splendid queen of every sorceress.

I am Ramin still, that Ramin you knew,
Still worthy of you, still in love with you;
I am still what I was, but you have changed;
Why do you act as though we are estranged?
Have you been listening to my enemies,
That you find bitter now what used to please?
Have you sworn them a lying oath, to break
The solemn promises we used to make?
Have you agreed with them to burn like straw
The Prince Ramin you loved and knew and saw?
　　　Alas for all the love and hope that I've
Expended hoping to keep love alive!
I sowed love in youth's garden, and I made
My soul an expert in the gardener's trade;
My gardening heart was happy in its toil,
My tears provided water for the soil,
I did not sleep by night or rest by day,
But with my labors wore myself away.
And when the spring came gillyflowers were there,
Tulips and lilies opened everywhere,
A hundred tufts of flowers sprang up and lent
Each passing breeze their fragrant musky scent,
Thick shade was found beneath the noble trees –
Willows and plane trees, myrtles, cypresses,
And fruit trees blossomed there, a welcome sight
To charm the heart with beauty and delight;
The trilling nightingale, the cooing dove
Sang with a myriad other birds of love.
Fidelity had built the garden's fence
That seemed a mountain made in its defense,
And at the mountain's foot a stream was found
Running through golden banks of grassy ground.
　　　But now estrangement's winter's here, a blast
Of faithless wind has swept away the past.

Misfortune's time has come, all we enjoyed
Is ruined now, uprooted, and destroyed,
The time of drought's upon us, the supply
Of water in the channels has run dry,
The fence is gone, the garden's razed and cleared,
The mountain and the stream have disappeared,
The wall's been ruined by our enemies,
Their malice has uprooted all the trees,
And all the birds that sang on every bough
Have fled, and flown away forever now.
Alas for all those flowers and cypresses,
For all my hopes and my anxieties!
Our love was made of clay, not gold; and when
It broke, it lost its value there and then.
Heart is severed from heart, and friend from friend,
Trouble and grief increase and have no end;
Our enemies rejoice to see our sorrow
(And may our wretched fate be theirs tomorrow!),
Our slanderers can rest content, since what
They wished for is exactly what they've got;
Now there's no need for friends or messengers,
Tale-bearers, confidants, or slanderers,
The nurse will not be hurt now, or Mobad,
And neither you nor I need now be sad.

    What sinner is there who compares with me,
Who's suffered such a blackened destiny?
It's bent me double, made me frail and weak,
I moan in anguish and can hardly speak.
Once I was brave and free; now, all I do
Is abjectly apologize to you.
The devil of disaster rules my fate
And has reduced me to this wretched state,
And someone with a devil in his mind
Becomes, as I am, penitent and blind.

Instead of aloes wood and musk my hands
Grasp useless willow twigs and desert sands,
And it is shards and gravel that I hold
Instead of perfect pearls and precious gold.
My love, leave your suspicions for a while,
Try kindness, and a welcoming sweet smile,
And if I once was thoughtless, try to be
More faithful and affectionate to me.
My love, you know the sin was yours at first
But finally it's me your sin has cursed.
You sinned that day, and now, a thousand times,
It's me who's asking pardon for your crimes:
How many times must I ask pardon? When
Shall I have cleansed your soul of rust again?
I always see the sin as mine; must I
Say that I'm sorry for it till I die?
        It's true, you are my goddess and my queen,
And capable of punishing Ramin,
But what of mercy and benevolence,
The pity that is shown to penitence?
If you deny my pleading and refuse me,
If you discount my crying and abuse me,
I'll haunt your doorway here, I'll weep and sigh here,
And mourn my life away until I die here.
How can I go elsewhere when only you
Can pardon everything I've done and do?
O moon-like love, don't do this, don't increase
My soul's despair! Have pity on me, Vis!
I sinned once, I admit it, does that mean
The only sinner in the world's Ramin?
Experienced men can sin, wise scribes can make
From time to time a terrible mistake,
Swift steeds slow down, and sharpest swords grow dull,
So why should you be so unmerciful

And threaten me with such distress and terror
Because I made an unexpected error?
You're beauty's goddess, I'm your slave, don't do
These things that mean I must despair of you,
And all because you're tired of me – I swear
This is the one thing that I cannot bear.
Blindness is better than for me to see
Exile again if you abandon me,
Deafness is better than for me to hear
Your voice insulting me when I appear.
My love, while you reproach me with such scorn
I hate my life, I wish I'd not been born;
You've turned to steel and stone, you're obdurate,
Your heart is filled with anger and with hate,
And love is something that you cannot feel
Since water's not a part of stone and steel.
Your hard heart's stone and steel have sparked a fire
That burns me with insatiable desire;
As people run to help a burning man
You should extend me all the aid you can,
Though even if you plunged me in the sea
This fire would smolder on incessantly.
The world's grown smoky from my soul's despair,
My blackened sighs that darken all the air,
And all the world will weep now for my pain
As night draws on, and with it snow and rain.
Inside, I'm like a temple's fire,[168] although
My outside's like a mountain slope of snow,
Which means that I am treated as love pleases –
Half of my body burns, half of it freezes.
Has God created, and can heaven show,
An angel made like me from fire and snow?
Fire does not melt my snow, and who has seen
Snow coexist with fire, as in Ramin?

This is an ugly deed, to murder me
With snow and ice for my fidelity!
I thought you'd quench my fires, I didn't know
You'd cast me out into the freezing snow.
Vis, I'm your guest; in two weeks I completed
A two months' ride – is this how guests are treated?
No! Guests are welcomed, they're not told to go,
They're not pushed out to perish in the snow!
At least don't murder me with cold, if you
Find killing me an easy thing to do."

VIS REPLIES TO RAMIN

When lovely Vis had heard him out she made
An answer like a poisoned dagger blade:
"Leave here, Ramin," she said. "Think of both me
And Marv as having no reality.
You took your fire, now take your smoke.[169] Don't plead,
As once you pleaded with me; there's no need;
Your pretty words deceived me once, but they
Can't do so now, whatever you might say.
You broke your word, your oath, your bond; what use
Could all the lies be that you might produce?
Go back to Gol, inveigle her, tell her
That she's the lover whom you now prefer.
You might be clever, glib, and eloquent,
But I'm not stupid, I'm not ignorant.
You know so many stories, you repeat
Your little tales to everyone you meet.
I know you well, Ramin, and I have heard
Those stories from you, I know every word,
My heart is sick of hearing them, I'm sick
Of all your disingenuous rhetoric,
I'm tired of all your smooth prevarications,
Of all your chopping, changing fabrications.

I've no desire to leave Mobad, and I
Will now be faithful to him till I die.
Mobad, and no one else, is worthy of me;
With all my faults he still contrives to love me,
He doesn't scorn my friendship, or decide
That one day he might take another bride;
He'll always love me, not like you, who break
The promises that you so glibly make.
He's drunkly happy as he rules our land,
Holding a crystal wineglass in his hand,
Enthroned in splendor in our audience hall
(You can make do with any place at all).
Now I'm afraid he'll see my empty bed
And think the rose he's looking for has fled,
He'll be alarmed, and search for me, and then
His old suspicions will return again.
If he finds out we're talking he'll conclude
This worn-out love of ours has been renewed,
And I don't want him hurt again – if he
Is angered now he might well murder me.

    I've had enough of fear and pain, Ramin,
The hundred hopes I've lost, the grief I've seen;
What have I gained from all this bitterness
This endless suffering, hardship, and distress?
What can I show now but my ruined name,
A broken oath, and hopelessness, and shame?
All that I've done has been offensive to
My God and king, and all because of you,
I gave my youth to you, and for your love
I lost both this world and the heavens above –
I wring my hands, regretting how I've sinned,
Knowing they'll close on nothing now but wind.
How often must I tell you that you'll see
No leaves or fruit develop on this tree?

Go back now; it's a waste of time to beat
On iron when it's cold; admit defeat.
Half of the night has gone, and it's still snowing,
Thick clouds are massing, and cold winds are blowing,
Have pity on yourself, go back now, go,
Before you're injured in this ice and snow;
And may the night pass well for you, and may
Good luck attend you with the dawning day;
May rose-faced Gol for evermore caress you
And bring you fifty worthy sons to bless you."

When Vis had chided him a while, her heart
Was quite content to see Ramin depart;
She said no more to him then but withdrew
And hid her face, and disappeared from view.
Neither the nurse nor Vis could now be seen,
No palliative was there to soothe Ramin.
He stood, as sad and as disconsolate
As enemies might wish, outside her gate,
Where everything was quiet and at peace
Except the turmoil in his heart for Vis.
Bitterly he complained to God above
About his blackened fate and faithless love:
"O God of purity and knowledge who
Is able to do all you wish to do,
You see me here bereft of company,
A wanderer with a wretched destiny –
Wild goats and sheep can trust the mountainside,
Asses and deer have lairs in which to hide,
But my poor heart's perpetually distressed
And I alone can find no place to rest!
But I will not go back, and if I can
Return so hopelessly I'm not a man;
No, if I have to perish I am sure
It's better that I perish at her door,

Then everyone, in all the world, will see
That it was love that took my life from me.
If this cold snow were sword blades hacking me,
This wind wild tigers' claws attacking me,
Not by a single step would I retire
Until I had fulfilled my heart's desire.
My heart, you've faced down lions and elephants,
You've never quailed before a sword or lance,
So why should you fear wind and rain, when they
Are both your images in every way?
Have I not breathed such winds for years in sighs,
And poured such raindrops from my weeping eyes?
And if that shining moon returns, these snows
Will be like petals drifting from a rose;
If my lips meet with hers, if she should place
Her arms about me in a sweet embrace,
These snowy clouds and winds will not alarm me,
And I'll forget I thought this storm could harm me."

And while Ramin described his miseries
His horse was sunk in mud up to its knees.
Ramin's eyes rained down tears all night, all night
As if white camphor fell, his horse turned white.
The horse was soaked, his rider's wretched state
Was even more distressed and desolate –
All night snows soaked his head, while round his breast
The cold winds whipped and would not let him rest;
His clothes, his cloak, his boots and breeches froze
As hard as iron beneath the swirling snows.

Within her room Vis wept throughout the night;
Her nails now made her face a fearsome sight
As she complained, "This snow, this cold, will be
As bitter as God's Judgment Day for me.

O clouds, that soak Ramin in this cold storm,
Have you no shame before his flower-like form?
You've made his cheeks like saffron, and your snow
Has made his nails as blue as indigo;
Your wailing seems to beg me to excuse him,
But it is you whose winds and snows abuse him.
Cease snowing for an hour, O clouds, oh, cease
From piling troubles on the heart of Vis.
O wind, why must you blow so violently?
Can you not lessen your intensity?
You're not that fragrant wind that gently went
About the world diffusing his sweet scent;
Why can't you pity one whose scent bestows
His fragrance on the lily and the rose?
O ocean depths, O surging, cresting waves,
Before Ramin you're little more than slaves –
However many jewels your darkness hides
His hand outdoes the bounty of your tides,
And you are jealous, which is why you've sent
These rainy clouds to fill the firmament.[170]
Your weapons are mere rain and pouring water,
But his are steel, inured to war and slaughter,
And if he gets away tonight he'll raise
An army's dust to choke your rainy ways!
How shameless I've become, that I allow
Myself to sit in warmth and comfort now,
While he, brought up with silk, brocade, and gold,
Waits shivering in the snow and freezing cold;
His face is like a lovely rose, and snows
Are fatal for the petals of a rose."

VIS RETURNS TO THE WINDOW
AND ADDRESSES RAMIN'S HORSE

Vis sat within her room a while, and then
She went back to the window once again,

Through which she saw the sun's first blade of light
That promised daybreak and the end of night.[171]
Again it was his horse that she addressed,
"Great steed, you're like my child, and I'm distressed
To see you suffer under these harsh skies,
I'd rather have you tread upon my eyes.
Why did you come with such an evil rider,
With such a hypocritical backslider?
Have you not heard the proverb wise men say,
'Choose your companion first, and then the way'?
If you were not with this vile rogue, I'd prize
Your being here, and you, above my eyes,
But as it is you'll get no audience
From me, no welcoming benevolence;
Go now, find rest and welcome where you're shown it,
And get your lost heart back from those who own it.
And as for you, Ramin, leave Marv and find
Some doctor who can treat your suffering mind.

     How often I craved audience from you;
I was your suppliant, constrained to sue
For mercy from you, and I was rejected;
All my sad supplications were neglected.
How often you slept soundly while I lay
Awake and restless till the break of day;
You slept in silk and fur, while I lay down
In all the filth and refuse of the town.
What once you handed me you now receive,
And as you made me grieve, so you must grieve;
My little lily flower, you might well be
Quite fragile, but you can't compete with me!
Drive hope now from your heart, and may you find
In your despair, as I have, peace of mind;
Hope brings us endless grief, but in despair
You'll find there is a kind of calmness there.

Once I was one who, filled with hope, would take
Her skiff upon the ocean, for love's sake,
But now I've left sea-going risks behind
And washed such expectations from my mind;
Now, in contentment, I choose chastity,
Contentment is the finest sovereignty.

      Now that your old love's yielded to the new,
Cherish the new, there's nothing here for you;
We like old rubies well enough, and gold,
But we prefer new lovers to the old.
You cut the head off from our love, and when
A head's cut off it will not grow again –
Even the grass upon my grave will keep
The memory of how you've made me weep;
Oh, I was wise, but I had not been told
That heartfelt love can wither and grow cold.
Don't seek for love from me again, in truth
Once we are old we can't regain our youth.
I am still Vis, that very Vis whose name
Your letter has besmirched with ugly shame
Although you are the only man I've kept
My faith with always, and with whom I've slept;
You were my only love, and of all men
Fate made you the most wretched specimen.
You're like a foolish mother who's been given
One child, a blind girl, by the ways of heaven,
And who can't see this fault, and tries to find
A perfect husband for a girl who's blind.
My heart's bent like a bow with grief, and you
Can hear my words are arrows, straight and true;
Your heart's my target now; take it away,
You'll be shot full of poison if you stay."

RAMIN REPLIES TO VIS

Ramin's heart writhed in pain, but he was seeking
A way to answer her while she was speaking.
"Sweet moon," he said, "is it your wish that I
Should be so crushed by sadness that I'll die?
I don't know any cutpurse who compares
With Love for catching people unawares:
He'll rob our hearts of patience; as he speaks
He'll steal the rosy color from our cheeks;
For him, to snatch a wise man's heart's no worse
Than for a thief to snatch a drunkard's purse.

My body's getting old, but love has stayed
Still young in me, and new songs can be played
On old lutes. Why should I be fearful of
Old age when it's my soul that holds your love?
Don't blame me for my love, no sick man chooses
His sickness and his pain, his wounds and bruises;
Don't laugh because you're strong, it wasn't me
Who asked Fate for this weakness that you see;
You saw me abject, waiting, in attendance,
And raised the banner of your independence.

Why did I tell you all my secrets, Vis,
And so ensure my sorrows would increase?
I rashly say my passions as I feel them,
You rashly spy on hearts and souls and steal them;
May no one say what's hidden in his heart,
He'll find that this is when his sorrows start!
Mercy belongs to greatness, and since you
Are Beauty's queen, you should show mercy too;
Now you've achieved such greatness, Vis, it's your
Responsibility to help the poor,
And if I've sinned for love, be lenient,
I don't deserve such scornful punishment.

While longing rules the universe, within
The heart of man there will be room for sin.
Adam once sinned, in Paradise, and I'm
The image of his essence at that time;
Sin's written on our foreheads, we are creatures
For whom sin's intermingled with our natures.
Learning lacks power and insight to remake us,
Courage won't save us when disasters take us,
Though no one, wise or foolish, wants to be
The victim of some cruel calamity.
The sins that I committed yesterday,
With yesterday itself, have fled away,
Tomorrow you will see my love at last,
And men plan for the future, not the past.
I broke the oath we swore, all I can do
Is abjectly apologize to you;
What city flourishes, or is at peace,
Whose people practice no forgiveness, Vis?
When wrongdoers and slaves apologize
Mercy in rulers is both right and wise –
Forgive my sin, and I will not commit
This sin again, or even think of it.
I've seen great beauty in you, but no sign
That you can be forgiving or benign;
I sinned as an experiment, to see
How merciful and gracious you might be.
Forgive me! Realize rewards are given
For good acts, both in this world and in heaven.
Isn't my shame sufficient punishment,
My grief an adequate admonishment?
I'm standing in the snow and rain here, but
Your eyes of chivalry are tightly shut,
Your heart is merciless, your eyes are dry,
Your tongue's a sword blade when you tell me, 'I

Have never seen you, I don't recollect you,
And, if I've seen you once, I now reject you,'
Ask what you will, but do not seek to be
Forever separated, Vis, from me;
I cannot drink this poison, Vis, or bear
This heart-destroying burden of despair.
And if my heart were made of stone I know
It would not have the strength to see you go,
No sorrows or catastrophes can hurt it
Only the awful dread you might desert it,
It doesn't pray for me, it doesn't pray
For anything except that Vis should stay."

VIS REPLIES TO RAMIN

And jasmine-breasted Vis said, "To your shame
All you possess of wisdom is the name;
Foolish Ramin, once spite has harmed a heart
The scar will not so easily depart;
Your spite has stayed with me, and it has driven
Out of my heart the love for which you've striven.
A man can't both deny God and believe,
A heart can't both profess love and deceive,
And when I think of your barbarity
No scent of love for you remains in me.
    You know what I once went through, you're aware
Of all my hope and subsequent despair;
You know you killed me when you went away.
You fed upon the carcass of your prey
And left, and found another love, and served her,
And you did well, Ramin, since you deserved her;
What else might you achieve, now that you've fed
Like some voracious vulture on the dead?
You gave your noble horse away and won
An ugly donkey in exchange. Well done!

Instead of palaces, it seems your tastes
Favor infertile plains and salty wastes.
I thought I had a noble lion here,
One that tracked only graceful, upland deer,
Not an old furtive fox, whose favorite habit
Is playing endless tricks to catch a rabbit.
Why, when you'd made your body pure and clean,
Did you defile it with such filth, Ramin?
You'd milk and wine, so what made you prefer
To dine on garlic and sour vinegar?
Or leave the lovely carpet where you sat
To sit yourself upon a threadbare mat?
And wasn't it enough that you should leave
My city and myself to mourn and grieve,
Without compounding your iniquities
By going to live with my sworn enemies?
That you should give another your affection
Without subjecting me to such rejection?
That you should write in such a way I bled
With every wicked word your letter said?
And then you piled another injury
On all the ruthless wrongs you'd done to me
By driving off my nurse and calling her
A dog, a termagant, a sorcerer;
It's you who are the cheat, not my poor nurse!
Whatever she's done, you have done far worse.
You called her ignorant, a willing tool,
A witch, a liar, and a scheming fool,
But it was you that tricked us with your crimes
And branded her and me a thousand times.
You are the wizard, *you're* Zahhak,[172] a weaver
Of spells and specious lies, a glib deceiver.
You were disloyal, not us; *you* broke the oath
That we had sworn was binding on us both.

Gurab amused you for a while, and yet
You've come back here, and with your eyes all wet,
Saying sweet things that have an iron sense
For all their golden outward blandishments.
I am the lovely garden you reviled,
I am the limpid stream that you defiled;
And now that thirst torments you, you've decided
To drink the waters that you once derided?
Men should not drink again from streams that they
Muddied with filth before they went away."

Ramin replies to Vis

Ramin replied, "Ah, Vis, sweet spring to me
Of China and of distant Barbary,
The world is like a millstone, God created
Its revolutions, they are fixed and fated;
One state is never permanent, and when
The summer's over winter comes again.
We are both children of this world, so how
Could one condition hold us then and now?
And, like the world, our bodies change; we're small
While we're still young, then gradually grow tall.
Or we grow sick and weak; before too long
We find that once again we're well and strong.
We're rich, then poor; we find we're fortunate,
And then we find we're in a wretched state.
Man's body has no strength, it's just a bit
Of flesh and bone, that's all there is to it:
It can't bear heat or cold, and, cold or hot,
It wants to be whatever it is not.
It longs to gorge itself, and when it's full
It whines it's bloated and uncomfortable;
Desire commands it, keeps it subjugated,
But then desire is all too quickly sated,

And pleasure soon turns out to be a master
Who seeks out weaknesses and brings disaster.
When once the heart attains what it's desired
It falters and immediately grows tired,
But when our hearts are thwarted they will rage
With vehemence no patience can assuage;
Restraint is absent when the heart's defied,
Passion is absent when it's satisfied.

  There is no happiness that ranks above
The glowing happiness that's found in love,
That makes hearts selfish, and estranges them
From sleep and rest, and so deranges them.
How much the heart endures! We cannot bear
Our lover's coquetry when she is there,
And when she's gone away the lonely pain
Of absence makes us want her back again
(We want her back, we long for her to stay,
And when she's here we long to get away);
Man is so helpless that he can't abide
In one condition and stay satisfied.
My love, I am a man, how could my soul
Escape the presence of desire's control?
Desire tugs at my reins, and now I've found you
I know I'll hover, Vis, forever round you.

  I sought you, following desire's direction,
Believing what was ugly was perfection,
But, with your stratagems and anger, you
Opened a door that was entirely new.
I left, so that I wouldn't have to see
The tricks and rage with which you treated me,
And took the partridge of my love away
Where she'd no longer be your falcon's prey.
How could the heart that had enjoyed your kindness
Endure your scorn, and rage, and willful blindness?

There, in the town I'd ruled once, I became
Contemptible, I lived in grief and shame;
I thought that if I left you life would be
An effortless and pleasant thing for me.
I'd find another love, and I'd forget you,
I'd cleanse my heart of you, and not regret you,
Since only love burns love, just as it takes
Iron to hammer iron till it breaks –
A new love saps an old love's fascination
As new coins drive the old from circulation.
And all my friends said, 'Only love can cure
The agonies of love that you endure;
If you're to make an anvil, to succeed
Another stronger anvil's what you need,'
　　I traveled to Gurab then, in despair,
Like one who seeks for water everywhere,
Searching for sympathy in every place,
Hoping for some reminder of your face.
And on the way I saw a rose, a sight
As radiant as the shining moon at night;
Lovelier than any idol that I'd seen,
Sweeter than any rosebud to Ramin.
I pledged my heart to her sweet face, and said,
'I have escaped my love for Vis; it's dead,'
I reasoned with my heart in every way,
Advising moderation and delay,
But what good were my words, when consternation
Welled in my heart, and grief, and lamentation?
The fire of love still burned in me, I felt
My body in its burning blaze and melt,
And still my longing for my absent friend
Flared in my restless heart and had no end.
　　If outwardly I seemed to be at peace
I still longed inwardly to be with Vis;

I could not eat or sleep, what could I do
In all this anguish but return to you?
    You are both good and evil now to me,
You are my sickness and its remedy,
You're all that's bitter to me, all that's sweet,
You're pleasure and disaster, cold and heat,
You're pain and kindness, sorrow, happiness,
Wealth's treasury and poverty's distress,
You are my world, my soul, my heart, my eyes,
My shining sun and moon, my turning skies,
My friend, my enemy – and in my sight
All that you've done to me is just and right.
Act as you will, my love, with poor Ramin,
You are my only goddess and my queen;
My heart is burning as I weep and wait
To hear your judgment on me, and my fate."

VIS REPLIES TO RAMIN

    And jasmine-breasted Vis, whose countenance
Made the roof glow with gentle radiance,
Wept as he spoke – but she did not relent.
When granite's carved by some hard instrument
The marks can't quickly be obliterated,[173]
And, though she pitied his distress, she hated
The things that he had done, and anger doused
The fire of pity that his pleading roused.
She said, "Ah, with what lying impudence
You strike the ball of specious eloquence,[174]
But begging won't entrap the wind, and mire
Cannot conceal the sun's resplendent fire.
And if you sought Gurab in your despair
Like one who seeks for water everywhere,
And took the partridge of your love away
Where she'd no longer be my falcon's prey,

Discarding me, in order not to see
My endless tricks and rage and sorcery,
Searching for sympathy in every place,
Hoping for some reminder of my face,
Finding a lover simply to forget me,
To dull your agony and not regret me –
Well, I'll accept all this, and I'll accept
That you could hardly eat and scarcely slept,
But why then did you act so odiously
By writing such disgusting things to me,
And drive away my nurse, and shout at her,
As though she were some irritating cur?
      If you have ears to hear and sense to guide you
I'll give you some advice to keep beside you:
When you declare your heart, see you leave space,
If need be, for a peaceful meeting place,
As wise men waging war will never cease
To leave a space within their plans for peace.
An angry demon has contrived to win you
And planted seeds of hatred deep within you,
Uprooting all the little seedlings of
Our reconciling and our mutual love.
Have you not heard that two cruel demons hide
Within our flesh, and prompt us from inside?
The first one says, 'Do it, don't hesitate,
You'll profit hugely by it, so don't wait!'
And when it's done we hear the second's voice
Asking us why we made this foolish choice;
The first one made you foolish and forgetful,
The second makes you sorry and regretful.
Why did you start out so belligerent
If now you say you're ready to repent?
It's easier not to sin at all than to
Have to repent for everything you do!

Not eating harmful food is preferable
To getting well with medicines once you're full.
If you'd been wiser then, when we were young,
You would have guarded your malicious tongue,
If I'd been wiser, I would not have seen
A lover in a scoundrel like Ramin,
And as you're sorry now, I'm sorry too,
And ask myself why I once favored you.
You're water now, and I am fire; you bow
Submissively, and I am angry now;
As fire and water can't unite, so we
Will never sing a single melody."

Ramin replies to Vis

And brave Ramin replied, "Your angry spite
Has made my daylight hours as dark as night.
I see two nights here now, one from this weather,
One from your spite, as they collude together.
How we have suffered, my poor horse and I,
Beneath this gloomy and tempestuous sky!
And why should Rakhsh[175] be punished, when he's not
A sinner or a part of any plot?
Deny me food and shelter, but allow
My Rakhsh a little straw and barley now;
You'll save his life, and hospitality
To him will reassure and comfort me.
And if I'm not your lover any more
Say I'm your guest; don't drive me from your door!
Everyone welcomes guests; no guests are told
They have to stay out in the snow and cold.
I've no excuses left, no abject pleas,
And no remorseful last apologies,
But everyone will say that you have been
Unchivalrous and cruel to Prince Ramin,

If you dismiss my suit and tell me to
Abandon any lingering hopes of you;
Men will say this was meanness, they won't say
That noble anger made you talk this way.
There's no blood feud alive between us, no
History of battles started long ago –
This is mere bickering, not a righteous war,
So what is all this hatred of me for?
You know that life's a serious thing, so why
Are you so keen to see me bleed and die?
    I'm not a man to run away from snow,
While I'm alive the cold won't make me go,
And while you're here I'll never leave this place
Not even if I die before your face;
And if I perish in this snow, my name
Will live on with an everlasting fame,
To die before you here will mean I'll be
Forever known for my fidelity.
Without you I've no life, since you alone
Are all the pleasures that I've ever known,
I tried the world without you when I fled
And though alive I felt that I was dead;
Why should I seek the world? If you're not there
My soul knows only sickness and despair.
    Come winds of winter, bring your snows, and sever
My soul's connection with my flesh forever,
Death in these snows is sweeter than existence
Made wretched by her anger's cruel persistence.
No matter how resilient and strong
A man is, in this snow he won't last long."

VIS REPLIES TO RAMIN

And jasmine-breasted Vis said, "Now, at last,
The sinner's trapped, and by his faithless past.

Wine that is drunk will not return, and when
A bird has flown it won't come back again;
You've no home here in Marv, and those you knew
Have no desire now to be friends with you,
Marv's not the place for you, and you'll receive
No kindnesses from me now; you should leave.
Don't waste your breath protesting, you won't find
That anything you say will change my mind,
Since eglantine and roses can't be found
In saline marshes or on salty ground.
You ended your first love, and now you're beckoned
To sit down elsewhere and enjoy the second –
Sweet Gol awaits you, why then should you be
Stricken with all this grief and misery?

     May King Mobad's great hall indeed be blessed
By some new visitor or princely guest,
A guest who's gracious, with a noble name,
And not, as you are now, a source of shame;
No, may his castle never welcome one
With no respect for all Mobad has done.
I cannot let you in, how could I give
You welcome where Mobad and I now live?
Or entertain a man unfit to wait
As a petitioner outside my gate?
I drive you from these walls, and you protest,
'In Marv, and in this castle, I'm a guest,'
Like some poor clod a village drives out who
Says, 'That's my home, and I'm their headman too,'

     You came here in the cold; didn't you know
That winter is the time for rain and snow?
Why did you take this journey then so lightly,
And treat the trials that lovers find so tritely?
Marv's not your home, and Vis is not your friend,
So couldn't you foresee your journey's end?

Your heart deceived you like an enemy,
But why does this mean you should shout at me?
But as Jamshid's vizier said, 'Don't waste breath
Applauding fools, or mourning for their death.'[176]
    Oh, how you cherished me, both day and night,
When you were still an unimportant knight,
Then you became a prince, and suddenly
It seemed you had no time at all for me;
You fixed a sign upon your door that said,
'No entry.' First you tricked me, then you fled.
Now I'm to save your soul? You should remember
You cannot have the spring when it's December.
I'm sweet to you, and so you leave me; when
It's cold and snowy, here you are again!
Forget me; you're a hero, as I know,
So set me free now, and for God's sake, Go!"

RAMIN REPLIES TO VIS

Heartsick, Ramin replied, "Bright moon, don't hurt me,
Oh, isn't it enough that you desert me?
That you have pierced my heart, and made my name
A laughing stock, and told me of my shame?
Forbear, bright moon, to shoot this ruthless dart,
You have already killed my soul and heart.
What could be worse for me, ah Vis, believe me,
Than hearing you're reluctant to receive me?
Why do you tell me I should go, and say
Mobad's home is no place for me to stay?
It's right to say that you're my enemy
When you deny me what is due to me,
And it's *not* right for you to drive me from
A place where friends and foes alike can come.
Did you not say illustrious men ensure
A place for peace when in the midst of war?

So where's your place for peaceful dealings then?
Or weren't you made from clay like other men?
    But if you won't be reconciled, if you
Are faithless now, whatever I might do,
I've no choice but to go from here, to grieve
In lonely desperation as I leave.
Give me a lock then of your lovely hair
To soothe and comfort me in my despair,
Perhaps its heady fragrance will revive
My fainting heart and keep my soul alive,
So that its scent will recompense the pain
I've suffered waiting in this snow and rain.
And when I'm free of you, eventually
You might be moved then to remember me.
I've heard the night is pregnant; who can say
What will be born here on the coming day?"

Vis replies to Ramin

And moon-like Vis said, "Sugar can't be made
From bitter cucumbers; and silk brocade
Can't come from stones, and no one can refine
Juice from a hemp plant till it turns to wine;
As iron won't turn to wax, you'll never see
A friend that's fashioned from an enemy.
Your windy words will not affect or shake me,
And all your strength won't topple me or break me.
I gain no happiness from being near you,
I lose no melancholy when I hear you;
You left an ache within my heart, no spell
Can ever cancel it or make me well;
Your rust corrodes my soul, no words can clean
This filth and leave me pure again, Ramin.
Your cruel words fill my ears still, and they've made
Against this talk of yours a barricade,

And you can boast and brag and beg and prate
And not a word of it will penetrate.
I laughed when I was with you, and I cried
When later you were severed from my side,
And now I neither laugh nor cry; my soul
Is free from love's tyrannical control.
The burning lamp of love and hope that shone
More brightly than the sun is spent and gone,
As has my heart, that was my enemy,
And everything is different now in me.
The eyes that saw your face, the ears that heard,
And so impatiently, your every word
(These thinking that they saw the sun, and those
They heard the news an angel might disclose)
Now see that sun as filthy pitch and hear
Your chatter as an arrow in my ear;
I did not know a lover's blind, that all
Her fortune's bitter and contemptible.
    'Good Fortune, tell me where you've been,' I say,
'Come, tell me where you hid until today.'
My body's healthy now, and I can start
To understand things with my waking heart;
I see the world for what it is, I feel
My spirit's new-won happiness is real,
And I have no desire to sacrifice
For fools my earthly life and paradise."

RAMIN REPLIES TO VIS

Ramin said, "Jasmine-breasted Vis, you gave
My soul to me, now take it from your slave.
What does it matter if you're sick of me,
Or if you've sowed the seeds of enmity,
Or if you're angry while I offer peace,
Or if you curse me while I love you, Vis?

I'll never take my eyes off you, I know
No one's like you, wherever I might go,
And if you pluck one of my eyes out I
Shall hand the other to you in reply.
What names you've called me! Though I grant that you
Have only said about me what is true:
Your condemnation of me is complete,
But curses said by you are sugar sweet,
They're blessings to my ears, and all you say
Resounds for me like songs musicians play.
And when you're silent how I long for when
You'll curse me, and revile me, once again,
Since all your speeches hurt me, and undo me,
And at the same time cure me, and renew me,
And in your anger as I hear your scorn
I hear the hope that love might be reborn;
And so I tell myself that it might be
That you'll relent, and once more favor me.

 I'm like a man who sees a lion ahead,
An elephant behind him; filled with dread,
He sees, both ways, disaster watching him –
Whichever way he turns, the prospect's grim!
If I stay here, my enemy is you,
Filled with contempt for everything I do,
And if I choose to leave I hardly know
If I'll survive this icy rain and snow,
And here I dither, and delay, and freeze,
Wavering between these two catastrophes.
But if death waits for me, at least I'll find
In such a fate some final peace of mind,
And though it takes my soul, death will release
My body from its pains and troubles, Vis.

 My body's drowned in tears, and like your hair
The world has shackled me to my despair;

Your fragrant curls enchain my heart, so how,
Without my heart, can I desert you now?"

VIS REPLIES TO RAMIN

And jasmine-breasted Vis, whose lovely face
Was like the full moon in its lambent grace,
Vis with her musky, perfumed curls replied,
"Leave me, Ramin, leave and be satisfied,
And pour the patient waters of content
On passion's flames now, and be penitent.
The less you say, the less of you I see,
For both of us, the better it will be.
      It's pointless torment to attempt once more
What's been attempted many times before –
I'm not so foolish as to try again
Something that's only brought me grief and pain;
You've branded my poor heart enough, you made me
Weep far too many tears when you betrayed me.
And if a Zoroastrian priest should tend
His sacred fire a hundred years, the end
Of all of his devotion is to learn
That fire will never change but always burn.
To cherish fools, to cherish wolfish creatures,
Has no effect on their essential natures;
I cherished you, Ramin, and found you were
A snake, a scorpion, an adventurer.
      Oh, you were gentle to begin with,[177] then
You showed yourself to be the worst of men,
And half my little life's been spent between
My pain and shame, because of you, Ramin.
And I can't bear the second half to be
A repetition of this misery;
I want my happiness, and I won't cast
My life upon the wind as in the past.

I sowed your love once, and for what? Why should
I plant what's never done me any good?
Why should I be my own worst enemy
And love a man who has no love for me?
Is ten years not sufficient? Ten sad years
Of unavailing misery and tears?
What can I show for all my faithfulness
But heartfelt anguish, horror, and distress?
   All men repent of sin, but I repent
That I was faithful and obedient,
Which made my drink a poisoned draught for me
And turned my friend into an enemy.
How can a heart survive in such a state,
Wounded by such extremes of love and hate?
If it were made of iron and stone I know
It would have split and crumbled long ago.
Even if I should long for love, no force
Could make my heart submit to such a course;
Once it's escaped from you, what heart would dare
To venture once again into your snare?"

RAMIN REPLIES TO VIS

Ramin replied, "Don't try so forcibly
To shake love's yoke off, and to wriggle free,
This talk will get you nowhere. I'm afraid
No soil's been turned by your contentment's spade,
And what your tongue says doesn't suit your heart –
The two could hardly be more far apart;
You talk of patience, but your heart denies it,
She hasn't heard of it, she never tries it.
You're like a drum that makes a hideous roar;
Within, it's merely wind, and nothing more.
You say you're sick of me, your words are brave,
But that's not how your heart and soul behave –

Your heart and tongue dispute and disagree,
And while one's bitter one is sweet to me.
If your heart feels no love for me, I swear
The skies are empty, Vis, and God's not there!
But luck's against me on this evil night
And treats me with malign, malicious spite.
It's left me in this freezing snow where I
Need only wait a little while to die,
And I won't stay to freeze outside your door,
No, Vis, I won't remain here any more.
You're foolish, and as even you must know
'A foolish friend is worse than any foe.'
Even a child should be abandoned who
Shows she's a fool whatever one might do.
         I'm in this snow and ice where nothing stirs,
And you're inside wrapped up in silks and furs,
You see the state I'm in and yet you chatter
About preposterous things that hardly matter,
Is this a time for idle conversation,
For silly coyness and inane flirtation?
My throat will tighten with death's dreadful rattle
Before you're done with all this stupid prattle.
I should die nobly, on a corpse-strewn field,
Ringed by dead warriors who'd refused to yield,
Why should I perish basely in the snow?
Why should I not have done with this, and go?
You don't want me, and I can't force you to,
But there are many other girls who do –
So may Mobad caress you and embrace you,
I've found another lover to replace you.
         When once I've gone you'll see who's hurt, you'll see
Who's suffered the more painful injury.
Farewell, I'm going, make the best of it,
Play the same tune until your lute has split!

I wish you patience, Vis, and peace of mind,
Just as we wish for sight to help the blind.
Mobad is yours and you're Mobad's, may you
Both find success in everything you do!"

And jasmine-breasted Vis said, "May you see
The thousand blessings that you wish for me,
May luck be yours, and may each day and night
Be filled with sweetness and your heart's delight.
But I am still the lover whom you knew,
Whose like has never yet been seen by you;
My brightness has not dimmed; my musky hair
Has not turned camphor white yet with despair,
My clustering curls are still as black and tight,
My shining pearl-like teeth as strong and white,
My silver breasts as firm and opulent,
My cypress stature has not yet been bent.
My face was once the moon, it's now the sun
Admired throughout the world, by everyone;
Rezvan[178] adores my lips, houris abase
Themselves before the splendor of my face,
I am the sun of beauties, and the queen
Of every potent sorceress, Ramin.
My face can look on roses with the scorn
With which a rose will look upon a thorn,
And as thieves pilfer purses from the sleeping
I pilfer hearts from clever men's safekeeping,
As lions and cheetahs leap upon their prey
My magic glances steal men's souls away.
My face is love's source, and idolatry
Comes from my curls' seductive sorcery;
I never saw a man who didn't prize me,
So why should you reject me and despise me?

Oh, you might slight me now, but I'm worth more –
Despite your scorn – than your new paramour.
Now you want both of us, but that's just silly,
A rose won't grow together with a lily;[179]
You should recall that proverb from the past,
'A town with two commanders cannot last';
Two swords won't fit in one sheath, day and night
Can never be a simultaneous sight.
You say I'm stupid when in fact what's true
Is that stupidity has captured you,
If you weren't such a fool you wouldn't be
Standing forlornly here in front of me.
And if I'm stupid, I'm not yours; my soul
Is God's, not yours, to conquer and control.
Thank God, Ramin, thank God now and be glad
You didn't wed a fool, like King Mobad!"

VIS TURNS AWAY IN HER ANGER AND LEAVES RAMIN

Vis spoke, and turned, impatient to depart,
And felt no love within her stony heart.
She left the window, hid her face and hair,
And called to all the watchmen posted there,
"Don't sleep tonight, each guard and sentinel
Among you must perform your duties well;
Tonight's a dreadful night that makes me fear
The world itself will drown and disappear,
The swirling sleet, the wind's ferocity
Thunder like hosts of charging cavalry.
My heart groans like a ship upon the ocean
Tossed by the waves' tempestuous commotion,
As if the winds and waves would split apart
The creaking timbers of my voyaging heart."

And when Ramin heard Vis expressly tell
The watchmen to protect her castle well,

He lost all hope he'd see her, and once more
He felt the freezing wind and heard its roar,
And dared not linger there, since every limb
Was numb now, and the cold tormented him.
He tugged at Rakhsh's reins, despairing of
His soul's survival and his former love;
His heart crushed by a craggy weight of woe
He moved off like a crag obscured by snow,
And cried, "My heart, what can you think or say now?
She's scorned your love and sent you on your way now;
But love involves its votaries in scorn
So often, it's for this that they are born.
If you survive today, never submit
To love again, or even think of it;
You're a free man, and free men shouldn't be
So ready to submit to tyranny.
Don't seek new lovers out now: no, remain
Aware of all your old love's burning pain,
Grieve for the life you lost to it, lament
The love you cherished and the time you spent,
And say, 'Alas for time and grief, alas
That I still suffer for what came to pass,
Alas for all my pains and struggles, all
Those vain attempts to intercept the ball,[180]
Alas for all that hope for which I sinned
That passed as pointlessly as does the wind.'
I told my eager heart, 'Turn round, go back,
A snare lies hidden on this dangerous track,'
I told my wagging tongue, 'Ah, don't impart
To her the fatal secrets of my heart,
She'll laugh at you and feel contempt for you.'
The day came when I saw that this was true,
Since when you told her what was hidden she
Was happy to torment and pester me.

She felt no love for me, and silence would
Have done less harm to me, and far more good.
How true that saying is, 'Even in birds
Silence is best; be sparing with your words.'"

How strange, how devious Fate is for us,
Leaving us powerless, pusillanimous,
Playing with us as players move the pieces
Upon a chessboard, till the contest ceases;
Treating us well at times, treating us badly,
Placing us happily, placing us sadly,
As though life had to be like this, and all
Alternatives were quite impossible.
(But if flesh didn't want so much, if we
Could stop our boasting, our immodesty,
The world could not oppress us with its weight.
If we could but escape our needy state,
If our ambition were to lose ambition,
If independence were our true condition,
We would not let the fleeting world abuse us
But treat it as a pastime to amuse us.)
        And so it was for Vis and for Ramin:
After such love, such hatred came between
The two of them that devious Eblis [181]
Could not have hoped to bring this couple peace.
But Vis regretted what she'd done, her heart
Reproached her that she'd let Ramin depart,
And in her eyes stood brimming tears that showed
Like pearls as they spilled out and overflowed,
Till, like spring clouds, she wept so fervently
She seemed to be a ship upon the sea.
Her cheeks were grey and tear-stained, as she beat
A stone against her heart in her defeat –

Ah, no, say rather with each heartfelt moan
She wildly beat a stone against a stone,
And all her cries rang like the plangent strings
A harpist fingers when he plays and sings.
She cried, "Why does misfortune stay with me
As though I were a bough from sorrow's tree?
Why have I made myself despair of life
And cut my own throat with this fatal knife?
I've done this evil to myself, as though
I had become my own remorseless foe;
Who'll douse this fire I've lit? What remedy
Could heal this self-inflicted injury?"

   Then to her nurse she cried, "Get up now, run,
Look what my foolish, wounded soul has done!
Has any other mother ever borne
A girl to be so hopeless and forlorn?
Good Fortune came back, and I slammed the door
On him and all that I'd been longing for;
I held the wine glass, and instead of drinking
I dropped it like a drunkard, without thinking.
Such black clouds gather round me now, and rain
Upon my head such horrors and such pain,
Three times this tempest's weight of sleet and snow
Has dropped on me tonight as grief and woe.
How fortunate I once was! Now I'm poor,
I've quenched the torch I held aloft before.
Go, nurse, go like the wind now and discover
The whereabouts of my dear, longed-for lover:
Clutch at his reins, make him dismount, and say,
'Yes, you were angry when you went away,
But nothing good's accomplished without fear,
And, where love's present, arguments appear;
Just as the soul knows yearning and frustration
So love involves reproaches and flirtation.

You acted cruelly, but I didn't act;
My cruelty was symbolic, not a fact;
Mine was mere words, and no one's ever seen
Love without words and arguments, Ramin.
Who'd want a love with whom one couldn't flirt?
And if my words hurt, your cruel actions hurt.
If all the things you did to me were blameless
How can you say the things I said were shameless?
If what you did was right, how can you dare
To claim that what I told you was unfair?'
Keep him there, nurse, until I come to tell him
How sorry I am now for what befell him."

VIS SENDS HER NURSE AFTER RAMIN AND THEN FOLLOWS HER

Quickly the nurse left, like a bird in flight,
Unharmed by all the perils of the night –
A heart that love makes vehement and bold
Fears neither wind nor rain nor heat nor cold;
The snow seemed petals, till she came to where
Ramin had ridden to, and kept him there.
      Now jasmine-breasted, cypress Vis made haste
(A snow-white body in the snowy waste)
To follow her; the sun's magnificence
Shone from her face, she smelled of springtime's scents,
She made the dark night day, and in the snows
Her face showed like a newly opened rose.
The silver of her body shamed the snow,
Smelling her curls, the winds forbore to blow;
Her eyes wept jewels upon the ground, her hair
Filled with its fragrance the surrounding air –
"A lovely houri's dared to disobey
Rezvan[182] and come down to the earth," you'd say,
"To rescue poor Ramin from his sad plight
And bring him safely to his heart's delight."

But when she reached him, still she could not hide
Her teasing arrogance and angered pride:
"Light of the brave," she said, "as clay formed you
The same clay formed all other people too.
We all have hearts that hurt, we all discover
The pains inflicted on us by a lover;
We all want what we want, we all feel greed –
The more we have the more we think we need.
I've hurt you now you say, but now you'll see
The many ways in which you once hurt me,
And if I've made your heart grieve think of how
You made me grieve; that's what you're suffering now.
Think of what pleases you; well, that applies
To everyone – you'll see this, if you're wise.
The world's our friend and then our enemy,
She favors you and then she favors me,
And if your enemy is yours today
You might be hers tomorrow, who can say?
      Why should a man whose acts are so unseemly
React to simple statements so extremely?
Think how you blackened all my reputation;
What would you do in such a situation?
Apart from ugly words and deeds, Ramin,
What have I heard from you, what have I seen?
You piled abuse upon abuse, and then
With every act abused me yet again.
Not only did you break the oath you'd made me,
You chose another love and so betrayed me,
And if this new love had to be, what spite
Provoked the letter that you chose to write?
Why were you so against my nurse and me?
Why did you mortify us publicly?
What did it profit you to spurn and shame us?
How did it help you to despise and blame us?

You felt no shame before your kindly love
Nor even shame before your God above.
Did you not swear a hundred times and more
You'd never break the oath of love you swore?
If you can swear an oath and, when you've sworn it,
Feel you're at liberty to break and scorn it,
Why can I not say once, and say again,
That you're the most despicable of men?
Why did you do such things that I'm ashamed
To say them to you now or hear them named?
Have you not heard that gossip molds and makes us,
And gives us honor in the world, or breaks us,
That all our faults are evil in so far
As those who watch and judge us say they are?
If you cannot abide men's blame, you should
Choose to do only what is right and good,
And in each act be mindful of the sorrow
That punishment for evil brings tomorrow.
Fighting brings retribution: 'Break a cup,
A jug will come along and beat you up.'
The violence that you sowed is reaped by you,
And those who talk too much must listen too –
You sowed and now you reap; you lectured me,
Now hear my answer; listen patiently.

     My lion lord, don't be so sensitive!
Don't ride away now like a fugitive,
This sulking is beneath you, so don't do it;
Your sin's not mine, and I don't have to rue it,
But it's quite right for you to feel the pain
You've made me feel, Ramin, so don't complain!
The fault is yours, and now you're angered by it,
Who gave you this idea? Who whispered, 'Try it'?
You be my judge, tell me my sin; I'm sure
I don't know what I should be sorry for.

Or you could list my body's faults, or share
With me what's wrong now with my face and hair.
But no, I'm cypress tall, my moon-like face
Still keeps its pomegranate blossom's grace,
My hair still holds its hyacinthine curls,
My mouth is sweet still, and my teeth are pearls,
And on my cheeks lilies and eglantine
Still mingle, blossom, blush, and gently shine,
My face still shares the sun's magnificence,
My mouth still breathes the springtime's sweetest scents.
So what fault can you find in me? Unless
You take exception to my faithfulness?
When friendship's needed I'm a trusted friend,
When help's required, my help will never end;
Thanks to my parents' noble ancestry
Beauty's my birthright, as is Liberty –
Am I not Shahru's daughter, and the queen
Of all the beauties that the world has seen?
The name of Beauty's mine, and Beauty's snare
Lies hidden in the ringlets of my hair,
And every hair within these curls and coils
Has trapped a thousand hearts within its toils.
The roses of my face are always fair,
The sweet scent of my curls is always there,
And when the blossoms of the spring perceive
My lovely cheeks they droop with shame and grieve;
No pomegranate blossom is as fresh,
As sweetly smelling, as my cheeks' firm flesh;
You won't find sugar sweeter than the taste
With which the beauty of my lips is graced,
So that all hearts desire this sweetness more
Than wealth, or life itself, for evermore.
        But if you're tired of love and loyalty,
If friendship's carpet's been rolled up for me,

Be chivalrous and hide it, don't allow
Your former friend to be made fun of now,
And in the midst of all your anger make
A space for moderation, for my sake,
So that the whole world does not come to see
Your lack of love and your contempt for me.
Not everyone who gnaws a bone then ties it
Around his foolish neck to advertise it!
And men say that a wise man's one who can
Keep secrets safe from any other man
(His own shirt doesn't know, he doesn't share
His well-kept secrets even with his hair),
So hide your enmity for me, don't be
So publicly contemptuous of me.

    Don't block the road to happiness with spite,
Or hastily snuff out love's candlelight;
Don't wholly leave my love behind, my friend,
It might prove useful to you in the end.
This fleeting world's unstable, it won't stay
Fixed in a single state from day to day;
If you feel hatred after love, love might
Come back again, once hatred's out of sight,
As, in a year, cold follows heat, and then
The heat returns, replacing cold again."

Ramin replies to Vis

Ramin replied as was appropriate
In their unhappy and distracted state:
"Ah, Vis, I've seen what you have done, I've heard
Your speeches, all of them and every word.
Now may a foolish man who has no sense
Escape from his delusive ignorance,
I'm not the kind of man who never tries
To rise up from the filth in which he lies.

A demon once misled me, I repent
Both that I trusted him and where I went;
I trod that path because he told me to,
I didn't know what sufferings would ensue –
I thought I'd find a treasure, not this vain
Accumulation of despair and pain.
In Kuhestan my life was glad and free,
No troubles, no concerns, tormented me.
I snatched my heart from all that happiness
And chose a path of sorrow and distress;
Oh, I deserve to suffer and be sad,
Why did I leave the happy life I had?
A fool thinks that he's wise, and good forsakes him,
And as good turns away so evil takes him.
Try giving something precious to a fool –
He'll ask for coal when he could have a jewel.
Fate handed me a jewel, and when I said,
'I don't want that,' it gave me coal instead.
Two months I rode, two hard months, and for what?
Look at the bitter welcome that I got!
But I deserved it, I deserve the worst
With which it's possible I could be cursed
Because I showed ingratitude to Fate,
And Fate now treats me as a reprobate;
I said, 'I don't want that,' and Fate said, 'Then
Don't think that I'll remember you again.'
        Yes, you were right to close your doors on me,
To call me 'fraud' and 'fool' so scornfully,
And yes, my heart is foolish; if it weren't
I'm sure that long ago it would have learnt
Not to feel longing for a person who
Is as unworthy and as vile as you.
Go back, forget me, as you said you would,
I'm leaving here, our talking does no good,

Till Judgment Day I swear I'll have no part
In linking one heart with another heart.
　　　Not that I didn't say your moon-like face,
Your musky hair, your silver arms, your grace
Make you the watchful chatelaine and queen
Of all the beauties that the world has seen.
No magic's like your eyes, and Loveliness
Looks on your face with envious distress,
Your curls and neck are musk and ivory,
And violets crown their dazzling panoply;
You are the joy of spring to look upon,
A Chinese idol, moonlight and the sun,
But I have no desire that you should shine
On me again, or make your splendor mine.
Ah, Vis, you cure with salves all lovers who
Have lost their grieving hearts because of you,
But, though my pain's intense, I'll die before
I once again come knocking at your door.
The spittle from your lovely lips revives
The sick and dead and gives them back their lives –
Before I seek for solace from you, I
Will suffer agonizing thirst and die;
And though my love is still a smoldering fire
You'll never see the glow of my desire,
May it be smoke, and not a sudden flare
That turns to ash and is no longer there.
You've found two hundred times more faults in me
Than could be listed by an enemy,
Now you forget the myriad things you said,
They've wholly vanished from your ears and head;
Can you not see you shame yourself in seeking
The love and faith from me of which you're speaking?
　　　O lovely, jasmine-breasted Vis, it's you,
Not me, who's like the foolish mother who

Has one girl, who can't see, and wants to find
A perfect husband for this child who's blind.
You're blind to all your faults, so your selection's
A lover who's possessed of all perfections!
And you find fault with everyone and say
Your way of acting is the only way.
So, what faults have you found in me that you
Are so enraged by everything I do?
It's you who's sick of love, so why taunt me
With all this talk of infidelity?
You're far more fickle than I've been, you've made
Cruelty and heartlessness your stock in trade;
And if you'd never heard of me, or seen
In all your life a trace of Prince Ramin,
You'd still no right to talk in such a fashion,
To act with such a lack of all compassion.

  Suppose we'd not been lovers long ago;
I was a man still, in the dark and snow,
My journey had been long, and I was friendless,
Caught in a blustery snowstorm that seemed endless.
I asked forgiveness for my sins, my pleas
Became a thousand begged apologies,
And still you couldn't bring yourself to make
A little show of kindness for my sake.
No, you denied me entrance, and you gave me
Nothing at all to shelter me or save me.
You left me in the snowy freezing night
And disappeared abruptly from my sight,
You wouldn't help me, no, you let me go
Assuming that I'd perish in the snow.
Your envy made you so enraged with me
You planned my death throes, like an enemy;
How faithless you must be, how inhumane,
To see friends die and only feel disdain!

Perhaps your heart rejoiced to see me dead,
But where exactly would my death have led?
The only thing you'd get from it would be
To be despised as you're despising me,
The profit would be mine – men would discover
Who was the faithful, who the faithless, lover.
And so disasters serve us – in the end
They show us who's a foe and who's a friend,
Now that I know you, I can truly say
I hate your stony heart in every way.
Your vaunted faithfulness puts me in mind
Of the great Simorgh,[183] which men never find,
Your heart is merciless, and Vis, I fear
Your eyes do not contain a single tear,
And God forbid men fall for you, since all
Your love is worthless and contemptible.
How grateful I am now to God above
That I've escaped the shackles of your love!

    From now on I'll love no one new; I chose,
And I rejoice in, my sweet-smelling rose,
I'll be her monarch till I die, and she,
Till death is here, will be the moon to me.
You'll walk two hundred roads before you've seen
A moon like Gol, a monarch like Ramin;
Good fortune joined us, and we live content
Where love returned is love's sweet complement."

VIS REPLIES TO RAMIN

And jasmine-breasted Vis now wept a flood
Of anguished tears commingled with her blood;
She ripped the bodice of her lovely dress,
And flung her veil off in her wild distress,
And cried: "Ramin, you are more dear to me
Than is my life for all eternity,

You are my heart's desire, the end and goal
Of all the longings of my heart and soul.
My fortune and my soul still trust in you,
Don't rip my wretched fortune's veil in two,
Don't make my soul love's slave, don't break the bough
Of happiness entrusted to us now,
Don't take the moon of hope and darken it
And thrust it deep within a loathsome pit.
If, in my joking, I have been too free,
And if I've shown a touch of jealousy,
Don't now abandon me, and then produce
My silly jealousy as your excuse.
Six months I've waited for you, haven't I
The right to make a spirited reply?
There's always pain when lovers are apart,
There's always anger in a lover's heart,
When hearts are blazing hot, a little teasing
Eases them of their anguish and is pleasing;
Reproaches between lovers will persist
As long as love continues to exist,
And I for one pray that my pains increase
So that my fond reproaches never cease.
        But if the heavens rain down stones, they'll fall
Upon the heads of lovers after all.
I'm sorry I reproached you, since I see
It's only made things even worse for me.
I thought that I was joking, and it ended
With you more irked and hurt than I'd intended.
If I was hard on you, consider how
I've braved this storm in looking for you now;
My brusqueness was all faked, Ramin, forget it,
It got me in this mess and I regret it,
And if my teasing you before was wrong
I'm snowbound with you now, where I belong.

If I was with you in your happiness
I've followed you, Ramin, in your distress;
I suffered in your absence so much pain
I'll never play at leaving you again –
I'll hold your reins forever now, and I
Will weep and groan for you until I die.
If you'll acknowledge my apologies
And not torment me with your homilies,
I'll be your slave till death, and all you say
Will be as God's word till my dying day;
And if my love is not like this, believe me,
Whenever you might wish to you can leave me.
But once you've left me, you can't then renew
The bonds of friendship linking me and you;
Cutting a tree down isn't hard, but when
It's cut it can't be planted once again.
You know, Ramin, I didn't want to hurt you;
Without good reason now I won't desert you."

RAMIN REPLIES TO VIS

Ramin, whose splendor lit the world, replied:
"I'll have no other lovers at my side,
What makes you think that I would want to see
Men taunting me and making fun of me?
Or have the world that is so sweet and bright
Darkened by melancholy's mournful night?
Why, when I'm happy, seek out misery?
Why make myself a slave when I am free?
I've spent so long derided as a fool,
The object of malicious ridicule,
It would be best if I did not pursue
This shameful story of my love for you.
Hell's all that I deserve if I once more
Try what I've tried and what has failed before.

I'm a free man: what free man would behave
So abjectly, as though he were a slave?
It is as bad for free men to submit
To wrong as for the wise to practice it;
Your face may be like sunlight, but I'll sever
Hopes of such sunlight from my heart forever.
If stones became so rare that they were worth
Six hundred times the jewels of all the earth
I'd buy a hundred pounds of them and heap
The lot of them upon my heart to keep
It weighed down so that I'd at last be free
Of all this shame that's so degraded me.
Being with you is worth a hundred treasures,
But all its anguish outweighs all its pleasures.
I'd rip my heart out if it ever tried
To bring you, or some new love, to my side –
Better to be without it, since I've seen
My heart loves everyone but me, Ramin!

    Perhaps luck's with me, and it was my fate
To see your love tonight mixed in with hate:
Many's the task that seems too hard at first
That turns out well, the outset was the worst;
And sometimes God can fashion a success
Out of what seems to be a hopeless mess.
And so it is tonight – it seems that He
Has fashioned what my friends would wish for me:
I'm done with talk, and with apologies,
With sorrow, burning, and love's miseries,
I was a slave, I'm now a king, and I
Who was the earth am now the moon and sky.
My soul's so free from pain and grief, you'd say
I've soared up from this world and flown away!
Once I was drunk: I'm sober now, I've woken
And all my long and foolish sleep is broken,

My blind fate sees again, at last I find
Wisdom once more in my benighted mind,
And now I've slipped the shackles of my lust
No onager will catch up with my dust.
　　　Don't think you'll see me as I was, despised,
Unhappy, helpless, and demoralized;
The man who's sure the world cannot now charm him
Has no fear that its blandishments might harm him,
His life's serene, profit does not attract him,
Disquiet over loss does not distract him.
May you find wisdom as I've done, and start
To know the peace of an untroubled heart;
Be wise now and content, contentment brings
A greater sovereignty than that of kings.
But sow love's seedlings for a century
And wind is all the harvest that you'll see.
A lover cannot rest, he's forced to tread
The hard and weary way that lies ahead,
And in this world, that way will never end:
And if you're wise, you'll mark my words, my friend."

VIS REPLIES TO RAMIN

Now jasmine-breasted Vis clutched at his hand
As, faint with longing, she could hardly stand,
And ruby teardrops touched her breasts as she
Shivered and trembled like a willow tree.
She cried: "My love, as dear as are my eyes,
Sweet moonlight, shining sunlight, of my skies,
Without your face I've no desire to live,
No wish for any pleasures life might give –
I hurt you, I was wrong, and I repent
And bite my hand to show I'm penitent.[184]
Don't draw your anger's bow, don't shoot the dart
That brings such misery to my poor heart!

Let us delight each other now and be
Each other's sweetest, dearest company,
And not repeat past words, but let affection
Wash our hearts clean of every imperfection.
Don't be aggrieved for what you've suffered through,
Don't brood on all the things I said to you;
That wife of yours might pester and oppress you,
But how could what a lover says distress you?
The greatest kings will bow to kiss the dust
Their lovers walk on, as is right and just,
And lovers' quarrels aren't like war, no shame's
Involved in all their teasing and their games.
So take my teasing, since you took my soul –
Calm yourself, exercise some self-control!
What will you do, Ramin, to hear men say
My blood is on your head, on Judgment Day?
What day is worse than this, when both my heart
And that cruel thief who's stolen it depart?
You took my heart, now you yourself are leaving?
You'll wear my life away with all this grieving!
Leave me my heart at least, and let me rain
Fire down on it and so destroy this pain!
How can you have the heart to leave me here?
To turn from my sweet face and disappear?
Are you Ramin still, whose firm loyalty
I used to praise? And now you're tired of me?
Alas for all the promises you made,
The binding oaths you've broken and betrayed.
I've told my foolish heart now to beware
Of any oaths a wretch like you might swear,
But she's strong-willed and obstinate, and who
Knows what the stubborn fool might say or do?
        Why do you hold me here so long, and keep
My eyes so bloodshot with the tears they weep?

Oh, if you're leaving here, then quickly go:
I'll soon have perished in this cold and snow!
But if it's true you're leaving, take me too,
And let me travel on your way with you.
Easy or hard, whatever might appear,
I'll ride a hundred parasangs from here
To stay with you, and if you slash my dress
A hundred times in your impetuousness,
And stab the hand that clutches at your hem,
I'll clutch your clothes still, I won't forfeit them;
I'll travel with you still, and I'll be glad,
I'll never stay without you, with Mobad.
If I'd a mountain for a heart, believe me,
It still could not endure to have you leave me:
O shining sun, how can you think to go
And leave me lost here in this cold and snow?
Ramin, you're like a beautiful brocade
Whose myriad lovely colors never fade,
How can you think to snatch away from me
All life and color, strength and dignity?
How shameless you must be, how pitiless,
That your hard heart's unmoved by my distress!"
And as Vis spoke, her tears cascaded down
Like rivers on the bodice of her gown.

Ramin's heart was indeed unmoved; you'd say
It was as hard as iron in every way,
Or that the snow and his fierce rage at Vis
Had made a pact that they would never cease.
Vis and her nurse retraced the way they came,
Her eyes were wet, her heart was all aflame,
Her cold flesh shivered like a willow tree,
Her soul was filled with hopeless misery.
She said: "How Fate pursues me now, as though
It somehow saw me as its mortal foe;

It fights against me always, and one day
I know I'll perish as its blood-stained prey.
Ah, nurse, is any fool like me if I
Should turn to love again before I die?
If I don't leave all thoughts of love behind me
Gouge both my foolish eyes out, nurse, and blind me!
My soul's as weak and as of little worth
As is a corpse that's buried in the earth,
And if my wretched life should now forsake me
There's no grave in the wide world that would take me.
I've lost my soul, I've lost my love, ah nurse
What sorrow can I face that could be worse?
No, Love has launched his last and worst attack;
There is no darker color than pitch black."

RAMIN REGRETS VIS'S DEPARTURE AND FOLLOWS HER

When Vis had left Ramin the skies became
Like some vast dragon breathing tongues of flame;
The snow was like a poison, since within it
Men's hearts would freeze and stiffen in a minute,
Black clouds were massing, blocking out the light,
Choking back breath, depriving eyes of sight;
The snow blew with such force that elephants
Could not have stood against its vehemence,
And hemmed Ramin in, as huge waves will force
An ocean-going vessel from its course.
His body was snowbound, but in his heart
Fire blazed that he'd allowed Vis to depart;
Tears fell like coral to his chest, and he
Regretted all his cruel discourtesy –
A cry burst from him, such a cry you'd say
His soul had fled his flesh and flown away.
He tugged at Rakhsh's reins then and turned back
And found Vis struggling on the snowy track

And like a drunkard tumbled down, and cried,
"Ah, Vis, my love, forgive my foolish pride,
Don't heap new grief on grief, ah, pity me,
A man who's doubled his iniquity,
Since what was evil seemed good in my eyes
And I did ugly things that I despise,
Twice over I have brought myself this shame
In front of you, and ruined my good name;
My eyes can't look at you, my tongue's too weak
And too abashed, now that you're here, to speak,
It's in a knot you'd say, and shame has made
My heart quake like a drunkard who's afraid.
Ah, Vis, I can't apologize to you,
Without you there is nothing I can do –
I'm helpless, friendless, and I have no peace
Within my heart or body now, dear Vis.
My tongue is silent and my soul is senseless,
Since love and shame have rendered them defenseless,
It was a devil who misled me, who
Made me so stupid when I raged at you;
How wrong I was! I'll labor to repay you,
You'll be my sovereign now and I'll obey you,
And I'll be pleased to be the least of all
The many servants at your beck and call:
And if you answer love with anger I
Will plunge my dagger in my heart and die!

    Ah, let me hold you in this snow till we
Together pass into eternity!
There's no one in the world for me but you,
If I'm to die my love, then you must too;
If I'm to die here in this freezing weather
I'll clutch your skirt and we shall die together,
We shall be friends in death, my love, and then
Together, after death, we'll rise again.

If you're to be my love, why should I fear
The fearful road till Judgment Day is here?
My heaven's you, my houri's you, and who
Would ever seek to be away from you?
I shall be yours, you mine, and I shall never
Give up my hopes of your dear love forever."

His heartfelt words were mingled with his sighs,
And mingled blood and tears flowed from his eyes.
The words they'd said a hundred times before
They now repeated word for word once more,
And all the cruel things that they'd said and done
Were once again gone over, one by one;
How long they talked! The world itself now gazed
In wonder at them there, and was amazed!
And Vis's heart was hard at first, although
Her face was like the spring when blossoms blow,
But as the armies of the day increased,
Unfurling dawn's bright banner in the east,
The fear of madness overcame Ramin
And Vis grew fearful that they would be seen.
They cut their talk short with the morning light
And sought a place where they'd be out of sight;
These lovers who had lost their way now learned
Their way again, and step by step returned.
They grasped each other's hands, and fearful of
The prying eyes that might perceive their love,
Took shelter in a hunting lodge, where they
Washed all their sorrows and their fears away.
Joy blossomed as they barred the door, and laid
Their bodies down on ermine and brocade,
One body with two souls, two jewels that shine
Together in the darkness of a mine,
Two jasmine-breasted lovers face to face –
You'd say those bedclothes were a heavenly place!

The moon and stars lay pillowed there, and posies
Of pomegranate blossoms and wild roses,
No picture galleries or gardens share
The charm of their sweet faces and their hair –
They were brocades of beauty, tangled skeins
Of loveliness deployed in musky chains;
Their faces lay on silks and rich brocade
From which it seemed their faces too were made.
    Now for a month they did not rest, but lay
Engaged in endless, amorous sweet play,
Mingled like wine and milk; and day and night
The arrow never faltered in its flight.
Two cypresses embraced, and then they'd hold
Two goblets filled with wine and made of gold;
Camphor and roses mixed, and each applied
Sweet salves to soothe the other's wounded pride,
And, though their hearts were hurt, their kisses brought
The love and pardon for which each had sought.

The king enthroned in all his golden glory
Knew nothing of these happy lovers' story.
He did not know that Prince Ramin now lay
In Vis's bed each night and every day;
That they drank water from one cup, that shame
Had drawn her sword and murdered his good name;
That these two lovers' hearts were purified
Of all the grief they'd known: that side by side
Each lay enchanted by the other's face,
Caught in the happy snare of love's embrace,
Content to give away both worlds to be
Each other's lovers for eternity.
One month of happiness made them forget
Six months of difficulties and regret.

And may there be no love at all unless
It's like this love, and brings such happiness.
How fortunate the lover whose sweet fate
It is to live in such a favored state –
Truly, this is the way that love should be,
Good fortune, followed by simplicity!
How many days I've loved, and never seen
A joy like that of Vis and her Ramin,
And time has passed me by now and I know
The best days of my life were long ago.

THE END OF THE TALE

پایان داستان

RAMIN PRESENTS HIMSELF BEFORE KING MOBAD

In love's sweet garden, for a month, these two
Were like a box tree flourishing anew.
Snow melted, warmer breezes blew; together
They were the first signs of more clement weather.
Ramin then said to Vis, "Time's getting short,
I should appear soon at the royal court,
I must announce myself again, before
Our secret's not a secret any more."
Stealthily then, that night, he stole away
And rode for miles before the break of day,
Then, turning back to Marv, he traveled straight
Along the highway to the city gate
And, with his traveling clothes unchanged still, strode
Into the palace, dusty from the road.
They quickly told the king, "Ramin is here,
The great sun's shining in its splendid sphere,
He's like a cypress in his elegance,
Topped by the full moon's glorious radiance,

Although the cold has numbed him, and his waist
Aches from the straps in which it's been encased."
And, entering, the silver cypress tree
Bent forward in respectful courtesy;
The king was overjoyed to see Ramin
And asked him how his journey there had been.

Noble Ramin replied: "Great king, whose might
And will accomplish what is just and right,
May victory be yours forever, may
Your enemies see many an evil day,
May you have all you long for, may your name
Reverberate with an unequalled fame,
May Fortune favor you eternally
With riches, prosperousness, and sovereignty.
I'd need a heart like Damavand[185] to bear
My mind's unhappiness when you're not there,
You brought me up when I was small, your love
Has raised my standing to the stars above;
You gave me life, position, everything,
You're both my father and my noble king.
If I could bear your absence you could say
My nature is defective in some way,
Saturn himself could be my chamberlain
If I were yours throughout your splendid reign!
And why should I pretend to patience when
I only long to see your face again?
I rule Gorgan for you, at your command,
I've cleared wolves from its rocky hinterland,
My sword's subdued its mountains, and its deer
Now live among its lions without fear:
The king's obeyed as far as Syria,
In Mosul too, and in Armenia,
And, by your power, the world itself to me
Is like a slave held in captivity;

God gave me everything, but not the thing
I wanted most – the sight of you, my king,
And when I'm somewhere that you can't be seen
I feel a dragon's swallowing Ramin;
God's generous, but He doesn't give each slave
Every last thing the slave might wish He gave.
And since I've longed to see you day and night
I've ridden here alone, as if in flight
From spring rains thundering down a mountainside
And flooding all the landscape far and wide.
I hunted as I rode along the way,
And, as black lions[186] do, I ate my prey,
But now I've seen your glorious court and you,
And all the splendor of your retinue,
My heart's a garden blossoming in the sun
And I've a thousand souls instead of one.
I'd like to stay here for three months, and then
I'll take the road back to Gurab again,
But if Mobad, my king, does not agree
His orders will be absolute for me.
If need be, I'll give up my life to do
All of the things that he commands me to,
Since he who does his king's commands and dies
Then truly lives, according to the wise."

To King Mobad his words seemed eloquent.
He said, "What you have done has my assent:
You are a lion among men, and you
Act righteously in everything you do,
And seeing you again so gratifies me
A one-day visit never satisfies me.
Now while the winter and the cold detain us
Songs day and night, and wine, must entertain us.
When spring comes, there'll be many courtiers who
Will ride as friends along your way with you,

And I'll come to Gorgan to hunt, since spring
Makes staying in one's house an irksome thing.
Go to the hot baths now, get yourself clean,
And change those traveling clothes of yours, Ramin."
Ramin rejoiced to leave the king, who sent
Him robes of honor, as a compliment.

Three months Ramin was there, and day and night
He spent in following his heart's delight;
Fate gave him what he wished; in secret he
Was closeted with Vis now, constantly,
And while his happy heart rejoiced he hid
From King Mobad all that he felt and did.
He took such care with Vis, none could detect them,
And King Mobad himself did not suspect them.

MOBAD DECIDES TO GO HUNTING

Spring's army pitched camp on the hills and plains,
And rivers ran with its reviving rains,
The world was like a garden now as though
Heaven had come down to the earth below.
The ancient world grew young and debonair,
Its cheeks were tulips, violets its dark hair,
Its lovely face a royal treasury
Of silks, brocades, and every luxury,
A thousand birds addressed the flowers in song
Like drunken lovers who sing loud and long;
Wild game descended from the hills to roam
The grasslands and to make the plains their home,
And every dawn new boughs were blossoming
As harbingers of the advancing spring.
Like brides who leave their litters, each new rose
Robbed countless nightingales of their repose,
It seemed that wine rained from the firmament,
The plain's dust took on ambergris's scent,

The gardens were heart-stealing girls, the trees
Shone with their blossoms like the Pleiades.
The air was like a glittering robe, the ground
A place where elegant, jeweled flowers were found;
The world became a banquet where a king
Might celebrate the glories of the spring,
And bright narcissi, where he sat to dine,
Were like exquisite goblets filled with wine –
And gold and silver filled the pleasant land
Like Khosrow and Shirin[187] sat hand in hand.
Mild zephyrs bore sweet-scented tidings of
The rose's and the jasmine's mutual love,
And petals drifted through the air as though
Silver and gold fell to the ground below.
All Marv's environs glittered like brocade
That skillful weavers from Shushtar had made,
And raindrops brought such pleasure as they fell
You'd say that they were drops of joy as well.

In such a time, when all the world was bright
With spring's return, and teeming with delight,
The king, irked by his house, sought fellowship
In outdoor pleasures and a hunting trip.
Quickly he sent out messengers to call
On all his courtiers, be they great or small,
To join him in his hunting expedition,
Saying, "Gorgan's our goal, and our ambition
Is hunting wolves and boar, or bringing down
Wild leopards from its mountains' rocky crown,
Or flushing out whatever monsters hide
Within the thickets of its countryside.
We'll loose our lynxes and our cheetahs there,
And hunted deer will be their daily fare."

When Vis heard of the king's intentions she
Saw joy turn instantly to misery,
And, in her anguish, to her nurse she said,
"What's worse than this? I might as well be dead!
I'm tired of life, I've been tormented by
A hundred sword wounds and I long to die!
May everything that's evil, all that's bad,
Curse this intended journey by Mobad!
Ah, how can I endure such separation
Or free myself from this new desolation?
If Prince Ramin goes I am sure my heart,
As he departs, will also then depart,
And may Rakhsh trample on my eyes tomorrow
If he sets out and leaves me to my sorrow!
With every step he takes, grief's brand will sear
The sweetness of my soul with pain and fear.

　　　As soon as he has gone you'll see me stay
As faithful as a watchman by the way
That leads here from Gorgan, and my poor eyes
Will be the cup of water that supplies
The wants of travelers when they drink and rest,
Or they'll rain pearls and rubies on my breast,
In hopes that God will see and pity me
And save my soul from this calamity.

　　　Go nurse, go now, and tell Ramin my state,
Tell him I'm wretched and disconsolate,
And find out what it is that he intends –
A fate my foes might wish me, or my friends?
If he intends to leave tomorrow I
Will cut short all life's chatter now and die,
Say that I say, 'How will I stay alive
Till you return here, how can I survive?
See you don't turn your face away from me,
When you come back it won't be me you'll see

Since I'll be dead; so find some way to stay here,
Something to justify a long delay here.
Stay in this house with me, Ramin, don't leave –
Be happy, let Mobad go, let him grieve,
You must enjoy good fortune now, while he's
Struck blind by months and years of miseries.'"

The nurse went straight to Prince Ramin and saw
Her news was salt in wounds still fresh and raw;
Repeating Vis's words, he looked as though
An arrow'd struck him from a well-aimed bow:
Convulsions seized him and he heaved cold sighs
While tears of anguish trickled from his eyes.
He felt he was the wretchedest of men
And wept to think of leaving Vis again;
Now pain, now terror, and now grief assailed him,
His heart was broken, all his courage failed him.
Then he addressed the nurse, "But King Mobad
Has mentioned nothing to me, good or bad,
He's sent no message either, it might be
That for some reason he's forgotten me.
        But if he says that I'm to go away
I'll find a plausible excuse to stay;
'My legs hurt,' that's a reasonable claim,
I'll say he knows I'm prone to getting lame,
And that I'd love to hunt with him, but sadly
With legs like mine I'd only do it badly;
I'll say I thought that he'd already learned
That this infirmity of mine's returned,
And this was why he hadn't let me know
I should be getting ready soon to go.
I was convinced that I would have to stay
Without him, here in Marv; that's what I'll say.
If things work out like this, nurse, I'll be given,
While I'm still here on earth, a place in heaven."

The nurse told Vis this, and you'd say Ramin
Had said to Vis that soon she'd be his queen;
Grief left her soul, her face forgot despair,
And happiness's roses opened there.

Mobad goes hunting and takes Ramin with him

The mountains glowed like gold, jeweled carpets shone
Upon the plains and glittered in the sun:
The castle rang with din, with drums and bells,
With bugles, brazen hooves, and ostlers' yells,
And mounted men emerged in companies
Jostling like boughs of blossom on the trees,
Surging from Marv like some great wave that rears
To fearsome heights before it disappears.
Ramin came forward to the king, and showed
That he was unprepared still for the road;
Before his men the king said, "What's this then?
Or are you up to your old tricks again?
Where are your traveling things? Is this a sign
That once again you're going to moan and whine?
Go, get things from my steward, I don't care
To go on hunting trips if you're not there."
Heartsick, Ramin did all he was commanded,
Like a snagged fish a hundred hooks have landed.
As he prepared himself, he looked quite beaten,
A shepherd whose loved sheep the wolves have eaten,
And as the crowd made ready to depart
Arrows transfixed his entrails, spears his heart.

When Vis learned that Ramin had left, her soul
Slipped wildly, suddenly, from her control;
The heart that had rejoiced now quivered like
A partridge when a falcon's talons strike.

Vis moaned to her poor heart the plaint of one
Who is alone, now that her lover's gone:
"Why should I not despair of loneliness
And weep red rubies from my heart's distress?
I'll never know a love like his or sow
Again the love that I sowed long ago;
Silence would be a fault; he's gone, it's right
For me to mourn his absence and my plight.
Nurse, if you doubt my anguish and my fears,
Look at my sallow face, my crimson tears,
These tears that are my words, that all unbidden
Tell to the world the secrets that I've hidden,
And how can my poor heart endure alone
A grief that makes all hearts that hear it groan?
It's not my lover now for whom I'm weeping,
It's for my soul, that's in my own safekeeping,
Since now my lover's gone I fear that she
Will follow him and slip away from me.
How can a heart that has no patience live
Through hardships even patience can't forgive?"

Then, from a corner of the rooftop, she
Watched Prince Ramin set out in misery.
The royal belt that's called Kayanid[188] graced
The silken contours of his lovely waist,
The road's dust settled on his musky hair,
His face was wan with longing and despair,
Remembering he'd had no time to tell
His love he loved her or to say farewell,
As though he drowned in oceans, tempest-tossed,
Or wandered deserts where the way was lost.
Now Vis's heart was wrung to see him there
And inwardly she cried in her despair,
"Farewell, my handsome love, my heart's delight,
Farewell, our army's most courageous knight,

Farewell, my dearest and my kindest friend,
Farewell, great lord, whose bounty has no end;
You did not say farewell, and it may be
You've taken all your love away from me.
        You've left now with a crowd of knights, a crowd
Of anxious thoughts is all that I'm allowed;
My heart was shackled by a hundred chains,
It broke them all (and nothing now remains)
To set out after you; my soul's still here,
Weeping and wailing till you reappear,
And I will send you sighs like clouds that bear
As rain the tears I've wept in my despair;
This rain will make grass flourish and streams flow
Before you everywhere you choose to go,
Since everywhere you are spring comes, and spring
Needs rain and cloudbursts more than anything."

The first stage of the journey was now done,
But Prince Ramin seemed lost to everyone –
Distracted and preoccupied, he showed
No sign of seeing what was on the road;
Instead, he moaned, and tears poured from his eyes,
But, for a sick man, this was no surprise.
Among his moans, he sang things worthy of
A man who's separated from his love:

"Kisses were all our arrows still, last night,
Our lips the targets of their eager flight;
And now, today, my soul's a hunted deer,
Your love the cheetah that pursues it here.
Ah, where are last night's pleasures, last night's teasing,
Those rubies and sweet pearls that were so pleasing?
What years of callousness we washed away
Where silk and silver pomegranates lay,
And where your face's loveliness was shown
Reflected in the garden of my own,

So that the secret darkness of the night
Was changed to shining day by our delight.
And now I've looked on such a night of bliss
How can I look on such a day as this?
This is no day, it is a temple fire,
A conflagration that destroys desire,
And may no lover have to look upon
A day like this when all is said and done,
That saps our patience and our self-control
And burns up in its flames the lover's soul;
And if Time measured time he'd surely say
'A hundred years are equal to today!'"

The king dismounted when the stage was over,
And Prince Ramin appeared, the wounded lover,
Within whose face a hundred signals said
That all his patience and good sense had fled.
He did not join the king for wine but claimed
His leg's old injury had left him maimed.
And so he was all day, all night, as though
His heart was now his soul's relentless foe,
His face made dirty with the journey's grime,
His wretched soul in anguish all the time,
His body now all heart, his heart all pain –
And so Ramin seemed likely to remain.

VIS COMPLAINS OF RAMIN'S ABSENCE AND ASKS THE NURSE FOR ADVICE

When Prince Ramin left Vis, contentment cleft
The bonds that bound him there and also left.
This moon became the sun, a constant yellow,
Not eating, sleepless, restless, sick and sallow,
Scoring her cheeks with blood, always repeating
Stories of her Ramin and their last meeting.

Then to her nurse she said, "Ah, nurse, contrive
To bring my faithless lover back alive,
Have pity on me, nurse, and show me how
I can be reunited with him now!
I cannot bear this new catastrophe,
I can't endure his absences from me.
Hear what I tell you, nurse, my words will flow
Like water as I tell you what I know:
Once, like a fool, I gave my heart away,
And now it's left me I'm quite drunk, you'd say,
But, ah, don't blame me, since this separation
Has brought a Judgment Day of consternation.
A fire has swallowed up my heart, and you,
Dear nurse, will soon be swallowed by it too.
Water will put out fire, but when my eyes
Weep watery tears these flames revitalize –
I weep like springtime showers upon a plain,
Whoever saw fire flare up in the rain?
Last night was just like this, as though I lay
On thorns and pins until the break of day,
And now it's breakfast time, but in my sight
This daylight is as dark as any night.
      My day's my lover's face, his lips will be
The only salve to sooth my agony,
And till he's here and I am sure he'll stay
I'll find no salve, and I shall see no day.
What's written on my forehead that my fate
Leaves me so wretched and disconsolate?
I'll seek out shepherds on the plains, I'll leave
The friends I've made to be alone and grieve;
My cries will make a tempest in this town
And boulders in the mountains thunder down.
I don't know what I'll do or who I'll see,
Who could replace my longed-for friend for me?
I'll bind my eyes, then nothing can attract me,
Since all I see serves only to distract me.

What is the point of everything I've seen
Except to make me restless for Ramin?
I've tried my luck so many times, for what?
Wounds and sorrow and pain were all I got!
Over and over I have tried, dear nurse,
Only to make my own undoing worse.
You've heard my story, now it's up to you
To bring me back to life. What should I do?"

The nurse said, "This is not the way to speak,
And no good ever came from being weak.
What do these tears and lamentations do
Except make everything much worse for you?
Your friends live happily, and day and night
Follow their pleasures and their hearts' delight,
And you are always suffering, wailing, sighing.
You've tried my patience with your endless crying!
The world is what it is, and there's a cure
For every injury that men endure;
The injury and cure are in your hands.
Why sit on them, Vis? Issue your commands!
God's given you unrivaled sovereignty,
A noble name and great authority:
Your mother is none other than Shahru;
Your brother and companion is Viru;
Your lover is Ramin who's worthy of
The royal throne itself, and of your love;
Your treasuries are filled with jewels, allies
Abound to help a daring enterprise.
Forget your whining and this foolish story.
You have the means, seek greatness, Vis, and glory!
The way you've treated King Mobad is ugly,
And constantly you've done it, cruelly, smugly,

While his demonic hatred of you, Vis,
Is like a mountain still and won't decrease –
He's what he was, you're what you were, both he
And you will be like this eternally.
　　　Before the anger in Mobad's cruel heart
Seeks out our blood, and tears us all apart,
Look for a way out, Vis, and don't delay,
You have the seed, the water, and the way.
He's like a lion, watchful, furious,
Waiting to set upon the three of us,
And mark my words one day he'll leap upon
The three of us and we'll be dead and gone.
You'll find no better partner than Ramin,
So crown him, do it now, and be his queen,
And when the royal crown and throne are won
You'll be the moonlight to his shining sun,
And there's no living king or noble who
Won't hurry to make common cause with you.
Your brother is the first man you should trust
Then other kings will see your cause as just
(They hate Mobad, they'd rather have Viru
And Prince Ramin as rulers here, and you).
Wisdom and you have been at odds too long,
Your heart has done you an enormous wrong,
If you let sense and knowledge help you, Vis,
The sorrows that have haunted you will cease.
So, if you can, act now; you won't discover
A better day than this one once it's over.
The king's left Marv, and all his men have too,
I'd say his treasures now belong to you
(What troubles he once went through to obtain them,
How effortless it's been for you to gain them!),
So use his gold to purchase his position,
Your wealth makes this an easy proposition.

Before he dines on you for lunch, attack,
And eat him as a tasty breakfast snack!
   If you agree to what I'm saying here
Write to Ramin and make your feelings clear,
Tell him to leave Mobad and to be twinned
For speed in coming back here with the wind.
Once he's arrived, we'll find some way to force
Mobad's life to a more ill-fated course."
And jasmine-scented Vis's cheeks grew red
As cheerful tulips at the words she said.

VIS WRITES A LETTER TO RAMIN

To write a letter to Ramin then, Vis
Asked for a pen, musk, silk, and ambergris,
So desperate were the words she wrote you'd say
Her heart's blood dripped onto the page that day
(O lover, writing to your love now, write
As Vis once wrote to Prince Ramin, her knight,
And you will hear stones weep like harp strings when
They hear the words that issue from your pen):
"From my affliction, from your faithful friend,
To one whose heart's harsh cruelty has no end.
From one who cannot sleep or eat to one
Whose sovereignty is like the moon and sun;
From one who groans for love, whose enemies
Delight in her heartbroken miseries;
From one who writhes and burns for love, whose fate
Darkens her world and leaves her desolate;
From a poor serving girl who weeps a flood
Of flowing tears commingled with her blood,
Whose soul has suffered and whose heart has bled,
Whose face is sallow and whose eyes are red,
Writhing and wretched, racked with grief and pain,
Whose every hair feels like a prisoner's chain,

Whose heart's disconsolate, who's wailing, sighing,
Whose eyes are rivers with her constant crying.
I write this letter now in such a state
No other mortal shares my wretched fate.
My body twists and trembles with desire,
My eyes weep, and my heart is seared with fire;
My body's like a candle from my tears,
While in my heart a cloud of grief appears.
Sorrow's my friend, my partner's misery,
I'm drowning in our separation's sea.
        One hand is on my heart now as I weep,
The other grasps my pillow where I sleep,
My ruby lips turn blue, and it's as though
The whole world sympathizes with my woe.
Your absence writes the secrets I once kept
Plainly upon my cheeks now, where I've wept,
And such a fire flares in my soul it's burned
Whatever patience my poor heart once learned;
My eyes are oceans now, and so profound
That in their watery chambers sleep has drowned.
        With the same hand I'm using now to write
I've rolled the rug of pleasure out of sight;
My body's melted from its pain, my heart
Is tired of grief and threatens to depart,
And how can I seek happiness when I've
No heart or soul to keep me here alive?
Away from you I live in such despair
That I'm as slender as a single hair.
The sun is like your face, and so its light
Comforts me in the daytime; in the night
The shining stars are like your teeth and they
Provide me comfort till the dawning day.
But no, my grief's of such intensity
That nothing can be said to comfort me,

And if it were a mountain, blood would flow,
Not streams of water, to the plains below.
    My friends are keen to counsel and advise me,
My enemies to blame me and despise me,
So much advice is mine now, so much blame,
That I've acquired an emblematic fame.
This is not love! No, it's a cloud whose rain
Is grief and sorrow and unending pain,
This is not separation, but a knife
Dipped in a poison that destroys my life.
Why do men give their hearts to love, and so
Ensure their souls an endless source of woe?
If every love's like mine, may love depart
From all the world now and from every heart.
How many days I laughed at lovers…How
I'm sorry for that foolish laughter now!
I laughed at them, just like an enemy,
And now, like friends, they weep and wail for me!
You saw me then, before love came, when I
Rivaled the sunlight of a noonday sky,
But now my cypress body is a bow,
And my pale cheeks have lost their youthful glow.
A laden branch bends downwards, and I bear
A heavy crop of sorrow and despair;
My body is a bow, its strings the streaks
Of blood and tears upon my wasted cheeks.
Rakhsh bore you off, you left me here to moan,
Bewailing your cruel absence all alone,
And all the dust kicked up by Rakhsh was spears
Thrown in my eyes, provoking yet more tears.
    Your image is before me night and day,
Incessantly I weep my soul away.
They say, 'Why weep and wail like this forever?
It's made you like an ever-running river;

A lover gone is like a day gone by,
Why should you long for what is done with? Why?'
But all they think and all they say is wrong.
When wine is spilled, its fragrance is still strong;
The sun has gone, it's dark now, but it's right
For me to watch for dawn's returning light.
Spring leaves us, and returns to us, and so
My lover will return to me I know.
Dear cypress-statured love, bright moon, brave knight,
Fierce lion slayer, glory's acolyte,
I am so deep in love, you know I'd give
My soul to death to have you thrive and live.
Each hair of yours is far more dear to me
Than is my soul for all eternity;
This world, my soul, they're not what I require,
It's you I want, it's you that I desire.
You know my love, you've tested and explored it,
For many years it pleased you, you adored it,
And look, my tearful eyes assure you of
The loyalty of this enduring love.

     Come now, look at my face, sallow like gold,
Down which too many precious pearls have rolled;
Come now, look at my eyes that overflow
Like Oxuses to fill the world with woe;
Come now, look at my back's deformity
That makes me shun mankind as joy shuns me;
Come now, look at my grief and say my tears
Declare I've had this sickness for ten years;
Come now, look at my fate that's so unkind
You'd say my eyes would shrivel and turn blind;
Come now, look at my love that like your beauty
Accepts no limits of constraint or duty.
Come quickly, or you'll find when you arrive
I lacked the fortitude to stay alive;

If you desire to see my face don't stay
To sit or rest or sleep along the way,
But in each day complete the distance gone
In three days, turning three days into one.
    Now, till you come, I'll weep and watch and wait
To see you enter at the city gate,
And if my wretched soul cannot restrain
My longing, I'll go mad with grief and pain.
I ask God for one thing now, day and night:
That I should see again your face's light.
More numerous than drops of rain, I send
Greetings to you, my knight, my radiant friend,
Greetings more large and lavish than the sea
To you, my shining sun, my cypress tree.
Grant me my life, O God, and I'll forsake it
When once I've seen Ramin; then you can take it,
Because if I die now the world will choke
And perish from my sorrow's clouds of smoke."

She sealed the letter, chose a messenger
From those who'd shown most loyalty to her,
And then dispatched him on a tireless steed
Of mountain toughness and unrivalled speed,
That like a vulture crossed the hills, and rolled
The plains up as a scroll whose tale is told.
The messenger, who did not sleep by night
Or rest by day, exerted all his might
To do the bidding of his lovely queen,
And brought her anguished letter to Ramin.

Vis's letter reaches Ramin

And when Ramin received it you would say
He'd seen his fate grow young again that day;
He kissed it with his ruby lips, caressed it,
And touched it to his eyes and head, and blessed it.

Then, as he broke its seal, he wept a flood
Of tears commingled with his crimson blood,
And as he read it through his smoky sighs
Exhaled his soul, and grief poured from his eyes.
Now, as he wept, the soulful tale he told
Was worthy to be written down in gold.

"My heart," he cried, "how many months and years
Must you endure calamities and tears?
My heart, the man who seeks for joy and fame
Can't do so calmly, or with fear and shame,
He's not afraid of swords or elephants,
Or of a roaring lion's belligerence,
Of snow or storms or rain or of the sea,
Of raging heat or cold's intensity.
      My heart, if you're in love still, why complain
So pointlessly of all your grief and pain?
Who hears your pleas? Who'll act for you if you
Don't act yourself and don't know what to do?
Love's not for weaklings! Few men will support you,
A multitude of foes will try to thwart you,
But you must brave it out now and reveal
The longings and anxieties you feel.
What joy can secret passions promise us?
A hundred minuses for every plus!
A single day of joy and happiness
Entails a year of sorrow and distress.
No, I must break love's shackles, or attack
Until my enemies are beaten back,
The best of brothers is a strong right arm,
A ready sword will keep it safe from harm.
      I can't continue to prevaricate;
If I'm a man, the world must know my state –
The worst that it can do is murder me
And, with a sword stroke, seal my destiny.

What valiant knight would shun his enemies?
What seeker after pearls avoids the seas?
Monsters guard pearls within the sea, on land
Poisons and sweetness can go hand in hand,
A sword can be the wine cup of success,
And lions guard the way to happiness.
Pass by the lions, drink the wine, remember
The New Year follows on from bleak December.
Ease will not bring you joy, you cannot gain
Your heart's desire untried by grief and pain.
  Think of the troubles of a trapper's way,
Traversing hills and plains to snare his prey;
What prey is there that equals sovereignty?
Why would I think I'd snare it easily?
Since sovereignty's my prey, and since possession
Of my belovèd Vis is my obsession,
Why do I fight with Fate and with Desire
And not pour water on this raging fire?
Why do I wait, augmenting my disgrace,
Instead of bursting from my hiding place?
My Vis and I are both ensnared, and we
Have lived too long in heartfelt misery,
And why not rip these snares to shreds, and tear
The roots up of our shame and our despair?
But everything that comes must come in season,
And all that happens happens for a reason,
And April's lovely blossoms cannot blow
When trees are shrouded by December's snow.
Perhaps the time to act has come at last
And all those other times lie in the past;
Perhaps our winter's gone and spring is here,
And our good fortune will soon reappear."

He spoke; his body quivered and resembled
A twisting snake, so violently it trembled.

His eyes saw only Vis, his flesh was there
But all his heart and spirit were elsewhere;
He could not rest, and till night came his heart
Was in his mouth as though it would depart.
He watched the east, and waited for the night
Whose gathering armies would conceal his flight.

RAMIN RETURNS IN SECRET TO THE CITADEL

And as light's fires died down, and smoky night
Rolled the day's splendid carpet out of sight
(A black horse bore the moon there, while the sun
Upon its chestnut horse was almost gone),
Only the stars and moonlight saw Ramin
Slip from the camp to flee to Marv unseen.
He rode with forty worthy warriors, men
Who'd fight an army and then fight again,
And Vis's messenger. In seven days
They dashed to Marv like wolves, by secret ways,
And when they were a day away, no more,
He sent her messenger to Vis's door,
To say he would arrive, as she had bidden,
But otherwise to keep the matter hidden;
No one but Vis should know, Vis and her nurse
Who'd be the venture's capital and purse.

He said to tell her, "Now our tale is on
The lips of anyone and everyone,
I'll never see Mobad again, since I
Deserve whatever way he'd have me die.
Stay in your rooms tomorrow night and be
Listening for when you'll have to welcome me;
Devise a covert trick for me to reach you –
I have a plan for victory I'll teach you,
But keep this secret till I come; I'll tear
The veil of secrecy once I am there."

The faithful messenger then sped away
More quickly than a hawk pursuing prey.

Meanwhile sweet silver-breasted, rose-like Vis,
Waited in Marv, in luxury and peace;
In the same castle, all the endless hoard
Of royal wealth and valuables was stored,
And their appointed treasurer and guard
Was King Mobad's vizier, his brother, Zard,
Who was the Korah[189] of his age and had
More riches to his name than King Mobad;
He also guarded Vis, and his commands
Were absolute throughout his brother's lands.

The messenger dispatched by Prince Ramin
Slipped slyly through the city gate unseen.
Wearing a woman's veil, he made his way
Upon a mule to where Vis gave, each day,
A banquet for the noble women who
She counted as her friends and retinue;
And by this pretty trick the messenger,
All unbeknownst to Zard, returned to her.
Who could describe the joy with which she greeted
Her envoy when Ramin's words were repeated?
As though bright pearls and sugared sweets cajoled her
With every word her clever envoy told her,
As though she were a beggar who had found
A wandering treasure deep within the ground,[190]
Or she was like a person, you'd have said,
Brought back to life again, who had been dead.
Immediately she sent to Zard to say,
"I had a dream before the break of day:
I dreamed Viru felt sickly and fainthearted,
But that his malady has now departed.

Today, to celebrate his health's return,
I'll go to where our fiery altars burn
And make an offering to the sanctuary
In gratitude for what God's done for me."
And Zard said, "This is just and right; may you
Act always as religion prompts you to."

Then, with her women courtiers, Vis went straight
To Jamshid's shrine,[191] beyond the city gate;
What quantities of fat sheep's blood were shed,
How many of God's indigent were fed,
What clothes, what jewels, what gold and silver, Vis
Distributed as if she'd never cease;
Night's shadows spread, and nothing could be seen,
As Vis's envoy went to fetch Ramin.

A room was cleared, the lovers were alone
And Saturn bowed to Jupiter's great throne.
Now, of their tryst, the world heard not a word,
No wind sprang up, and not a blossom stirred.
When Fortune's with us, obstacles we fear
Can suddenly dissolve and disappear,
And so it was for Prince Ramin and Vis –
The fruit of trouble's tree was joy and peace.

The noblewomen all departed then
And Prince Ramin's force joined with Vis's men.
The Prince's forty warriors had ridden
As Prince Ramin had, with their faces hidden
By women's veils, and in this covert state
Rode undetected through the city gate.
Torchbearers went ahead and cleared the way,
And servants kept the populace at bay,
And by this trick the veiled Ramin was brought
Into the castle and to Vis's court.

The castle gate was barred, and guards called out
Upon the rooftop shout for answering shout;
For all their watchfulness they did not see
That Vis's rooms now held their enemy.
Night came, as dark as faithlessness; you'd say
That pitch and smoke obscured the shining day;
Dark as the ocean depths, the depths of night
Shone like the ocean depths with jewels of light,
And from the east night's forces rose, as when
Sekandar[192] came back from the dark again.
The warriors swarmed out from their hiding place,
And with drawn swords like myrtle leaves gave chase
To any of the castle's men they found,
And cut them down and left them on the ground;
Now like a fire they raged, eager for slaughter,
And like a raging fire they gave no quarter.
And like a leopard Prince Ramin now crept
Into the chamber where his brother slept.

Ramin kills Zard in combat

Zard bounded from his bed (in combat he
Was like a lion for ferocity)
And snatched his falchion up, as truculent
And angry as a maddened elephant,
But Death had come for him, fell Death whose hand
No soul can free itself from or withstand.
Ramin cried, "Listen, throw your sword down, hear me,
No harm will come to you, you needn't fear me,
I'm Prince Ramin, your younger brother, I
Have no desire to see you fight and die.
Throw down your sword, submit, better a chain
Bind both your wrists than that you end up slain."
But when Zard heard his voice, black rage and spite
Made all the world for him as dark as night;

He cursed Ramin, and like a lion roared,
And aimed a blow with his uplifted sword
Against Ramin's head, which was unprotected;
But, in an instant, Prince Ramin deflected
The massive thrust, which sheared off half his shield,
And it was Zard whose life was forced to yield
As Prince Ramin's great blade came crashing down,
Splitting Zard's head wide open at the crown
And spattering his brains and rosy blood,
With one tremendous sword stroke, in the mud.

When Zard's good fortune failed him and he fell
The castle sentries' fortunes failed as well.
The dead were thrown from rooftops, and the way
Around the walls was blocked where corpses lay;
Some, fleeing death, leaped from the roofs and found
What they had fled from as they reached the ground;
Some, too, of those who fought at Vis's side
Gave up their valiant souls for her and died.
The enemy was vanquished, and their night
For Prince Ramin was like the morning's light,
And when three watches of the night were done
All of Zard's power and sovereignty had gone.
This darkness brought Ramin his heart's desire,
And jewels and treasure, all he might require,
But in the midst of its tumultuous fray
It also took his brother's life away;
Such is the world – the sweetness handed us
Obscures another gift that's poisonous;
Its flowers have thorns, its sweet caresses sadness,
Its profits losses, and its passions madness.
And when Ramin perceived Zard lying there
He ripped his shirt to rags in his despair
And cried out, "Ah, my brother, dear to me
As sight is and my soul's eternity,

May both my hands be cut off, may a spear
Impale me through the gut and kill me here,
Why did I slay you, brother, and so break
My own back for my angry passion's sake?
I can find countless treasures, but I'll never
Come on my brother Zard again forever."
And when Ramin had wept a while and thought
Of all the pointless grief repentance brought,
He saw that this was not a time for shame
Or grieving, but for war and martial fame.

When Zard, the shepherd of his flock, had died
Wolves quickly closed on them from every side,
Swords plunged into their skulls, as though swords said
A sermon as they severed every head,
Proclaiming that Ramin was king, and then
The heavens blessed this prayer with their "Amen."[193]
For Prince Ramin no night could rank above
This night, as dear to him as Vis's love,
Since it had cleared his enemies away
And scattered darkness with the break of day.
And with the dawn Good Fortune's light made plain
That King Ramin had now begun his reign;
Ramin rejoiced, sat side by side with Vis,
Together, and in public, and at peace.

RAMIN STEALS MOBAD'S WEALTH
AND FLEES TO DAYLAMAN

Each camel, every mule, in Marv was brought
At his command now to the royal court,
And all the wealth the treasuries contained
Was loaded on them; not a thread remained.
He paused two days in Marv, no more, and then
With Vis, and his new wealth, set off again.

Vis in her golden litter's draperies
Shone like the moon among the Pleiades;
Ten thousand mules and camels bore more gold
And jewels and luxuries than could be told.
Now day and night the caravan made haste
To make its way across the desert waste –
Within a week they passed the stages for
A journey that should last two weeks or more,
And in two weeks, before a soul could find them,
The desert they were crossing was behind them.
Before the king heard tell of all Ramin
Had done to him, Ramin was in Qazvin
And pushing on to Daylaman; his fame
Had made a fluttering banner of his name.

This Daylaman is hard, forbidding ground;
Here armies from Daylam and Gil abound,
Their warriors' war cries echo through the night,
Their arrows, and the spears with which they fight,
Can strike through armor, and their champions throw
Javelins as far as others' arrows go.
They fight like demons, and the world abhors them,
It hates them and it fears them, and ignores them.
They have huge shields, like walls, that they display
Colored and stained in every kind of way,
And since they covet fame they persevere
In constant civil wars, year after year.
From Adam's time, unnumbered kings have tried
To conquer them, and to subdue their pride,
And still no monarch's ever made them pay
The tribute of the vanquished, till today;
Their maiden borders are unbroken still,
No king has bent this virgin to his will.[194]

Urged onward by the promptings of his fate
Ramin arrived in Daylaman in state,
And spread an ox hide on a patch of ground;
Then, on the opened hide, he made a mound
Of fifty purses filled with coins, and poured
A golden goblet's gold and silver hoard
Of glittering coins upon the little hill,
Showing he had both riches and the will
To follow through now with his royal mission;
He did not lack for wealth or for ambition.
And with this shower of wealth the springtime came,
A sudden blossoming of Fate and Fame;
Men flocked to him, more numerous than wishes,
Than sands, or leaves, or water drops, or fishes.

    The world came running (not, if truth be told,
For Prince Ramin so much as for his gold).
Noble recruits assembled there to aid him
And to a man they all of them obeyed him,
Men like Keshmir, Azin and Sam, Viru,
And like Bahram, Raham, and great Gilu;
Now other kings from other countries sent
Armies to show him their encouragement,
And in a month so many joined him there
It seemed that soldiers jostled everywhere;
The general of these forces was Viru,
Ramin's vizier and champion was Gilu.

MOBAD LEARNS THAT RAMIN HAS TAKEN HIS WEALTH AND VIS

When King Mobad's nobility first heard
The news of everything that had occurred
They didn't tell him, since Mobad by nature
Was an impulsive and ill-tempered creature
(This is the worst of frailties for a king).
For three days no one dared say anything;

During this time Ramin's affairs went on,
And flourished like new blossoms in the sun.

And when at last he learned of this you'd say
That for Mobad the news was Judgment Day;
As Fortune turned on him, his reason fled,
Whether he looked behind now or ahead
All roads seemed sealed to him, and he had no
Idea of what to do or where to go.
At times he said, "I'll go to Khorasan,
Damn Vis, and damn Ramin, and damn Gorgan."
At times he said, "If I retreat, it's clear
The world's contempt is all I'll ever hear;
They'll say I feared Ramin's success, they'll say
I went to Khorasan to run away."
At times he said, "And if I fight this war,
Will my good angel help me? I'm not sure;
My own men hate me, if they had the choice
I've no doubt that Ramin would have their voice;
He'd be their king, he's young and fortunate,
His tree of glory's in a splendid state,
He's valiant and strong, and furthermore
He's taken all my wealth now, and I'm poor.
That wealth was useless then, I hoarded it
And he's the one who'll reap the benefit.
My mother got me in this mess, it's she
Who tried to reconcile Ramin and me;
It's my fault if Good Fortune is denied me,
I let a woman's foolish chatter guide me."

A week passed, and the king stayed out of sight,
Unsure if he should run away or fight,
And in this time he crossed two hundred seas
Of thoughts and fears and possibilities,

Till finally he said, "I can't go back;
Willing or not, my plan is to attack."
Ashamed to flee, he left Gorgan and went
West to Amol,[195] and pitched his royal tent,
And there his camp made all the world abound
With colors, as though flowers obscured the ground;
The tents were like bright hills, the hills were bright
With flower-like spots of beauty and delight.

KING MOBAD IS KILLED BY A WILD BOAR

How well we think we know the world, although
Its ligatures are things we never know.
How well they're hidden, and how strong the Fate
That keeps the world's transactions in this state!
The world is sleep, we're dreams, and why should we
Imagine this is where we'll always be?
The world's conditions alter, and renew,
And won't stay always as we wish them to.
        When love appears, the world can't tell apart
Goodness and evil in the human heart,
And it won't stay the friend of any lover
Until his love's accomplished and is over;
To trust the devious world with love's to tell
A blind man to become your sentinel.
Its various meretricious trinkets hide
The truth, which stays unseeable inside,
It's like a conjuring trick, and what we see
Is not in fact how things turn out to be.
It's like a caravanserai, which men
Pass through, never to pass that way again;
A moment's all that anyone can stay,
No longer; then he too is on his way.
It's like an archer who, year after year,
Shoots endless arrow shafts that disappear

Into the dark; he has no notion where,
Or how, they strike, or drop down from the air.
Or you would say it's like a crone whose face
Has somehow kept its youth's bewitching grace,
Who every moment thrusts into the grave
Another husband who's become her slave.
We struggle for its wealth, with so much pain,
Till neither we nor any wealth remain;
We see an army, and we see a king,
Time passes by, and we see no such thing.
　　　And in our day our generation thrives,
The group of men with whom we share our lives,
And this day passes by, it goes, and then
Another comes, and with it other men.
This is so strange to me now, and I find
It breeds black melancholy in my mind;
I don't know what time passing is, or what
Its tricks on us betoken in its plot –
That such a king as King Mobad, whose reign
Had brought the world such pleasure and such pain,
Should end his days so wretchedly! Alas
That all that he had hoped would come to pass
Should stay as figures in his heart and eyes,
Which he perceived, but could not realize!

He pitched camp in Amol, and spent the night
In drinking wine, in pleasure and delight,
Giving his nobles robes, handing the poor
Money and weapons for the coming war:
Wine gave Mobad the happiness he sought,
Now see the hangover that morning brought.
The king was seated with his nobles when
A cry came from the tents that housed their men;
It happened that the camp was pitched beside
A place where various streambeds coincide,

And here a boar appeared, an animal
As violent and as uncontrollable
As is a maddened elephant; the boar
Was in the midst of men, behind, before,
All yelling at it, as it ran and found
The entrance to the royal camping ground.
The king came from his tent now to confront it,
And mounted his quick polo horse to hunt it;
The javelin that he held within his grasp
Had pitch black feathers fixed upon its hasp,
And it had shown a myriad foes the way
To death's black door, before that fateful day.
Now, like a raging lion, King Mobad
Hurled the black lance with all the strength he had;
It missed its mark, and with tumultuous force
The boar attacked the legs of Mobad's horse,
And got its tusks beneath the gut, and gored
The horse's belly as it reared and roared;
Rider and horse together now, pell-mell,
As though the moon and sky had fallen, fell.
The struggling king could not escape before
He was impaled there by the charging boar
Whose thrusting tusks now tore his flesh apart
Up from his navel to his beating heart,
Ripping the place where hate and love are housed;
The lamp of love, the blaze of hate, were doused.
The king of kings was dead, and darkness fell
Upon the noblemen who'd wished him well:
How easily this king, who had enjoyed
Such homage and such glory, was destroyed!

O world, I will not hear your voice repeat
Its everlasting message of deceit.
And since I've witnessed everything you do
To other men, I'll turn aside from you;

I've scoured my heart now of the scraps of trust
And love I felt for you, like so much rust.
It seems as though you hate us, it's as though
Contempt for us is all that you can show.
What have we done to you to make you grieve?
We eat two rounds of bread, and then we leave!
  Has any evil skinflint ever been
As miserly as you are or as mean?
You take back what you give; you let us stay
Two days with you, then snatch our lives away;
It wasn't us who said, "Please entertain us,
Then turn your heart against us and disdain us!"
What do you want from us, what recompense,
That you should shed the blood of innocents?
If you're a jewel, why does your splendor shine
Nowhere but in the darkness of a mine?
Why in your millstone-turning do you blend
Earth's winds and dust and waters without end?
You've thrown me in a pit, why should I care
How proudly you enjoy the upper air?
Oh, I could look on you eternally
And you would be what you will always be –
This sky, this water, and this earth, these seas,
These forests, and these mountain fastnesses,
And always, everywhere, each living creature
Enduring your abominable nature.
No man who knows your flaws and faults denies
You're anything but fraudulence and lies.
I do not know the world, O God, it's you
I know and need for all I'll say and do.
The world's not worth our knowing, and its name
Should be unspoken and a source of shame.

Now when he heard that King Mobad had been
Brought down by his declining star, Ramin
Gave orders to his followers that they,
For seven days, should mourn for him, and pray.
In secret he thanked God for how He had
Brought to an end the life of King Mobad;
There'd been no battle when his blood was spilt,
And such a death absolved Ramin of guilt.
A thousand times he bowed in prayer and said,
"O God, who sends down blessings on my head,
Who opens doors to men, and who contrives
The hidden ways and workings of our lives,
Who drives men from the world, and who has given
To others thrones as high as Saturn's heaven,
I swear to you, O God, that I will strive
To please You for as long as I'm alive;
I shall be just in my authority,
In deeds and words a man of honesty,
I shall be generous in my reign and give
The indigent the wherewithal to live.
Help me, great God, since only You are fit
To guide me to what's right and requisite,
Be my companion, my support, defend me
From any evil enemies intend me.
You are my lord, I am Your slave, You gave
This sovereignty to your devoted slave:
You are my lord, I am Your slave, and I
Shall be your messenger until I die.
You've made me regent of the world, oh spread
The shadow of Your grace above my head!"

These were his prayers, and in this humble fashion
He asked for God's protection and compassion,

Then gave the orders that his men prepare
To leave the campsite they'd constructed there;
And to the din of drums and trumpets they
Stirred like the Oxus, and got underway,
And as a cloud, when April's winds have started,
Scuds through the sky, the column now departed.
From Daylaman then to Amol, you'd say
The frenzied clamor was like Judgment Day;
What signs of victory and joy were seen
By lovely Vis and radiant Ramin,
As on Ram's day,[196] still glorying and glad,
They reached the camping ground of King Mobad.

Nobles and courtiers rushed to gather round
And scatter jewels on him as he was crowned;
They hailed him as the king of kings, and gazed
In wonder at him, awestruck and amazed –
His hand was like a cloud that seeks to rain
Not rain but pearls upon the parched terrain.
He rested in Amol a week, to dine
And down continuous goblets of red wine;
And then to young Raham (whose deeds and name
Already brought him an unrivalled fame,
Whose ancient lineage was from Kian)[197]
He gave the province of Tabaristan,[198]
Then to Behruz he gave the town of Rey[199]
(Behruz who'd helped him on that fateful day
When he had fled with Vis from King Mobad;
He'd put at their disposal all he had,
Hiding them in his house, and he deserved
To be rewarded by the man he'd served).
Cast goodness on the waters, and the ocean
Will bring you pearls to honor your devotion.
He gave Gorgan then to Azin, who'd been
Unwavering in his friendship for Ramin.

The general at his court was Prince Viru,
The master of his household was Shiru,
Two elephants, two lions like no others,
Both champions were Vis's noble brothers.

When all the towns had kings, and all the borders
Lords of the marches faithful to his orders,
Ramin set off for Marv, his shining face
The cure for all its horror and disgrace.
All Khorasan was filled with decorations,
With stands where beauties watched the celebrations;
The roads became like gardens you'd have said,
And every hand poured jewels upon his head –
Men hailed him as their king and swore they'd be
His faithful subjects for eternity.
As King Ramin went into Marv, his sight
Was dazzled by a heaven of delight,
As beautiful as blossoms in the spring,
As happy as the fortunes of its king.
A thousand voices sang, the women's clothes
Glistened like blossoms or an opening rose,
A cloud of musky fragrance filled the air
And gold and silver coins fell everywhere;
For three months golden coins and jewels rained down
And celebrations filled the happy town.

All Khorasan joined Marv in welcoming
The advent of Ramin as their new king.
For years the country's subjects had endured
Mobad's reign, now deliverance was assured;
And in their freedom from his unjust ways[200]
They showered Ramin with gratitude and praise
As though they had escaped hell's misery
To sit in heaven under Tuba's tree.[201]

(The evil come to evil ends, their name
Eternally evokes eternal shame,
And let this be a warning; if you do
Evil, evil will surely come to you.
As Khosrow[202] said so justly and so well,
"God made the evil from the stuff of hell,
And in the end they will rejoin the same
Substance and origin from which they came.")
Ramin ruled justly, and he strove to keep
The world more peaceful than a man asleep,
And everywhere his conquering generals went
They spread the glories of his government.
Failure dogged all his foes, his sovereignty
Prevailed from China now to Barbary,
Each province had its king, each borderland
A war lord under King Ramin's command.
They built a thousand villages, remade
Old buildings that were ruined and decayed,
And built new caravanserais beside
Well-traveled roads, each with its guard and guide.
Criminals died on gibbets, or they spent
Long years in prison as their punishment,
The world was rid of footpads and marauders,
Of Kurds and Lurs,[203] and raiders across borders.

     Ramin made gifts of such a quantity
Of gold and silver coins that penury
Was turned to wealth, and avarice's name
Now vanished from the world, for very shame.
Injustice was forgotten, and the poor
Became more strong and stalwart than before;
Wolves did not hunt for sheep, and sheep no longer
Acted as prey because the wolves were stronger.
Each week Ramin advised his followers,
Promoted and reproved his ministers,

Advanced the upright, and eradicated
Those who were villainous or dissipated.
In all his audiences he took great care
To judge impartially and to be fair –
Whether a monarch or an old crone came
The justice they received was just the same.
Religious men who visited were treated
With courtesies with which great kings are greeted,
And cultured men were welcomed with delight –
They were as precious to him as his sight,
And Persians followed learning, since he loved
To hear points argued and see matters proved.

Ramin lived for a hundred years, plus ten,
And, of these years, this paragon of men
Spent eighty-three as king, in luxury
And wealth, with absolute authority.
The age grew fruitful during his long reign,
His glory vivified the world again.
Three things were lacking while he ruled – these three
Were pain, and sorrow, and anxiety.
He fed his mind on wisdom and on truth,
His body's pleasures gave him back his youth;
He toured Tabaristan and Khorasan
Or hunted in the hills of Kuhestan,
Or to his royal progresses he'd add
The plains of Khuzestan, and then Baghdad.
He built a thousand waterways, and so
Allowed a myriad villages to grow;
Ahvaz is one such town (and its old name
Of "Ram's Town" still perpetuates his fame,
Since, in official records, this is how
The town is designated, even now).
Ramin's name suited him, because "Ram" meant,
In that time's language, what he was: "Content."[204]

No king was ever like him, no musician
Has ever shared his skill in composition,
And who has ever made a harp as fine
As those made following Ramin's design?
(And they're still called "Ram's harps," in honor of
The man who made them with such skill and love.)

Kingship was his, according to his wish,
He ruled now from the moon's sphere to the fish,[205]
But handed all his kingship to his queen
Who governed both the world now and Ramin.
He had two sons by her; the world could see
Her beauty in them, and his bravery;
Its hopes lay in their glory. Prince Jamshid
Was one's name, and the other's Prince Khorshid.
He gave Khorshid his eastern lands, and blessed
His brother with the countries of the west;
To one he gave Khorazm, Soghd, and Choghan,
One received Egypt, Syria, Qayravan.
Vis ruled the world, but certain countries were
A special appanage reserved for her,
So that Azerbaijan, and Arran's lands,
And Arman, were entirely in her hands.

Contentment came to Vis and her Ramin;
For many years they ruled as king and queen,
And lived so long that they survived to see
Their children's children reach maturity.

THE DEATH OF VIS

When eighty-one long, happy years had passed
The cypress tree declined her head at last,
And Vis's lovely body bent as though
Its slender straightness had become a bow.

The world is a sufficient foe for those
Who have, in all the world, no other foes;
As Nushravan[206] said when old age's dart
Had lodged itself within his failing heart,
"Now that I'm old, the world has done to me
Things unperformed by any enemy;
I leant against the world, it broke my back,
Now it destroys me with its last attack."
The world was sweet to Vis, its love repaid her,
But, as it turned, its treachery betrayed her;
The world revolved, new weaknesses assailed her,
The seven members of her body failed her.[207]
Death stepped out from his ambush; all too soon
He snatched away that lovely waning moon.

Ramin's heart was a mine of grief, his eyes
Were weeping sources where new rivers rise.
"Sweet love," he cried out in his misery,
"Soul of my flesh, dear as my soul to me,
The brand of loneliness has seared my heart,
You've urged the horse of parting to depart;
In all the world I've witnessed no one who
Has kept faith with her lover here like you –
What made you tire of me? Did you not say,
Did you not swear, you'd never go away?
Why did you break your promise then, and tether
Fidelity and treachery together?[208]
No, you were faithful, it is Time who's made me
Suffer like this, whose cruelty has betrayed me;
What wonder that Time's hurt you? Tell me, who
In all the world has Time been faithful to?
And now you've gone from here, the world's bereft
Of faithfulness – there isn't any left.
Old age supplied me with sufficient pains
But you have bound me in a captive's chains.

Why should you now augment my agony
And let disaster find its way to me?
My eyelashes once cleansed the dust that lay
Upon your feet and swept it all away,
And now, dear helpless love, you lie asleep
Beneath the dust, and I must wail and weep.
Your sweet voice used to say, 'Ramin, allow
My flesh to be the dust you walk on now.'
And now I see that day's come, when I must
See your sweet silver body turn to dust.
How splendid wealth and kingship were to me
When you and I could share our sovereignty!
The world's a sickness for me now; Ramin
Can seek no pleasures here without his queen.
        Should I now tear my clothes, and should I heap
Dust on my hapless head now as I weep?
You know such actions, such wild grief and rage,
Do not become men when they've reached old age;
My eyes weep jewels of grief, my heavy heart
Is stricken to have seen its love depart,
Long may they suffer! But I must refrain
From visiting my hands and voice with pain;
It's right my heart and eyes should grieve, but I
Won't rend my clothes, or shriek and scream and cry –
Patience becomes old men, especially
When lovers have to part. But if you see
My silent tongue is patient, you should know
My heart's impatience cannot cease to grow.
My heart's grief seethes, but I am old and weak,
And silence holds my tongue: I will not speak."

He had a tomb erected for his queen,
Within the temple precincts at Borzin;[209]
It touched the stars, and it was worthy of
The splendor of a princess, and his love,

Studded with jewels, as though men might be given
An image in its loveliness of heaven;
And both the temple and the tomb would make
Rezvan feel envious for their beauty's sake.[210]
And now the tomb's erected, you will see
How he made ready for eternity.

RAMIN GIVES HIS SOVEREIGNTY TO HIS SON AND
BECOMES A RECLUSE AT THE FIRE TEMPLE
UNTIL THE DAY OF HIS DEATH

On New Year's Day,[211] when all the world is bright
With springtime's triumph over winter's night,
He called to him his splendid son Khorshid,
Who was a princely man in word and deed,
And set him on the throne, and hailed him then
As king of every country and all men,
Placing the royal crown upon his head.
"Resplendent monarch of all lands," he said,
"Now may this crown and throne be fortunate
And win you glory in your royal state.
God made me ruler of the world, I hand
To you this kingship over every land;
I've taught you all the royal skills you need
(And I've rejoiced to teach you them, Khorshid),
And given you this crown now, since I see
That you're deserving of such sovereignty.
More than a hundred years I've lived, my son,
The world's gone by for me, my deeds are done;
For eighty-three years now my friends have been
Made happy, and my foes sad, by Ramin;
And now it's right that you should reign, since you
Are young still, and your government is new.
You've witnessed how I ruled this land; maintain
The usages I ruled by in your reign,

And when the world and men are judged, you'll see
I'll ask of you the things God asks of me.
Desire is sweet, but sweeter is the name
A good man leaves behind him as his fame.
Act well, my son, and when you come to die
You'll be content to bid the world goodbye."

When he had given King Khorshid the throne
Ramin forgot the glory he had known;
He left this world's throne then, and went to where
The other world's throne rose into the air,
And in the hallowed temple he became
A poor recluse, beside the sacred flame.
He gave his heart to God, and he was given
Another sovereignty, derived from heaven.
He'd been a great man, but he'd been a slave
To all his heart might hanker for and crave,
And while he ruled the world Desire had been
The ruler of the heart of King Ramin.
But now he left the world, his heart was freed
From sorrow, and his flesh from lust and greed,
And this new freedom from the world's lusts meant
He had escaped eternal punishment.
For three years, while he watched and prayed, Ramin
Hid from the world's eyes and was never seen;
He sat by Vis's tomb, and there he kept
His daily, nightly, vigil while he wept,
Or bowed to God, beseeching Him that He
Forgive him for his sins' enormity.
He didn't cease to weep and pray, despite
His frailty, for three years, by day and night,
Asking forgiveness, filled with penitence
For all his sins and worldly insolence,
And you would say that smoke rose from the flame
Of all his sorrow, and remorse, and shame.

His body was a saffron thread, his tears
Of grief fell every night for three long years;
And when his strength was gone, one sunrise, he
Was called by God to His eternity.
His foes had sorely hurt him, but Ramin
Rendered to God a soul washed pure and clean.

His son, the sun of kings,[212] Khorshid, now brought
A crowd of noble mourners from the court,
Who laid the royal body of Ramin
By that of Vis, his lover and his queen.
Their souls were reunited, side by side,
In heaven, where Vis was once again his bride.
So Vis departed, and Ramin; and so
We, every one of us, will one day go.

The world has laid its ambush, night and day,
It's like a cheetah, we're the cheetah's prey;
We're like wild deer, we wander without fear,
Imagining it doesn't know we're here –
We say, "How wise we are! Who could trick us?"
What "Wisdom" could be more ridiculous?
Where we've arrived here from we never know,
And we have no idea where we will go.
We live in two worlds, one flies quickly past,
The other one's the one we know will last,
But it's the passing world we've always sought
(We hardly give the other one a thought).
We see this world, we know that we must leave it,
And steadfastly refuse still to believe it;
How foolish, how bewildered we must be,
To choose this world, and not eternity –
We hope for an eternity spent here,
A place from which we have to disappear!
Why do we curse the world, when all man's nature
Shows he's a foolish and befuddled creature?

The world's a chain, we love it, and we never
Turn from this chain to God, who lives forever,
Our God who made two worlds for us, the one
Eternal, and the one so quickly gone.
Happy the man who chooses Him, who lives
According to the orders that He gives,
Happy the man who makes a noble end,
Whose fame survives, who has God as his friend.

We hear of those who've long since passed away
As others will hear tell of us one day;
We hear of stories from the days of old
And we'll become the stories men are told,
We'll be a tale one day, as we have seen
This tale unfold, of Vis and her Ramin.
I've told a story that's as sweet and fine
As springtime, and as lovely in each line.
My handsome friend, so wise and elegant,
Whose nature's pure, whose voice is eloquent,
Recite my story now; you'll see it bless
Your listening friends with smiles and happiness,
And studious men of letters will proclaim it
Sweeter than springtime orchards when they name it.
Recite my verses, I want you to see
Their value, all their strength and fluency.
And as you read my poetry I ask
That you now undertake another task:
Seek pardon for my sins. Say, "God of glory,
Forgive the youth who wrote this pretty story;
You who acknowledge all your slaves' repentance
Don't make him suffer for each word and sentence!"
And may God's noble blessings light upon
The Prophet and his household, one by one.

To Vis

I came to you, how many years ago,
And felt the stirrings of
A puzzled sympathy I could not know
Would turn, in time, to love;
Love that took on the idiom you taught
The foreign heart you'd caught.

And how insistently you chivied me ...
"When will you get to work?"
"A little time, Vis, give me time, you'll see".
"Dick, all you do is shirk
Your promises ... Why did you make them then?
You're weak, like other men!"

And so I sat, before day dawned, each day
And parsed your words, and turned
To English rhymes the words you'd have me say.
And page by page I learned
The life I gave was yours alone to give,
And yours the life I live.

DD

NOTES

1   Korah is the Qarun of the Qur'an; a contemporary of
Musa (Moses), known for his fabulous wealth. Kasra is
Anushirvan the Just, a Sasanian monarch (531–579 CE)
famous for his justice and also his wealth. Many medieval
Persian poets bracket together figures from Islamic lore
and pre-Islamic Persian history in this way.

2   The poem opens with a celebration of the return of
spring – when the Persian New Year falls – at a king's
court. This became a traditional way to begin romances,
and other kinds of narrative poem, in both medieval
Persia and medieval Europe.

3   Violets and jasmine signify beautiful hair and breasts
respectively. There are a number of conventional
comparisons for the body in medieval Persian poetry,
almost all based on features of the natural world or
precious stones and metals; a list of these is given in the
appendix on page 517.

4   Khuzan is Khuzestan, in southwestern Iran.

5   The onager is the wild ass of Iran and central Asia.
Onagers were a favorite prey for hunters in pre-modern
Iran. Herds of them still roam parts of their ancestral area.

6   Gorgani excuses his lovers in much the same way that Chaucer does in his *Troilus and Criseyde*. Despite many obvious differences, *Troilus and Criseyde* is the closest English poem in its sensibility and details to the world of *Vis and Ramin*.

7   Rezvan is the angel who guards the Islamic paradise; in Persian poetry much is made of his being in charge of paradise's beautiful houris who welcome the souls of the faithful.

8   Sorush is a Zoroastrian, pre-Islamic angel, whose name continued to be used in poems written in the Islamic period. He is known for his splendor and as the bringer of good fortune.

9   Zard's clothes are mainly Parthian (especially the breeches and boots), but the turban is probably an anachronistic Islamic element. A long cloth was sometimes wound around the Parthian cap, and it may be that Gorgani is referring to this, but it seems more likely that he is envisaging an Islamic turban. Later in the poem Ramin's turban is also mentioned.

10   Milk and wine are often coupled together in the poem, sometimes as separate contrasted or complementary entities, sometimes as two entities mixed together. When separate, they either represent two lovers (as here with Vis and Viru, or later in the poem Vis and Ramin) or they function as one of a number of images that place red and white side by side in descriptions of a body's beauty. Often a drink made from a mixture of wine and milk is referred to, and the drink represents the union of two lovers. This drink also existed in medieval and renaissance Europe; it was called a "posset." The great seventeenth-century English diarist Samuel Pepys was especially fond of it and often mentions it.

11   Ahriman is the evil principle of the universe in Zoroastrianism. The devil.

12 Minorsky suggests that the name Manikan implies a
    claimed descent from Manizheh, a central Asian princess
    who figures in a romance in the major Persian epic the
    Shahnameh, written by Ferdowsi some forty to seventy
    years before Gorgani's poem.

13 Damavand, an extinct volcano in northern Iran and the
    highest peak in the country. It has numerous mythological
    associations. In the main, Gorgani uses it simply to signify
    a huge mass of something.

14 Nahavand is the plain near Hamedan. It was the site of a
    major defeat of the last pre-Islamic dynasty of Persia, the
    Sasanians, by the Arabs in 642 CE.

15 Daylaman, also called Daylam, is a mountainous
    and wooded area to the south of the Caspian Sea,
    famous for its remoteness and the independent spirit
    of its inhabitants.

16 See note 8.

17 A magical bird from Persian mythology, the Simorgh
    appears in a number of medieval narrative poems, most
    notably Ferdowsi's *Shahnameh*, and Attar's *Manteq al Tayr*.
    As here, one of its appearances in the *Shahnameh* is on a
    chieftain's banner.

18 See note 11.

19 Tokharistan is a remote mountainous region east of Balkh,
    in what is now northern Afghanistan.

20 Elements of this long and involved astrological
    description were much imitated by later Persian poets,
    especially Nezami.

21 See note 7.

22 Eblis is an Islamic name for the devil, probably derived
    from the Greek word *diabolos*.

23 A traditional saying, meaning to attempt the impossible.

24 See note 7.

25 A parasang was the distance that could be traveled by a
    laden pack animal in an hour, and so varying in length

with the nature of the terrain. It is usually taken as meaning around three miles.

26 Farkhar is a Buddhist temple in Tibet.

27 This is one of a number of references in the poem that imply that as well as being Mobad's younger brother, Ramin was also his son, which would be just possible according to Parthian marriage practices. It may be that the appearance of these moments is a survival from an earlier version of the poem in which Ramin was unequivocally both brother and son to Mobad; or it may be that "father" is being used by Gorgani merely to mean "protector"; or it may be both. The fact that Tristan is the nephew of King Mark is perhaps a garbled echo of this brother/son moment, in that someone who is referred to as a son and a sibling in the Persian story has become a sibling's son in the Western tale.

28 Khorrad and Borzin are famous Zoroastrian fire temples.

29 The Persian word for chivalry is "Javanmardi," which literally means "young-manliness." This code is apparent in the earliest Persian poetry and seems to pre-date the appearance of chivalry as a major preoccupation of medieval European poetry. This makes it very ironic that the concept of "chivalry" came to be regarded, in the West at least, as a wholly European phenomenon.

30 A pun on Ramin's name; one of the many meanings of "Ram" is "tame."

31 A legendary pre-Islamic Persian monarch, Jamshid brought the arts of civilization to mankind.

32 A legendary pre-Islamic Persian monarch, Khosrow is famous for his integrity, sagacity, and statecraft.

33 Hushang is a legendary pre-Islamic Persian monarch.

34 See note 5.

35 Large talismans against the evil eye, and placed prominently on a roof to protect the building, are also recorded from ancient Greek culture.

36 Noshad is a legendary pre-Islamic palace with gardens famous for their beauty.

37 See note 10.

38 Gems are referred to as "faithful" because they don't change color and are virtually indestructible.

39 Khosrow and Shirin were a pair of Sasanian lovers; if *Vis and Ramin* is indeed a Parthian tale, and all the evidence indicates that it is, this is an anachronism, as Khosrow and Shirin would have lived long after Vis and Ramin. This is not the same Khosrow who is referred to in note 32, but the historical king Khosrow Parviz (died 628 CE).

40 "Ram" was the twenty-first day of each month of the Zoroastrian calendar and was regarded as auspicious.

41 It's clear from the poem that Gorgani is using "Kuhestan" to mean the area round Mahabad (modern Hamedan, the ancient Ecbatana), although it was more usually applied to an area further east. The word means "mountainous area".

42 See note 7.

43 A convention that also appears in other Persian medieval romances; the lovers first meet by the young man entering his beloved's home via the roof.

44 See note 7.

45 The metaphor is from polo, as are all the metaphors in the poem that involve a ball. Polo was extremely popular at the medieval Persian courts.

46 The metaphors' meaning may not be immediately obvious; the "ermine cap" is the snow on the mountain's summit, the "Byzantine brocade" is the wild flowers of spring (which are spectacular throughout much of Iran, particularly on the mountain slopes).

47 On the Caspian Sea.

48 Armenia.

49 A proverb, meaning that a bad guide will lead you to a bad place.

50 Vis intends a double meaning here, and a double insult. She means "When you are as powerful as God," but also "When you are no longer impotent."

51 This combines three occupations traditionally associated with Jews in medieval Iran: moneylending (for the same reason as in Europe, usury was forbidden to the dominant religious group), the production of wine (forbidden to Moslems, and undertaken by members of the religious minorities), and music making. The last is well attested and survived into twentieth-century Iran.

52 To a Western reader brought up within the Christian tradition this will recall Matthew VII, 6. The reading is present in only one manuscript and it depends on a single letter. The other manuscripts read, "Was casting pearls (i.e., weeping) on the earth." The parallel with Matthew makes more sense in the context of what is happening in the poem at this point. The phrase, presumably in Matthew as well as in Persian, comes from the practice of casting precious items in the pathway of a king; this was seen as an entirely appropriate and even useful thing to do (as it might lead to a reward); whereas casting precious items in the pathway of a pig is clearly pointless.

53 Bilqis is the Islamic name for the queen of Sheba, who was King Solomon's lover.

54 The "uplifted mammoth foot" is his anger, not Vis.

55 The bearer of good news was traditionally given a gift.

56 The real sun and Vis.

57 The moon escaping from a dragon is a conventional metaphor for an eclipse.

58 This was an actual Zoroastrian oath: "I swear by my hatred of heresy that…"

59 Flowers and coral refer to their cheeks and lips.

60 Having a wine cup in one hand and the beloved's hair in the other is a conventional topos in Persian erotic poetry.

Rumi gives it a mystical meaning in one of his most famous ghazals.

61 See note 22.

62 The equivalent of "Cutting off one's nose to spite one's face."

63 This seems to be a proverb, but if it is I have been unable to trace its meaning.

64 See note 11.

65 This depends on a play on words, since the phrase for "to take an oath" literally means "to drink sulphur," which seems to refer to a pre-Islamic trial of veracity.

66 The turban is probably an anachronism.

67 It seems possible that the magic love potion of the *Tristan* tale had its origin in this passage, or in similar places in the poem. Wine is strongly associated with the erotic in *Vis and Ramin*, and the nurse's magical skills (as in her fashioning the talisman) would provide a context for turning the drink into a magic one.

68 Wearing someone's earring denotes that one is that person's slave.

69 Mehregan is a Zoroastrian festival held at the autumn equinox.

70 Cheetahs were kept at the Persian medieval courts for hunting, as they were later at the Mughal courts in India.

71 In Tunisia.

72 Tears are often referred to as bloody or red, or compared to red things like wine or pomegranate seeds. Weeping blood is a Middle Eastern topos generally (it occurs in the New Testament of the Bible) and turns up in some Western medieval and Renaissance texts (e.g., Chaucer's *Troilus and Criseyde*, and Burton's *The Anatomy of Melancholy*).

73 I.e., in prayer.

74 Camphor is white.

75 See note 10.

76 The pomegranate flowers are her complexion, the hyacinths are her curls.

77 See note 22.

78 Vis and her nurse.

79 Bizhan is a young hero in the *Shahnameh* known for his impetuous bravery.

80 An example of Gorgani playing with conventional metaphors to produce a paradox. A golden bow seems much more valuable than a silver arrow; but the silver arrow is the straight white body of an elegant young person, whereas a golden bow is the bent sallow body of an old sick person. So it is the silver arrow that is preferable.

81 Dark blue (or black) was the color of mourning in ancient Iran.

82 See note 23.

83 Felt is made in water, and during the process grows waterlogged and extremely heavy.

84 This speech draws on two separate topoi common in medieval Islamic poetry. One is the "ubi sunt" topos (where are...), the other is the addressing of a place where someone absent, whom one loves or admires, once lived or stayed.

85 See note 8.

86 Saturn is the planet that denotes power and authority.

87 The world was thought to rest on the back of a huge fish. From fish to moon therefore means from bottom to top. The phrase (which is common in the medieval period) is a pun in Persian as the word for "fish" is "mahi" and that for "moon" is "mah."

88 The third one is the nurse.

89 Musk, her hair; silver, her body; pomegranate blossoms, her cheeks; pomegranate fruits, her breasts.

90   Hyacinths and musk, her hair; lilies and roses, the pink
      and white of her cheeks.

91   The name means "blond-haired." On the rare occasions
      in medieval Persian poetry that someone is mentioned as
      having blond hair this characteristic implies malevolence.

92   I.e., from bloody tears.

93   Arran is to the north of what is now Iranian Azerbaijan.

94   Leveled by the weight of the army passing over them.

95   A legendary archer of pre-Islamic Iran, Arash shot an
      arrow from Mount Damavand to the River Oxus, in order
      to establish Iran's northern border.

96   See note 11.

97   Both worlds – this world and the world to come
      after death.

98   We've been told a few lines back that she is already on the
      ground. Gorgani quite often makes small slips like this.

99   Camphor is white, cinnabar is red.

100   In this speech Shahru clearly thinks her daughter is dead.
      This topos, of lamenting as dead someone who is in fact
      still alive, is fairly common in the Hellenistic romances
      that are contemporary with the Parthian period, and
      thus in all probability with the origin of the story of *Vis
      and Ramin*.

101   There was a Zoroastrian belief that everyone had an
      angelic representative in heaven.

102   A remote and inhospitable area in northern Afghanistan.

103   A pleasure dome is a structure in a palace garden for
      picnics and the like. A rather fancy summer house.

104   This refers to wine drunk at the Festival of Mehregan.
      See note 69.

105   A people from the northern Caucasus region.

106   I.e., in comparison.

107   See note 25.

108 Clearly there are no bars on the windows that look into the inner courtyard.

109 "Harem pants" worn under a skirt.

110 Zahhak is a demon king who, in the *Shahnameh*, is chained forever beneath Mount Damavand as punishment for his evil rule over Iran.

111 The name Bimashi is not cited anywhere else. Minorsky suggests that it is the name of a demon.

112 "A moon above a cypress tree" is a conventional image meaning a beautiful face on an elegant body. To sever the moon from the cypress is to cut someone's head off.

113 This seems to be an Islamic angel, as green is an auspicious color in Islamic culture and Islamic angels are often said to be dressed in green.

114 Whether she is claiming this as part of the dream or as something real after she awoke from the dream is as ambiguous in the Persian as it is in the English. She is teasing Mobad, and then backs away at the last minute.

115 Baghdad, which appears quite often in the poem, is an anachronism; the city was founded during the Islamic period, in the eighth century.

116 Layla is the heroine of the originally Arab romance *Layla and Majnun*, which was versified by a number of Persian writers, though we have no versions of the story from as early as Gorgani's poem.

117 Gilani buffalos were famous for their massive size. Gilan is a watery, humid province south of the Caspian Sea.

118 It's unclear what is meant here – possibly a golden hairnet, or a snood made from gold wire.

119 This second song is present in only one manuscript.

120 There are references to pre-Islamic Persians facing the sun in prayer in various medieval texts.

121 "Behgui" means "eloquent."

122 See note 13.

123 The sea is Passion; hell is Separation from the beloved.

124 See note 25.

125 The place names Gorgan, Isfahan, Amol, and Gurab are used to generate a series of puns. Gorgan can mean "wolves," and Isfahan comes from the word meaning "army." When Gorgani mentions Amol he puns on "mol," one of the many words in Persian for "wine." He splits Gurab into two words, "Gur" meaning "onager" and "ab" meaning "water." In general the place names in this passage are in western Iran stretching as far as the Euphrates, which the Parthians and Sasanians saw as their western border.

126 Archers from Abkhaz and scorpions from Ahvaz were both referred to as deadly.

127 By "musk" here is meant down on her upper lip. The pearls and wine are her teeth and lower lip.

128 A pun as "Mahabad" can mean "place of the moon."

129 Cf., Vis's gift of violets when she and Ramin swear eternal love.

130 See note 8.

131 "Gol" means "rose." Throughout the episode involving Gol, Gorgani constantly puns on her name.

132 Silver, ermine, eglantine; sight, touch, scent.

133 Shushtar, in Khuzestan, was famous for the production of fine cloth, especially brocade. Kharkhiz, in what is now northern Afghanistan, was known for its musk and its silver mines.

134 Scorpions are curls, narcissi are eyes.

135 See note 7.

136 Though it is hinted at, no make-up is actually mentioned or described when Vis is dressed in her finery by the nurse. The implication is obviously that Vis's beauty is natural and that Gol's is to some extent "applied."

137 This is not entirely fanciful; there is a tradition of Persians decorating particularly beautiful trees with gold and other ornaments. It is what Handel's famous aria, from *Serse* (sc., *Xerxes*), "Ombra mai fu" is about.

138 The silk is to write on; musk is added to the ink to perfume it and to add blackness.

139 I.e., a useless exercise.

140 Again he puns on Gurab (see note 125), this time using the syllable "Gur" in a different meaning: a channel or pit, or the grave.

141 The box tree is Vis.

142 Rose water is tears, blossoms are cheeks.

143 That is, he does not ask the traditionally polite questions of someone who has arrived after a journey.

144 A proverb, meaning everything comes to those who are patient, but it may come too late to be of use.

145 Arvand is a mountain near Hamedan/Mahabad.

146 Striking steel against flint was the most usual way of starting a fire.

147 It's clear that her scribe, Moshkin, composes the letter in Vis's name, rather than Vis doing so herself. Perhaps this was sometimes the case when scribes were employed, though often in medieval narrative poems the "I" of the letter actually dictates the message, rather than allowing the scribe to phrase it as he thinks best.

148 A pun; "Moshkin" means "musky."

149 See note 53.

150 Whether the soul was made of blood or not was argued over in both Islamic and Christian countries during the medieval period, as they shared the same medical and physiological systems.

151 See note 31.

152 See note 95.

153 The Romans recorded (to their horror) that the Parthian male nobility used make-up, including kohl.

154 The "hair of the dog" for a hangover is obviously not only a Western concept.

155 This indicates that it was known in medieval Persia that the moon's light was the sun's light reflected.

156 See note 13.

157 The "seven members" of the body are (1) the head and neck; (2) the chest and all that it contains; (3) the back and lower torso; (4, 5, 6, and 7) the two arms and two legs.

158 Without a knowledge of the Arabic alphabet on the part of the reader, this passage can only be translated approximately as it refers to the specific shapes of Arabic/Persian letters.

159 See note 87.

160 I.e., at the other end of Iran.

161 This is the third time he has been handed violets by a young woman; by Vis, and then by Gol, and now by the young woman he meets while hunting.

162 The hero of the romance *Layla and Majnun* (see note 116).

163 See note 95.

164 Rakhsh is the name of the horse ridden by the chief epic hero of Iran, Rostam, whose exploits are recorded in the *Shahnameh*. At first Gorgani seems to use "Rakhsh" generically for a hero's horse, but later he implies that Ramin's horse, like Rostam's, has the name Rakhsh.

165 See note 7.

166 Vis is clearly back in her room at this point.

167 See note 55.

168 The Zoroastrians worshipped before a sacred flame kept burning in a temple.

169 The fire is his passion, the smoke is his rhetoric.

170 This indicates that it was known that rain came from evaporated sea water drawn up into the clouds.

171 Further on in this scene Gorgani clearly forgets that he
  has said at this point that the night is about to end, just
  as it seems to have slipped his mind that he has Ramin
  hunting in a spring landscape, near Gurab, and then it is
  immediately deep winter when he sets off for Marv a day
  or two later.

172 See note 110.

173 The granite is her heart.

174 The metaphor is from polo.

175 See note 164.

176 See note 31.

177 One of the meanings of "Ram" is "gentle."

178 See note 7.

179 The rose is Gol, the lily is Vis.

180 The metaphor is from polo.

181 See note 22.

182 See note 7.

183 See note 17.

184 To bite the back of one's own hand is still an action that
  signifies penitence or apology in Persian culture.

185 See note 13.

186 Black lions are as mysterious in Persian as they are
  in English.

187 See note 39.

188 Kayanid was the name of a legendary pre-Islamic dynasty.

189 See note 1.

190 Korah's buried treasure was said to move from place
  to place.

191 Ancient buildings were often assigned to the mythical king
  Jamshid. The modern Persian name for Persepolis is still
  Takht-e Jamshid, which means "The Throne of Jamshid."

192 Sekandar is Alexander the Great. In the medieval Asian
  versions of his legend he travels to the darkness at the edge

of the world to seek the waters of eternal life, but loses his way and returns empty handed. The story is included in Ferdowsi's *Shahnameh*.

193 The metaphor refers to the practice, common during the Islamic caliphates, of announcing a new ruler at evening prayers in the mosques of a town or kingdom.

194 The area (to the south of the Caspian Sea) was notorious, throughout the medieval period and beyond, as being difficult to bring under the control of a central government.

195 Amol is on the eastern border of Daylaman, the area to which Vis and Ramin have fled.

196 See note 40.

197 Kian, or Kayanid was the name of a legendary pre-Islamic dynasty.

198 Tabaristan refers to the lands to the south and east of the Caspian Sea.

199 One of the major cities of medieval Iran, Rey has recently been almost absorbed by the southward expansion of the modern capital, Tehran.

200 This is the first indication we have had that Mobad was not a good ruler.

201 Tuba refers to a tree in the Islamic paradise.

202 See note 32.

203 In medieval Persian texts the Kurds and Lurs (who inhabited the ancient province of Media, in western Iran) had a generally bad press. They were seen largely as freebooting bandits, who descended from their mountains to loot the sedentary and civilized peoples of neighboring areas. Their reputation in the rest of Iran had much in common with that of the borderland Scots in England throughout the medieval period.

204 "Ram" had numerous meanings; among them were, contented, gentle, tractable, happy, considerate.

205 See note 87.

206 Nushravan is Anushirvan the Just, also known as Kasra. See note 1.

207 See note 157.

208 Distracted reproaches to the dead for leaving one alone in the world are commonplace in medieval and subsequent Persian literature.

209 See note 28.

210 The poem ends as it began, with a dual reference to Islam (Rezvan) and Zoroastrianism (the fire temple), and with the celebration of spring at the king's court.

211 The Persian New Year falls at the spring equinox, in late-March. See note 2.

212 "Khorshid" means "sun," which means that the line involves a rather obvious pun in Persian, as it does in English.

COMPARISONS FOR THE BODY

With the exception of gender specific characteristics, and the massiveness of a hero's body or his bravery (often compared respectively to an elephant and a lion), stock comparisons are used indiscriminately for women and men.

AN APPLE	the chin
AN ARROW	an elegant and straight young body; often contrasted with a bow (q.v.); the male sexual organ
A BOW	a bent and ugly old, or sick, body; often contrasted with an arrow (q.v.)
A BOX TREE	the body's slender elegance
BOX TREE LEAVES	curly hair
BROCADE	the mingled red and white of the face; the face's or body's softness and beauty; also a stock metaphor for the flowers in a spring landscape
BUNCHES OF GRAPES	curly hair
CAMPHOR	an old person's white hair, sometimes contrasted with musk (q.v.)
CORAL	the lips
A CYPRESS TREE	the body's slender elegance

EGLANTINE	the pinkness and softness of the face
FILBERTS	fingernails (painted with henna)
GARNETS	the lips; ruddy or blushing cheeks; spilled blood
GOLD	a yellow (i.e. sick and ugly) body or face; often contrasted with silver (q.v.)
GRAPES	fingernails (painted with henna)
HONEY	the lips' sweetness
HYACINTHS	curly hair
JASMINE	breasts (color and scent); skin (color and scent)
JUDAS TREE BLOSSOMS	rosy cheeks; spilled blood (the American name for this tree is the redbud)
A KEY AND A LOCK	the male and female sexual organs
MILK	the whiteness of skin; often coupled with wine (q.v.)
THE MOON, ESPECIALLY THE FULL MOON	the face
MUSK	hair (black color and scent); sometimes contrasted with camphor (qv)
NARCISSI	the eyes (white outer petals, with a dark brown center to the flower)
PEARLS	tears; teeth
POMEGRANATES	breasts (shape); ruddy or blushing cheeks (color); spilled blood (color)

POMEGRANATE BLOSSOMS	the cheeks
POMEGRANATE SEEDS	the lips; drops of blood
ROSES	the cheeks; the face generally; flushed skin
ROSE WATER	tears
RUBIES	the lips; ruddy or blushing cheeks; spilled blood; also wine
SAFFRON	the yellow color of sickness; the thinness of a sick body
SCORPIONS	curls
SILK	the softness of the face and body
SILVER	the body's (desirable) whiteness; often contrasted with gold (q.v.)
STARS	the teeth
STRAW	a sallow complexion and/or frailty (during sickness)
SUGAR	the lips' sweetness
THE SUN	the face
TULIPS	ruddy or blushing cheeks; spilled blood
VIOLETS	hair (color)
WINE	the redness of skin; often coupled with milk (q.v.)

Printed in the United States
by Baker & Taylor Publisher Services